GODS OF LOVE

THE COMPLETE SERIES

JEN KATEMI

GODS OF LOVE

THE COMPLETE SERIES

Platinum Passion
Aphrodite Calling
Sex Club Secrets
Immortal Seduction
Demon of Envy

JEN KATEMI

ISBN 13: 978-0-6484045-0-7

Gods of Love (The Complete Series)
includes five previously published novellas:

Platinum Passion, first published 2011
Aphrodite Calling, first published 2012
Sex Club Secrets, first published 2013
Immortal Seduction, first published 2013
Demon of Envy, first published 2014

First Edition
Published by Flourish Books
Edited by Deadra Krieger
Cover by EmCat Designs

ACKNOWLEDGMENTS

To my amazing readers. What is a writer without readers?
Knowing that someone out there enjoys what I write makes
the long hours and hard work worthwhile.

And of course, to my beautiful family. You are my world and
you mean everything.
Thank you.

AUTHOR'S NOTE

In Greek mythology there are many versions from which to pick and choose, and researching the erotes was no exception. The most popular belief seems to be that the erotes were a group of winged gods who were the children of Aphrodite, the Greek goddess of love and sexuality who was born from the foam of the sea. The Greek god Eros was either their father or one of their brothers.

Another belief, and the one that resonates best with me, is that the erotes were in fact different aspects of the primal god, Eros. Erotes is the plural of eros (desire), and I am fascinated by the idea that love is so complex it must be personified across several beings.

While the erotic author in me applauds the idea of the greatness of Eros, I also love the idea that his power, and therefore that of the erotes, stems primarily from a woman—the Olympian goddess Aphrodite (sometimes called Venus in Roman mythology).

Thus the concept of the Gods of Love series was born—stand-alone novellas that can be read in any order, but that also share a common theme.

The first three novellas in the series focus on the erotes (Pothos, Himeros and Anteros). The fourth novella introduces Aphrodite and her insatiable hunger for love. The final novella in this set focuses on the black sheep of the family. Phthonos (Thon) is the god of envy and jealousy, brother to the erotes and wayward son of Aphrodite.

Each of these sexy Greek gods of desire is skilled at satisfying the erotic needs of humans who cross their path. But where do the immortals turn for sexual healing when loneliness strikes at each eternal yet world-weary heart? I hope you enjoy these unique love stories.

PLATINUM PASSION

BY JEN KATEMI

PLATINUM PASSION

POTHOS, GOD OF SEXUAL YEARNING

Three people. One erotic fantasy. A twentieth wedding anniversary like no other.

Jeannie yearns for the return of passion in her marriage. Jake craves new excitement in the form of another man. Pothos is an aspect of Eros, the ancient Greek god of love, and this couple's distinctive yearning has called to him. By the power of the erotes he intends to rekindle the flame of Jake and Jeannie's passion in a night of desire that will be the ultimate platinum anniversary gift.

And when the gods of love decide your marriage needs a boost, they never do it by halves.

CHAPTER ONE

He came to her on the night of their twentieth wedding anniversary.

Jeannie was lying in bed, straining to read the last page of her book in the weak circle of light cast by the bedside lamp. Jake snored gently as he lay beside her fast asleep. She sighed with that mix of contentment and regret that she always felt when a good book ended, and was about to remove her reading glasses when he was just...there—standing in the doorway of her bedroom clad only in faded denim jeans.

She gaped, too stunned by his appearance to even think about being afraid, though afterwards she wondered what the hell was wrong with her that she hadn't made a sound. Not even a squeak of terror, though it wasn't terror she felt as she stared at the stranger in her house.

The stranger who had just stepped straight off the cover of the romance novel she was still holding was standing there smiling and beckoning.

The picture in front of her shook as she looked down and then back up at the real deal in her bedroom. Almost exactly the same, with unruly black hair curling down into eyes that pale emerald color of the sea on a fine day, sharply cut cheek-bones that gave him a sensual air, and a darkly tanned body so honed to muscular perfection she could see why he was currently the most popular model of the day for romance book covers. Including the one in her suddenly vice-like grip.

She squeezed her eyes shut then popped them open again. Yep. Still there. Still looking as hot as an ancient warrior. In fact, far hotter in the flesh than he appeared on the printed page.

A sudden contraction deep within her belly created a pleasurable ache. One that she hadn't felt in a long time.

"F...Federico?" She tried out his name, her voice a whisper that finished on a high note of panic, but he just smiled and held out his hand.

"Jeannie. Come." The faintest hint of an accent laced his words and enticed her all the more.

Why was she not screaming her head off? Or reaching for the phone to call the cops? Why am I even considering stepping out of bed to accept this stranger's hand? "Because it isn't real." She cast a glance at Jake to see if he had woken up when she spoke. Nope. Still asleep. Still snoring.

Jake's brown fringe flopped across his face and gave him a more youthful look than she was used to seeing lately. Setting up his own software company was what he'd always wanted and finally, eighteen months ago, he'd taken the plunge and stepped out into business for himself. But the hours had been long and stressful as he fought to build up a client base, and she could see the toll it was beginning to take in the deepening lines around his eyes and the faint smattering of grey in the shorter hair at his temples. A wave of tenderness had her reaching out to caress him, and then she glanced up to see the stranger watching her with an approving smile.

"Okay," she said. "So I'm asleep too, and this is definitely a dream. A damn good one, mind you." Then she frowned briefly. "Isn't it?"

"If that makes it easier for you," he said gravely, "then think of this as a dream. Now come."

"What about...um..."

"Your husband will not wake just yet," he said, correctly interpreting her hesitation. The look he directed briefly at Jake held such warmth that it set off a faint throbbing directly at her core, even though he was not, for those few seconds, concentrating on her. "There will be plenty of time for Jake...later."

"Really?" His words intrigued her, inviting thoughts of Jake and this stranger together in a sexual way. She was unsure why her dreams might be filled with such images, but the heaviness that intensified in her womb was a welcome result. It was an ache she hadn't felt in quite some time and, secure in the knowledge that this wasn't real, she raised one hand to her breast to explore her burgeoning nipples.

"Jeannie." There was a faint chiding now in the stranger's —Federico's?—voice. "Jake is for later. I promise you, he will have his turn. Now it is your time, beautiful woman. Come." On the last word his lips curved up in a sensual grin and he shifted slightly in the doorway. The sheen of his caramel skin glistened in the golden light cast by the reading lamp, and she had the urge to run her fingertips over his body and find out if it really was as smooth and sleek as it looked.

Her legs slid out from under the covers almost of their own volition, but then her breath caught and she felt her cheeks heat up. "Damn! I forgot, um, well..."

He cocked an amused eyebrow. "I can see past that flannelette nightgown, Jeannie," he said. "You are beautiful

7

beneath it, but I will fix your attire before Jake joins us. His vision may not be so...x-ray."

She glanced again at Jake, who shifted slightly in the bed, then down at herself. Beautiful? That was definitely stretching the truth. The flannel nightie hid the persistent little pot belly and also the cellulite that had recently begun to appear on her thighs, both of which were courtesy of two children, and she knew without having to look in the mirror that a few streaks of grey had begun to silver her previously golden-blonde hair. Managing their home, her job as a secretary at the local medical center, and raising two teenage kids almost single-handedly while Jake was stressing over the new business in this difficult economic climate, had probably taken its equal toll on her.

She and Jake hardly spoke these days, let alone had time for anything more intimate than a quick peck on the cheek. Feeling good about her body—feeling desirable or even remotely beautiful—was just not on the agenda. Maybe, she realized, it wasn't just her husband who'd forgotten how to be romantic.

Federico reached to remove her reading glasses and drop them onto the bed, before holding out his hand, and despite the pang of guilt, she leaned forward to clasp it. Heat assailed her as strong fingers closed over her own. Heat and power.

It felt as if her body was standing to attention, energized by a burst of electricity that made her feel more alive than she had in years. But still she hesitated. "Jake's my husband," she said.

"I know."

"I love him."

"I know that, too. And he loves you. You have been married twenty years and your love for each other is just as deep today as it was the day you met. But things have not been the same lately, have they? The physical spark...it does not appear to be there at present, does it?"

She stood in the doorway and looked back at the man she loved. "No." The frustration filled her, twisting her lips. "I want it to be! And so does he; I'm sure of it. It's just...we're so tired all the time!"

Federico placed a finger under her chin, lifting her face until she was staring into his eyes. They really were the most unusual color she had ever seen. Almost translucent green, it reminded her of her favorite place in the world—the deserted white beach in far north Queensland where she had first made love with Jake on their honeymoon.

Twenty years ago tonight.

And he hadn't remembered.

Tears welled involuntarily and Jeannie bit her lip as she fought them back. I don't want to cry in front of this man. I know it's my dream, but still...

He was caressing her now, running a strong thumb down her cheek and over trembling lips. His touch left a ribbon of warmth behind. "Shush," he said. "He will remember, and the spark is still there, I promise." Laughter lit his features. "Tonight we will nurse that spark back to life until it becomes a raging fire once more."

A wash of joy crossed her skin, and even though she sensed it was being forced onto her rather than generating from inside herself, she sank gratefully into the emotion. The need to cry receded and a growing sense of excitement took its place.

Butterflies. I'm thirty-eight years old and I have butter-flies in my stomach. For heaven's sake!

"Tonight I am going to ignite your fire, Jeannie. First you and then Jake will have his turn. Eros sent me to—"

"Who?"

"Ah." He frowned, and then sighed dramatically. "You people in this modern age. Never mind. It is of no consequence right now. We need to focus on you, Jeannie, and your upcoming pleasure at my hands."

The way he said her name, with that faint accent softening the "J" sounded slightly European. And the idea of him pleasuring her with those strong fingers, which were even now tracing small circles down the column of her neck and along her collarbone, created damp heat in her sensible cotton panties.

She took a deep breath, trying for composure. "I've never had a fantasy without...well, without Jake in it."

"Really?" He went very still, and she got the feeling her admission had genuinely surprised him. "That is most unusual. But...rather endearing." He looked across at Jake, then back at her, and the hint of astonishment in his features morphed into determination. "Do not be concerned, darling Jeannie. It is in my nature to inspire many aspects of yearning. And to sate them. I will ensure that Jake joins us soon, and that you both have the best time tonight."

Thoughts of herself sandwiched between Jake and Federico—or perhaps it could be Jake in the middle, sinking himself into her while Federico pounded him from behind—sent a wave of pure lust crashing through her body. She let out a tiny moan and saw those strange green eyes light up as he watched her. "Why am I picturing these things?" she asked.

"Because you are with me! It inspires you."

Now it was her turn to raise a brow. Even figments of the imagination needed to behave. "I didn't actually expect you to answer that one, you know. It was rhetorical. Anyone ever call you on that self-confidence thing?"

He laughed then, the sound pure and rich, and her heart

filled with delight. Was he manipulating her emotions? Maybe later she'd have an issue with that, but for now, she didn't care. She just felt young and happy again, like when she first married Jake.

"Often," he admitted. "But I have no need for humility. I am a..." He hesitated, and then said, "Well, I am Federico, at least for tonight. So—" he pulled her forward into the dark hallway— "where would you like to go, beautiful woman?"

He stood a full head taller than her own five foot six inch height, and she had to crane her neck a little to meet his questioning gaze.

"I like the beach," she answered, and then could have kicked herself. The beach? At night? Why had she said such a stupid thing? "Well, I guess it is my dream," she added with a hint of defiance.

He tilted his head and studied her. "A good choice. I, too, enjoy the beach. So base, and raw, and elemental. Especially at night, with moonlight silvering the water." He leaned forward and warm breath lifted the hair near her ear. "Close those gorgeous blue eyes, little one."

A moment of dizziness assailed her when she did as requested and then fingertips grazed her cheek. "Okay to look, now," he said.

She did so, and gasped when she saw where they were standing. The long, sandy curve of beach near Port Douglas in northeastern Australia was straight out of her imagination. Balmy air caressed her skin, despite the fact that it was the last night of winter. It had been a cold, wet evening in Melbourne, but here, in the warmth of the tropics, her flannel nightie was instantly too much.

She stared wide-eyed at their suddenly exotic setting. The full moon bathed everything in a flattering silver-blue sheen. She bent down and grabbed a handful of sand, wanting to feel

11

the reality of it, and let the still-warm grains leach out between her fingers. The texture in her hands and between her bare toes recalled the delicious memory of her wedding night. Jake's firm hands had ignited eager anticipation in her body and his weight pressed her down into the small sandy depression beneath the palm trees. Their kisses mingled as youthful passion made them forget they were still in a public place, however dark and deserted it might be.

It was the only time they had ever made love on the beach, the night they both gave up their virginity, and she'd cried with joy afterwards. Jake, she remembered, had caught her tears on the tip of his tongue and then kissed her with salt-flavored tenderness.

"How?" she said. "It's two thousand miles from Melbourne! Where, I might add, it was freezing."

He laughed. "The power of the gods is immense. Tonight, this country shifts from winter into spring. And the influence of the erotes is strongest at the changing of the seasons. I plucked this location from your place of yearning. It called to me, that yearning of yours."

"The influence of the...erotes?" She stumbled over the unfamiliar word. "Just who the heck are you?"

He raised his head proudly. "I am Pothos," he said, and it was as if the statement vibrated the air around them. All of a sudden he seemed taller, stronger, and more otherworldly. He looked like a god of old, shimmering with power; the golden skin alight with moonbeams and his face a study in supremacy as he stared at her down his nose. A frisson of fear touched her heart in tandem with the mounting desire.

If I touch him now, will I self-combust?

Like a moth with a death wish, she stretched out her fingers anyway, ran them over his chest that did indeed feel like satin, and felt the charge of an electrical current coursing through her veins.

Her lips parted and she let out a gasp.

Power. So much power.

But then he shook his head and grinned, and the momentary spell was broken. She dropped her hand and surreptitiously rubbed her still-tingling fingertips.

"I am the one who has been sent to fulfill your fantasies, Jeannie. Yours and Jake's. This is the night your marriage gets back its passion. Twenty years. It is worth celebrating, and tonight will be my platinum anniversary present to you both."

He stepped forward and swept her into his muscular embrace, then bent his head so that his lips were only a whisker away from hers. "So—" his breath heated her mouth —"are you ready to begin our celebration of passion?"

"No! I mean...platinum? I thought...isn't twenty years china?" She was stalling, torn by a combination of lust and guilt. He leaned so close she could practically taste the sweetness of his breath. Yet, her need for Jake was as strong as ever.

Pothos knew it, too, and his eyes darkened to a stormy green before he finally let out a dramatic sigh.

"You are stubborn, woman," he said, but then he conceded. "China is the traditional gift for the twentieth, but platinum is the modern interpretation of this anniversary. Platinum is the symbol of something very special. Almost unattainable. At least in this day and age."

Those last words sounded unaccountably cynical, and she wanted to soothe this strange yet compelling being. She wanted his playful good humor back again.

"A platinum anniversary present? Sounds...very generous. But...what about..." She hesitated, hating that everpresent practical side that reared itself even in a dream. Then she glanced at the gently lapping water a few meters away and blurted out, "What about crocodiles?"

He snorted. "Hmm, maybe Eros should have arrived a few seasons ago. You are rather wound up. No crocodiles, Jeannie, or sharks, or anything unpleasant to worry about tonight. I will make sure of it. You really need this, do you not?"

Her heart sped up. "Th-this?"

"Yes, you stubborn, beautiful woman. This."

As if aware that she couldn't bring herself to make the final move, he bent the few millimeters required to connect with her lips, and claimed her with a kiss both unfamiliar and incredibly intoxicating.

The heat, she thought. The heat and the seductive mastery. Oh, my God! How do you resist someone like this? Someone who makes every cell in your body scream out for more?

The corded strength of his muscles rippled beneath her fingers as she clutched at him in shocked pleasure. The sheer power in Pothos' kiss was its own aphrodisiac, and she moaned deeply into his mouth before returning the favor, lips and tongue mingling with his as she sought to learn the taste of someone new.

"You must get a lot of practice at this," she gasped, when they finally broke apart.

She felt the vibration of his chest as he chuckled. "Some," he admitted. His dark hair fanned her cheek as he leaned in and nipped her bottom lip again, before capturing her mouth in another potent caress.

His penis began to harden against her belly and despite its confinement in his jeans, she knew it would be of breath-taking proportions if she was game enough to free him from his scanty clothing. Her sex, already aching, throbbed anew. What would it be like to stroke the organ of someone other than her husband? What would it be like to taste him? Would his sexual juices taste the same, or have their own unique flavor? What would it be like to have the contained power of Pothos pounding away inside her?

And Jake...what would it be like if he was here, too, watching as she writhed in the sand with another man? Would he want to join in? Had he ever wondered what it would be like...to taste another cock...or to feel the completeness of receiving someone's body inside your own?

"Oh, Pothos," she moaned, fumbling for the fastening on his jeans. "I want..." Her voice broke. What did she want? Jake, her familiar, dark-haired husband of twenty years? Most definitely. And Pothos, the golden-skinned Adonis who had seemingly materialized straight off the cover of a romance novel, clearly a manifestation of everything she was missing in her life right now?

Yes, God help her. She wanted him, too. Badly.

But somehow, it wasn't quite enough to have one without the other.

She stopped trying to unfasten his jeans and rested her cheek against his chest, enjoying the hardness and the heat. Turning slightly, she inhaled the delicious aroma of his skin. Different to the clean citrus smell of her husband, Pothos smelled exotic and sensual. Not quite musk, not quite spice, but altogether it was heady and enticing.

"Like someone bottled pheromones and sprayed you with it," she muttered, wanting to bury herself deeper in his embrace.

"You like it, of course," he said, and now it was Jeannie's turn to laugh at that supreme confidence.

"I love it," she admitted, and at her words the aroma intensified around her, as if she were immersed in a sensual river, almost drowning in pleasure. Her knees buckled as erotic images began to assail her. Images of herself crammed between Jake and Pothos, the three of them somehow entwined on the sand, moaning and rutting, and taking it in turns to love each other in the silvery light of the moon.

That's what I want, she thought, and the ferocity of her longing had her hands reaching up to fist in his hair. "Can you bring Jake here, too? I want you both."

"Good," he said, voice rough with desire. "That is how it should be. The three of us, sharing a platinum night of passion. Together."

His decadent words sent a delicious shiver across her skin, but before she could respond Pothos bent down to grasp the bottom of her nightgown and rip it up and over her head. Moments later and those cotton panties were gone too. She stood naked in front of him as he threw the underwear aside, but strangely, she felt no embarrassment. A light breeze tickled her flesh and puckered her already aching nipples. Pothos reached out a finger and lightly grazed one of the expanding nubs. "Beautiful," he said, and now his voice had a deep huskiness. "Jake should see you like this. Bathed in moonlight and sensuality."

His finger left her breast and traced the rest of her body in a delicate caress, skimming across ribs moving rapidly as she struggled to breathe evenly, down through the curve of her waist and over her abdomen to rest, feather-light, at the very top of her slit. Her mons was bare except for a tiny heart shape of hair right where Pothos' index finger now rested. The Brazilian had been done only last week and she'd left the heart in a display of whimsy in the hope Jake would enjoy the new look. But he hadn't even noticed.

Unlike Pothos, who now had a crooked little grin on his face as he traced around the heart. "A genuine blonde," he said.

She nodded in a distracted fashion. It was becoming more

and more difficult to draw a breath. Her gaze fell to his jeans, the denim now clearly stretched to its limit across his groin. Not fair that he should still have clothing on, while she stood here dressed in nothing but her pussy heart.

"Would you...please...remove..." Her fingers trembled as she reached out to touch his straining bulge, and his intake of breath was audible. She enjoyed the momentary power, mimicking his delicate exploration of her body with a fingertip adventure of her own. The shape of his penis, up over ripped abdominal muscles and then down again. All were new, and unfamiliar, as was her flare of pleasure at the increasingly irregular pattern of his breathing.

So this...god of love, or whoever he was, could be moved by desire, too.

She fumbled again for the fastening on his jeans, but he shook his head, then stepped back to remove his clothing in a fluid movement that was far quicker than she'd have been able to achieve with her shaking hands.

His cock sprang free and she gasped at the enormous size and inherent power in his organ. Pothos was longer and wider than Jake, but not unduly so, as her husband was rather well-endowed. But it was not only his erect appendage that had her eyes wide and her whole body aching for sex. Though his shoulders were built for power, his body tapered down in a long, lean arc to narrow hips. As he turned toward the water for a moment she got a view of tight buttocks and impressively muscled thighs.

Had he done that twirl on purpose? So that she'd see and appreciate the perfection of his body from every angle? Yes, she decided, as he glanced back at her over his shoulder and grinned boyishly. He most certainly had. "Nice butt," she managed, in the understatement of the century, but it was worth it to see the affronted look on his face.

"Nice?"

"Very nice, in fact."

He moved so fast she only had time for a quick yelp before he was standing over her, gripping her shoulders. The head of his organ was almost, but not quite, touching her stomach, and she could feel the radiant heat leaching out from its proximity. "Nothing about me is nice, Jeannie."

Instant moisture pooled between her legs as she imagined that erect cock inside her, sliding up and down her passion-slicked passage as she clenched her muscles around him. No man but Jake had ever been inside her before. With Pothos, there were so many inches she doubted he would all fit. If he did thrust up and into her, she knew it would be an experience like no other. And she definitely knew that nice would not be the word to describe such an experience.

It would be pleasure and pain.

Agony and ecstasy.

She reached out to press a trembling finger onto the base of his cock, and then ran it lightly up to the tip. A drop of moisture poised there above his tiny slit, and she hesitated before continuing through the droplet with the cushion of her index finger. He shuddered and groaned, and the heaviness in her womb intensified, even as the ache of guilt almost over-whelmed her.

How could she be standing here with this stranger, wanting to sink herself onto his massive shaft, and not betray her husband? Even in a dream, wasn't this...wrong? Her mouth twisted and she began to step back, but Pothos tight-ened his grip on her upper arms.

"Do not feel guilt," he said, leaning into her hair. "It is in my nature to seduce. You are human and therefore physically unable to resist, should I want you. And make no mistake, Jeannie. I want you."

"But Jake—"

"I want him, too, Jeannie. Does that shock you?"

"No. Well, yes. Maybe a little." Her voice was faint. I want you, he'd said. And I want your husband. In her world people didn't say things like that. Shouldn't she be jealous as well as guilt-ridden? Shouldn't she be feeling more afraid of this intoxicating desire?

"Jake has already been tempted by my influence," Pothos continued. "When he arrives, you will find that he has no more mind to resist his deeply hidden desires than do you."

"So this is not of my own will? Nor Jake's?" She frowned up at him. That would explain the earlier sensation of something 'other' pressing in on her from the outside and influencing how she felt. "You're manipulating us into wanting what we don't really want? That's wrong, Pothos. Just…wrong."

His cheeks flushed and those delicious lips thinned. "I never force anyone into anything they do not want. That is not why I am here." He let go of her arms and paced a few feet up the beach, then back. Clearly her words had agitated him. "No one has ever rejected me before. Are you rejecting me? Me?"

"Well…"

He was staring at her, confusion written all over his features when she didn't immediately deny it. "I am here because you yearn for something more in your relationship. You yearn for passion, and desire, and all the things you had in the beginning that have been lost along the way. Jakes yearns, too. He wants excitement back in your lives just as keenly as you do. I am here because your longing called me, Jeannie. I am Pothos. I am the personification of everything you and Jake need to complete your relationship and truly become soul mates."

He ran an aggravated hand through his dark hair. "Am I... by the gods, am I...mistaken?" That last word came out so reluctantly, so agonized, that she couldn't help but smile.

Despite her feelings of guilt, his explanation called to her very essence. She did want more in her relationship with Jake. So much more. And if her husband felt the same and would be joining them shortly...

"You're not wrong," she admitted. Her hands gravitated back toward him, drawing him into her embrace, caressing the stricken look from his features. "Can you at least turn it off?" she asked. "So I know that what I'm feeling is genuine." He felt so hot and so hard against her body, in many ways just like Jake, and yet infinitely different.

"I cannot." His voice was strained. "I am what I am, Jeannie. I cannot change it. But I would not be here if you and Jake did not want this. Even if one of you wanted this and not the other, I would not be here. It has to be both of you, yearning for wholeness, for desire, which calls forth the power of Eros."

His fingertips were working their way down her spine as he spoke. She shivered beneath his touch. "I do want this," she said, rubbing her cheek against him, enjoying the unusual feel of a chest without any hair. Jake had a smattering of hair across his chest and while she loved the springy feel of it when she stroked her fingers down her husband's body, following that line to his groin, the smooth sensation of Pothos was new and exciting.

His organ pressed against her, and she imagined this enormous cock together with Jake's, her hands encircling them both as she bent down to run her tongue across their dual, straining, moisture-tipped heads.

Jake and Pothos.

Citrus and spice.

What a perfect, delicious blend.

"Maybe nice wasn't the best description for you," she admitted. Certainly not if he had a hand in the wicked images flitting through her mind.

His eyes shimmered in the moonlight as he met her gaze. Then a flash of white teeth as he grinned signaled his intention even before he bent to lift her into his arms. She squealed in mock horror as he began to wade out into the water.

"I take it back! You're better than nice! You're damn near perfect!"

"Damn near?" He lowered her until she could feel the ripple of gentle waves on her ass. The water was warm, not the harsh cold she was expecting. In fact, she realized, that felt...really good. Better than good.

She stopped struggling, but her voice was breathless as she said, "If I admit you are absolutely and utterly perfect, will you lower me...just a touch?"

He pretended to consider. "Like this?"

His arms dipped and she was a few inches lower in the water now, the undulating wetness against her bare pussy like a gentle tongue lapping at her clit. Darting in and out and around every part of her sex in a persistent erotic tease like nothing she had ever experienced before. "Oh, yes," she gasped. "Just like that."

"Admit it, then."

"I do, I do," she moaned. "Perfect. Your butt...your body...your face...everything about you...turns me on so bad—oh!"

He'd dipped her again, a little deeper this time, yet his arms were not even straining at the effort of holding her weight. She could feel his phallus pressed against her hip, her body stroking up and down the length of him as he repeatedly raised and lowered her into the water.

He was doing that on purpose. And it felt so…damn…good.

One of her arms was around his neck and she clutched at dark strands of silken hair.

"Pothos," she gasped. "It's like you're…manipulating the waves…or something. It's…I—"

"The erotes command the power of Aphrodite," he said, dipping and lifting, over and over. "Our desire, like our mother before us, was born of the sea."

The words made no sense to her, but the foaming crest of each small wave continued to caress her like a lover until she couldn't concentrate on anything but their touch. Now it felt like his fingers, now his tongue. The warm night air and the contrasting cool ripple of water. Over and over. Until she couldn't take any more.

"I can't hold on." She gasped. "I think I'm going to…" A wave once again whispered along her slit. "Oh God, Pothos, I'm going to come—"

"Yes!" His voice was fierce, triumphant, and at the sound she came apart in his arms, bucking and shrieking through her orgasm as he continued to hold her in the path of the gentle but insistent tide.

When she finally quieted, he moved further out into the ocean and lowered her all the way until she was immersed up to her neck. He was still holding her clutched against him, but now she could feel a trembling in his arms. "That is only the first of many tonight," he said.

She reached up and touched his cheek in wonder. "What about you? I can feel your need, Pothos."

"My need is enormous," he admitted, and she chuckled.

"I know that," she said drily. "But—"

"Shh." He placed a brief kiss on her lips. "My needs will be sated this night. Do not worry, little one."

He put her down and she stumbled in the waves before strong arms pulled her close and held her. She rested her cheek against him, enjoying the vibration of his strong heartbeat. They stood like that a moment longer before he took her hand and led her back to the water's edge. The sand was so fine it felt like silt beneath her feet. They stood in the balmy air, moisture dripping off their bodies, listening to the relentless slap of the sea as it met the shore. The folds of flesh along her slit, caressed only minutes earlier by that same tide, were still so heavy it almost felt like her womb was about to fall out. His unsated cock jutted out in front of him, a stark reminder that there was more to come in this encounter. Again she was assailed by the scent of musky passion.

The scent of Pothos.

She wished even harder that her husband was here to enjoy this moment with them, and as if he sensed her thoughts, Pothos smiled.

"Now we are ready for Jake," he said, and pointed back up the beach.

CHAPTER THREE

J ake rubbed his eyes and padded barefoot along the sand, not sure why he was dreaming of this particular stretch of beach but recognizing the location. His cock shifted as he remembered the night of their wedding. The night he'd made love to Jeannie for the very first time, right in the center of that sandy knoll over there among the palm trees.

Shit. I forgot to give her the ring.

It was probably still sitting in his bedside drawer, where he'd hidden it last week in readiness for tonight. A platinum eternity ring had seemed fitting for their twentieth, but he'd crawled into bed earlier and fallen asleep practically as soon as his head hit the pillow.

Poor Jeannie. She probably thinks I forgot altogether. It's just…I wish I wasn't so damn tired all the time.

But the funny thing was, he didn't feel tired right now. In fact, he felt downright horny.

He looked down at the black silk boxers Jeannie had bought for him a couple of months ago, the material starting to tent in front as an erection grew out of nowhere. Shifting uncomfortably, he glanced around to see if he was alone, wanting to unbutton the front and take his rapidly rising cock into an eager hand. Out here in the open, it would pay to hold off from touching himself until he confirmed whether or not there was anyone else around.

If only Jeannie was here to share this moment with him. It had been so long since they made love, and he couldn't even pinpoint the last time they had actually been out on a date. Lately, though, his fantasies were twisting in a new direction, one that he shied away from most of the time, and only gave in to when he was somewhere like this. Safe within a dream.

It began at the gym one day, when he was drying himself off after a shower. Another man had walked into the change room and stripped off, still slick with sweat from his workout. There was something attention-grabbing about the rounded dips and curves of the man's well-muscled arms and shoulders, and the lean strength inherent in his deeply tanned body. Jake found himself checking out the other guy's naked form and wondering what it would be like to taste another man's cock; what it would feel like to fuck or be fucked by a man.

The thoughts shocked him and he had quickly sat down, bunching his towel to hide the slight arousal. Admittedly, sex with Jeannie was off the agenda lately, with both of them so tired, but...jeez, he'd never before entertained homo-erotic thoughts.

Why now?

The other guy had walked into the shower room seemingly oblivious to the scrutiny, and Jake watched him go, wondering what would happen if he followed the man into the private cubicle and they quietly took it in turns to suck each other off under cover of the falling water.

He couldn't understand where such lewd thoughts came from. He loved Jeannie, with all his heart, and even though it had been difficult for them lately with all the time he'd spent trying to set up the business, he still enjoyed making love with his wife. She turned him on like no one else had ever been able to, and sated his desires in a way that continued to intrigue him even after two children and more than half a lifetime together.

And it was more than sex, with Jeannie. That old adage about someone else "completing" you might have made him squirm when he was forced to watch that Jerry Maguire movie with his wife and daughters, but there was something to the concept. He and Jeannie were meant to be together. He'd always known it, ever since he met her on their first day of high school and something in him recognized that she was the one.

Thank God she loved him back. There was no one else who knew every single thing about him, even the really gross, disgusting bits, yet she loved him anyway.

Well, almost everything. These new homo-erotic cravings hadn't been shared with her as yet. He wasn't quite sure how she'd take it. Hell, it was hard enough to know how to process the feelings himself. Where had it come from, this yearning? Why? He'd never had desires like this before. And it wasn't like he didn't want Jeannie any more. Yet how could he reconcile his enormous need for his wife with this budding curiosity to try something new?

The guilt wracked him, even though he was certain he would never do anything sexual with anyone other than Jeannie, be it man or woman who tempted him. Unless she was there with him, of course. Though he knew deep down she would never go for it, he found that once the idea of a threesome came into being he couldn't stop thinking about it.

Images of himself and Jeannie letting another man into their life filled his head. They danced across his vision until all he could think of was the three of them in a heap of angles and tangled limbs on their king-sized bed as they took it in turns to love each other. Images of tasting another man, of being fucked by him even as he made love with his wife, had his cock rising to attention. What would Jeannie think if he pleasured her in tandem with another man, one from the front, one from behind, his gorgeous wife writhing between them until the pleasure burst out of her with a complete lack of restraint?

That night he had gone home and made love to her with so much energy that she ended up screaming her release, quite different to their usual quiet routine, and he had emptied himself into her in such a rush of juice that it threatened to drown them both in volume.

There'd be double the fluid with an additional man in their bed. He was damn near ready to shoot his load right here on this beach as a new fantasy began to build in his head. A fantasy that involved Jeannie, and the man from the gym. Right here on the sand. Right now.

He shivered in need, reaching down to stroke himself through the silken material.

I want Jeannie. I want…more.

His vision blurred and he shook his head to clear it, and then realized he was not alone on the beach after all.

Fuck! Impossible to hide this boner. His hand instantly shifted away from his cock.

He could see the silhouette of a man and a woman standing further up the curve of the coastline, hand in hand, ankle deep in water by the looks of things. But then he frowned. Were they…surely they weren't…naked? That would be too weird, given the nature of his latest fantasy. He took a hesitant step forward, then stopped, cheeks flushing with embarrassment. Hell. They were. And the guy had a hard on even bigger than his own.

Clearly, they wouldn't want anyone else raining on their privacy parade right about now. He turned to leave, but as he did so the couple held out their arms toward him, gesturing, and something about the woman, the way she stood, the way she flicked her hand in a come-to-me type gesture, the way she tilted her head just that little bit to the right...

No way. "Jeannie?" His voice came out on a squeak of amazement and there was no chance she could have heard him, but he saw her nod and gesture again. Thank God this was a dream, or he'd be pretty damn shocked to see her standing naked like that with another man by her side. Ridiculous, he knew, given his recent train of thought, but still...

He took a faltering step toward them, then another, and then with a deep, shuddering breath he began to run toward the couple on the beach.

Toward his beautiful wife and the unfamiliar man with a hard on the size of a baseball bat.

Toward his ultimate sexual fantasy in the flesh.

Ω Ψ Ω

Jeannie felt the tears trickle down her cheeks and mingle with the moisture from the sea. "Thank you," she whispered, without taking her eyes off her husband now racing up the beach.

"De nada, little one." Pothos' voice was husky, and he squeezed her fingers tightly before letting go. "Now go get your husband, and bring him back to me."

She did, flying down the sand to meet him, jumping into

his arms and finding herself twirled around in his strong and familiar embrace as he sought to slow her momentum. "Just like a corny movie," she laughed, and he chuckled too, before nuzzling the delicate skin of her neck.

"Not quite like a corny movie," he murmured, suddenly nipping her.

"Ow! Jake, that hurt!"

"Not with him in the picture, too." He lowered her to the sand and gestured toward Pothos, and Jeannie felt her cheeks begin to heat up. So. Maybe the bite had been a form of punishment. But she could see he was aroused, and it confused her. Was he jealous? Was he disgusted to find his wife standing stark naked in the arms of another man? Or did it somehow turn him on?

Then he spoke, and he sounded so wistful she reared back to get a better look at his features in the moonlight. "This dream, Jeannie, it's…" The aching need in her husband's eyes said more than his words and her guilt began to turn to hope. Was Pothos right? "It's my fantasy coming to life," he blurted out, and her mouth dropped open.

"Um, I think…" Deep breath, Jeannie. Take a deep breath. "I think that's my line, Jakey. Isn't it?"

Pothos was watching them with a knowing smile lighting his gorgeous face. Yeah, okay, smarty pants, she thought, and gave him a conceding shrug. His smile widened and her heart leapt. She turned back to Jake.

"He's here tonight…for both of us. If…if you want it?" She finished on a hesitant whisper and held her breath, afraid of how this might go.

His fingers tightened almost painfully against her hips. "I want it," he said roughly, and with those three words her body grew heavy with arousal. Again. She took his hand and they began to wade back through the shallows, water splashing around their ankles, but Jake suddenly stopped short and turned to face her.

"Let me look at you," he said. "It's been so long since I've actually seen you naked."

Her heart skipped a beat. Had it really been that long? Yes, she realized. It had.

Shyness gripped her for a moment, but in the light cast by the moon she could see his brown eyes darken almost to black. A sure sign that he liked what he saw. Her shyness receded, and she ran her hands over her breasts and down her stomach toward her mound. "You like?" Her husky voice reflected her need.

"God yes, Jeannie. I like. You look so gorgeous tonight. Glowing. And...when did you get that Brazilian? Man, you look so damn fuckable."

Her womb contracted with an ache she felt all the way to the tip of her breasts. "So do you, Jakey. At least—" she dropped to her knees in the wet sand and shimmied off his boxer shorts—"now you do." She couldn't resist leaning forward to take the tip of his cock into her mouth, running her tongue around the familiar, hot flesh, tasting the pre-cum juice that had already begun to leak from him. He let out a sharp gasp and hands fisted in her hair, the prickle of pain in her scalp sending a delicious message throughout her body. But Pothos—where was he? When she raised her eyes from Jake's sexual arousal it was to find their new companion scrutinizing them intently and Jake now sporting a slightly embarrassed grin. Time for introductions, it seemed.

Standing up in the wet sand was slightly awkward, but Jake automatically leaned forward to assist her, before capturing her mouth in an unexpected kiss. He'd always loved tasting his own fluids on her lips, and right now there was plenty to taste.

She drew back, laughing. "Pace yourself, darling," she said. "I want to introduce you to Pothos." The throatiness of expectation laced her words as she met the sea-green eyes of their soon-to-be lover. "Pothos, this is my husband, Jake. I want both of us to experience your passion, tonight."

"You will." Pothos stepped forward and cupped Jake's cheeks in his hands. She saw the tenderness in his touch, watched her husband half raise his hands in an instinctive response before letting them drop awkwardly back by his side.

"The gym?" Jake queried.

"Yes." Pothos smiled. "It was preparation. For tonight."

She wasn't sure what Pothos meant, but her husband seemed to understand. Moonlight traced his features and she could see his pulse beating so fast in his neck she wanted to reach out to calm him down. His erection, she realized, was not dissipating. If anything it was getting bigger.

Well, well. A faint ribbon of jealousy flitted through her and she hugged herself, knowing the irrational nature of the emotion given her own desires, but unable to feel completely comfortable with the idea that someone else was able to arouse her husband so fully.

As if sensing her disquiet, Pothos glanced sideways at her, the corner of his mouth curved up in a crooked grin, and as simply as that she felt the tension slip away. As long as it was Pothos, it would be okay. She wanted this. For herself. And for Jake.

She nodded her acceptance of the unspoken query. "Yes," she answered. "Love my husband, Pothos."

CHAPTER FOUR

The tanned Adonis claimed her husband's lips in an embrace that seemed both tender and fierce. Their lips and tongues met, and clashed, and laved each other violently as muted groans from two aroused males quickly filled the air around her.

Testosterone doubled, she thought. Tripled, if you took into account the potency of Pothos' essence.

He was taller than Jake by a couple of inches, younger-looking and clearly stronger in build, but Jake still looked pretty damn hot as he leaned in to give as good as he got. Their kiss had more harshness—more desperation—than the one she had shared with Pothos, and she began to understand something about the strength of Jake's need.

Observing the magnitude of their mutual desire was such an erotic turn-on that Jeannie's legs gave way and she sank to the sand. Eros, he'd said. And Aphrodite. Now that she was watching rather than participating, she had the mental space to think about his words. Wasn't Eros the god of all things erotic, or something like that? And she vaguely recalled a picture of a goddess on a scallop shell floating on water. Was that Aphrodite?

She'd definitely never heard of the erotes before tonight. Whoever he was, this Pothos—erotes or otherwise—he and Jake were creating an intensely sensual display of physical desire right in front of her eyes. Their chests were pressed together, one dark golden and heavily muscled, the other lighter in skin tone and slightly more lean. Pothos' pelvis surged into Jake's and she could only imagine what it felt like to have two hard cocks mashed up against one another like that. Her husband clutched at the firm buttocks of his new partner and moaned in a way she knew well.

"Oh, Jake," she whispered, parting her legs to touch herself as each of the men grabbed for the other's cock and began to drive their fists up and down. Fast. So fast.

Her finger circled the nub of her clit, slipping in the creamy moistness coating her sex as she listened to the moans coming from above and watched the unfamiliar image of her husband pumping another man's penis. Jake's head was tilted back slightly, lips parted in a rictus of concentration, and Pothos, his eyes narrowed and cheeks flushed, was working equally hard on Jake.

The rhythmic tightening action of Jake's buttocks as he rode Pothos' hand in increasing tempo had desire raging through her system. She whimpered, imagining a fountain of seed from both of them like a milky shower over her body, and slipped a finger deeper inside herself to simulate the act of sex.

Then Jake was moving, dropping down to his knees in front of Pothos. The two men were silhouetted against star-kissed water that reflected the vast night sky. They looked beautiful—one the embodiment of power, the other in a more submissive pose, like an erotic picture on an ancient Greek urn, and she felt the rightness of what was about to come next.

"Jeannie, I want to suck his cock," Jake said, without taking his eyes off Pothos.

Pothos looked at her, though, desire written across his features. "I find myself wanting this, more than I expected," he admitted in a hoarse voice. "Something about the two of you is making this experience...more."

"More what?" The two men were waiting for her go-ahead, and perversely, she wanted to make them wait. It felt pretty damn exciting to be in control, even if only for a few seconds.

"Just...more," he answered. "I cannot explain it. I do not ordinarily experience the emotional side of loving, not often at all. But here, with the two of you..."

His eyes were pleading, and then Jake was looking at her as well. "Jeannie, for the love of God..."

She raised her chin. "All right," she agreed. "Go for it, boys."

Jake bent forward and Pothos slid into his mouth. She saw Jake flinch at the first taste of another man, then the initial hesitation disappeared and he groaned and took the organ deeper, sucking and licking and moving his head, slowly at first and then faster as he found the right rhythm. All the while these incredible grunting noises were emanating from his throat, as Pothos growled his own enjoyment from above.

Jeannie sat up, wanting to join in, and Pothos beckoned her. On hands and knees she scooted over to Jake and shuffled in behind him, pressing her mons into his rear and thrusting hard. She reached around his body to find and stroke him while she did so, matching her rhythm to the one he was using on Pothos.

Her lungs didn't seem to be working properly and her heart pounded frantically in her chest. Jake's back formed a pillow for her breasts as she rode him while he mouth-fucked Pothos. Never in a million years would she have imagined doing this with her husband. And what they were doing was driving her right to the edge.

When Jake finally came up for air she could hear his ragged breathing almost matching her own, and even Pothos looked as if he were having trouble staying on two legs. She took her hands off Jake and reached forward to trace the trembling thighs of the other man, and then Jake turned awkwardly and reached for her hips. "Jeannie. As much as I wanted to taste another man, it doesn't feel right without you. I love you. I want the three of us to be in this together. Equally."

"Wasn't planning on missing out, Jakey." She ran her thumb over his now swollen lips. "Did you like the taste?"

He dropped his gaze, cheeks flushed. "Different to what I expected, but…yeah."

"Look at me, Jake," she said, knowing exactly what he was feeling by his actions. "Don't be ashamed. This is a fantasy for both of us, not just you."

He looked up then, with such love in his eyes that her breath caught. She leaned in and kissed him, tasting second hand the musky sweetness of Pothos on his lips.

"Mm, nice," she murmured, and looked up at Pothos to see his eyes flash with humor at her comment.

"And I think it would be nice to make love with you, Jeannie," he said. "If you will have me."

Her glance flitted to her husband, who looked like he

couldn't decide between a smile and a scowl. "Jake? Equally, you said."

He settled into a sheepish grin. "Yeah, I'm up for this. It's just…" He sighed. "A little part of me doesn't want to share you. I know that's not fair, but that's how I feel. Especially with, well, someone who looks as good as—"

"Jake." Pothos spoke with a calm authority from above. "She desires you. That will not change after tonight. In fact…" He dropped down on his knees to join them, placing one large arm around each of their waists. "From tonight your love will be even stronger. Renewed. With the power of the erotes to help you along, your desires will be completely fulfilled. No more yearning for what you cannot have, Jake. Nor for you, Jeannie."

As he spoke the scent of passion rose around them, only this time it was citrus and musky spice intermingled.

Nor for me. The words were full of wonder and they whispered past her on a wave of scent, almost not there at all. As she opened her mouth to query whether he'd spoken, Pothos leaned across and touched a finger to her lips. He shook his head.

Words were forgotten as power surged through her. Power and the heady fragrance of love. Citrus and musk. It smelled like Christmas.

She closed her eyes and inhaled deeply, then opened them to see both men staring at her. One was the partner she had spent most of her life loving, the other the epitome of romance and eroticism that had been conjured presumably out of her somewhat warped imagination. Their heat and their hardness along the curves of her body felt so right. She was cocooned and completely safe, and incredibly turned on by this unique ménage situation.

She reached up and traced a finger around two sets of lips, first one, and then the other. "Just kiss me already, guys," she said.

Pothos raised a brow and looked across at Jake. "She is feisty, our Jeannie, is she not?"

Jake's eyes were liquid heat as he grinned. "She certainly can be," he agreed. "So we'd better do as she says."

In perfect accord they swooped in to capture her mouth. There was no hard and fast connection, though, just a delicious ballet of lips, tongues and teeth as they began a three-way kiss that sent a shudder right through to her soul. Oh, God, that felt so good. The gentle persuasion of Jake's familiar mouth was a perfect counterpoint to the masterful power of Pothos. She took one tongue into her mouth in a darting thrust, then the other, then both were there dancing together in a blaze of heat and moisture.

The men had turned their bodies as they kissed her. She could feel Jake's organ against her right hip, Pothos' pressed to her left. Both were hot, and hard, and thrusting almost in unison against the softness of her flesh. Her hands traced down over muscled backs and cupped their buttocks, encouraging the rapid movement. Scents assailed her, the scent of musk and spice, a hint of citrus, the fresh smell of the sea as a soft breeze caressed her. Wetness pooled in a creamy film along her slit. She was so damp it was surprising she wasn't dripping down her legs.

Could it get any better than this? Yes, it could, she realized, as they both rained kisses down her neck and over her collarbone until each found a breast and began to suckle. Moist suction on both breasts at once pulled the moan from her throat. She collapsed backward toward the ground, but somehow a strong arm—not sure whose—supported her descent until she was laying on her back on the beach, right at the very edge of the tide's reach, with one man on each side of her, still suckling and licking and teasing her nipples into pebble-hard nubs that reached up toward the star-studded sky whenever the men paused to steal a brief kiss from each other.

She clenched her fists in their hair to encourage them further, one brown tousled head next to the darker one, as they continued to suckle her into submission. Hands reached for her pussy, fingers circling her clit, teasing apart the swollen folds of flesh and sliding inside her body. She bucked beneath them, unable to tell which of them had a finger inside her—or maybe it was both of them—unable to contain herself, panting and moaning and... "Oh, yes," she cried out. "I'm going to explode, oh yes—" Her shrieking cry went on and on, gushing hot slick juice onto his hands, whoever he was...

Jake.

It was Jake whose hand now cradled her hot mound, holding her lovingly while her body continued to spasm, and it was Pothos whose hand stroked her cheek and pushed a sand-crusted lock of blonde hair out of her eyes. She read the love in her husband's face as he bent to kiss her lips, and tasted the flavor of Pothos in his mouth.

She felt almost complete, at this moment, surrounded by the essence of these two incredible men, but she wanted more. She wanted them both inside her, not just their fingers, but their sexual organs, in a proper joining of their bodies.

As usual it seemed as if Pothos could read her mind. "It was good that you came," he said. "You needed to be that wet, first, to properly accommodate me."

Laughter bubble up of its own volition. "Really?"

Jake shook his head and chuckled. "Pothos," he said. "You're not supposed to boast about, well, about size."

"Why not? It is true, Jake. When I make love with you, I will call on my power to adjust my size so that I do not hurt you. But now, for Jeannie, I need...I really need...to be inside her."

Jake looked to Jeannie first and, breathless, she nodded her approval. "Yeah," he said. "Make love to my wife, Pothos."

He plunged up and into her and she screamed.

Agony and ecstasy.

Just like she'd imagined.

This was a joining like nothing she'd ever felt before. He was so huge he filled her to bursting point, and still there was more in reserve. "Pothos," she sobbed, delicious pressure on every part of her insides as she squirmed to better accommodate him.

"Is that easier?" Pothos shifted a little, and the pressure eased. Agony disappeared and only ecstasy was left as he began to move in earnest.

"Oh, yes," she wailed, as her hips lifted to meet him. "Much better." She flung her head to the side, letting out a whimper when she saw Jake up on his knees beside them, pulling on his cock in a fast and furious fashion. His cheeks were flushed and his eyes were almost black with a passion that she hadn't seen in her husband's face in so long.

"I remember that look," she cried out. "I remember."

She moved her hips faster, matching Pothos thrust for thrust, focusing her gaze on the tip of her husband's cock as it slid in and out of the slick gap between his fingers and thumb. She moaned as her body began to build toward climax.

"Jeannie," Pothos growled, swooping in to claim her in a

rough kiss. Her heels clutched more tightly around his buttocks, pressing him home, and she took his shuddering groan deep into her throat before he released her mouth. "Keep squeezing me like that and I'm not going to last, beautiful woman."

She tried reaching out to Jake as she saw the tell-tale signs of fluid on his cock shining in the moonlight, but was pinned too effectively beneath Pothos. He was so close to coming and she wanted him inside her.

She wanted both of them sheathed inside her.

Pothos saw what she was striving for. "Come, Jake," he said. "Join us."

He rolled to the side, stilled impaled inside Jeannie and taking her with him, and then her husband was behind her, the juicy head of his cock pressing into her rear.

"Okay?" Jake's voice was hoarse and she knew what he was really asking. This was something she'd never let him do before, and she bit her lip. Could she do this? Could she take both of them at once? Would it hurt?

"Yes," she sobbed. "Do it, Jakey."

And he did, gliding into her with an ease she wasn't expecting, so slick with pre-cum that it made his entry relatively painless.

Pothos groaned, possibly at the pressure of Jake's entry tightening her vaginal passage around him. She was so full of man she was afraid she might burst. Then they both began to drive into her body, first one, and then the other, tag teaming, separated only by a thin sheath of her inner flesh, and the world as she knew it splintered around her. Sensation became everything as she was fucked from every direction at once, hands on her hips, hands on her breasts, lips against her neck as she flung her head from side to side, hot, hard bodies rutting against and inside and behind her, desperate groans in her ear as she gasped and moaned her own need in equal abandon.

"I can't help it, guys," she sobbed. "I'm going to come... again...oh, my God..." She broke apart between the two of them, arms flinging out to grip handfuls of somebody's hair and her body rocking as she came in an orgasm so strong it clenched every part of her body, back passage, front, clit, all the way up to her womb...

My womb feels like it's going to explode from this ecstasy.

Even her breasts ached to the very tips, with a pleasurable pain so fierce that she wouldn't have been surprised to see a spray of seed streaking out of her nipples.

Then the men were climaxing, too, both at the same time, with a wordless roar from Pothos and a gasping, groaning, "Fuck, yes," from Jake, and twin streams of heat flowed into her passages in a pulsing, bucking experience that sent her oversensitive sex over the top yet again and her body into spasms that she felt throughout every inch of her being.

She went limp, breathing raggedly, unable to move to save herself, and heard Jake behind her sounding like he was about to have a heart attack. *I know how you feel, dude,* she thought, but didn't have the strength to say it. Pothos had his eyes closed, and even he was breathing heavily, a funny little smile lifting the corners of his lips.

Eventually the sea began to make itself felt, little rivulets of water darting in and out around their slack bodies, cooling the heat and washing away sweat and sand and sexual juices in a soothing rhythm. After a while she was strong enough to roll onto her back and felt the two men do the same. The three of them just lay there, looking up at the stars, and Jeannie couldn't keep the massive grin off her face. "Well," she said, after a lengthy silence, "that was...nice."

She felt the rumble in Pothos' chest and heard Jake's snort of laughter and realized, dream or not, that this instant in time would be etched in her memory forever.

"Who are you, really, Pothos?" she asked. "And what are the erotes?"

He laughed, the sound rich and full. She felt the joy like a presence, and looked across to see Jake's face light up. So he felt it, too.

"Google me, Jeannie," Pothos answered.

"Google you?"

His grin was wide. "You do not know how much I have wanted to say that to someone. It has been a while since I have been sent on an errand such as this. Certainly not since the advent of computers. Yes. Google me."

Jake raised a brow. "Just how old are you, man?"

He shook his head. "Older than time." For an instant he looked weary, and then the laughter returned to his features. "But on nights like tonight, with the two of you, I feel as young and as carefree as I did in the beginning."

Jeannie frowned. "The beginning of what?"

"Everything, darling Jeannie. The beginning of everything. But come—" he sat up—"let us play."

"I thought we had been, already," Jake murmured, and Jeannie chuckled.

"I meant in the sea." Pothos looked out over the water. "I have some friends I would like you to meet. Look!"

He flung out a hand as Jeannie reluctantly sat up and Jake followed suit. They looked out just in time to see a pair of dolphins break the water in an arcing jump about a hundred meters from the shore line.

"Oh!" Her hand went to her throat at the perfection of the moment.

"Aphrodite's companions. They have been waiting for us

to finish, and now they are calling," Pothos said. He was grinning like a boy, and Jeannie felt her heart lift in response to his delight. Jake's arm went around her and she leaned back into familiar warmth. "Come and play, beautiful couple, and let the delicious embrace of goddess-blessed waters soothe our bodies in readiness for the next round of loving."

CHAPTER FIVE

Next round? Jake mentally rolled his eyes. He wasn't sure how he'd possibly get it up again tonight, after that extensive rush. I'm thirty-eight, man, not eighteen. And he'd never shot his load in quite such a violent manner before. He must have had mountains of seed building up in his system for his orgasm to have been so vast.

Even as the thought crossed his mind, Jeannie was saying quietly in his ear, "I've had more orgasms tonight than I've had in the past three years, Jakey. And my body sure does ache, right now. Not sure if there's anything left in the tank for more loving!"

He gave her a quick kiss and held out his hand to help her up. "I know what you mean." Pothos had plunged ahead of them into the sea, his eagerness to swim with his dolphin friends abundantly clear. "Let's just enjoy this for what it is; an incredible chance to swim in the tropics at night, perfectly safe for once, and with dolphins, no less! Beats a rainy night in Melbourne, with me no doubt snoring beside you."

"True." Her fingers closed over his, and they waded out together.

"Are you okay?" he asked. "I mean…you know…because of the…you know…"

"Anal sex?"

"Yeah." He was blushing; he could feel it in the heat of his cheeks. And the embarrassment of blushing made him burn even more.

"I wouldn't want it all the time, hon, but—" she stopped thigh-deep in the water and looked up at him—"at that time, in that particular moment, it felt right. And don't forget the usual path was already taken. By Pothos."

When she smiled he let out a huge sigh, not realizing he'd been holding his breath. "I guess," he said, matching her grin. "So, we can just enjoy this?"

"Yes," she said, and suddenly he was being splashed, then she was off, plunging beneath the next wave and emerging further out with laughter coloring her voice. "Come get me, if you can."

He chased after her, diving beneath the surface of the water, not expecting to be able to see in the darkness but when he opened his eyes the visibility was as good as it would have been during the day. From beneath the water this time, he saw Jeannie do another duck dive. Then there was a flash of male leg as Pothos swam past with powerful strokes. He popped his head above the water with the intention of grabbing another breath but felt a sudden bump against his leg.

"Shit!" His yell of fright was matched by a shriek from Jeannie, but Pothos was there, laughing, shaking water droplets from his hair, and he realized they had just been introduced to the dolphins.

"They only want to play," Pothos said, and Jake again felt the nudge against his thigh.

He reached a tentative hand into the water and felt the

slippery smooth body of one of the dolphins glide through his fingers. He broke into a grin and looked across to see Jeannie's mouth shape itself into an 'o' of surprise and wonder light her eyes as she, too, touched a dolphin for the first time ever.

"Pothos," he said, looking at the man who was floating nearby and wanting to share what he felt. "This is—" A sudden shove beneath the waves knocked him off his feet and when he emerged a few seconds later, coughing up salt water, he came face to face with a chattering dolphin that looked as if it were teasing him. "Priceless," he finished, laughing.

Pothos stood, neck and shoulders above the sea, watching him with shadowed eyes. "The dolphins like you, Jake. A lot. Jeannie too. More than they expected to." He was unusually serious and Jake felt there was a hidden meaning in the words that he wasn't quite getting.

"That's good," he said awkwardly. Jeannie would have got it. Whatever it was. Then Pothos was shaking his head and grinning again before arching back into the water with a graceful move.

He turned his attention to the waiting dolphin and sent a handful of water splashing in its direction. "And you, mischief-maker…better watch out…"

There ensued an enchanting game of chase that ended up including all three people and two dolphins, Jake shouting with laughter and listening to Jeannie's carefree giggles and remembering the way it used to be for them, when they were still young and the stresses of life had not yet taken over.

We can be like that again. I know we can.

A sudden lick of arousal stirred through him and he reached down through the water to touch himself with a sense of disbelief. A hard on. *Again? I've never gotten one that quickly after making love. How can I want it again so fast?*

But he did. He wanted to sink his cock deep into his wife, reclaiming her body as his, and this time, he wanted more than that. This time he wanted to feel what she felt when he fucked her. He wanted someone to sink their cock into him while he made love to Jeannie.

No, he corrected. Not just someone. Pothos. Other than Jeannie, only Pothos could get him this damn horny.

He swam across to where Pothos had just ducked his wife under water. She emerged with intent in her eyes, but when she saw Jake she stopped short.

"Jake?" Her tone was uncertain, and she glanced back toward Pothos, who was looking at him with a knowing grin.

"Are you ready again, Jake?" Pothos asked, and he nodded.

"Yeah." His voice was hoarse.

"Jake." Jeannie spoke his name again, but this time with understanding. She could probably read the rampant desire in his face. Her lips parted and she asked hesitantly, "Who do you want?"

He reached for her beneath the water, felt the curve of her hip and pulled her close. She gasped when she came into contact with his cock. Hell, he felt like gasping himself, he was so ready. "I want you, Jeannie," he said. Then he looked over his shoulder. "And I want you, Pothos. I want you to fuck me, hard, while I make love with Jeannie."

He didn't wait for a response from either of them, confident that the ache of desire was about to be amplified by Pothos. However their new lover did it, Jake didn't care. He just knew that this night was like no other he'd ever experienced, and the heady lust that filled his nostrils had just gotten stronger as Pothos' eyes flashed bright and his wife let out a faint moan and shifted impatiently against him. He lifted Jeannie, taking her weight easily with the help of the water's buoyancy, and settled her warm pussy onto his dick. She immediately wrapped her legs around his waist and her arms around his neck and clung like a limpet while she kissed him. His hands kneaded the rounded cheeks of her buttocks and he pushed up into her hot center, taking her resulting gasp into him as they continued to kiss. The tip of his cock connected with her body in that deep, dark place inside her.

He broke off the kiss. "You're mine." He thrust again, not sure why he felt he had to stake his claim, and she let out a strangled cry.

"Always, Jake."

Then the hardness of a male body cradled his back, pressing into his thighs, and he buried his face in Jeannie's golden hair, almost overwhelmed with a mixture of fear and excitement at the realization of what was coming.

"And you're mine, Jake. You and Jeannie. Mine." The deep voice rumbled in his ear as the hardness of Pothos' organ poked and stroked him, from that sensitive place behind his balls all the way up to press into his rear opening, then back again. Down and up, back and forward, stroking with such a measured pace that the movement threatened to send him over the edge of a cliff.

Or, more accurately, into a wave.

He locked his knees as his legs threatened to buckle, but then strong hands were there, holding his hips, steadying him even as he drove again into Jeannie.

Mine.

Fear and excitement. Like a knife edge, with the promise of pleasure on one side, the threat of pain on the other. God, he wanted this so bad.

Jeannie was whimpering now, lunging up and down in his arms, riding his cock and clenching herself around him. Thank Christ for those pelvic floor exercises she did religiously every day. The muscle contractions were so strong it felt like her body was trying to milk him as she said, "Fuck me, Jake."

He growled. "Yes! And you fuck me, Pothos."

The pain crashed over him as Pothos drove into Jake's body, the unfamiliar intrusion like an assault on all his senses at once. He let out a harsh panting gasp and his fingers tightened so hard on Jeannie's hips that she also cried out.

"Oh, my God!" He was afraid to move, afraid not to move, but then the pain began to recede as Pothos slid out and in again. It was gentler this time and the stroking pressure against his prostate was both soothing and erotic. It was centered deep within him, this sensation of fullness that began to grow into something more.

So this is what it felt like to be fucked. This strangeness of having someone else inside your body, the ache of desire making you forget everything but the need to move your hips in the age old rhythm of love, the feel of lips suckling against the back of your neck, the caress of fingers around your waist, the taste of your wife in your mouth as you lean in to take everything she has to offer...and more...

Thrusting, pounding, riding each other in the deliciously tepid embrace of the sea, until you can't hold on any longer...

Jake released Jeannie's lips and let out a piercing cry as he came, emptying himself into her as she matched his orgasm and came around his pulsing cock. Then there was an echoing roar in his ear as Pothos lost it, too, and the feel of hot liquid filling him gave his orgasm even greater impetus. He continued to moan and release yet more fluid into his wife.

She was sobbing, her face buried in the crook of his neck, and now Jake was crying, too, silently, with hot tears that dripped down his cheeks and were lost in Jeannie's already sea-drenched hair.

Too much.

Pothos was holding them both up; he must be, because Jake's legs were no longer working and he felt drained and shaky and ready to keel over. They were still joined, all three of them, and he leaned back into Pothos' hard chest as Jeannie leaned into his.

"Pothos," he began, but his throat was too tight to continue. *How do we ever thank you for this moment? This sense of utter fulfillment?*

"You have, Jake. You already have." Lips grazed the top of his head, and he was truly at peace for the first time in his life.

I think a little part of me loves you, Pothos. I love my wife, but somehow, I love you too.

At that moment the two dolphins broke the water further out, and their joyous jump silhouetted against the lightening sky seemed somehow a manifestation of everything he had experienced in the dual embrace of Pothos and his wife.

"Jeannie," he whispered, when he could finally speak again. "Look at the horizon. Dawn's coming."

She lifted her head and looked, and another sob escaped her. "I don't want this night to end," she said in a quiet voice. "I want this to last forever."

"Yeah. Me too."

The sky was growing lighter, streaks of pale gold beginning to strobe the edge of a few puffy clouds, turning the midnight blue to a paler hue. Apart from the jutting ends of the cove they were in, the horizon out to the Great Barrier Reef was untouched by land as far as the eye could see. From the shore he heard the first warbling call of bird-song as creatures that'd been sleeping through the night began to stir. The moon was still up, though, and its silver sheen warred with the gold of the coming day to coat the sea in a shiny metallic blanket.

"Like platinum," he said, and tightened his grip around Jeannie. "Our anniversary night together. With the god of love by our side."

"Pothos," Jeannie said. "Thank you."

"Shh," said their Adonis, his arms still around them both. "My beautiful couple, it is all good. You have taught me something, too, this night. It was something that I knew in the abstract, but not in a real sense. Until now. Through your love for one another, and your generous acceptance of Eros into your relationship, you have shown me the true power of the erotes." He laughed suddenly, with an exhilaration that Jake felt resonate through his body. "I think I am in love with you both, a little. Me…in love!" He spoke with the wonder of a little boy on Christmas morning, and Jake saw Jeannie's lips curve up in an indulgent smile.

"Welcome to our world, Pothos," she said.

"Thank you, beautiful couple. So much. Happy anniversary."

CHAPTER SIX

The dolphins played nearby as they spent a few minutes more in the water, and then Jeannie staggered out and lay on her back at the shore line. She looked up at streaks of gold extending across the sky, and listened to the nearby splashes of the men chasing after one of the dolphins. They would never catch it, she knew, unless it wanted to be caught, but it sounded like they were still having fun.

She couldn't join in if her life depended on it, though. Her body ached in places she'd never even dreamed of, replete but utterly exhausted. Thank goodness the kids were away this weekend, staying with friends. It meant she and Jake could sleep in. But...she was probably asleep right now, she remembered. The magic of this night could only have been a dream.

Why that thought filled her with sadness she wasn't sure, but this was one dream she didn't want to wake up from. She felt as if she and Jake had taken a momentous step forward in their relationship. Even after twenty years, it seemed there were aspects to each other—or maybe in the end it was just aspects of herself?—still to be discovered.

And Pothos, what of him? Would he now disappear back into the depths of her imagination, or would he stay and continue to enhance their relationship? Real or not, if he chose to leave, what would she do when he disappeared? How would they survive without this wonderful man to complete them?

"Jeannie." He materialized beside her and traced gentle fingers over her curves. In their electrically-charged wake, her strength returned and the confusion in her mind begin to settle. "You and Jake will be fine without me. But I am not going far. Not for long. I will return whenever you need me. Or maybe"—he paused—"whenever I need you." His grin held an element of sheepishness. "Not something I expected, I admit," he said. "But these…feelings I am having, I confess I rather like."

"Oh, Pothos," she laughed. "You'll have to learn some contractions."

"Contractions?" He frowned.

"You can say 'I'm' instead of 'I am,' 'don't' instead of 'do not,' and so on."

"Ah." His frown disappeared. "Are you…teasing me, Jeannie?"

"Maybe a little."

"So. Maybe I will tease you a little, now." His voice held the hint of laughter that she loved, and as he stood up his vibrant presence began to shift and fade. "Next time, I will appear in a way that satisfies even those desires you have not yet begun to be aware of. Maybe something like this?"

She blinked as his image seemed to have another super-imposed over the top. Then Pothos was gone and a tall woman stood in his place, her long, wavy dark hair cascading over her shoulders. She was clearly naked under a see-through, floor-length white nightgown, with generous breasts almost spilling out of the low cut top and supremely feminine curves adding delicious shape to the unexpected vision. But familiar green eyes lit with laughter invited her without words to enjoy the view.

This is what he called teasing? Jeannie's breath caught in her throat. She couldn't stop her gaze drifting down over the curved figure to focus on that dark triangle clearly visible through the diaphanous material at the apex of the woman's thighs. What would it be like to caress the slit of another woman? Would it be as moist as hers suddenly was, right this minute? What would it be like...to dip her tongue in there and taste?

"M-maybe," she managed, and the woman threw back her head and let out a tinkling laugh.

"Definitely," the night gowned beauty corrected drily, and then her gaze shifted over Jeannie's shoulder. "What do you think, Jake?"

Jeannie turned to see that Jake had joined them on the sand, his gaze flickering between herself and the other woman. She saw his cock shift and begin to swell, and the moist heat between her thighs deepened as she witnessed the speed and the strength of his arousal.

Really? Her lips curved upwards. Ten years of sex in one night. Yep. I'll take that, thanks.

"If this is what Jeannie wants, then I'm more than happy for you to visit again." Jake's voice vibrated with desire, and he knelt down to slide an arm around her waist. The trembling in his touch mirrored her own. "Jeannie?" he queried, pressing a light kiss on her temple. "Is it?"

She took a deep, shuddering breath, and leaned in to Jake's embrace. "Yes," she admitted. "But only if you're there, too."

"Baby," he growled, turning her so she was more fully

enclosed in his arms, "I wouldn't have it any other way." The full impact of his erection now crushed between them was a heady promise, but it wasn't enough.

How the hell can I still want more after the night we've already had?

A moan left her lips. She wanted Jake inside her, cocooned in the tightly sheathed embrace of her body, and by the way his muscles were tensing, as if getting ready to shift his weight up and over her, she knew he was there, too.

But Pothos—well, not Pothos anymore; the woman—was speaking in a feminine, lilting tone. "It is time for me to leave you now, beautiful couple."

"No!" Panic raced through her, and Jake's heart jolted beneath her cheek as he echoed her plea.

"Stay. Please," he said, and as if they were one, both held out a hand toward Pothos.

"I cannot," said the woman who had loved them both as a man. Regret laced the words. "I wish I could. It turns out you are my favorites, Jeannie and Jake. This night has been everything a man—or a woman—could possibly wish for. But our night's work has been most successful, would you not agree?"

She stepped forward and put an arm around both of them, and Jeannie shivered at the swish of the gown against her side while familiar fingers traced down the curve of her back. She felt an answering shudder in Jake, and though she hadn't known it was possible, his erection swelled further. Wetness slicked her where the tip of his cock rested. He was more than ready to pound into her. She sighed her pleasure, taking one last moment to enjoy the thrill of a threesome embrace, before looking up to meet raging hunger in her husband's eyes.

"Yes," she whispered, "I think you're right. The spark is well and truly back, Pothos. Thank you."

"I will return," the man/woman promised. "At the changing of the seasons, when you need me...now make love, my beautiful lovers. Make love like it is your first time once again. With all the wonder and anticipation and passion that you had in the beginning. No more yearning."

The voice washed over them and Jeannie let out a cry as Jake slid into her. She wrapped her legs around him. "I want you, Jake. I love you."

"And I love you. So much..." Then they were lying on the cool sand, limbs entwined, and Jake was pushing into her, groaning as her hips rose to meet his, and the sheets tangled...no, wait...the sand beneath her back...no, it was the sheets on their bed...

She froze at the same moment Jake did, and looked around in shock to find herself back in her own bed, cocooned beneath the covers, her husband's sweat-slicked body joined with her own, and his cock filling her to bursting point.

Pothos?

She glanced around, but of course they were alone in the light of dawn. It had been a dream. An unbelievably erotic dream that must have been so strong she had attacked Jake even in her sleep.

"Hi," she said, blinking up at him, a hint of embarrassment in her tone. He was staring down at her with a bemused look. If he knew what she'd just been dreaming, what would he think? The ache in her womb began to increase at the remembrance of her fantasies and her legs tightened involuntarily around him. She felt the shudder go through him as he shifted on top of her. He was still inside her, still massively erect, and that tiny movement, not quite a thrust, had such an effect on her body that she let out a faint moan.

His breath hissed out. "Hi, yourself," he growled, and

then he captured her lips with his own. The kiss was deep and lasted several seconds, his mouth and tongue almost punishing her with a newfound mastery and purpose.

Newfound mastery?

He was Jake, her husband of twenty years. Nothing new about that. Was there? She swore she could almost taste Pothos at the edges of her husband's kiss.

"Jake," she began, when he finally broke the connection. "How—"

"I want to fuck you so bad." His voice was guttural. "You smell like the beach."

Her heart jumped, and her own sense of smell kicked into play. "So do you," she realized. "Why? Why do we both smell like the beach?" When I've just spent a whole night dreaming of us having sex on the sand. With Pothos.

Jake rolled over and brought her too, so she was sitting astride him. He was smiling, reaching out to circle her nipples with his thumbs. "I dreamt of the beach," he said, and her heart sped up. Was it possible he'd been having erotic dreams, too? She doubted they'd be as debauched as hers were, though. But then, incredibly, she saw a faint blush darken his cheeks. "I want to tell you what I've been dreaming, but…" His fingers tightened on her nipples and he pulled on one of the erect buds almost fiercely.

Her breath caught for a second. "But what?"

"But you'll think I'm…no, just forget it." He turned his head away, but not before she caught the flash of self-loathing in his eyes. And as he continued to look away she saw the faint smattering of white on the arch of his neck, almost at the dip of his collarbone.

"Jake!"

Her cry had his head whipping back in shock. With a

trembling finger she reached out and touched his neck, then brought her finger up to show him.

Sand.

Grains of white sand.

In their bed.

On her husband.

"Oh, my God, Jeannie! Did you...did we...Pothos?"

Was it real? How could such an experience be real? "I...I don't know." She wasn't sure whether to laugh, or cry, or scream with shock.

"Did last night really—"

"Shh." She placed a sandy finger over his lips, her heart racing madly, but not with fear. How to process this? How to deal with what they had exposed in each other? How to deal with the impossible being real? "I think maybe...we did."

His shock was palpable, and she knew, seeing again that faint flash of fear, of self-loathing, that he needed something from her. Whatever had transpired this night, they would deal with it later. Right now, Jake needed her. Needed acceptance for who he was in every way. And she needed the same from him. They were soul mates, and soul mates didn't judge, they just...embraced their other half...

"I love you, Jake," she said, and began to slide off him.

"Wait! No!" He grabbed at her hips to hold himself inside her, but she laughed.

"I'm not going anywhere, Jakey." She settled her mons at the base of his still erect cock, pressing her clit gently into the angled flesh between his organ and his balls. "Was your... experience...something like this?"

They both looked down at his almost vertical appendage. It appeared, from the way she was sitting astride him, as if it had grown out of her pussy. She heard the hissed intake of his breath and knew she was right.

"Yes," he said, and shuddered. "Do you hate me now?"

"Of course not." She took his cock in one hand and began to stroke. It looked like she was pleasuring herself, and he watched her movements with an avid desperation. "I love you even more, if that's possible," she said. "I feel like you finally let me in. To see all of you. Do you hate me? Because I tell you, this turns me on."

He groaned. "God, no! How could I hate you?" His hand joined hers on his cock, and she began to thrust into him with her pelvis as they stroked together. Her clit swelled as it pressed against his hardness. "I'm so sorry I didn't remember our anniversary," he said. "Well, I did, but—here. I bought something."

He stilled her movements, and then reached over to the bedside table to remove a small package from the top drawer. He pressed the package into her palm. "For you. To say thank you for the past twenty years, and to ask if you'll put up with me for the next twenty."

Her heart skipped a beat. He'd actually bought her a gift? "Twenty?" Her voice was breathless. "I was thinking another forty. Maybe even fifty."

"I hope so." He rested his hands on her hips. "Open it."

She clicked open the tiny velvet covered box, and nestled inside was a ring. Not quite gold, not quite silver.

"Platinum," Jake said. Jeannie's eyes filled with tears. He hadn't forgotten.

"I got something for you, too," she said, "but you fell asleep before I could give it to you."

"I'm sorry—"

"No." She reached down and touched his lips with the tip of her finger. "No more sorry. Only…my gift's breakable, so it'll have to wait a bit now." China. She'd thought it was a china anniversary, but Pothos had set her straight.

At the thought of Pothos she automatically rocked her pelvis a little and felt Jake's hips twitch beneath her. She knew the signs. After all these years, she knew. He was aching to be inside her, pounding away, and it was a place she was happy for him to be. She shifted until she was over his cock, ready to plunge down onto him. But first she paused and looked down at his contrite face.

"It's okay," she began, but he frowned.

"No. It's not okay. I've been putting the business ahead of you and the kids for the past year and a half. I'll make sure it doesn't happen again." He gripped her hips and eased her down, and she groaned at the completeness of their joining. "You deserve better. Pothos reminded me of that, tonight."

"That goes both ways, Jake." She grinned and began to ride him. "I promise not to wear my flannel nightie for a while, and I'll shave my legs, and…ah…that feels good…"

Her husband's thumb was twirling small circles around the nub of her clit as she rode his cock, and then thoughts and words went out the window as his hips lifted beneath her and they began to move in unison.

The peak, when it came, was violent and prolonged, and she arched her back and let out a ragged cry at the same instant he convulsed and emptied himself into her. "Oh, Jeannie, I love you so much…"

She collapsed against his chest and burrowed her face into the crook of his neck. "And I love you, Jake," she whispered against his warm, sex-scented skin. "Happy anniversary, darling."

Curled up against her husband's body, she thought again of the Adonis who had changed the course of their lives in this one, short night. "Thank you, Pothos," she whispered, and felt Jake's arm squeeze her a little tighter in response.

"That man is pure gold," he murmured.

"No." She hoped Pothos could hear them, wherever he was. "Pure platinum. See you on the first night of summer, precious man."

Ω Ψ Ω

Please read on for the next instalment in the GODS OF LOVE series.

APHRODITE CALLING

BY JEN KATEMI

APHRODITE CALLING

HIMEROS, GOD OF SEXUAL DESIRE

Gina Deveraux is forced to confront her painful past when she attends a high school reunion. Born into a male body, she spent her childhood and teen years living as a boy, and has only now returned in an effort to put the past behind her so she can begin to live life without the continuing fear of loneliness and rejection.

Himeros is one of the erotes, an aspect of Eros, and as such it is his duty to answer the call of sexual desire whenever a human needs him. But he has been living among mortals too long and his interest has waned. When he decides to accept one last call he finds a woman who is unique. A woman who encapsulates the whole human experience in her body, and her soul. Has he finally discovered the one with whom even a god of desire could find fulfillment?

This story is for everyone, transgender or otherwise, who has ever struggled with identity or felt as if they are outside the "mainstream" of society—it takes enormous strength of character to fight for what you know is right when others say the opposite.

CHAPTER ONE

Desire. He could sense it. Wafting up from below to his current vantage point on the landing. His shoulders wanted to slump, but he couldn't allow it. No matter how weary he was of this calling, he was a god. Their god. It was his duty to respond.

Perhaps his brother had the better idea. Reside with the gods, not the mortals, and come out to play only when the mood took him. That had been at the changing of the seasons, for Pothos. It was when Aphrodite's power was at its strongest and when they all felt the mating urge most intensely.

Himeros suspected that the seasonal visitation schedule was likely to change a little for Pothos, now that his brother had found his pair. A smile curved his lips as he recalled his brother's astonishment and joy, but then the smile faded.

There was no joy here, for him. No pair of lovers such as Pothos had found. No one to tantalize and entice him out of his lethargy. But he stayed anyway, hoping, searching. Answering the endless calls to Aphrodite from those seeking sexual gratification.

So. He squared his shoulders and looked down at the sea of mortals stretched out before him on the ground floor below. Which of them was the seeker this time?

He sampled the air, testing, and his fingers tightened on the handrail. There was something different about this one. Desire, yes. Stronger than any he had felt in years. For that alone, he knew he would answer this call. But the sexual nature of the desire was edged with more. So much more. A desire for... He frowned, slanted his head to the right, and focused his gaze on the person in need.

Well, well. This was one call he had never experienced. And he thought he'd seen it all.

Excitement rippled through his body, replacing the ennui to which he'd grown accustomed.

Sweet mother.

Aphrodite, could this possibly be the one?

$$\Omega \, \Psi \, \Omega$$

"So, which one's your husband?" The bane of Gina's teenage existence looked expectantly around the room and then back with an unpleasant smile. "You are married by now, aren't you, G? It has been fifteen years."

"That is why we're here tonight, Maris. Our fifteen year reunion." Gina's teeth were beginning to clench and she'd only been here twenty-two minutes. She worked her jaw reflexively. "And, ah, no, I'm not married, actually."

"Gay partner then? Or..." The other woman's eyes flared with curiosity. "Maybe you don't call it that. What do you call it?"

I call it sheer stupidity for thinking things might be different fifteen years on. She took a deep, calming breath before she spoke, but the words that came out were not the ones she'd intended. "I call it...engaged, just like anyone else does. He's...there. Over at the bar. The one with the dark hair waiting for the bartender."

Shit! Why had she lied? So much for facing her past with honesty and truth. The moment she experienced that cruel gleam in Maris' eye she reverted right back to teenage immaturity.

"But which one?" There were several guys milling around the bar who could fit the dark-haired description she'd given, and this was Maris, after all. Thorough, if nothing else. Gina found her arm clutched in a tight grip as the woman tried to pull her across the room. "Show me. I want to know who was brave enough to take on the Amazon ball breaker."

At the old and hated nickname Gina stopped dead, and with her ten inch height advantage over Maris, the latter had no choice but to come to a screeching halt beside her. "Oops," Maris giggled, "didn't mean to call you that, Gerry. It just slipped out, you know. Old habits and all."

"Yeah. Sure. And it's Gina." Why the hell had she decided to come along this evening? Fifteen years was not long enough to put the horrors of her past behind her. Fifty years would never be long enough to get over what Maris and her crowd had inflicted on Gina during high school.

And she could feel them staring, every last one. Not openly, of course. Most people weren't actually that rude. But human nature being what it is, they were curious, and the surreptitious glances and raised eyebrows punctuating their own conversations were almost impossible to miss. It was what she'd expected, of course. Still, it was so hard not to turn around and walk straight out again.

Deep down, she'd always known the Eastwood High reunion was going to be a difficult evening. In the end, though, that was precisely why she decided to accept the invitation to this cocktail function. She wanted to challenge herself to face her fears of the past, and to put it where it belonged—in a great big "this is history" basket, so she could start a fresh chapter of her life as Gina. A woman who was strong enough to get through almost anything and look to the future without being tied down by what had gone before.

Yeah, right. And you're doing real well with that so far, sister.

Maris had latched onto Gina as soon as she arrived at this upmarket city hotel on the banks of Melbourne's Yarra River. No sooner had Gina picked up her name badge from the registration desk than the other woman was there, hovering. Had she been watching to see who picked up the Deveraux name tag? They all knew, of course. People talked. But none of them had seen the new Gina Deveraux, formerly Gerry, since graduation.

Drawing her into the function area and talking about her husband who worked in investment banking and their three young children, and asking about Gina's life in the last few years. All the while with that spiteful gleam in her eye. What the hell was she going to do if Maris didn't detach herself, but insisted instead on meeting the so-called fiancé?

You could just tell the truth. She took a deep breath and opened her mouth to admit the lie, but she never got the chance as a darkly tanned hand reached down to loosen Maris' grip on her arm. "Darling," purred a deep voice that rolled over Gina's skin like warm chocolate sauce. "There you are. I've been looking all over for you. Here's the drink I promised."

She looked up—and up—into a pair of blue-green eyes that sparkled with compassion. The sensory blast caused by the sound of his voice intensified as she took in the setting in which those gorgeous eyes resided. A mess of dark hair itching to be finger-combed into submission topped a face straight out of Hollywood, with strongly defined eyebrows and cheekbones slashing down at an angle almost too severe to be sexy. A wide mouth that would look slightly cruel if it wasn't currently curled up at one corner screamed sensuality, while that body...

Hmm, she thought, raising an eyebrow. Whoever the hell you are, that body is just...yum.

His broad shoulders tapered down to narrow hips before flaring again into thighs whose muscles were evident even beneath the material of an expensive-looking charcoal suit. A suit that fit him perfectly, though it seemed almost a waste to cover assets as faultless as those with mere fabric. His were the kind of looks that made a woman want to check her lipstick and straighten her clothing, and she resisted the impulse to reach up and touch her hair, knowing she'd put enough product on the neat brown bob to keep it immaculate right through the evening.

Instead, she stretched out a hand to accept the drink he was offering, not sure of his game but willing to play along for now. As her fingers brushed his, a flare of sexual awareness flickered deep inside and her breath caught momentarily.

There was something in the stranger's demeanor that suggested the opposite of civility. A sense of untamed wildness that made his suit seem slightly out of place and gave her the impression that he did not really...belong.

Among us, but not of us.

The thought darted out of nowhere and she had no idea

what it meant, but the nerve endings in her body didn't care. They sparked to life while her stomach flip-flopped in a pang of excitement that she hadn't felt in a long time.

She gave a surreptitious tug with her free hand on the red dress she was wearing, settling its skirt more smoothly around her hips, and managed somehow to smile politely, even though she wasn't sure who the hell he was, but willing to run with whatever he had in mind if it would help her get away from Maris.

Who, come to think of it, did not look quite so attractive now that her mouth was hanging open in that look of frozen astonishment.

Gina couldn't help it. Her lips twitched, but she managed to turn her gulp of laughter into a polite little cough. *Whoever you are, I love you for creating that look on Maris' face.*

She raised the glass to her lips to hide the grin, and the stranger met her gaze over the rim, a hint of mirth brightening the blue of his eyes. Unaccountably, she felt as if he were reading her mind, or at least, sharing the joke in a strange moment of camaraderie. The warmth of his regard enveloped her, like a protective blanket.

"Thank you," she said, tipping her glass toward him and adding a belated, "Darling." When she took a sip her eyebrows rose. Not quite the same as a nice smooth glass of red, but this white wine had a piquancy she'd never experienced before. Sweet, and yet not sweet at all. It tasted of peaches and honey, and...flowers? What sort of wine was this?

She took a bigger sip this time, enjoying the unusual flavor and the warmth as it coursed down her throat, and realized the stranger was watching her closely as she drank. His regard made her nervous and she darted out the tip of her tongue to moisten her lips and capture the last of that tantalizing wine residue.

His pupils flared.

Desire. The air between them suddenly crackled with tension and she found herself unable to breathe at all.

"Gina," Maris spluttered. "Is this...who?"

The moment broke and her heart thumped painfully. What was I thinking? It had been indulgent, even if just for a few seconds, to imagine this god-like creature had arrived to rescue her from Maris and everyone else who judged without empathy. To imagine a fleeting sexual chemistry with someone who actually understood.

As if someone like him would be interested in me.

Had they gone to Eastwood High together? She recognized nothing about him, and couldn't imagine any of the people with whom she'd attended school turning out like this. So blisteringly hot.

Now, of course, he would introduce himself and they would all get back to realizing that Gina was on her own. Sorry, Maris. No fiancé in the building.

Her lips tightened. Alone in the city, in a sea of people.

"Maris, this is..." Her voice trailed off.

"Himeros," the tanned Adonis said, reaching out to shake Maris' hand. "Gina's fiancé."

Three things happened in quick succession then. So quick that later, Gina couldn't even say what had transpired first. Maris' intake of breath so deep she choked on her own saliva, the wine falling out of Gina's suddenly numb fingers, and the man—Himeros?—reaching forward with almost superhuman speed to catch the glass two feet from the ground. His free hand snaked around Gina's waist, pulling her in to the warm curve of his body and anchoring her there while Maris recovered from her choking fit.

He's taller than me, she found herself thinking. For once, there is someone in this world who is taller than me.

He leaned down and nuzzled her hair, and she felt a spark like she'd been walking on carpet before touching a piece of metal. Sharp. Unexpected. Energizing.

"Trust me," he murmured, and she gave a tiny nod.

"For now," she clarified after a moment, and he gave a delighted-sounding laugh.

"Oh, Gina. You and I are going to enjoy one another so much more than you know." He glanced at the now-recovered Maris staring wide-eyed at them both, and then focused that wicked gaze back on Gina. "You know, darling, after that delightful love-making session we had this morning, I want to refresh my memory. I need your passion again. Right now."

"Oh! No, I don't think—" Her protest turned to a frightened squeak as his mouth covered hers. He didn't understand...he couldn't understand...he'd hate her if he knew...oh, my God, but that feels good. Almost...almost normal...

Her lips parted against his insistent coaxing and she let him in. It's been so long since I did this. Since I did anything approaching normal.

But now she could feel his tongue, just the tip of it, skating across her teeth, teasing her own tongue with a gentle invitation to dance, their breath mingling, suction growing stronger. A moan now. Was it hers? Or his? Or was it both of them? Low groans forming deep in the backs of their throat, the throat that he was now caressing with one finger, the other hand in her hair, tightening like a fist...

Where did the wine go? she wondered, then didn't care as their kiss deepened and she felt an unexpected heaviness in her pussy area. She gasped as the ache intensified, inadvertently drawing the sweetness of his breath further into her body. The sweet breath of a stranger whose lips against her own were turning her on in a way she had never thought possible.

It's okay. It's okay to do this in a crowded room, surrounded by people who couldn't give a shit about me as a woman, who couldn't know the journey...who couldn't know.

The kiss ended, and she looked up into a gaze so wise she felt that anything might be possible. "I know," he said. Two simple words, and she was caught.

How could he know? What did he mean?

"Maris," he said. "Please excuse us. Gina and I are going to be busy for the next several hours. Aren't we, darling?" The voice vibrated with craving and Gina's cheeks heated up.

"Well, I—"

"Let's go." He spoke with sudden authority and the people milling around them stopped trying to hide their furtive glances and gaped openly at the loud command. Gina felt a flash of antipathy at the way he'd called extra attention to them both. As if she needed more. But the antipathy was coupled with something else. Something primitive that responded to his authority and had her lips parting in anticipation even as she raised one eyebrow at his tone.

"And where might we be going?"

His eyes smoldered as he met her gaze, the flash of merriment her only warning. "To our suite upstairs, of course. I want to make love to you until your screams of release raise the roof on this building. Until everyone at this reunion—" he looked around at the sea of faces staring unashamedly, "—can understand what they've been missing and crave it madly for themselves." He drew himself up to his impressively full height, and the voice also seemed to grow, reverberating around the room. "I promise you all one thing. Tonight, when you are home in bed with your partner of choice, or perhaps alone with only your imagination for company, you will crave what Gina has to offer."

His fingers traced a pattern along her collar bone, right above where her racing heart was debating whether or not to jump out of her chest. His lips parted in a wide, wolfish grin. "But I am the only one who will get to take it."

CHAPTER TWO

"**O**h my God! I cannot believe you said that!" Gina's face, when she caught sight of her own reflection in the mirrored elevator, was beetroot red, but she was laughing. Hard. Maybe I'm hysterical, she thought, and that made her laugh even harder. "Jesus."

She leaned against the wall and watched as Himeros pressed the button for the top floor. Figured he'd actually have a hotel room, and of course it would be the penthouse. Who was this guy? And why did she not feel afraid to go upstairs with him? Just because he looked like a romance novel hero didn't mean he wasn't ten different kinds of weird. Something deep inside her was responding to this man in a way that was unlike anything she had ever felt before. She couldn't explain it, but she felt safe with him.

Despite the fact that he'd just told everyone in the room he was taking her upstairs to fuck her brains out. Only he'd said it slightly more poetically than that.

She reached up and rubbed her temples. "That's the last school reunion I'll ever be able to attend!"

Himeros pouted, looking slightly put out by her response. "Would you have wanted to attend another?"

"Well, no, but that's not the point, really, is it?"

"Why not?"

"Well, because...I don't know, it just isn't!"

"Aha! So you don't have an answer, then." His triumphant smile made her laugh again.

"Who are you, Himeros, and why are you doing this? Helping me escape, I mean. Though," she paused and looked at the numbers flashing past as they ascended in the elevator, "maybe I'm not escaping out of here, as such. Am I going from the frying pan into the fire?"

He shifted a little, and the confined space suddenly seemed a lot smaller than it had a few seconds ago. She had the impression of vibrating energy, reaching out to encompass her. If she hadn't known better, she would have said his tanned skin held a strange shimmer that made him look as if he were lit from within. She blinked, but the light intensified.

"I am Himeros, god of sexual desire, and I am here to answer your call to Aphrodite," he said. "You are most certainly heading into the fire, but this is one fire you won't want to extinguish, once you've savored the heat of these flames."

"My call to Aphrodite? What exactly do you mean by that?" It's certainly getting hot in here, she thought. Why am I so aware of him? I've been around men before. Sexy men. But it's never felt like my body is finally waking up...

"Gina." When had he moved closer? Why was he now standing directly in front of her, his arms raised to press a hand against the elevator wall each side of her head? Had he answered her question? She couldn't remember. Aphrodite...

"We will wake you up, together."

Her breath caught. He was now leaning forward, almost

touching her, his face so close to hers she could see the flecks of green in the blue of his irises. So close that if she raised her hand, she'd be able to brush the delicate end of his long eyelashes, or trace the angled shadows cast by those gorgeous cheekbones.

"We're here." His words whispered in a puff of warmth across her lips and she parted them involuntarily.

"Are we?" How she was managing to keep talking was beyond her. She wanted to close the few centimeters of distance between them and explore that mouth again, to feel the firmness of his body up against hers, to enjoy the heat of a hard cock that wasn't her own pressing against the soft curve of her stomach.

"You have a choice, now, Gina," he said. "Join me here, tonight, and I promise you will not regret your decision. But if you don't want that, tell me now, before we step over the threshold..."

"Himeros," she whispered, not sure what she was asking, and at the same time knowing what she needed to say. "I want to, so much, but there are things about me you don't know."

"I know everything, Gina. I told you, I heard your call and I am here to answer it, if you wish."

She shook her head. "I'm afraid." She closed her eyes to avoid seeing the revulsion and started when she felt the touch of his fingertips on her cheek. A touch that sent shockwaves right through her body—unfamiliar shockwaves in places that had been numb for too long. She'd been wrong. She wasn't strong enough to handle everything. She wasn't strong enough to handle this.

"Himeros." She took a deep breath and pressed back as far as she could against the wall. "I'm not, well, I wasn't..." Just say the damn words. Get it over with. "I wasn't always like I am now. I used to be—"

"You were born with male genitalia, and you lived as a man for the first twenty-four years of your life. You were Gerry, and now you are Gina. I know, gorgeous woman. I told you, I already know. Open your eyes and see how much I want you right now."

Ω Ψ Ω

Himeros watched as her eyes flew open and she stared at him in what appeared to be shock. She really had the most unusually colored eyes. Blue like his own, and yet they were nothing alike. Gina's were a pale icy shade, rimmed with long black lashes. Right now her dilated pupils and slightly parted lips were obvious signals to the desire seething below the surface. It was so intense he could almost taste it, and he felt a responding lick of heat to his groin.

With so much sensuality simmering beneath her translucent skin, that thick, dark hair cut into a chin-length style that framed her face, her long limbs that spoke of strength and a contrasting vulnerability lurking behind her eyes, she was simply stunning. But she didn't yet know how to manage that beautiful femininity.

He reached out and captured one of her hands, guiding it not to his already hard cock, but to his chest. Her fingers were warm beneath his grip and he pressed them over the area near his heart, hoping she could feel the racing at his core beneath her cushioned fingertips.

"This is what you are doing to me, Gina." He inhaled deeply and was surprised to hear the tremble of emotion in the breath. "I want to show you what you can be. What you can feel. And...maybe..." An ache began in his chest, some-where beneath her touch, and he frowned. What was this ache? He could almost make out the haunting laughter of Aphrodite ringing in his ears and his lips twisted.

Yes, sweet mother. Wicked mother. Leading me here, now, when I've been so weary of this time and place. I hear you.

"Maybe your sexual need will bring me back to life, Gina. Remind me that I am capable of feeling, too. It's been a long time since I...felt. We need each other tonight. Please?" That last word slipped out before he could control it. Where had it come from? He had never begged for anything in his life.

I am a god, and this woman is simply another human in need...

His fingers tightened over hers. No. He would not lie to himself. This woman was not simply another mortal. She was different. He could sense it. And she could well be his ulti-mate saving grace, if he could only bear to let her in.

She needed to connect on a physical level. He needed it on an emotional level. Would they...could they...make it work?

He bowed his head over her hand, thinking about the power of Aphrodite. Thinking about loneliness.

Seems like it has been forever.

Ω Ψ Ω

And he thought his heart was racing? Hers was pumping so hard she thought she might faint. He knew her secret, and he wanted her anyway? Desire made her body ache with need, but the craving still warred with fear in her mind. She was afraid of what he wanted, afraid of what he expected from her. Afraid she couldn't ever really be normal. What if she couldn't be with a man in that way? What if she couldn't feel in a physical sense?

I'm so tired of being on my own.

It had already been far too long. Eight years since the procedure. Even longer, since she'd been with anyone in a sexual way. Back then, she had still been pre-op, though she'd been living as a woman, already on the hormones.

A chick with a dick.

Amazing how many men were excited by the idea of having sex with someone who had tits and a cock.

Including James, her boyfriend of over a year. She'd thought they had something special. Like The Crying Game in a way, only better, because she'd told him straight up she was a transsexual woman so there'd been no surprises when they ended up in bed and her dick was as hard as his. He told her he'd never been with a guy before, even one living as a woman, and she let that slide, even though she wanted to scream it at him. "I'm not a guy. I am a woman. Can't you see it? Can't you see me?" But his eyes had already been feasting on her cock, and he'd nearly put his neck out when he'd moved downward so fast to take her into his mouth.

"Always wanted to taste another guy. I want you to cum in my face, baby." She remembered how his hoarse words had washed over the tip of her before he sucked her in, and she had immediately closed her eyes, pretending it was her clitoris he was teasing into orgasm. When the pressure and the heat built to an almost unbearable peak she felt him shift, and opened her eyes intending to return the favor and give him some oral pleasure, but he flipped her over and plunged into her ass from behind. No gentle teasing of her entrance to ready her, either. The dress she'd bought only that morning had ridden up in a bunched mess as she knelt on the edge of the bed. He'd reached one hand up to fondle her breasts, and the other down to pull on her cock in matching rhythm to his own increasingly fevered thrusts.

That had become the pattern of their love-making. The last time had been after their anniversary dinner to celebrate one year together, and even though by that time he always preferred taking her from behind, he still enjoyed reaching around to fondle her. She wished her breasts were bigger for him, but the hormones had given her only a smallish B cup and she was determined to avoid an augmentation if she could.

When he took her, she always tried to imagine something different between her legs; tried to visualize his hard cock sliding between the moist, twin folds of her pussy and the nub of her clitoris swelling in response. But every time Jamie eased his heated rod past the sphincter of her ass and began to thrust and grunt, the flush of warmth that flooded her own cock as his balls slapped against hers were an instant reminder that she was still physically a male.

She remembered reaching down to stroke herself, trying to match her pace to his as the sense of urgency took them both and the tempo increased. Then came the full feeling, that moment when she knew she was about to explode and her partner yelled triumphantly as he came inside her. The seed of her own cum spurted out between her fingers in a hot, creamy jet. She remembered the shuddering of his thighs against hers, the collapse onto the bed as he lay atop her, still sheathed inside her ass, and the relief of pure physical release coupled with the faint sense of wrongness at the act. She didn't want to fuck or be fucked as a man.

Who knew that night would end up being the last time

she'd ever had sex with anyone bar herself? She'd certainly had no inkling that the phone call she got the next day, confirming her surgery procedure date, would set off such a chain reaction.

Jamie. Ah well. His loss.

But her whole body now trembled as she stared at this Adonis-like creature in front of her. He had appeared out of nowhere to rescue her from further humiliation at the hands of her high school cronies, and he wanted to have sex with her. As a woman.

Despite the fact that he knew her secret.

This person who called himself a god and looked like her idea of the perfect man, and who incited unfamiliar sexual feelings that were aching to be explored further, desired her.

And that thought scared the bejesus out of her.

Right this second she might not have her hand around his cock, but she couldn't miss the trouser material straining at his groin. As she stared up at him she could see the faint flush in his cheeks and the telltale glitter in his eyes. Oh, yes. This man desired sex. As soon as possible, by the look of him.

Something inside her eased. Her fingers, still resting against his chest, fisted beneath his. "Please?" she repeated, raising her eyebrow. "Oh, Himeros," she admitted. "You had me at 'I know'!"

She felt the thud of his heart at her words, then he was taking her hand into his and drawing her into the suite. I'm actually going to have sex tonight. Expectation edged with anxiety filled her being, and her breathing was shallow as she looked around the room.

It was a huge expanse rimmed with floor to ceiling windows that looked down on an iridescent sea of city lights. Melbourne, spread out before them in all its evening glory.

Beneath her feet, thick white carpet swallowed her black

stiletto shoes. At home she preferred flats, or even better, bare feet, but here at the reunion she'd wanted to make a point with the red dress and the high heels.

"Should I, um, take them off, or—"

"No. I want those heels to be last thing you remove, Gina. If you remove them at all. I like long legs in the women I bed, and your legs...in those heels...divine. Now come."

She followed him through the lounge area and into the bedroom. A bedroom like nothing she'd ever seen before. This one had a raised dais in the center, with an enormous bed covered in purple satin as its centerpiece. A large, ornately carved box sat at the foot of the bed. Around them, in every direction, she could see the lights of the city sparkling, and she wondered if there might be a peeping Tom in any of those tall buildings. Himeros didn't seem to have any curtains in the suite.

The thought of being watched as they made love added a tinge of spice to a situation that already had her breath coming a lot faster than usual.

"I like looking out over this part of the world from up here," he said, as if in answer to her wide-eyed staring. "And if anyone is game enough to watch in return, then I am sure they will enjoy what they see."

She laughed at the confident tone. "So sure of yourself."

"Oh, yes. Most certainly. And especially tonight. Now turn around, Gina, and enjoy the view while I do the same from behind you."

Her brows came together. He wanted her to turn around? "I—"

"Trust me."

She took a deep breath and let it out slowly. Her sexual drought had to end sometime, and there were only so many times you could make love with a dildo or vibrator and not get bored. This man called himself a god. He certainly looked like a god. An incredibly sexy one. If he only wanted her ass like all the others, then so be it. Her drought would be broken with more of the same from her past. Which certainly hadn't been bad sex, by any means. Merely...less spectacular than what she'd imagined might be possible.

"You keep telling me to trust you, but...all right. I will." She turned to face the window, focusing her gaze down toward the river wending its way through the center of Melbourne. With the lights reflecting off the water, she could almost imagine that an ancient god had indeed decorated the scene with a handful of jewels thrown in a glistening cascade across the landscape.

She started when she felt his breath warm against her neck. "I am going to take your virginity, not your ass. Unless you want me to take both, tonight?"

Virginity? "It's been a long while, I admit, but I'm not...I mean..." Pop my cherry as a woman? "I suppose, technically, I've never made love as a woman, but..." Oh, God, we're really gonna do this? Another pang squeezed her belly, and her voice shook when she added, "I probably do want both, I guess, if I'm being really honest—"

"Shh." His chuckle stopped her nervous chatter. "Just enjoy the moment, my love."

She felt the zipper on the back of her dress begin to wend its way down her spine, and her breath caught when the warmth of a fingertip followed in its wake, urging the edges of her dress to slither away with greater ease until the material pooled at her hips. Then his lips were against her skin, branding her with heat, just at that dip where her neck melted into shoulder.

Gina let out a shuddering breath, one she hadn't even known she was holding, and arched her head to one side to allow him better access. So hard to think straight, when his hands were spanning her waist like that, caressing the edge of her ribs. When his lips and tongue were doing the most incredible things up the line of her neck to nuzzle in such an intimate manner at her earlobe.

"Himeros," she whispered, as her knees threatened to buckle at the heat and the heaviness between her legs. And it felt different, this time, from what she remembered of past encounters. It wasn't just centered in her groin, that familiar feeling of an impending explosion. It was her pussy that was hot and heavy, and aching to be stroked, yes, but she also felt the ache throughout her whole body, like a stream of spreading warmth. She hadn't realized it could feel this...damn...good.

She reached back to find his hips and pull him closer in against her, wanting to share this newfound sensation of desire.

"I do desire you," he growled in her ear. "So much."

"I know," she said, emboldened by these new feelings, wiggling her ass against the rock-hard core of him. "I can feel how much you want it. Me."

As she turned in his arms, she caught the momentary grin that lit his features before his mouth swept down to claim hers. And if she'd thought the sensations before were unique, they were as nothing to the onslaught that swept through her when his lips and tongue forced their way in to brand her with his essence. The power behind his kiss was so intense she couldn't even respond, other than to let out a moan that he swallowed then continued on.

Demanding more.

Dominating.

CHAPTER THREE

Her knees buckled as she capitulated to that power, but strong arms were there supporting her even as she collapsed against his muscular frame.

The power gave pleasure. And pain.

They merged into one until there was no thought, only feeling. Heat and light and energy flowing through her from him, filling her even as the ache and the need intensified.

Release.

She was desperate for it; needed it with every fiber of her being. Felt the elusive edges of it curling through her body and heard her own frantic whimpering as if from a distance. She was drowning in pleasure; in the scent of lust that surrounded and invaded her whole being.

What the hell was happening? Had he disconnected her from reality? Was she going mad? The thoughts coalesced then fragmented as the exquisite, yet punishing, kiss went on and on.

Then, just at that moment where she couldn't take any more of this agonizing embrace, the searing nature of his kiss eased and she had the space to react. And to breathe. "Wow."

Her heart was racing and she was almost fully supported by his encircling arms. She planted her feet more firmly on the ground, trying to take back some semblance of control over her own body.

"Was it too much?" His tone was apologetic and she shook her head.

"No. Yes." She reached up and clutched at his hair, needing the physicality to fully re-ground herself. "I don't know. But that felt like no kiss I've ever experienced before." She pulled his head down toward her. "Whatever it was, I want more of it."

This time though, it was as though he held himself slightly in check and she had the space to kiss him back properly. When she broke the connection to nip at his bottom lip then tease him with the tip of her tongue, he let out a groan of his own. It emboldened her, that groan, and she repeated her action. Then they were kissing fully again, but this time she was giving as good as she got, equal in their connection and in their feverish response to each other.

She hadn't even realized she had loosened his shirt from the trousers until she found herself able to reach up into that warm space between fabric and skin, to stroke the muscled contours of his back with eager fingers. Gina wanted to learn the feel of him. Who was he, this god-like man with the physique of a bodybuilder and skin as smooth as satin?

What was he?

His hands in turn were already on their own intimate exploration and she felt his caress across her waist and down. His grip tightened as it traversed the curve of her hips and buttocks before he suddenly lifted her. She instinctively wrapped her legs around his middle, the dress pooled between them around her hips and rode up to expose the garter tops of her stockings. The position widened her vaginal folds enough to allow the swelling in his trousers to press against her slash. She felt the heat even through the material of his clothing and her G-string underwear.

He was standing in front of one of the full-length windows. It would be hard not to, in this room of glass walls. She wondered if there was anyone watching them right now, perhaps with a pair of binoculars. The thought of being watched ramped up the situation ten-fold. Maybe those at the reunion downstairs would hear her screams of release after all.

Maybe some of them were even now watching from one of those rooms across the street...

She tightened her butt, pushing her pelvis more firmly against him, rubbing on his hardness and using it to increase the pressure on her mound. Gina hoped they were watching, those bastards from her past. Watching, and wanting what she had between her legs right now. Not her own cock, anymore, but someone else's. Himeros, cocked, loaded, and ready to fuck.

And he's going to fuck me.

"We do have a couple of onlookers."

His soft words, murmured into her hair, had her thighs tightening involuntarily around him as the burning excitement grew. Who was watching? And what show did they want to see? Straight sex between a man and a woman, or sex between two people who both had a penis?

Are you wondering if I really had the op? If there aren't actually two hard dicks here right now, hidden by my skirt, sliding up and down against each other and dampening my panties with all that leaking pre-cum?

Too bad.

A sudden flare of anger ignited inside of her toward the peeping Toms, whoever they were, and she dug one of her heels into the crease of his ass, rubbing it up and down with just enough pressure to elicit a moan of protest from Himeros.

She stopped. "Sorry."

"Ah, but I enjoy the lick of pain, Gina."

"Oh." She liked how her voice got all husky when she was aroused. When she was home alone with her vibrator there was no call to speak. She hadn't realized it would sound like this, all deep and throaty. "Really?"

"Yes."

She reached up and caressed his face, following that angled cheekbone with one finger. "Then it's a pity you're still wearing trousers, Him."

"Won't be for long." Dang, now his voice is all gruff. Sexy as hell.

"Good." Her head dropped back and she felt the touch of his lips like butterfly wings along the line of her neck, then lower.

Maris, are you watching this? Are you imagining what it feels like to have your legs wrapped so tight around someone like Himeros? Are you wondering what it feels like to be me? About whether I have sensation in my whole body like you do? In my breasts, in my nipples...when he kisses me like that along my collarbone...when his hands grip my ass so firmly that I want to cry out in pain...and pleasure? When his fingers skim my slit, from back to front, over my asshole and further forward, circling around my vagina, tracing his own hardness at the same time as he is pleasuring me? When his middle finger slips beneath the fabric of my underwear to find the engorged nub of my clit and teases it, oh, just there...

She moaned. "God, Himeros, I feel like I'm going to—" His rough growl of encouragement tipped her over the edge. "Yes!" she cried out as the sudden orgasm took her further than she'd ever been before. "Oh, yes!"

Sensation rolled through her body and she bucked in his arms. So unexpected, and so all-encompassing. This was pure heaven, and hell, and all things between, where feeling was everything and nothing else mattered. She whimpered at the startling shock and the joy, and fell forward against his chest.

Having an orgasm as a woman was nothing like shooting your load as a guy.

She lay boneless and trembling in his arms.

"That was amazing," she said at last.

Himeros was breathing heavily, too, but not, she realized, from any effort required to hold her up during her frenzied release. He seemed to have managed that without any problems at all. No, he was breathing as hard as she because he was now fully aroused—she could feel it between her legs and up into the curve of her stomach, pressing against her and demanding release from his trousers, just like her own cock had done when she still had one.

Only his was bigger. Hotter. Harder. And much more manly.

His chuckle, then, was as full of humor as it was pent-up lust. "That was nothing, Gina. We haven't even taken off our clothing, yet. I will make you scream before this night is done."

And just like that, her body reignited. How? she wondered. How is it possible to feel so much so quickly? I know the hormones changed the balance of everything, but this? Again?

He shifted her weight in his arms. "I am the god of desire, gorgeous one. I want to release you from the prison of your own fear. I want to show you everything you can be as a woman."

His eyes glittered, more green than blue, in a framework of eyelashes that were longer than her own. He was so beautiful to look at, she thought. But there was something else now...an edge of vulnerability in his features that evoked an answering pang of tenderness. She reached up and traced one of his eyebrows. "What is it I can see there, Himeros? When I look into your eyes and you let down your guard?"

A flash of something, quickly hidden.

"Nothing." He frowned. "You should be seeing my desire for you. Nothing more, nor less than that. Can you not feel it?"

A wave of sensation washed over her and she wanted to melt in his arms again. No bones, that's how it felt. As if he'd sucked out her skeleton and replaced it with a river of need that ran through every part of her body, from the top of her head to the tip of her toes. She let out a faint moan. "I feel it," she whispered, but managed to add after a moment, "But I still see your fear."

"I am not afraid."

"Aren't you?"

"No." Now he didn't sound so certain, and the tide of sensation that continued to wash over her lessened a touch. If she were being fanciful, she would say that he really was a god. A god whose concentration on the flow of desire was being interrupted by uncertainty.

"Fear can be crippling," she said, not sure where her words were coming from, but confident she was on the right track. She knew what fear felt like. What it looked like. Fear had faced her in the mirror every day of her life. "It stops you from doing so much."

"I know."

"But what fears would a god of desire have?" She wasn't trying to be sarcastic, throwing that god title back at him. It was just that she couldn't comprehend how someone who looked like Himeros, and who had his level of self-confidence, could ever be crippled by fear or vulnerability.

"Too many to name."

Oh, God, it was loneliness she heard in his voice. He was lonely. She knew how that felt. She'd been alone on this journey of self-discovery for most of her life. Even her parents, supportive though they had been during her teenage years, through the hormones and the surgery, didn't fully get it. They supported her, yes. But they didn't get it. And outside of her parents, people neither understood nor supported her. They thought she was a freak. The "Amazon ball breaker" as they had called her at school. The boy who wanted to be a girl.

The boy who was a girl, deep down inside. Only she was buried so deep, no one else could see her.

It sucked, feeling lonely. Big time.

She cupped a hand around his jaw and leaned in to press a kiss to his chin. "When you're with me, Himeros, you're not alone. Neither of us is. Whether this is a one night only deal, or whether we see each other again, please, remember that." She looked up into his eyes, not letting him pull away even when he stiffened. "I'm beginning to see you. Really see you."

Gina wasn't even sure what she meant by those words, but they felt right. It was almost as if someone were guiding her to say the right thing. And she could sense his essence. It was beautiful; a shimmering vitality that surrounded him, like an aura of golden light.

Was he a god? A real one? In that moment, with his features frozen in surprise and a sudden energy that had come out of nowhere snapping at her pores, she could let herself believe it was true. It was as if the woman inside had finally found her voice, and she was calling out to the man inside this god.

She felt empowered by the realization. "I see you," she whispered again, brushing her fingers at the edges of the strange golden light. His aura. It was warm, all-encompassing, and its effect flowed through her veins like liquid fire. She gulped at the clout it contained.

"And I hear you," he answered. "Aphrodite was correct. I hear you."

The wonder in his tone swelled her heart. With that vista of twinkling lights spread out behind him, the purple blue of the night sky peppered with stars as a backdrop, and that joyous astonishment etched across his face, she could let herself believe that anything was true right now.

Her very own Greek god. For tonight, at least.

Ω Ψ Ω

He wasn't familiar with these feelings; with the emotion running through his system. It made him feel vulnerable, and that was not a state to which he was accustomed. But with Gina, he couldn't seem to help himself. By the gods, he had shown her a trace of his power, without even realizing he'd done so until she reached out and touched it.

The erotes did not lose control, ever. Even in the midst of passion, they remained somewhat detached. Emotion was for mortals. The erotes controlled their desire.

The erotes were desire.

And yet, he had let his power leak out like wine from a

cracked vessel the moment she reached for him. He had behaved like a mortal, not a god.

He tried to lean back, away from her delicate breasts pressing into his chest. Away from her influence. "Well," he said. "I—you..."

But she followed him, leaning in and poking him with those twin mounds. Her bra rasped against his skin, denying the familiar distance, and he felt an unexpected surge of happiness. It bubbled up from nowhere and he let out a bark of laughter. "It is not often that I am lost for words, Gina."

"Really?" Warmth lit her voice and she laughed, too. She arched her back, wriggling her pelvis back and forth against his cock, and the need to sink into her in one huge thrust grew almost unbearable. But she needed finesse, at least for tonight, and he would not be so crass as to split her in two with his need. He couldn't resist, though, when she pressed into him like that and cradled his hardness deeper between the thin folds of her flesh. He let out a trickle more of the heady power he kept within, trying to keep it controlled this time, and fought the urge to envelop her in it completely.

Gina. You are driving me toward humanity faster than I can step away from it.

Ω Ψ Ω

She wanted to experience more of that golden heat even as she needed to ease her own ache within. It was an ache that had intensified as his life force—or whatever it was—flowed through her. When she pressed into him it felt different, doing this as a woman. She could get closer, for one thing. And it was so much more intense.

"Perhaps tonight," he said, "we will help release each other from whatever prison we have made for ourselves."

"I hope so," she answered.

Then his lips were skating down the line of her neck until they met her bra strap. He chuckled against her skin before the graze of teeth eased the strap away to expose one of her breasts. "Oh, Gina," he said. "You do know how to choose your lingerie, don't you?" And then his mouth closed on her already hard nipple in a sensation so good she didn't even know how to process it.

"Yes," she said. "I was just...trying to make a point this evening about...being a woman." She could hardly speak as his rhythmic suckling intensified. Hell, she could hardly string two words together in her head. Then he paused, and reached up in one deft movement to unclip her bra altogether, sliding it off first one arm, then the other, with a grunt of satisfaction.

"You don't need to make a point. But you do look good in black lace. Even better out of it."

She found herself chuckling at the ease with which he did it. "A bit of practice showing, there, Him."

"A little. Naughty minx." As if in punishment he grabbed her nipple between his teeth and pulled, then his tongue flicked her, hard.

She let out a gasp. Pleasure and pain. There it was again. The touch of his mouth, like a hot brand, rippled from her breast outward until her whole body yearned for his touch.

"Himeros! I didn't know—it could be like this."

"We are only getting started here, Gina." He had carried her across to the bed without her even realizing it, and now he lay her onto the purple satin and shimmied her dress down over her hips until she was wearing only her G-string, suspender stockings, and her high-heeled black shoes. The sheets felt cool and slippery beneath her heated skin.

He stood on the top step of the dais, looking down at her, and for a moment all her fears came rushing back. It was the first time she'd been undressed by a man since before the surgery, and she instinctively looked down to double check that everything seemed as it should. No appendage jutting up where it shouldn't be, at least. Her mound instead was pure pussy, laid bare beneath the see-through underwear by a recent Brazilian, her body and thighs maybe a touch too long for a woman, but then she'd always been tall and there wasn't much she could do about that. But...what if there was something out of place? What if she didn't look normal?

"You look sexy as hell, woman," Himeros said, and the affirmation of her as a woman, articulated in that rough, almost urgent, tone, sent a pleasurable shiver right through her and eased the creeping fear.

"And you have too many clothes on," she answered.

He tilted his head, considering her words. "Easily remedied."

His tie was gone already, she realized, and he made quick work of his shirt, shucking it off and letting it fall to the floor. His torso was everything she had already known it would be from her brief exploration of his body a few minutes earlier. Chiseled muscle and smooth caramel skin, the nipples small and hard like decorative brown pebbles in a chest so magnificent she'd never seen one like it before outside of a cinema.

"Whoa." She scooted onto her elbows, then sat up fully to watch as he removed the rest of his clothing. "So, you work out how many hours a day?"

He was facing slightly away from her, sliding off his underwear, revealing a tight butt and strong thigh muscles that flexed as he bent then straightened. He turned his head to stare at her over his left shoulder and her breath caught at the look of sheer desire in his eyes. *He does look like a god,* she thought. *A sex god. How the hell did I get so lucky?*

"I don't need to work out, Gina. I am a god of love. I get all the exercise I need in other ways."

There was no mistaking what he meant. The fire from his gaze suffused her body. He turned to face her fully, then, and the breath she was holding escaped in a gasp borne of panic and craving. He was enormous; there was no other word for it. The cock jutted out and up, fully erect. His balls beneath were large as well, but pulled up tightly near his body. Clearly he was almost ready to release himself. She remembered what that felt like.

No wonder he's breathing so hard.

She focused on the network of veins beneath the darkened flesh and the glistening drop of pre-cum crowning his cock. She wanted to lean over and take him into her mouth, taste the juice of this gorgeous Adonis and suck him into abandon. The musky smell of impending sex surrounded her.

But the panic that edged her need refused to go away. There was no way she'd be able to take him inside her. He was just too big. He'd rip apart all the good work her surgeon had done. And yet...he looked just as she imagined a god of love might look. So tempting. So incredibly, fucking hot. So exactly what she needed to really make herself feel like a woman.

"I want to taste your cock, Himeros." Maybe he'd come in her mouth and she wouldn't have to take him into her pussy. She wanted to, though. Oh, lord, how she wanted to feel Himeros deep inside her body; his rock-hard dick sheathed tightly in her vagina. A man inside her properly for the very first time.

He stepped toward her and she felt the wave of longing wash over her anew, even as she shrank back in alarm. "I do want you to taste me, Gina," he said. "But not yet, my darling. First, I want to banish that fear of yours. And I intend to try something new."

She laughed, albeit a little breathlessly. "It's all new to me, Himeros! But...what did you have in mind?"

One eyebrow lifted as he studied her. Then he looked down at the large box at the foot of the bed, tapping a finger against his perfect white teeth in a thoughtful pose before reaching down to open the lid. She could see now that the carvings on the box were some kind of ancient-looking decoration, similar to what she had seen carved into urns and other bits of pottery at an exhibition at the National Gallery last year. An exhibition of ancient Greek artifacts. "Um..." She found herself clutching at handfuls of purple satin, and consciously made an effort to ease her grip. "Is that your magic box of tricks?"

"Don't be nervous, Gina. I will not hurt you; I promise." He considered her over the top of the lid, before humor lit his features. "Believe me, there are many things in here that could hurt you, if you wished it that way."

What the heck is in his mysterious box?

"I get the feeling you do like an edge of pain to your pleasure at times. Am I correct?" His eyes shone with a wicked glint, and a lock of dark hair flopped over his brow. He looked like a mischievous boy about to play a naughty trick on someone.

She had the urge to reach up and push his hair back into place, but couldn't move a muscle to save herself. Yes. Just not today. Not for my first time as a woman.

When he nodded, eventually, as if she'd answered him aloud, it felt like he had deliberately released her from some kind of frozen trance. She sat up straighter and shifted her shoulders to ease the sudden tension.

"I enjoy many different things, Him, but—" Gina glanced down at his cock and couldn't help herself. She reached out to touch it, stroking one finger from the base to the hot tip and dipping in to the tiny slit to collect that tempting drop of clear liquid on the cushion of her finger. "—I don't want to be hurt today." You're just so damn big. She lifted her finger to her mouth and slipped it between her lips, sampling the flavor of his cock juice, savoring the thick, musky taste.

It was as good as she had expected. Better. Nectar of the gods, indeed.

He let out a low groan as he watched, and she smiled and sucked some more.

"I cannot think straight when you do that." His voice was hoarse. "But today, I think, we are going to start simple." He held up a long piece of black lace, then let one end of the fabric fall until it drifted across the tip of his cock. "Today, I am going to bind you with this."

CHAPTER FOUR

More juice had already replaced what she'd taken from his cock, and it sparkled there before soaking into the lace. She saw his eyelids flutter briefly at the drift of material across his member, and was hooked.

Okay. A little bit of binding. I can deal with that.

"I want you to stop being afraid of who you are, Gina, and learn to embrace it instead. It is time that you stopped thinking and started to feel. And it is time you really mean it when you say that you trust me." He cupped her chin in his hand, the thumb stroking over her slightly parted lips. It felt like heaven, and she reached out to moisten his digit with her tongue.

His grip tightened. "I will not hurt you. But right now, I am going to take away your sense of sight."

He lifted the piece of black lace from where it lay still draped over his penis and leaned forward to place it across her eyes.

With her vision gone, other senses rose to the fore. She hadn't even thought about it before. About how one might use one's senses to process the world. But when Himeros fastened that scrap of black over her face, tying it firmly behind her head to ensure it didn't slip, she fell instantly into a world of darkness in which sensory processing became everything.

The first thing she noticed was his scent. Surrounded by the musky sweet smell of Himeros, there was also something deeper and more wild that she couldn't identify. Rosemary? Oregano? The fresh clean scent of mountain air? She inhaled deeply, relishing the unidentified yet delicious aroma, knowing that if she bent down to take him fully into her mouth, this is what it would taste like.

Next she noticed the smooth feel of the mask against her face. Was it lace? Or perhaps there was a satin backing. Multi-purpose, then. When she reached up and discovered the front was in fact, lace, her fingers toyed with the rough material, going still when she found Him's hand there already.

"Him," she said. "You don't even know what I do for a living."

"Does it matter, right now?"

She nodded. "I'm a photographer. I see everything in pictures. Visually."

"Ah." His breath was warm in her ear and she heard the laughter in his voice. "Not tonight you don't."

"Seems not."

He lifted her hair to one side and she felt the press of his mouth against the side of her neck, just below her earlobe. Who knew that spot could be so sensitive?

"Lie back down, Gina." The voice had a commanding air and she immediately complied, shifting back until she thought she might be in the center of the enormous bed.

"Like this?"

"Yes. Now I am going to remove the rest of your underwear. I want you naked bar those shoes. When we make love, I want those heels digging into my back. Hard."

"I think..." She swallowed and nodded. "I think I can manage that."

Hands brushed lightly at her hips and she wriggled to help him out. She felt one of his fingers slide beneath the strap of her G, and lifted her pelvis a little, but instead of the clothing being removed straightaway, she felt a ribbon of moist heat frame the triangle of satin. His tongue. She parted her legs wide to give him better access, reaching down in fumbling fashion until she found and gripped a handful of his silken hair.

Without sight she could only imagine what he would look like, the tip of his tongue sliding along her flesh that was already swollen with need, that wayward hair flopping down over his brow, his gaze intense, probably flecked with the shade of green that for some reason reminded her of the sea, looking back up her body as he teased around and over her mound. When the graze of something hard—presumably his teeth—nipped at her clitoris through the material she yelped, then pressed upward to enhance that exquisite pressure. Hot lips met her thrust and played with her, moistening the material. Lips, tongue, and teeth worked in unison to torment her core while his fingers slipped beneath her G and went exploring along her slit.

A gasp escaped as she felt one of his digits slide into her. The first person other than her surgeon or herself ever to breach her pussy. She didn't have the creamy moistness of a biological woman, but somehow, with Himeros, it didn't seem to matter. She rocked back and forth against his face, adjusting to the feel of having someone inside her, even if it was only his finger.

"Yes," she managed on a shaky exhale of breath. "That feels fucking fantastic."

He chuckled against her clit. "So tight, Gina. I look forward to entering you properly."

She felt the words and the laugh as a welcome vibration and it escalated her senses into overdrive. She moaned. Having her cock sucked in the past had never felt like this. The intensity of what she was feeling now was more—so much more—than she was used to. Even through her underwear.

The pressure suddenly disappeared and so too did the scrap of material covering her pussy. She couldn't see his reaction to her full-on nakedness and a flare of panic had her reaching up to rip off her mask, but found her hands imprisoned beneath larger ones. "No. Leave it on, Gina. Go with your gut, and feel. Feel your need. Feel mine."

She whimpered, wanting to do as he asked. "Okay," she whispered. "I can do this."

"Of course you can. And for the record, you are beautiful." That last word came out husky, and she felt tears prick at her eyes at the genuine tone of his voice.

But still she hesitated. "Normal?" she asked at last.

"Yes, darling. Perfectly normal."

She bit her lip, glad the telltale tears were hidden by the black lace. At this moment she felt incredibly vulnerable. "Thank you, Him."

Then she gulped when she felt the warmth of his lips on her inner thigh, trailing a moist path from her knee up to the edge of her muff. "I love your legs," he said. "They're so long." The scrape of her suspender stockings as they were eased down and off was as nothing to the heat of his words on her vulva lips. "Trust," he whispered, and she felt the word rather than heard it, right at her core.

"I do," she moaned, and his lips connected with hers, mouth

to slash, no material restraining him this time. Kissing her in the most intimate and incredible connection she'd ever felt. "Yes," she cried, making no attempt now to stop the moistness leaking from her eyes at the joy of feeling a real live person—perhaps even a god, no less—touching her in such an intimate way. At feeling Himeros touching her, kissing her, that way.

Her hips thrust up and into him, and she hardly noticed when he eased off her shoes to remove the stockings fully, then placed the heels back onto her feet. Because the whole time he did that, he was doing things with his lips, and tongue, and teeth that she had never dreamed could feel so wonderful.

He wanted these heels pressing into him? He'll get that, and far more, tonight.

She wailed when his tongue slipped inside her, licking, and tasting, and creating a rim of moisture.

"Oh, God, Himeros. I want your cock inside me."

"Soon, Gina." His mouth left her then, and she felt the impact of cool air replace his warm breath. The contrast of wet heat, then cold, added intensity to her need, but then he was over her, flesh to flesh, pressing her down into the sheet and searing her with the warmth of his body against hers. He was hard muscle and soft silken skin, a juxtaposition of angles and curves. He was everything at once. She blindly reached out and found the arc of his shoulder, traced around the muscle and down to his bicep, then dipped beneath to find and follow the line of his ribs.

"Your fingers feel like butterfly wings," he said, the playful tone encouraging her to explore further.

She felt the heaving of his chest against her body and beneath her fingertips. He was ready. The familiar scent of aroused male flowed over and around her, and then she found herself rolling with him as he turned on the bed. Finally she was atop him, straddling his hips.

A rush of sound assailed her then. The sound of her own ragged breathing as she tried to control the crazy beat of her heart. The muted roar of traffic from city streets far below, and the wailing of a siren signaling an emergency somewhere out there in the real world, beyond the four walls of this suite. It was like he really was a god, and he'd invited her up to his abode in the sky, far from the petty rush of everyday life. This could be their Mount Olympus, this penthouse suite.

She continued to run her fingers over his body and down an undulating six-pack, encountering the dip of his navel and circling it before going lower to find and stroke his cock. She felt the shudder run through him at her action. He was so large it was difficult to hold him with one hand so she brought the other forward to join in. Thick moisture coated her fingers; he must be leaking pre-cum in earnest now. She raised one hand to her mouth and lapped at the residue. Yes. Salt, and musk and a hint of something sharp, almost spicy. The taste of Himeros.

The taste of sex.

"I want you to fuck me, Him," she said. "But first..." She reached up and ripped the mask off her face, throwing the scrap of lace off to one side of the bed. She blinked at the sudden infusion of light and looked down to see the hard planes of his face etched with longing as he stared back up at her. His caramel skin looked lighter against the dark purple satin of the sheets. Her thighs, nestled on each side of his hips, were almost white in comparison.

She wanted this so badly, but in the end, it had to be on her terms. "I refuse to be blind when you enter me. I need to see you when you sink yourself into my body for the first time."

"Good." His grin was instantaneous and some of her ferocity faded. He wanted it this way, too. "You have begun to accept who you are, Gina. You have opened your heart to Aphrodite and found her essence inside you. It is time for us to make love."

"Aphrodite? You've mentioned her already tonight. She was a goddess, wasn't she? The goddess of sex?"

"Is," he corrected gently. "She is the goddess of so many things. Love, beauty, pleasure. She is all things woman. And you have found her. In here." He touched the valley beneath her left breast, and her eyes filled with sudden moisture.

Not again. She looked upward for a moment in a futile attempt to prevent them spilling out, then gave up and let the tears fall down her cheeks. "Yes, I think I might have. At last." Two wet splotches rained onto Himeros and she reached out, intending to smear them away, but he caught her hand and raised it to his lips. As she felt the press of his mouth in the center of her palm she smiled. "You're right. It is time for us to make love."

She lifted her hips as he centered himself at her vaginal entrance. The flinch was instinctive; she couldn't help it, and he paused. "I have enough cum in my balls to sink a ship. I have wanted to try your body ever since I saw you, and the wait has had me leaking juice all evening. It will be a well-lubricated joining, I assure you."

Her laugh was throaty. "Enough to sink a ship? That actually sounds a little scary." She let out a squeak as he thrust with his groin and at the same time tightened his grip on her hips, compelling her downward.

The head of his cock was now inside her, and she panted with a mixture of aching pleasure and apprehension. It felt hot, and hard, yet slick at the same time. She wanted him deeper inside, and took a breath before sinking down without any further urging.

Full. Wet. Everything inside stretched so tight she was afraid to move more than a millimeter or two. But oh...my...God...it felt so good to have a real live man inside her, shifting now, slight movements that she could feel deep within her body. The ache was so deep and all-consuming that she couldn't even compare it to the clit orgasm she'd had earlier. This was real, and she was about to fuck as she'd always wanted to, as a woman, with a man who saw her. Really saw her. And it felt so right.

A moan made its way out from deep within her gut, and he shuddered in response beneath her. She began to move, slowly at first as she sought to learn the feel of Him inside her, then more urgently, giving in to what she felt and riding harder. She saw her own need reflected in his face as he began to thrust back and heard his groans mingle with her own sobs as the momentum built.

Then he was reaching up to pull her forward onto his chest, her long torso a distinct advantage as it allowed his mouth to reach her breast easily. He sucked and licked first one nipple, then the other. She could almost imagine a fountain of milk spraying out over them both, he sucked so damn hard. When their mouths met, tongues mimicking what their bodies were doing, thrust for thrust, the sweet taste of him mixed with her own pussy flavor on his lips tipped her over the edge.

Pressure. Unbearable pressure.

A primeval keening sound tore its way out of her throat as she exploded around him. In, and around, and everywhere at once, then nowhere at all, until the reverberating echoes of her scream brought her drifting back to reality. It shocked her, that high-pitched scream at the moment of her release. She had never screamed when having an orgasm before, and the instinctive and uncontrolled nature of it was new and rather unnerving. As she lay atop him trying to recover her equilibrium, a little part of her wondered if she had actually been loud enough for those downstairs to hear her. Just as Himeros had predicted. Wouldn't that be something?

"I made sure of it," Himeros said, and her heart skipped a beat. She didn't question how he could read her thoughts, nor whether he was telling the truth. Somehow, she knew he had done it. He had ensured they all heard and made them regret what they were missing. Her face was tucked into the curve between his neck and shoulder, and she didn't even attempt to control her grin at the thought of Maris and the shocked look she would be sporting right about now.

Then she realized that Himeros had not released his mother lode. She struggled to a sitting position. "You—you never came—"

"Shh. We are not done." He flipped her until he lay on top, took his weight on his elbows, and looked down at her. His hair was a wild mess, and it matched the look in his eyes. It made her shiver, that look. "Now dig those heels in, my darling Gina. The ride has only just begun."

Ω Ψ Ω

A wave of tenderness washed over him at the startled expression in her eyes. Then he sucked in a breath when she suddenly did as he requested and jabbed those spiked heels into his butt. One into each cheek. Hard. Tenderness was replaced by a pleasure so intense he shuddered.

"Good," he said in a low voice he hardly recognized as his own. "Again."

She did, a mischievous grin erasing the surprise in her features, and he began to thrust, trying to remember to keep it gentle for her this first evening. It was so hard to maintain control, especially when she kept jabbing over and over in perfect rhythm with his hot, plunging cock. She moved one of her feet and began to stroke his ass crack with the stiletto heel, from the top of his cheeks down to that sensitive spot just behind his balls and back up again. Down and up, over and over. He couldn't help the groan that rasped out of his throat.

"Gina..."

"Yes, Himeros?" Her slow question held all the innocence in the world, and he groaned again.

"I can't hold on if you keep doing that, especially if you...yes. Just there." His breath hissed out between his teeth as she found his asshole and teased the entrance with the tip of her shoe heel.

"I don't want you to hold on," she said. "It's two for none already, in my favor. Your turn to come, Himeros."

She hesitated then, and he ascertained her intent. Excitement flooded his system, banishing the last traces of ennui. He nodded his head. "Do it," he demanded, and she rammed home the shoe.

He bellowed at the intense rush of pleasure as she fucked him with the shoe. He bucked crazily as the liquid heat in his balls was finally let loose and he came inside her. Forever, it seemed, he came, totally out of control despite his best efforts, thrusting and moaning as wave after wave of exhilaration washed over him. Dimly he could hear her sudden gasps and knew the heat of his cum inside had set her off again, and she cried out too as she came around his cock. Her convulsing body sucked him dry in the way that Aphrodite had always intended it for this woman. Yes. He collapsed on top of her. They trembled in unison and clutched at each other like two drowning souls seeking freedom from struggle.

Aphrodite, he thought, when thought was again possible. Thank you for sending this woman my way.

The echo of knowing laughter at the edge of his mind was the only response.

CHAPTER FIVE

G ina couldn't remember ever feeling so sated. When the heat of their bodies had cooled and her heart rate returned to normal, she kicked off the offending shoes and stretched. It felt like pure luxury in this bed; satin beneath her, an Adonis beside her, her body aching in new and unfamiliar ways, and this massive grin on her face that probably looked ridiculous but refused to reign itself in.

"Not bad, Him," she said. "Not too bad at all."

He snorted and slapped her lightly across one hip, but his lips were curved up at the corners in an indulgent manner. Then abruptly, he rolled away and off the bed. She watched as he paced over to the window and stared out at the night. Gina enjoyed those fluid movements that reminded her of a ballet dancer. Not a spare ounce of fat, anywhere. And even flaccid, his tackle looked impressive. She could see his dick now in the reflection of the window, and wondered how the hell she'd managed to fit him so easily inside her. How did he even walk comfortably with that between his legs?

And yet he did, with a smooth grace that was fascinating.

A muscled Greek god shouldn't have that level of elegance. But he does. It's a joy to look at him.

"I guess you'll be going soon," he said, the voice slightly muffled as he leaned his forehead against the glass. A puff of white fogged the window when he exhaled.

She frowned. Sated she might be, but he looked far from it. In profile, right now, he just looked...sad. The sudden shift in his mood confused her. "Do you want me to go?"

No! The word seemed to reverberate around her mind like a scream of protest, but in front of her he just shook his head in silence.

When she stood up and stretched there was a click in her spine as her body began to protest the unfamiliar activity. Not as graceful as you, Himeros, that's for sure.

She padded over to where he was standing by the window, curling her toes in the thick carpet as she went. Everything in this room was over-the-top luxury. Even the soles of her feet were being treated to something special. The dimpled line of his spine called out to her and she ran her fingernails over the dips and curves and down to his hips. A trail of goose bumps appeared on his skin in the wake of her caress. How can I have such an effect on him?

"What is it, Him? You've just given me the best few hours of my life. I don't want to leave. But I will, if you prefer it."

He shrugged. "You found her, the Aphrodite inside you. You have what you need, now, to survive out there." Himeros gestured toward the city spread out below them. She looked down. Red, green, blue, golden, and white. Reflections shimmered along the winding line of the river. Movement and muted noise. Beauty, and energy, and life. Yes, she had what it took to survive, and he had helped her realize that.

But she stiffened when he added, "And I'm a god. I need no one. No mortal, to continue on."

The ache of loneliness was there again in his voice, and with a flash of insight she suddenly got it. "Him." She wrapped her arms around his waist and pressed a kiss to the back of his shoulder. "I'm not going anywhere. I could never have enough of what you've shown me tonight. Even if I could survive out there, why would I want to, without you by my side for as long as humanly possible?"

"You mean that?"

"Of course." He turned to look at her then, and one arm snaked almost reluctantly around her waist. She tilted her head as the uncertain smile hovered on his lips, before breaking through fully. And there it was—that zing of elation; the quiver that she felt right at her core every time he showed signs of delight.

"How do you see it?" he asked.

See what? She almost asked, but there was wonder in his tone, and she knew what he meant. So instead of playing dumb, she took a deep breath and let it out slowly. "Your aloneness? I don't know. I just...feel it, I guess. I recognize it." Her lips twisted as she added for good measure, "I've lived it."

His arm tightened around her. "Not as long as I have."

"No. I suspect not."

She snuggled into the curve of him, enjoying the unusual feeling of being dwarfed by her partner. His height and strong build could have been daunting, had she been shorter, but instead she felt as if they fit together perfectly. He made her feel more womanly, simply by his large presence beside her. They stood like that in companionable silence for several minutes, looking out and down toward the lights and scurrying activity far below on the city streets.

At last she spoke. "I've only had one real relationship in

my life, Him. His name was James. He left me when I decided to go ahead with the reassignment surgery."

"Why?"

"Who knows? I think maybe he didn't really love me, you know? He loved my body, my man bits, coupled with the woman bits. Not the real me inside. He never saw me, I don't think. Not really." She didn't even know why she was trying to explain it. But there was something about his isolation that called to her. "I get loneliness," she added.

He shifted, then she felt the caress of his lips on the top of her head. "I know you do," he said quietly. "And for the record, that man was a complete idiot."

Poor James. "Maybe he was." She sighed, needing something to break the somber mood. "So," she said, "given that we're standing here in front of this window buck naked, is there really anyone watching?"

He chuckled. "Right now, three people are staring at us from that building across the street. Two men and a woman, each alone in their apartment. One of the men," he stared out into the darkness, "yes, he was standing there in a bath towel a few minutes ago, but now he has dropped the towel and exposed his erection. He is not young, but his cock points up toward the sky like a more youthful man as he takes in the length of your limbs. He is very enamored of you, beautiful Gina."

"Really?" Her breath caught at the thought of someone wanting her from afar.

"Oh, yes. And the woman," he continued. "She has torn one of the buttons off her nightgown and one of her breasts is exposed. She is toying with her nipples. Pulling on them, over and over. Quite desperately, in fact. She wants what is over here, that woman. She wants to watch as you and I make love again. Oh. Hmm."

Gina glanced up at that quizzical noise, and had to laugh at the smug satisfaction in his features as he added, "She wants to have sex with me, of course." He looked down and met her gaze, and his eyes flashed with unexpected light. "She wants to be you."

She wants to be me? Another woman was identifying with her, and even wanting to change places with her? She let out a sudden laugh. This night was crazy, and like nothing she'd ever dreamed of when she set out for the reunion several hours earlier, but by God, it was delivering. In spades.

"Well, she can't have you. Tonight, you're mine, Himeros."

Standing here in plain sight, with her nakedness on display to anyone in the vicinity who chose to look into their lighted and uncurtained suite, was an alien activity for her. Yet her pussy grew heavy with anticipation at the knowledge there was sex going on all over the city tonight, and that some of it might be inspired by herself and Himeros.

"There's a couple watching too, from that hotel room over there. He has a set of binoculars trained on your milky-white body as we speak." Himeros lifted his chin to indicate the direction, and though she could see the window with its two dark silhouettes, she couldn't make out any detail inside the darkened room. Unlike Himeros and herself, framed in this well-lit rectangle of glass, the other couple had chosen to keep their antics in the dark.

"But I see everything, even in the dark," Him said, and she found herself trusting that he told the truth, even as she didn't understand how. "Do you want to know who they are?"

Yes. "Um..." Did she, really? What if it really was Maris, watching them? Would that increase or decrease her pleasure? Her labia lips swelled, suddenly so heavy with desire she wondered if they would start to hang down. Okay, she thought. So that answers one question at least. I want her watching. I want her to see when I come. When I scream my release to the world. As a woman.

"It is Maris," Himeros murmured, and Gina's lips parted at the intense rush of pleasure that shot through her. "And her husband."

"Oh, God," she whimpered. "What are they...are they—"

"He has handed the binoculars to her, now, and she is studying you very carefully through the lenses. Her husband, after all, has been turned on quite badly by your nakedness."

It was getting harder to stand upright. She wanted to sink to her knees at the thought of that woman's husband becoming sexually aroused by her. The...what was he again? The investment banker?

"Oh, yes, Gina. He is. So is Maris, though she is fighting it. Her husband has already unzipped his trousers and released his member. He is touching himself. Pulling quite frantically. His face has that look."

"What look?" There was greedy curiosity in her whispered question. What did Maris' husband look like when he was aroused?

"His eyes are half-closed and his mouth is tight in a rictus of concentration. His cheeks are flushed. If he is not careful, he will shoot his creamy load all over that window before his wife has a chance to kneel down and take him into her mouth. You know, she is imagining you when she does that. She always has."

"But...I..." Her heart was pounding and her clit felt as if it had swollen, jutting out from her vulval lips like a ripe red berry just begging to be eaten.

"And now she is looking through those binoculars at your clitoris, wanting to see you pressed up against the window, and that turns her on, too. She sees that you are a woman, after all, and she is very churned up inside, Gina. You are driving her insane with desire. First as a man, now as a woman—"

"I was never a man."

"No." He spoke quietly. "But she didn't see it that way. She desires you, Gina. And she hates you for it, in a way."

As he spoke, the birth of understanding dawned. Anger and hurt—literally years of pain—now had the chance to filter out through her pores and escape. Not in an instant. It could never be that easy to let go of the resentment, but the possibility of freedom from the weight of what had been holding her back was now there in front of her. If she wanted to accept it.

"Himeros." She shook her head. "I don't know what magic you're weaving tonight, but thank you!"

He grinned. "Don't you want to know what she's doing now?"

"No. I—" A pang through her breasts illuminated the lie. "Yes," she amended. "Okay. Tell me."

"She has fallen to her knees in front of her husband, and she is sucking that hot, hard cock of his. He is still wearing his trousers; she is accessing him through the gap that his zipper has made. But she has the binoculars in her hand, and even as she licks and sucks, bobbing her head up and down, she keeps twisting her head to the side to check on you. Touch yourself, Gina." There was suppressed laughter in his voice. "Show some compassion for the poor woman."

She shook with the strength of all the bottled-up emotion that was itching to be released, then reached down to stroke her core. Once, twice, then she pulled away again. She was ready to shatter already and she wanted to wait. Wanted it to be about Himeros and herself, not about Maris.

But still she was curious, like an insect attacking a flame.

Mesmerizing, yet deadly. "What is he like, her husband?" She didn't mean his personality, of course, and Himeros shrugged.

"Meh," he said, suddenly sounding more like a man than any god she could imagine. Her lips twitched at his next words. "Quite hard, reasonably sized, but he is not as magnificent as I."

She snorted, but even as she did so, movement in the area of his groin had her glancing down and she let out a sharp puff of breath. He might be smug, but he was right. She'd never seen a cock like his before. It was magnificent, and it definitely seemed as if Himeros was enjoying the moment as much as she. He was standing up almost vertically already, his member so tall it almost reached his navel and wide enough that a small woman would have trouble getting her hand around its girth.

Lucky I'm not a small woman, then.

Already dark with the rush of blood pulsing beneath its thin membrane of skin; his cock called to her with its need. Then he stepped forward and pressed the end of it to the window, leaving a kiss of moisture where it touched, and his boldness encouraged her. She stepped forward too, right up onto the window ledge, gripping with her bare toes and balancing herself as she pressed hot breasts against the cool glass and tilted her pelvis to show off her slit.

"Wait." His command halted her, but then he was stepping in behind her, reaching around to spread her labia just a little wider before pushing her even harder against the glass. "Show them how much woman you are," he whispered in her ear.

She giggled and dropped her head back into the crook of his neck, still looking out at the night. "I am woman," she said.

"I don't hear you roaring."

"I am woman!" Her sudden scream fogged the glass and she felt the rumbling in his chest as he laughed.

"That's better," he said. "Makes me want to fuck you all the harder."

She lifted up her arms and placed her hands on the window, spread eagle in a star-shape with Himeros molding his body to her rear. Never had she felt more alive than in this moment, right now, looking out from what seemed like the top of the world, surrounded by the essence of love, and desire, and need. Framed by a man, and proclaiming her womanhood to everyone.

"I am a woman," she screamed again. "Hear me now."

"By the gods, you are the sexiest thing I've ever held in my arms," Himeros muttered. "I want to fuck you until there's nothing left but you and I. Until Aphrodite is sated, and I think you are beginning to realize that will never come to pass."

She was breathing raggedly, her chest heaving against the glass and her pussy heated by his long rod that was nestled along her slash, as well as by the thought of their voyeuristic audience out there in the dark.

"Then fuck me, Himeros. As hard as you like. For as long as you need. Forever, if that's what it takes. I'm going nowhere until the Aphrodite you've unleashed inside me is sated." She didn't know where the words were coming from. The timber of her voice was lighter than normal, more husky than she usually sounded, too. But she was filled with a sense of freedom that she had never felt before. Her laughter filled the room as she repeated his words back to him. "And we both know that will never come to pass."

His moan in her ear sounded almost animal-like, as if it had been forced out of some deep, dark place inside him that she wasn't privy to, and it sent a delicious shiver down her spine.

She gasped when determined fingers grabbed her by the hips and then he was plunging up and into her, parting her vulval lips like a hot knife through butter as he surged inside her body. She screamed at the force of the impact as he touched her core, and her body exploded around his cock in a raging orgasmic fury.

And then the world as she knew it imploded as the glass she was leaning against shattered into a million pieces and she plunged out into the blackness of the night with Himeros still riding her back in a roaring frenzy and the orgasm convulsing her now airborne body. She screamed again as blind terror overlapped her orgasm and they plummeted down toward the earth, several stories below.

CHAPTER SIX

An eternity, a milli-second, and all time in between. The fall could only have been a few seconds long, but it seemed to last forever. Despair filled her even as her body continued to convulse around Himeros, too far gone in the throes of passion to stop the orgasmic release. The wind buffeted her face and body as they plummeted, whipping the keening scream from her lips and carrying it up to the clouds and out of earshot.

She closed her eyes against the inevitability of the ground rushing at them. Kept them closed even as he tightened his arms around her, cradling her body into the warmth of his flesh, keeping the chill away even as they plunged headlong toward death.

I've found myself at last. And I'm about to lose it all.

Not fair.

A moment in time, etched forever in her mind, in which to rejoice in what he had shown her.

A milli-second in which to acknowledge everything that had gone before. A milli-second in which to regret what might have been. A milli-second in which she could still wish for a future containing happiness and love.

Containing Himeros. Her god.

And in the space of a heartbeat it would all be gone.

For both of them.

Desire filled the void left by shock. Desire for life above all else.

In the last remnants of life she clutched at his arms. Falling. Still falling. But safe. Always safe in his arms. At the end, she would not be alone, after all.

"You may fall while you are with me, but I will never let you crash." Were they real words in her ear, or an echo of hope in her mind? Still hoping, even as they fell. Her lips twisted at the futility.

But...shouldn't they have reached the ground by now? Shouldn't they...

She forced her eyelids open, determined at the last to face their destiny head-on, and sucked in her first breath in...how long? There was no ground rushing up at her, no concrete below. No city buildings around them. Only Himeros, holding her, surrounded by a golden light, energy vibrating off his skin. Suffusing her with heat. And they were no longer falling, only...something. Hovering in mid-air? What the hell was going on? And why weren't they...?

"Are we dead?"

Her voice came out on a hoarse whisper, and her throat ached like it did on those days when the loneliness took over and she had to hold in the tears while desperate to cry. When she held in so much emotion she wanted to burst from the need to let it all out.

She pressed closer to Himeros, wanting his strength and his hardness to prove them—or at least him—was still a physical entity. "Are we alive? What the fuck happened, Himeros? Where are we? Why are we not..."

Dead on the pavement. She couldn't say the words aloud. She was afraid if she did, it might make it real.

"Look at me, Gina."

His voice commanded, echoing around her and through her body all the way to her bones.

She did look. She had no choice; that voice compelled her to do as he bid. And what she saw filled her with awe.

His hair was moving like it was electrically charged; the eyes flashed like green beacons lighting up the golden aura surrounding them both. Green and gold. His aura. It emanated from his caramel skin, that golden light, and bathed her in warmth and a strange, drowsy kind of sexual energy. It made her want to fuck the nearest living person, but at the same time it enticed her to snuggle in to its heat. Power and desire. Strength and security. Above all, acceptance. His aura accepted her for who she was.

Disbelief, ridicule, everything negative was gone from her head as reached out a trembling hand and caressed his granite cheek. "I..." She shook her head and tried again. "I see you."

Now it was his turn to suck in a breath. "I don't show myself often," he said, and the voice was no longer compelling. Instead it held a hint of uncertainty. "Ever, actually."

She loved that uncertainty. It gave her the strength to lean in and kiss him. Beneath her lips she tasted the heart of him. A unique, delicious experience.

To taste the soul of a god.

"Then I'm the luckiest woman in the world, aren't I?"

He nodded gravely. "You are."

She burst out laughing, and if there was an edge of hysteria to her laughter, who the hell could blame her? She didn't even know where they were, nor how he had saved them. Maybe she really was dead, and that would mean he was, too. Yet even in this moment, he still had that ego. It was a part of him, though, and she wouldn't change it.

"I see you," she said again. "And I accept you, Himeros, god of sexual desire. I accept everything about you."

He bowed his head for a moment, then looked up into her eyes. There was raw emotion contained within that gaze. "Then I am the lucky one," he said. "Now I am beginning to understand what my brother Pothos was trying to explain."

Who?

She frowned, about to ask, but he added, "He found the ones. A couple in need of love. And in helping them, he discovered the true meaning of Aphrodite's power. I..." His voice broke and Gina's heart skipped a beat at the desolation in his tone. "I have been looking for so long, Gina."

"Shh." She reached up and stroked his hair. Silken, clean, and still wayward with that sparking electricity. Or whatever it was. He moved into her caress, clearly enjoying her touch. "I'm here now," she said.

"I was so weary, Gina. I was ready to return to my home with the gods and leave these mortals to their own devices. Burnout, I think you call it here. But then, Aphrodite sent me to find you and I am weary no longer."

"As much as I love hearing this..." She paused, unsure how to say it, but then just blurted it out. "Why, Himeros?" she asked. "Tell me. Why have you shown yourself to me? I'm not special. I've never done anything important. I've never saved anyone's life. I'm an adequate photographer, but I'm not the best there is. I'm full of bitterness about the past and I'll probably never quite get over all the things I've been through over the years. My only real partner...he, well, he wanted a chick with a dick. He didn't want me. And now that I am finally who I'm meant to be, physically as well as in my soul, well, I'm just not that unique."

Hell, I can't even string the right words together to speak properly.

"Oh, but you are." He picked up a lock of her hair, rolling it gently between his fingers before letting it fall. "You have the whole human experience contained in here." He touched her temple. "And here." He moved his hand over the place on her breast just about where her heart sat.

"You know what it's like to live as a man. You know what it's like to be a woman. You know what it's like to be lonely. You know what it's like to fight the whole damn world for your own identity. Gina, that takes so much strength! You have more soul in you than any person I've ever met, man or woman. Two-spirit, it is called in some cultures."

He paused before adding, "I think Aphrodite sent you to me, or perhaps vice versa, because she knew you were the only one with whom I might be able to find fulfillment in your world."

"Wow. You do know how to make a woman feel important." Her smile felt like it would split her face in two. "Kiss me, Himeros. Please?"

Gina braced then, waiting for the onslaught, but his kiss this time was feather-light, and the tenderness as he pressed his lips against hers brought yet more tears to her eyes. She'd never cried so much in her life, but this time, she didn't care. He wouldn't see her as weak. He'd said he thought her strong.

She closed her lids and the tears trickled out beneath them, coursing down her cheeks. The moist heat of his tongue lapped them up before they reached her jaw, then he was back to her mouth, and she could taste the salt of her own crying as he teased open her lips and shared his soul with her.

Really shared his soul.

It felt as if she were drowning in ecstasy as wave after wave of happiness filled her being. She had never felt so alive than in this very moment, suspended in the midst of, well, wherever the hell they were.

Reluctantly she turned away from his kiss, but she had to know.

"So, um...are we actually....dead?"

His laughter bellowed out of his chest. "No, my darling, we are not dead. I extended my essence to protect you. I would never let you crash to the ground in that way. Never."

"You extended your essence?" she repeated. "Hmm. You could have told me a few seconds earlier, maybe. I could have enjoyed the ride without nearly wetting myself in terror."

"Oh, Gina. You and I are going to have so much fun in the days and weeks ahead."

"Days and weeks?" Is that all?

"Oh, we will have a lot longer than that, Gina. Months. Perhaps years. We will have as long as you wish. I have been waiting forever for you, my love, and forever is such a long time to be alone."

"Himeros."

She wrapped her arms tightly around his waist, never wanting to let go. "Take me home, beautiful god. I want to make love to you again, but I want to do it in the real world, surrounded by things that I can relate to. A bed again, maybe, instead of that damn window."

His arms slipped around her too, and they clung together in the extraordinary golden light a moment longer, before she felt the touch of his lips on the top of her head. "Your home? Or mine."

"Oh." Where was his home? The penthouse suite? Mount

Olympus? Maybe the clouds above? Would she ever really get to see his home?

"You will see my real home, Gina. When the time is right. But for now, let's make it yours. I'm thinking you have some interesting sauces and toppings in your kitchen that I would like to try out before this night is over. I am hungry."

She looked into his laughing face and read the hunger there. It wasn't for food, and Gina was suddenly ravenous herself.

"Let's go home, then, Himeros."

Ω Ψ Ω

Please read on for the next instalment in the GODS OF LOVE series.

SEX CLUB SECRETS

BY JEN KATEMI

SEX CLUB SECRETS

ANTEROS, GOD OF REQUITED AND UNREQUITED LOVE

Ella is in love with her best friend Kade. But her love has not been returned, and when bisexual Kade shows no signs of becoming romantic toward her, she decides to call a halt on her unrequited love and accept an invitation to a celebrated Melbourne sex club.

Kade is distressed when the woman he is beginning to see as more than a friend decides to visit Secrets before he can tell her how he feels. He follows her into the club and witnesses her at play with the enigmatic Anteros, a sexy god-like man who seems to know exactly how to satisfy her innermost cravings. But Anteros also feeds the hidden desires within Kade. How can he admit his feelings for Ella when he's not sure he can commit with his whole heart?

Anteros is one of the erotes, an aspect of Eros and the ancient Greek god of requited and unrequited love. He has heard the call of these would-be lovers and intends to show them that friendship can sometimes be the best place to kick start a lasting romantic relationship.

But love cannot flourish unless it is returned, and how will he convince Kade—a man who occasionally enjoys other men—that he can be true to the woman he loves? What will happen to this couple when the night ends and they return to the real world outside the door of Secrets?

PART I
ELLA

CHAPTER ONE

One too many margaritas and she was about to spend the first night of her thirties holed up in a sex club.

Hmm. Not much of an excuse, really, when she thought about it. *Not like I'm drunk or anything.* Three drinks, mostly laced with watered down lime juice, did not a crazy woman make.

So why the heck was she standing here on the street in front of a door covered in padded black leather, about to accept the dare that her friends had automatically assumed she'd refuse?

"Do it," Theo had insisted, and the other three echoed his laughing plea. "You're thirty, now, Ella; it's time you did something exciting in your life. For once."

Only Kade was silent, his long, slim frame rigid, staring at her with those penetrating hazel eyes that reminded her of an amber gemstone bracelet she'd recently assessed. He'd been so quiet tonight she couldn't read him, even though they'd been friends for close to ten years. A third of her lifetime.

"Kade?" What was going on behind that dead-pan expression? "What do you think? Should I go ahead with it?"

He shrugged and shook back the light brown hair that always threatened to flop down into his eyes. "It's not you, Ellie. You're too…vanilla for what's behind that door. I think you should go home."

Too vanilla? The muscles across her shoulders and neck began to tie themselves into an unpleasant knot. Oh, Kade. You should have known better than that.

She smoothed her hands down her short black dress, adjusting the hem of the skirt over her hips and giving herself a moment to gather courage, before pressing the buzzer set discreetly into the wall beside the door. "Right then," she said. "Guess I'm going in."

The nervous ache in her gut had nothing to do with Kade's hurtful comment and everything to do with the small peep window that opened up above the buzzer as a pair of assessing eyes looked out into her own. At least, that's what she told herself as she gave her name and waited while they checked their list of bookings for the night. Or whatever it was they did before letting people in.

No one gained entry to Secrets without a pre-approved booking, she knew that much, at least. When the personalized invitation had arrived on her desk at work two days ago, its black glossy paper inscribed with silver writing and a "happy birthday" message from the management at Melbourne's most celebrated sex club, she'd stared around the mostly open-plan lab in disbelief. Which of her work colleagues would give a woman a visit to a sex club as a birthday gift?

Jared in research, maybe? He was the one most likely to play a practical joke. But when she looked across the room he wasn't at his work station, and he'd surely have wanted to see her reaction if he'd done this. She picked up the invitation intending to throw it in the trash, but something stayed her hand, and instead her thumb stroked across the raised silver letters as she re-read part of the message.

The truth of your unrequited desires will be revealed... the most exciting night you ever have...from the moment you step through our door your life will be forever changed...

Did she want her life to change forever? It wasn't too bad as it was. She loved her job as a gemologist at the Melbourne Museum, evaluating gemstone donations and potential acquisitions. It was different, and exciting, and a far cry from where she had started in a jewelry retail store all those years ago. Outside of work, she had family and friends to keep her occupied.

What would Kade think of this invitation? Her lips twisted at the thought of his reaction. Would he approve of her visit to a sex club? She suspected not, but found herself imagining what it would be like if she did go to the club, and if Kade accompanied her. Would they go their separate ways and meet up afterwards, or...

The truth of your desires will be revealed...

She knew Kade was bisexual. He'd had a girlfriend when they first met, and a boyfriend for the past two years, at least until Kade had abruptly broken things off about four months ago. Would he want to watch if she had sex with another man? Would he stand by and do nothing, or want to join in? And if he did join them, who would he want to be with? Her? Or the other man?

A frisson of desire contracted her womb at the thought of sharing another man with her sexy-as-hell friend, and instead of throwing out the invitation she tucked it into her handbag. The invitation was for Friday evening. For her and a friend, if she wished to bring someone, and the only proviso was that she had to call and confirm the name prior to arriving at the appointed time.

A small group – including Kade – was taking her out for birthday drinks after work that night. Would she dare to do something so decadent, so…unfamiliar?

Her heart threatened to jump right up out of her throat as the doorway opened in front of her and an attractive, dark-haired woman in a long silver dress gestured for her to enter.

Oh my God, is that a studded collar she's wearing? Seriously?

She took a deep breath before stepping inside.

I'm thirty, I'm single, I haven't had sex in two years, and the guy I think I might be in love with prefers his dates to have a cock instead of a vagina. They're my dirty little secrets. Not so bad, really. So, what have I got to lose?

She glanced back at Kade just as the door was about to close behind her. "I gave them your name, too," she said.

The disbelieving laughter of her friends filled her ears. "God damn!" That was Theo. "She really did it!"

Kade though, was not laughing. She caught only a glimpse of his face before the door closed him out, and he looked seriously unhappy. His eyes had turned more emerald than amber; glowing so bright they looked like twin traffic lights staring her down.

Last time he looked like that had been the night he broke up with his boyfriend and turned up at her apartment three-quarters drunk and needing a sympathetic shoulder.

Her fingers twitched and she almost extended her hand, but the woman with her was already speaking and drew her attention back to the present. "Welcome to Secrets, Ella. We're really glad you decided to join us this evening."

Wow. Her voice was husky and sensual, and a primitive quiver darted across Ella's skin. "Thank you," she answered, her skittering heart lending a slight breathlessness to her own voice. "My, ah, friend decided not to join me this evening, so—"

"That's fine." The woman's mouth curled up at one corner in an expression that was almost sly. "Quite often we find it better if patrons come alone, anyway. Less chance of inhibitions getting in the way. Come through, Ella. There's someone here who's been waiting to meet you...very impatiently, I must say."

Her tone was indulgent. Whoever was waiting was clearly a favored...what had she called it? Patron.

Ella's curiosity grew as the other woman wrapped long, crimson-tipped fingers around her upper arm and drew her further into the venue. Would whoever was waiting to meet her be the one who had sent the invitation? Would it be someone she knew?

I hope not.

The only person for whom she had sexual feelings had been left outside the door of the club seething with displeasure at his vanilla friend daring to try something new. And without his approval, either.

Bad luck, Kade. I'm here tonight for me. No one else. Just me. And my unrequited desires, apparently.

The flip-flop of her stomach sent a wave of warmth spiraling downwards and her womb squeezed in nervous anticipation of what might lie ahead.

I'm in a freaking sex club! I can't believe I'm here.

She stared around, trying not to appear too wide-eyed and open-mouthed, but keen to take in as much as she could of the atmosphere. They were now in a large, red-carpeted room with a huge bar built in a circular shape in the middle, all black and silver chrome and reflective walls. There was a dance floor off to one side, filled with people swaying in time to music that played softly in the background. At each corner of the floor was a raised dais containing a pole, and on each dais was a person in pretty much no clothing whatsoever performing a range of acrobatic feats up and down their pole. Two women and two men, with—oh! One of the latter was in an advanced state of arousal. She looked down at the floor and felt the heat invade her cheeks. At least they embrace equality here, she thought, trying to focus on the positive.

The rhythm of the music was a slow, sensual tempo that seemed to reach out and caress some hidden place inside her she hadn't even known existed. She shivered, not used to such a primal response. It was only music, for heaven's sake.

Okay. Concentrate on the room.

It didn't look anything like what she'd imagined. In fact, she hadn't known quite what to imagine. A dingy room full of weird-looking contraptions and implements that looked like they belonged in a torture chamber? A row of beds, maybe partitioned off by curtains? Men seated on chairs being given lap dances by well-endowed, topless women? Whips and chains in abundance? People in gimp masks rutting indiscriminately everywhere she looked?

Instead, deep and comfortable-looking lounge chairs in intimate conversational groupings dotted the room. The cavernous place was filled with men and women dressed in various types of attire, from conservative formal evening wear like she was, right through to more risqué BDSM-type wear, including one woman on hands and knees beside a couch chair who was wearing nothing but black stiletto heels and a studded black collar attached to a lead. The lead was held by a man in a James Bond-style suit, who was sipping a drink and staring nonchalantly around the room.

The woman's rear faced Ella directly and she couldn't help her gaze falling to that rose-pink slash with a creamy pearl offering at its center. Clearly, the woman was in a state of excitation, despite the uncomfortable pose. She felt the dampening of her own panties and didn't understand why another woman's pussy would turn her on. Especially when that woman was forced to endure such a submissive pose, while her partner – probably her Dom – sat so comfortably above her in his position of power. The man's gaze fastened on Ella and his eyebrows rose slightly when she lifted her chin and stared back at him down her nose.

Anyone tries to put me in a collar and I'll bloody well bite them.

The BDSM lifestyle, and that book series, the one everyone was talking about lately, was definitely not her cup of tea.

If being in a sex club is all about becoming someone's submissive then I won't be staying long.

She stopped in the middle of the room, forcing the other woman to stop with her. "Maybe I should make this clear from the outset. I'm nobody's sub," she said. "I'm not signing any contract that gives someone control over my body. Not like that." She nodded at the nearby couple.

The woman snorted, but she did let go of Ella's arm. "You won't have to, hon. Your secrets lie in other areas, don't they?"

"Well, um…" Yes, but how would anyone else know of my secrets?

"Come. I promise you won't be disappointed with tonight's pleasures. He is awaiting you in one of his private viewing rooms."

A private viewing room. Isn't that an oxymoron?

But anticipation mounted when she followed the other woman. As she walked she felt the rub of her labia lips against each other, lips that seemed to have swollen since she stepped inside this strange new world and left reality behind.

Who was He? It seemed appropriate, based on how the silver-dressed woman spoke, to add a capital "H" to the pronoun. Guess I'll soon find out.They stepped through a doorway near the rear of the bar area and into a long hall with a number of rooms leading off it. Each room boasted a large observation window with a bar-style counter running beneath it, and each counter had a couple of chrome and black leather bar stools tucked in beneath as well as neat baskets of condoms sitting on top.

Peep shows? Each viewing area had the ability to be curtained off for some semblance of privacy if the person watching through the window desired it, though she could still hear muffled groans coming from behind some of the curtained areas that were clearly in use.

Despite the obvious purpose and the subtle sounds of sex it still seemed as expensively styled back here as it was out in the main bar area. The muted hum of that primitive music seemed to suit the ambience and her hips swayed more than usual as she walked. The pang in her womb spread lower to center directly between her legs.

A few of the bar stools were occupied by people who hadn't bothered to close their red velvet drapes, including an older-looking man who had released his penis from his trousers and was pumping hard with his fist as he watched three women in a triangular formation on a large bed in the room beyond.

Ew! She averted her gaze from the man only to encounter the women, whose gently-moving heads were concealed deep within the valley of each other's legs. From the sounds of the inarticulate whimpers that echoed from the room they were clearly enjoying both the giving and the receiving of pleasure.

Sudden anxiety added a sharp edge to the desire flowing through her system as the reality of where she was began to hit home. This was hard-core. This was going to be sex with a stranger. Maybe with other people watching. Could she do this? Did she really want to do this?

As if the silver-dressed woman sensed her discomfort, she spoke quietly when they moved past the watching man. "One of those women in there is his wife, you know. They visit once a month and take it in turns with their chosen lovers."

"And...she doesn't mind?"

"By 'she', do you mean either of their lovers? Or the wife? The answer is no, in any case. The couple met the two women at Secrets about three years ago, when they came here looking for a way to spice up their love life. One of the women is a high level executive in marketing, too busy for a full-time relationship. She was thrilled after that first time with them, when they wanted to meet up again. The other is a divorced single mother who came here looking for something uniquely her own. The no-strings approach suits them all perfectly, and they've been meeting here regularly ever since. They've all grown to genuinely care about each other."

"Oh." Ella glanced back at the guy, who was so fixated on what was going on in that room that he hadn't even noticed them walk by. The expression on his face was definitely lustful, but there was softness there too, that she could almost describe as loving. She hadn't noticed that at first. Knowing it wasn't just a seedy one-off event but something meaningful to all of them made her look at him in a slightly different light.

Maybe I'll find what I'm looking for, tonight. Even if I don't yet know what that is.

"Here is where I say goodbye, hon. This room is yours for the night. Enjoy." The woman leaned forward and pressed a light kiss onto Ella's mouth, just the very tip of her tongue darting in to stroke lightly against Ella's teeth before releasing her.

She gasped at the contact and her nipples puckered in an unexpected reaction. Before she could say or do anything in response, the woman gave her a small push. "Go. Have fun." The door snapped shut behind her.

A room lit by what seemed like hundreds of candles confronted her, as did a large four-poster bed taking up much of the space in the center. On one side of the chamber she could see a shelf that contained all manner of unusual-looking toys. She recognized only a few of them, including dildoes of varying sizes, some silver balls, handcuffs and other more complicated restraints as well as a whip and something that looked like a feather duster.

Around the edges of the room, almost hidden in the shadows, were pieces of furniture that reminded her of gym equipment. But her gaze was irresistibly drawn to the largest piece of furniture other than the bed. A huge, almost throne-like chair carved out of some kind of darkened wood sat facing her, and it was currently occupied by a giant of a man wearing black leather trousers and nothing else.

His legs were thrust out in front of him and casually crossed at the ankles, one arm resting over the edge of the chair while the other supported his chin. He studied her in silence.

Holy moly! The potency of his personality swept over her like a powerful magnetic pull, and her feet of their own volition shuffled closer towards him.

Even though his face was still mostly in shadow she caught a flash of white teeth as his lips parted, and her womb constricted in an ache so intense a tiny whimper escaped. It was as if the involuntary sound let loose an even stronger barrage of invisible sexual energy. She was drowning in awareness of her own body's needs, like flowing molten lava encasing her in its heat and forcing its way in to touch her soul.

What the heck? She tried to tamp down on the crazy thoughts, clasping her fingers together tightly to still their sudden trembling. Nerves. It was just nerves.

Then he leaned forward, into the light, and she stopped breathing altogether at the beauty of his face. So. It wasn't nerves. It was pure, unadulterated lust.

"Welcome, Ella," he said. "I've been waiting for you a very long time."

CHAPTER TWO

She had never seen anyone like him before. Not even Kade was this good-looking, and with his six foot plus long sleek body and tousled brown hair her friend was the most handsome guy she'd ever met. But this man...

He looks like perfection.

His hair was thick and dark and invitingly rumpled, and it framed a face that could only be described as chiseled. But that inadequate term didn't do justice to the hard yet sexy lines of his cheek and jaw. The flickering candlelight accentuated the curves and hollows of his face and the strong, patrician line of his nose in a way that created an alluring sense of mystery. As if she couldn't quite perceive all of him at the one time, and couldn't get a grasp on exactly who he might be.

But his eyes... oh, lord, his eyes stood out like beacons of brilliance without any flickering whatsoever. They were a clear blue-green aquamarine color, framed by thick dark lashes that created a sleepy, almost heavy-lidded shape. The clarity of his gaze was what had stopped her breath and it was hard to stare back at him without feeling like she was drowning in their delicious depths.

Who had eyes like that in real life? She studied gemstones every day that weren't half as dazzling as this. Even photoshopped celebrity shots didn't look this good.

Her quick intake of breath was a deliberate attempt to try and break the bedazzled spell, and his wide mouth flicked up at one corner as if he knew the difficulty she was having controlling her bodily responses.

Decadent pictures centered around that mouth immediately flooded her mind. Imagine those lips on me, on my breasts, suckling at my nipples until the blood beneath rises to the surface and turns them a beautiful dark rose in contrast to my pale skin, or on my clit, working it loose from the folds of my pussy until it hums with heat and engorges to the point where I can't even close my legs anymore...

She blinked and shook her head. Lord, where had these imaginings come from? His grin grew wider then, as if in unison with her thoughts. He couldn't know, of course, but...

"I'm glad you're a redhead," he said. "Makes it easier to see the blush of arousal light up your skin."

Of course she flushed even darker then, the embarrassing prickle of heat travelling all the way to her toes. She wiggled them in her new high-heeled shoes, aiming for calm, and made a concerted effort to ignore her body's betrayal.

"I'm blonde," she corrected, and he tilted his head, studying her.

"Really? I could have sworn that visit to the hairdresser last week gave you those cascading golden locks. I love the blonde, mind you, but knowing you're a redhead underneath adds an element of spice to the occasion."

How the hell...? She closed her gaping mouth before he classified her as a simpleton. "Well, okay, maybe I did get a little help from a bottle but—"

"I know everything, Ella." His voice was rich and deep

and her skin quivered at the delicious sound, despite his outrageous claim.

Everything? I don't think so.

His eyes danced as if mocking her thoughts.

Now that he was sitting forward in the light the rest of his body was displayed more clearly. He was tanned and buff, his chest hairless, with not an ounce of excess fat anywhere that she could see. And she could see a long way down. His trousers sat low on his hips, the chiseled 'v' indentation inviting her eyes lower. The leather was so tight it left little to the imagination and she swallowed hard at the thought of fitting all that was clearly on offer inside her own body.

Was there a condom in this world big enough to cover him? Would it hurt, if he entered her? Would she even care about pain, if it meant coupling with a man this gorgeous-looking?

Her mound ached and the urge grew to jump onto his lap and rub against that enormous penis. She could feel her nipples popping out and hardening like twin miniature erections of her own. When he glanced down at her breasts then back up again, she knew they were visible through the thin material of her dress.

He leaned back again, relaxing into the chair like a king at ease in his throne room, and she felt the need to regain some level of control.

"I...um...are you the one who invited me here tonight? We haven't met before. Have we?" She was amazed her voice still worked, even if it was a little squeaky.

Instead of answering her, though, he asked a question of his own. "Why did you accept the invitation, Ella?"

She opened her mouth to respond then closed it again, considering. Why had she accepted? "I...well..." She took a deep breath, tired of pretending all the time. What was so wrong about speaking the truth, for once? From what she had read about this club in the past couple of days, it was supposed to be a discreet environment where secrets could be expressed or indulged, and they would stay safely within these four walls after the night was over.

A couple of well-known actors and a sports star or two were reputed to be regulars, but nothing had ever leaked to the media about what might or might not have gone on once that padded leather door closed behind them.

"I'm in love with someone who doesn't love me back," she blurted out. "And I'm sick of waiting for him. I know it's never going to happen. When I got the invitation I had this idea that we'd both come in to the club together and somehow find our way to each other. But now…I know that was stupid, and I think maybe I'm here to finally do something for myself. I'm here to put a line under the past and start fresh. With something—maybe with someone—completely new. I want to challenge my boundaries."

Her cheeks were aflame yet again; she could feel the burning as she spoke. Why had she just divulged all of that to a complete stranger? He was here as she was, no doubt, for sex and nothing else, and he probably didn't give two hoots as to what her real motives might be. "Look," she corrected, "basically, I'm just here to have a good time. Like you are. And…actually, I don't even know your name."

He chuckled and shook his head. "I liked your first explanation better. I especially like the part about pushing your boundaries." He held out his hand then, and a compulsion to step forward into his embrace washed over her. "Come here, Ella, and let's get to know each other properly, at last. You want to know my name? I am Anteros. Some call me the god of requited love. For some it starts as unrequited. All who open their hearts in my presence will have love returned, in the end."

Anteros. That sounded Greek, and would explain his exotic Mediterranean coloring. The rest of his words made little sense, but she moved forward anyway and clasped his right hand in hers. "It's a pleasure to meet you, Anteros."

"Yes, it is."

A laugh escaped her at his unexpected arrogance, uttered in such a cordial tone. "Most people would respond with, 'and you'."

"Ah. My mistake. Of course it is lovely to meet you also, Ella. That goes without saying. But it will still be your pleasure, tonight." Warm fingers wrapped around her hand and held tight, the touch igniting her whole body in a way that she couldn't fathom. Like an electric current flowing out of him and into her through their connected flesh, heating her blood and washing through her veins like wildfire.

"Suspend your disbelief, Ella. Anything is possible at Secrets, tonight."

Suspend disbelief? I can do that. She closed her eyes for a moment. Need grew, intensified…Kade…

"If your lover were here right now, what would you want from him? From this…Kade?"

Had she spoken his name out loud? She must have. "I don't know."

"Yes, you do." He was close enough now that his words whispered across her temple, disturbing the shorter tendrils of hair around her face. "Look into your heart. Tell me."

She shivered, and glanced back at the large viewing window with its heavy drapes drawn to each side. "I want…"

"Do you wish the curtains closed before we begin? I am amenable to that, if it is your wish."

"No." She looked hard at the glass, not having realized until this moment that it was one-way. A whole football team of people could be out there, observing them, and she would have no idea. Instead, her reflection stared back at her, pale and ethereal-looking, her newly blonde hair long and wavy rather than frizzy-looking for once, and the whiteness of her limbs an interesting counter-point to the powerful darkness of Anteros standing behind her. Even with five-inch heels on, he topped her by a good six inches, and she wasn't short to start with. They looked good together, she realized. Dark and light. Strength and delicacy.

I feel different already. No more flat-chested beanpole. I feel…kind of sexy, for a change.

Time for truth. She took a deep breath. "I wish that Kade were here, watching me right now. Watching us, wanting us, while we do things here in this room that I've never done before." She leaned back into Anteros as he let go of her hand and began to stroke down and up her arm and then lightly across her left breast. He paused for a second at the tip, rolling his thumb over the hardened nub, before dipping below to hover near her rapidly beating heart. "I want him to see me in a new way. I want him to want me, the way I've always wanted him. I want him to love me, the way I—"

"Ella." Anteros pulled her away from the mirrored window and dipped his head in towards her throat. A caress like butterfly wings tickled her skin along the edge of her collar bone. "Shall we assume he is there, and he is watching, and give him a show the likes of which he will never forget?" His words vibrated against her and need grew in her belly. "Shall we punish him a little, or maybe quite a lot, for making you feel so lonely, all these years? Shall we do that, right now?"

"Oh, yes, Anteros. Please, yes."

He moved without warning and captured her mouth in a

kiss like none she had ever experienced before. He was hardness, and power, and masterful strength, and yet there was also a delicacy to his touch that thrilled her. She opened her lips and let him in and his tongue danced across her own as a firm grip tangled itself in her hair and tilted her head back, hard. He tasted of honey, cinnamon and citrus, fresh and clean and delicious. She imagined Kade watching them and mimicked his own action by fisting her hands in his hair, grateful it was long enough to thread easily through her fingers. She clutched hard at the silken strands and darted into his mouth with her tongue.

He groaned and the erotic sound emboldened her. She forced her body into the unyielding curves of his with a desperation she hadn't known she possessed, pressing her mons into his groin until the heat and the hardness already there grew impossibly larger.

There was no doubt about her effect on Anteros.

Are you watching, Kade? See what I can do to a man, if only you would let me?

She reached down to touch him but Anteros suddenly broke off their kiss and gripped her wrist. "No. I am in control in this room, Ella," he said. "Not you, for once."

What did he mean? "I...I don't want all that Dom/sub stuff tonight. I already told the woman—"

"I know." He stared down at her with a gaze that was just so damn...endless. She could drown in the depths of those eyes. "I don't need a submissive. Or a Domme, for that matter," he said. "Neither does Kade. We need a woman who is willing to relinquish internal control every once in a while. Someone who lets us be the boss, when we feel the desire. There is a vast difference between the two."

What was he talking about? No one in their right mind would ever think about bossing this man around. He was too powerful. Too much of a testosterone-filled male to let anyone else be in charge. Especially a woman.

He laughed suddenly. "You'd be surprised, Ella," he said. "Aphrodite is one hell of a woman and she most certainly does not like to hear the word, no."

She frowned. "Aphrodite?"

"The mother of us all. I am one of the erotes, her child of unrequited desire, and I am here to fulfill your yearning for love, as I have done for so many others before you."

"I…" Don't even know what to say. Did he really think he was a Greek god? She didn't want to turn back now, not when she'd already committed to using tonight to mark a changing point in her life, but what if she'd picked the one crazy guy in the club in which to entrust her first step into the sexual unknown?

Panic threatened and she gulped in air, forcing herself to count slowly to ten. I'm fine. I'm absolutely fine. It's nothing like…that other time.

She thought of the woman in the silver dress and the warmth she'd displayed on mentioning him. … Four…five…six…

Secrets had a well-known reputation for protecting its clientele, in every sense of the word. The rumors that this was a place where even celebrities felt safe to visit if they were so inclined, knowing that their secrets would not disappear out the door, gave her some measure of reassurance.

…Seven…eight…

The woman would not have introduced them if this man were intending to harm her in any way. It was okay. Even though her gut instinct was telling her that he could well be dangerous if he were riled, she had the feeling that it could be her emotional health that was at risk, not her body, this time.

…Nine…

A wave of desire washed over her and guided her thoughts into chaotic overdrive. She could feel it pressing in on her, not from within but from outside of herself.

Suspension of disbelief.

"Ten, Ella. I won't hurt you. I am here for your pleasure, and to help you find what you seek."

"How is that possible?" she whispered.

He smiled with such warmth that his whole face lit up. "Anything is possible." A caress danced across her cheek but he had not moved, other than the flick of an eyebrow. His gaze settled on her mouth and she felt the moist pressure of a kiss. A recently familiar one that tasted of citrus and cinnamon, and perhaps a hint of honey. She raised a shaking hand to her lips and traced their aching fullness.

"Who are you?"

He raised an eyebrow. "You know who I am," he said. "Look deep into your heart and you will find me there. I care, Ella. I heard your call of need, and I care."

"Show me more. Please."

"I will. You are mine until dawn, you know." He looked over her shoulder toward the viewing window and his expression become mocking as a hint of cruelty twisted his lips. "Mine!"

The possessive tone sent a throb of desire directly to her clit and a flood of juice coated her. She made her decision. "I will be yours tonight, in every way you want me."

"Good." He turned her to face the window. "Right now, I want you to undress yourself, and I want you to do it slowly, so that Kade can appreciate every little detail as you remove your clothing and reveal that lean white body of yours. Then, when you are fully naked, I am going to bind you to this chair with your legs spread wide and your sex open to whoever wishes to imagine plunging into you."

"Oh, I'm not so sure—"

"You are going to let me do that, Ella, because it is time you learned to trust again. It is time you learned that handing over control to someone else does not mean what it did for you in the past."

PART II
KADE

CHAPTER THREE

He hadn't intended to follow her in. He was so damn fucking frustrated that she would choose to do something so vastly out of character. A sex club, for God's sake. What the hell was she thinking?

But then she'd looked back at him in those last few seconds before the door closed, and her face had altered, as if the Ella he knew was slipping away and there was nothing he could do to stop it. She was about to go have sex with a stranger. Or even more than one person if she got talked into some group stuff. If she did, things might change irrevocably between them and he would never have the opportunity to crush her in his arms and say all the things that were rushing through his brain right this minute.

"I gave them your name, too." Ella's final words sent a startled jolt to his heart, and it took all of three seconds before he made his decision.

"Fuck it. I'm going in to get her." He punched the buzzer and held it down until the peephole opened once again and a pair of accusing eyes stared out at him. He took a deep breath and willed his heart to slow down. "I'm invited." After a few minutes of invisible consultation behind the door, he was finally in. "Don't wait up for us," he called out to Theo and the others.

"He's going after Ella? I thought he was gay," one of them said, but Theo's laughing response was cut off abruptly when the door closed them out and he entered this world full of secrets.

They thought he was gay? He rolled his eyes. Everyone thought he was gay, but he wasn't. He was bisexual. There was a hell of a difference between the two. Why did people not get that?

The woman who guided him through the crowd in the bar area was tall and slim, dressed in silver clothing and with some kind of weird collar adorning her neck. She speared him with an assessing look when he mentioned Ella. "I've agreed to take you in because you were her invited guest and as such you've already been security screened, but I'll only do it on one condition." Her fingers splayed on his chest. "You must promise not to enter the room unless invited. If you do so without such an invitation, you will be forcibly removed from the premises. Is that clear, Mister Kade Devlin?"

He nodded. "Crystal, ma'am. Guess I'll just have to make sure I get an invite, then, won't I?"

She laughed and the severity of her features softened. "I suspect this night could get interesting, after all." She led him down a hallway and stopped before a large window. "Here's your Ella. Now take a seat, if you wish, and enjoy the show, Kade."

She toyed with her collar for a moment, observing through the window, and he felt a surge of proprietary anger at someone else watching his friend in such an intimate situation. As if she felt his emotion, she chuckled. "I'm leaving now, Kade. If you want food or drink, press this service button and we will attend you. If you wish to listen in on the room, just push this button over here. The sound, like the vision, is one-way only, so they won't hear or see you in return."

She melted away into the darkness of the corridor, and he looked into the room to see Ella – his beautiful, stubborn Ella – standing only a few feet away. An exceedingly attractive man stood just behind her and he appeared to be staring directly at Kade while doing something behind her back. Unzipping her dress, maybe?

Can he see me? The woman said it was one-way.

He moved to the left a little, testing, and the man's eyes flared vivid blue-green as they followed him.

Crap! It wasn't one-way, then. But Ella didn't seem to have noticed him. It was only that man, whose lip was now curling up at one corner in a sardonic grin. "Mine." The word was impossible to miss, even without sound, and Kade's cock jumped to immediate attention despite the resentment roiling around in his stomach.

She's not yours. Not yet, man. I don't give in that easily.

A half-lidded look of sensual abandon softened her features and her head dropped in a dreamy fashion to one side as she began to shimmy her dress down. The clothing peeled away from her shoulders, one slow inch at a time, to reveal pale skin with its faint smattering of freckles dusting the surface. There now was that slight hollow at the base of her throat, the one he had almost kissed last week until he chickened out at the last moment.

There too, were her breasts, and they were even better than he'd imagined. Small and pert in shape, they were topped with long rosy nubs pointing right at him. So the little minx had not worn a bra this evening. She'd sat beside him all night, laughing and drinking her salt-encrusted margaritas, not letting on that the black velvet material of her dress must have been rubbing directly against those nipples all that time.

Had it felt good, that abrasive sensation?

His jeans grew tight around his groin.

Jesus, God, it was like his ultimate sexual fantasy right here, seeing the two halves of his craving come together in one divine moment. Pure muscle, masculine strength and an exciting, rock-hard body on the one side, and the familiar softness and feminine beauty of the woman he wanted to love and cherish on the other.

But the exquisite beauty he found in the couple before him was the very reason he hadn't spoken up before now. How could he commit to any sort of relationship with Ella if his orientation meant he might never be completely fulfilled? What if he hurt her unintentionally, simply because he couldn't control his impulses or his need for cock every once in a while?

He couldn't put her in that situation. It was just too unfair.

How can I be sure I'll be faithful, if we end up together? How can I put her through that hurt if I can't help but stray from the straight path?

He leaned forward and touched the glass, spreading his fingers wide against the cool surface and wishing instead he could touch the heat of those crimson nipples.

What would it feel like, to take one of Ella's breasts into his mouth? What would she taste like? He ached to suckle on his friend, run his tongue over her skin, inhale her perfume and hear her moan in the way he'd been imagining in his dreams almost every night for the past few months.

She didn't know it, but she was the reason he'd ended things with Will four months ago. Every time he was with his male lover, even as he was enjoying the power and the hardness of Will's superbly muscled body, he had found his mind wandering to the tantalizing softness of Ella's skin, the brush of her hair against his cheek when she hugged him hello or goodbye, the flare of happiness lighting up her gentle grey eyes whenever she saw him, the surprising steel in her touch when he dropped in to visit after a hard day at work and convinced her to massage his neck and shoulders.

He spent his day manipulating other people's bodies back into alignment in his osteopathy clinic, but she was the only one who ever did the same to him.

Little snapshots of Ella, flickering through his mind at the most inopportune moments, took his attention away from Will and he began to wonder what it would feel like to sink into her welcoming body instead.

What would it be like to have her thin legs wrap themselves around him? Would her thighs hold deceptive strength in their length, just like her fingers? What noises would she make if he bent over her and slipped his tongue along her slit or curled it around her clit? Would she taste like salty passion if he used his mouth to bring her to orgasm? What would be the expression on her face if he lay back and let her ride him as hard or as gently as she liked?

Maybe she'd look something like this. His breath fogged the glass. Oops. Too close. He pulled back a little, not wanting to obscure anything about this tableau playing out in front of him.

The man she was with, the one who seemed to be looking straight at him with that knowing and slightly malicious grin, extended a hand around to tweak one of Ella's nipples between a powerful finger and thumb. He stretched her out, hard, over and over, as if he were trying to encourage milk from a recalcitrant udder.

Did it hurt? His jaw clenched, even as the thought of white spray streaking out the end of her long pink nipples and decorating the window in front of him sent more blood racing to his dick. But then her mouth parted and her tongue flicked out to moisten her lips. God damn. She was enjoying what was being done to her.

His knees buckled and he sat down hard on one of the bar stools.

Dear God. She looks so much sexier than I could ever have imagined.

He hadn't thought he could get any harder and yet here he was, rigid now and threatening to explode in a sea of cum just like a teenager with a dirty magazine.

He pressed the button to enable sound to release from the room.

She was mewling in a way that sounded like it was being forced out of her from somewhere deep inside. The man was murmuring in her ear. He could hear the low thrum of a male voice without being able to make out individual words, and his hands fisted on the bench top in front of him.

I want to be the one to whisper in her ear until that incredible sound is forced from her throat. And I want to be the one to have erotic words whispered in my ear by that dark, mysterious male...

It felt like he was being pulled in two directions at once. He wanted to be this man, the one who was giving her so much pleasure, and yet part of him also wanted to be where Ella was right now, on the receiving end of this amazing-looking Adonis's attentions.

Where the hell had she found him? That physique was close to perfection with those wide shoulders, undulating stomach muscles, tight butt and the flex of powerful thighs as he bent to help Ella shimmy her dress over her hips and down. It was everything he had ever thought he wanted in a sexual partner. Until recently.

Oh, Ella. Wish I was man enough to tell you how I feel right now.

He wanted to. His stomach burned with the need to tell her, but how could he, when he wasn't sure he could give her the future she deserved? Even while falling in love with her he was still attracted to this man who was running proprietary hands over her body and who looked hot enough to eat.

But then, so did Ella.

Her dress was gone now, and she looked damn sexy as a blonde. The color change suited her, but he hadn't got around to telling her that, yet. She was wearing only her new five-inch sparkly silver heels and a see-through lacy G-string.

I gave you those heels, Ellie. Remember? For your birthday.

Peeking through the see-through fabric was her bare mound and the start of her slit, and he wanted to sink his tongue into that dark, secret place and tease out the essence of her arousal.

"What do you taste like, Ellie? I wonder. Is your cream spicy or sweet?" His erection threatened to burst free of his trousers and he was tempted to unzip himself and pull. But he knew what others were doing, up and down this hallway. He could hear their panting excitement, even if he couldn't take his eyes off Ella and this man pressed up now against her rear as, together, they shimmied down her G-string.

He shifted uncomfortably, trying to ease the ache in his loins. He didn't want to be like all these others, wanking at a peep show like it was not a potentially life-changing moment. He kept his rigid cock in his pants, hoping to savor it a bit longer. He wanted to wait until he was with Ella. He wanted to bury himself in her beautiful body and not burst until he was deep inside her.

And if he were being truthful with himself, he wanted to

do that while this gorgeous Adonis did exactly the same thing to him.

He couldn't help it. He let out a tiny whimper, and the Adonis's eyes blazed as if he'd heard the sound.

Not Adonis, Kade. My name is Anteros. God of requited and unrequited love. Do take out your beautiful cock. I want to see it.

He shook his head. Anteros? God of unrequited...Where were these thoughts coming from? It felt like someone else had taken over inside his head. Maybe he was crazy with lust?

No. You are not crazy with lust. But you will be by the end of this. I am Anteros, and I hear your need. Every facet of it. Show me your erection and I will release mine for Ella to enjoy. She needs this, Kade. Desperately. You know what happened.

She needs this? Yes. He knew what had happened, and maybe she did need this at last.

His hand crept to his pants and slowly released the zipper, but there was nothing slow about his member. It sprang free the moment it was allowed to, hard and hot and pointing skywards. His lips parted at the relief of cool air on his burning skin. When he looked back into the room, though, he was conflicted. Jealousy and fascination warred within him as the man stepped back from Ella, turned her to face him and removed his leather trousers with a fluidity of movement that seemed almost impossible.

She gasped and the sound echoed out through the speaker system in the hallway at the same time as Kade's sharp intake of breath.

Jesus! He'd known that with trousers off the view likely would be delicious, but... That hard-on was the most magnificent he'd ever seen. Bar none. Huge and hard and quivering, even through the glass he could make out shiny juice leaking from the engorged tip. The man was primed and ready to fuck and Ella hadn't even laid a hand on him, yet.

He glanced down at himself and met the eye of his own member staring straight back up at him. His lips twisted as pot, kettle and black came to mind.

"I want to taste you, Anteros."

Ella's voice was low and rough. He'd never heard her talk like that before, and the sound sent his body into overdrive. He desperately wanted to hear that vibration of sexual need when she next spoke with him.

Where had this wanton version of his friend come from? And why had it taken him so damn long to see what had clearly been right in front of his nose?

She was leaning forward now, dipping her head towards that enormous hard cock, and her tongue slipped out to run itself over the tip. He knew what that pre-cum would taste like, spicy and sharp, and he yearned to take her mouth in a kiss that would reveal the dual flavor of her own nectar coated with Anteros.

A bead of moisture tipped his own member and he ran a thumb lightly over the top before bringing it up to his mouth. He sucked on his thumb for several seconds; imagining capturing her lips and lapping on her tongue, and couldn't help the moan that rasped as it came out.

The bastard must have heard him again. He'd looked up at the involuntary sound and turned slightly, giving him full view of Ella's lips wrapped around him. She was moving up and down, a little hollow forming in her cheek as she sucked, her hand working the bottom half of his member that she couldn't quite reach with her mouth due to the length.

And the guy was enjoying it, too. A rictus of absorption transformed his features and the brilliance of his gaze was hooded now behind half-closed eyelids. A deep groan escaped the man's lips and a shudder wracked his body as he clutched at Ella's hair, pushing her down, forcing himself deeper.

Kade had that strange sense of being split in two again, of wanting her beautiful ruby red lips wrapped around him instead of this stranger, and at the same time wanting to taste what she was tasting. Wanting to be both giver and receiver of such exquisite pleasure. He dared not touch himself again. If he did his cum would flood this hallway and likely drown everyone nearby.

What he wouldn't give to be in that room right now, sharing their passion, sharing their desire. Sharing the woman he loved with this sexy stranger. Sharing the stranger who seemed to have invaded his head with the woman he loved.

Taking the two halves of what he needed, even as he gave everything that he had.

Oh, God, I want you both so fucking bad.

Cruel laughter teased like an echo at the edges of his mind.

"You didn't want her before, Kade. And now it's too late. She's mine. Mine."

CHAPTER FOUR

E nough!
      He lunged for the door like a crazed lunatic, but at the last moment something stayed his hand. That voice was buzzing inside his head again, telling him to wait, and to watch, for just a few minutes more until the time to enter was right.

He scowled through the glass, one hand clenched on the door knob, willing her to sense that he was here and ready to join in their sensual play. Or to rescue her from it if that's what she preferred.

Ella. I want to wrap you in my arms, kiss you hard, see the glazed look descend as I lead you to that large chair and shove you down into it. We could have so much fun in that chair...

His breath caught as the stranger did exactly what he'd just imagined, leading Ella by the hand and seating her. He noticed the restraints then, hanging from the top of the chair, with more around the armrests, and the chair legs. What were they made of, those restraints? They didn't look like metal handcuffs, but more like...

He craned his neck. Some kind of jewel-encrusted bracelet? Delicate and pretty, but presumably still firm enough to hold her in place. He'd used handcuffs with Will a time or two, but just the standard issue ones you could get at any sex shop. He'd never seen anything that looked so... well...sparkly and pretty.

But Ella? He didn't think she'd be willing to say yes to any kind of restraint, regardless of her fascination with beautiful gemstones. He knew her history. Knew what had happened when she was barely out of her teens. It was how they'd met, the night of that party, when he walked in by mistake while looking for the bathroom and saw her being held down on the bed, tears squeezing themselves out of her soft grey eyes and her hands pushing ineffectually against the guy scrabbling around on top of her. He'd reacted on instinct, seizing the bastard and throwing him across the room until he hit the wall and crumpled to the floor, too drunk to get up and fight back. She was still fully clothed, so he hadn't been too late. But...almost.

He flexed his fingers for a moment, remembering how hard she'd been trembling when he tried to help her up. Since then she never lost control. Ever. He suspected that would especially apply in a sexual situation.

Even as the memories ran through his head her features lost that glazed look and she gripped the ends of each chair arm. "Anteros, I'm not sure I can do this—"

"You can, my girl. You are stronger than you think. And we are in a very safe place, here in my bedchamber at Secrets."

Anteros peeled her grip off the chair and raised her hands to his lips, kissing each of her palms in turn. Kade couldn't decide whether to race in and save her, or let this play out a bit longer. What would Ella want him to do? Did she need a knight in shining armor?

Anteros raised his head and looked straight out through the window, and though he didn't say anything aloud Kade could hear the voice echoing inside him.

Wait. Just a minute or two more. You will be joining us soon, and she needs to make this decision on her own. I will not hurt her, or push her further than she is able to go.

A fleeting grin tilted Anteros's lips at the corner. And you are already her knight in shining armor. You have been since the moment she met you.

Kade's mouth dropped open, at a loss to explain what was happening and how the hell this stranger was fucking with his mind.

And what did he mean; you've always been her knight? Did it stem from that night? Had she always loved him? Had he truly been blind for that long?

He'd had several lovers in the time they'd known each other, both men and women. Ella had only had two that he was aware of, and the most serious of those had only lasted a few months.

Oh, Ella. How I must have hurt you over the years, without even knowing it.

She was clearly considering the man's words, her head tilted slightly to one side. He recognized the moment she made up her mind. Her chin firmed and her chest rose and fell in a couple of quick deep breaths, before her arms lifted above her head and she let him fasten the bracelets around her wrists.

"Do it. But...not too tight. Please." Unease laced her words, but so did determination. It was right that he'd waited, then, and let her make this decision on her own.

Anteros finished securing her wrists then bent to raise her legs, first one, then the other, so that her knees were splayed over each of the chair arms in a position that displayed her pink pussy lips in all their naked glory. His heart sped up at the sight. It called to him like no other sex ever had, that pussy. It was the core of her, the physical center of the woman who knew him better than anyone else in this world, and he desperately wanted to connect with her and experience her fully exposed offering.

But Anteros stepped in front of her then, like a deliberate reminder of his presence, and in a couple of quick movements he had her ankles fastened, too. She was still wearing those spiky silver heels, the weight of them pulling her feet down in what looked like an uncomfortable position and clearly making it impossible to close her limbs.

"It's funny," she said, studying the restraints and pulling on them experimentally. "They look like real rubies, to me, but I know they can't be. I must be getting slack in my old age."

He could hear the edge of anxiety in her voice and saw the rapid rise and fall of her chest. His jaw clenched. I won't let him hurt you. I won't let anyone hurt you again.

"Trust your instincts, Ella." Anteros fondled the red stones briefly. "Your eyes are only thirty years old. You are but a babe by my reckoning, and you can see perfectly well even without your gemology tools." He moved off to one side of the room, near the bench, and his voice became muffled. "The restraints were a recent gift to me from Pothos, one of my brothers. The day he found his pair. The rubies are as real as his love for Jeannie and Jake. He wanted to share some of his joy."

Was that regret lacing his tone? Or…hunger? Kade frowned, trying to guess at Anteros's mood, but then the latter was back at Ella's side and he was holding a glass container of ice and a large black feather.

Ella's features relaxed noticeably when she saw the feather. Her eyes half-closed and her head dropped back against the seat. "No whip. You're really not going to hurt me, Anteros." She sounded more confident now, and the tension holding Kade's shoulders tight began to dissipate.

"No, my dear one. I will not hurt you. You are bound, and you are safe, and you will enjoy the experience." He put down the ice and brandished the feather, a wicked gleam lighting up his eyes.

Kade couldn't help it. His gaze kept sliding back to her slash as he imagined that black feather tracing its enticing contours. It began to glisten as if in anticipation of being touched and he shuddered with desire, almost losing his load right then and there in the hallway, aching to taste her now abundant juices but unsure what she would think if he just barged right in and sank his face into her privates.

"I wish Kade really was out there right now."

Oh, God! Ella! She wanted him here, watching her. Watching them.

He grabbed for the curtain around his viewing area, shoving it closed as fast as he could along the smooth, almost noiseless track built into the ceiling.

Damned if he'd let anyone else share this vision of perfection.

Ella's fanny was not for public show.

He reached for his cock.

Now, Kade. His head whipped up and the man was staring at him and nodding toward the door. You may enter. It is time.

PART III
ELLA

CHAPTER FIVE

Helpless. She felt utterly helpless and vulnerable in this crazy position, and it should have had her screaming to get out. In the past it would have. But here in the privacy of this club she felt safer than she had in a long time. There were rules here, and security checks, and the people who came to Secrets would abide by those rules, however unusual or kinky their needs.

She could trust Anteros.

She knew it in her heart, and it gave her the courage to relax into the moment. "If Kade were out there, watching, I wonder if he'd want me right now."

Anteros laughed, a quiet chuckle that flowed over her skin and left goose bumps as effectively as that feather would, if only he would lean forward and touch its delicate end to her quivering flesh. "Look over there, my girl." He gestured toward the doorway and she gasped at the sight of the handle turning.

"No, I don't want anyone else to see—Kade! Um. You're…Kade." She must sound like a half-wit, repeating his name over and over, but she couldn't comprehend that the subject of her imaginings was actually here in the room with them, right at the instant when her fanny was laid out like a Christmas turkey on a plate.

Sweat broke out on her forehead as her whole body flushed dark and she began to struggle against the bindings. "Kade, no, don't stare at me! Anteros, please. Let me—"

"Shh." Her dark-skinned companion laid a gentle hand on her ankle. "He is not repulsed. Look at him."

She couldn't. It was impossible to meet Kade's gaze. What would he think to see her trussed up like this? She stared instead at the window, biting her lip and willing herself not to cry. But then he stepped in front of her and his swollen penis was directly in her line of vision. It poked out of the gap in his trousers in a manner that was clearly far from revulsion.

"Do what he says, Ellie. Look at me." His voice was familiar and gentle, yet the fingers that slipped under her chin and forced her gaze upwards were firm and uncompromising. When she finally looked into his eyes she read the truth in their brilliant depths. Not hazel right now. Green. Like the August birthstone, peridot.

A hesitant grin decorated his face. "You've never looked more beautiful to me than right here in this moment. I want you, Ella Harris. Please don't send me out of this room."

She looked past him to Anteros, taller than Kade and looming over his shoulder, only to find the same truth embedded in his features. Both of these men wanted her. Right now. Like this. Helpless and bound, and somehow with enough power to evoke desire in two very different yet equally sexy men.

Anteros stepped up beside Kade and slid his arm around her friend's shoulder and then stood in silence, staring down. Kade's fists at his side clenched and unclenched themselves. He was shaking and clearly trying to disguise it. Twin phalluses jutting outwards proclaimed their mutual arousal and the musky aroma of pending sex was strong in her nostrils. But neither man made a move toward her.

Oh, God! They were letting her choose.

Her clit began to throb in a way that infused her whole body with an overwhelming need.

Choice. What a heady aphrodisiac.

When she was twenty, and drunk, not bound like this but tightly held against her will by an equally drunk guy she'd met at that party, she'd not been allowed a choice and her shoulder had been almost dislocated in the process of trying to get away. But here, tied up in the most vulnerable position possible, she was being given the freedom to make her own decision on how to proceed.

She smiled. A trembling one; she could feel the quake in her chin, but yep, it was a smile nonetheless.

"Well then, gentlemen." She ran her tongue around her lips and focused on the titillating sight directly in front of her. "If you step forward about, oh, say, seven or eight inches, I might have a better chance of reaching you both."

CHAPTER SIX

They complied as if they were one, and though she couldn't fit both of them into her mouth at the same time she tried her hardest. She had never realized till this moment that each person had their own distinctive flavor, but as she licked and sucked and moved between the two she identified both the cinnamon honey of Anteros and the new and excitingly musky taste that must be uniquely Kade.

Then Anteros was gone and it was purely Kade as he plunged more deeply into her and she really had the chance to taste and suckle her friend. He was big, not as long nor as wide as Anteros, but plenty big enough for her mouth and later, if things went well, for her passion-slicked vagina. And he was hot. Hot and hard. So hard it was like sucking on wood that just happened to be coated in a delicate velvet-skinned casing.

"Ella." Her name on his lips was almost animalistic, gruff, like nothing she'd ever heard from him before, and her hips spasmed involuntarily as her sex threatened to explode.

Then he was gone and she cried out, but he hadn't moved

far. He had dropped to his knees in front of her and bent forward to sink his face between her legs.

"Wait!" The command from Anteros gave him pause and she bucked against the restraints, trying unsuccessfully to force contact with Kade as the latter waited for permission to touch her.

"Please don't make me wait any longer for him." Her voice came out pleading. She looked down the length of her body to Kade's eyes flaring bright and his face taut and strained. She couldn't seem to catch her breath properly, but he didn't seem to have the same problem. Puffs of heat against her flesh signaled the rapidity of his breathing.

Then Anteros reappeared above her and leant over to press a gentle kiss on her lips. It felt peculiar to kiss someone from that angle, weird and exciting, but then she forgot the weirdness as someone's fingertips fluttered over her stomach and down, flicking the already sensitized nub of her clit and exploring along her exposed slit all the way to her anus. The questing digits circled there and she pressed up into them, relishing the unfamiliar sensation. No one had ever touched her back there before. If he entered her now, with only the wetness from her own body to ease the entry, would it hurt? And who was the intrepid explorer? Anteros, or Kade?

She had her answer in the glee of Anteros's crooked grin. She gasped when his thumb grazed directly over her rear entrance. "I will breach you there, later, when Kade is inside you," he murmured.

Is that...oh! Is that a promise? Even her thoughts were breathless and disjointed.

"Yes, Ella, that is a promise." He kissed her again but only briefly and she strained for more as he pulled away.

How is it possible to want two different men so badly? Is

there something wrong with me? I know I love Kade, but Anteros...

"There is nothing wrong with having secret desires, and every now and again it is important to have those desires fulfilled." Anteros caressed her scalp. "You will have me too, if you wish. But for now, I plan to slip some ice deep inside your vagina, before Kade tastes you there. It will heighten your response, and I want your first experience of his mouth on your sex to be...perfect. Is that all right with you?"

Perfect? "Uh huh. Yep. That's...yes." She nodded frantically, unable to speak further, then yelped when a blistering coldness orbited her vaginal entrance and spread upwards, deep inside her passage. "Oh, my God!" She felt Kade lurch crazily between her legs.

"Okay, Ellie?" he asked, so close to her core that his hot breath vibrated across her clit, warring with the aching cold that was now burning her from within.

She arched her back as much as she could in her limited situation, angling her hips toward his mouth. "God, yes, Kade. I've been waiting for this too damn long."

"I don't want to hurt you."

A chuckle slipped out of her and her eyes closed. "I'm already hurting, hon. I burn. Right there."

His inarticulate response was absorbed by her body as his mouth met her pussy lips and she cried out at the intimacy of his touch. "Yes!"

Finally.

She lurched as her best friend laved her, the heat of invasion a prolonged and incredible torture as his tongue darted up and into her then out and over her clitoris. His hot suckling while the intense cold seared her insides had her womb folding in upon itself until she couldn't differentiate between fire and ice and it was just one exquisite pain that threatened to blow her wide apart.

Nothing had ever felt like this before.

Nothing had ever felt so good, or so right.

Kade was there between her legs. The man she loved was dipping into her body, tasting her, loving her, and it was a million times better than she'd ever imagined.

Blood rushed to the area, swelling everything she had, magnifying the sensations until her breathing grew loud and ragged. She writhed against her restraints, frantic to be free, but the bracelets held firm and her inability to move only added to her ardor.

"Anteros," she cried out, opening her eyes and spying him behind Kade, stroking purposeful hands over her friend's body and efficiently assisting the removal of his clothing. "Good," she gasped. "It's only fair that we're all naked. I want all of us to lie together, tonight."

"Oh, we will, Ella. Believe me." He tickled the crevice behind her knees and she could feel the shaking of his touch. So. He was affected by this moment, too. His eyes darkened suddenly and he sank his fist into her friend's brown hair. Clutching tightly, he forced Kade up and exposed his mouth swollen and glistening with moisture. Her moisture.

"Kade?" Anteros put a wealth of meaning and a myriad of questions into that one word.

She went still, waiting for Kade's response. "Yes," he said after a pause. "I want that more than anything. I'm falling for you, Ellie. You'd have to be crazy not to have worked that out already. But…I want him, too. A lot. I can't help it. It's part of who I am."

There was apology in his eyes, and sorrow, and she shook her head. "I know, Kade, and I don't care. Stop apologizing, or worrying about hurting me. I'm an adult and I get to make my own decisions. I want to be with you in whatever way makes you happy, and if this is what we need to do in order to be together, then I'm in. I…want…this as much as…oh! It feels so…good…"

Anteros had retrieved that giant black feather from God knows where and was finally stroking it over her skin. He circled her breasts, flicking across the nipples, then down her ribs and over her stomach. The delicacy of the touch titillated her senses and she shivered violently. How could something so light create such a storm of awareness inside? How could it center itself so completely in her womb, like the gathering of heavy clouds right before a massive storm breaks loose?

When the movements of the feather grew faster and more frenetic she cried out, unable to contain the tempest. "Kade. Get up here, please. I want to taste you again before I…quickly!"

Kade jumped to do her bidding and his member was there in front of her, so close she could see the engorged veins winding their way around the outside of his shaft. She parted her lips and he slipped inside, pumping back and forth in quick, concise movements that were punctuated by little whimpering noises from his throat.

So that's what he sounded like in the throes of passion.

It was like being invited into the abode of the gods. She sucked and licked, desperate for more, but the pressure and the ache in her pussy grew too much to bear. She turned her head and he popped free for a second.

"Anteros," she gasped. "Please. Take Kade's place down there. Take me in your mouth. Drink in my…I'm going to… please!" A hard body slipped between her legs and Anteros plunged into her with his tongue. She shrieked and began to sob as the explosion of a pulsing orgasm burst forth from her sex. She rode him through the involuntary contractions, his mouth maintaining contact and lapping up the liquid spurting out of her. It was likely a mix of melted ice and her own body's juices, and she rocked back and forth within the limited constraints of her position, her muscles clenching and vibrating against Anteros for many seconds longer than she expected.

Then Kade let out an agonized shout and she lunged for him again, drawing him back in as he began to buck frantically and the spurt of hot seed filled her mouth.

"Fuck, Ella," he said at last, raising his head. His eyes were still hazed with desire and his voice was croaky. "That was better than anything I've imagined."

"I know. Same for me."

"That, my friends," said Anteros from between her thighs, "was only the beginning."

PART IV
ANTEROS

CHAPTER SEVEN

His cock burned like a bitch and his balls were heavy and full. If he were to release his load right now, there would be not a dry spot in the room. He would have to watch himself with these two. He wanted to pleasure but not over-whelm them. They were babes in the woods when it came to love. They called it vanilla. He called it sweet innocence.

Kade picked up a lock of Ella's hair and ran it through his fingers as she smiled up at him. Their goodness was obvious. Such consideration of each other's needs and the desire to please one another on so many different levels was a breath of fresh air in his otherwise jaded world. Perhaps that was what came of being friends before lovers.

He would have to hold much of himself back in order to create pleasure without scaring them away.

A pang in the area of his heart made him frown as he glanced around the chamber. Somehow his existence had reduced itself to this room in a sex club. When had his world become so small and walled-in? And how had it happened without him noticing? But there were so many mortals who desired his assistance. So many who yearned for love and didn't quite know how to get there on their own, and this place was as good as any for finding and servicing those people.

Normally cynicism burned beneath the surface of his skin, growing stronger in his veins each time he was called upon for help. Soon, he might need to leave this world for a while, and return to the heights from which he had descended. But for now he was still here, and this time for once it felt different. This time, with Ella and Kade in the room, the cynic was quiet and instead he felt the stirring of something completely new.

Something that lightened his mood and made him want to skip and clap his hands. As if he would do that, of course, but still. The alien feeling was there and it was difficult to deny.

What was this new emotion? Was it…happiness?

He tilted his head, watching the two mortals clasp hands and recover from their orgasm. What if, just this once, he could be something more than a mere tool to bring two people together? What if there was an actual place for him in their lives?

His smile faded. He was being fanciful.

They were a perfect match without him.

His role was simply to bring them together, and to help overcome this niggle of guilt that remained in the mortal man's mind every time he looked at Ella.

So Kade needed a man every once in a while. Why did he not just act on it? She had already said she would accept that non-heterosexual part of him, and she had the inner strength to do so. He had seen it. She was as beautiful on the inside as she was on the outside, except for her tendency to want to control things, but Anteros was used to that in a woman.

Aphrodite. The most dominant woman ever to descend from the heights of Olympus, though she had not visited this world for a very long time. Not since her tryst with Anchises, and that must have been... He calculated quickly. That had been way back in the time of Troy.

Mother. He closed his eyes, giving Kade and Ella a few moments more to recover, sending out a snaking current of power to unsnap the bracelets and free her. Her surprised relief tickled his mind and he opened his eyes to find them both staring up at him blankly.

"How did you do that?" Kade asked.

"Suspension of disbelief," he answered.

"Huh?"

Amusement dawned in Ella's eyes and she grinned and bit her lip.

His chest swelled at their regard. What if, for once, he really wasn't just a means to an end? What if, for once, he could be...more? "It is nothing, just a small snippet of my power." He cleared his throat. "Would you like to see it again?"

"Yes, please," Ella said.

"Sure," echoed her companion.

His heartbeat accelerated and he sucked in a surprised breath at the emotion sweeping through him. Concentrate. He sent out tendrils of influence and allowed the wisps to become visible, chuckling at their squeaks of shock when the power leached out towards them in its earthly form, like an electrified dancing wraith.

He allowed the surging force to lift and transport them to the center of the bed before easing off, but then an unexpected heat suffused his cheeks and he lowered his eyes in confusion. Was this what Ella felt when she blushed that delightful pink color? He touched his face, exploring the warmth that seemed to be getting stronger with each passing second. It was...intriguing.

"I'm sorry," he said. "I didn't mean to show off." Ye gods, why had his voice turned brusque?

Ella was clutching at Kade's arm. "Could it be true? Could he really be...a god?"

Ah, this one he could answer. "It is true, Ella. And for tonight, I am your god. Yours and Kade's. We have many more hours until dawn, so we should make the most of our time together. Do you not feel the beginnings of a new lust already meandering through your blood?"

Kade's eyes went round and he looked down. His member was stirring again, and Ella extended a trembling hand to stroke him. A tiny whimper left her lips and her other hand cupped her abdomen.

Oh, yes. They felt it, alright. Craving. Their burgeoning desire ramped up his own many times over.

Things were going according to his plan, and he should feel complete satisfaction. If he got these two together, then his work for the night would be a success. It was always the way, and there was no reason why this time should be any different to all the times that had gone before. So why did it irk him, the thought of succeeding with Ella and Kade and watching them leave Secrets without a backward glance?

Pothos had found his pair in Jeannie and Jake.

Himeros had bonded with the delightful Gina and their loneliness would be eased for many years to come.

I have no one beyond this night.

Until the next person in need called for his services, but he was okay with that.

I am always okay with that.

He moved to the bed and ran his hand up and down one of the ridged wooden posts, taking comfort in its solid strength. He loved this bed. He had brought it with him from Olympus and it had lasted throughout the eons he had been here. So much loving had taken place on its extra-deep mattress. So many lessons in love and almost endless healing of heartache. And yet, he had always been the teacher whose students would graduate his sexual classroom and reenter the real world. A world where there was no place for Anteros.

When Kade and Ella reached out to him now, it felt different. For the first time ever in his memory, he did not wish to be the teacher.

He wanted instead to be an equal amongst them. Not a Master, nor a superior, nor for a little while, a god of desire.

He just wanted to be a man who loved and was loved in return.

Requited love.

Unrequited love.

Gods above, these were supposed to be his areas of specialty.

He frowned and gripped the bed post harder.

PART V
KADE

CHAPTER EIGHT

He still couldn't figure out how he'd gotten onto the bed, but right now he had more important things on his mind. Impossible to believe he had another hard-on so soon after the first was sated, and by the look in Ella's eyes she was feeling much the same way.

Not that I'm complaining. I like being a superman of sex.

"Kade, Ella. Come here. I want to kiss you both."

Anteros had climbed onto the bed, too, kneeling up and holding one of the posts with a grip that looked strong enough to break a lesser piece of wood. Was he all right? He had the strangest expression on his face. Almost wistful.

But…no, whatever it was had disappeared, if it had ever been there at all. Anteros looked absolutely fine. Not wistful at all. Instead his face was hard and purposeful, and that magnificent cock jerked upwards, drawing attention to its unrequited lust.

A flood of desire directly to his dick had it lurching in response as it filled with throbbing heat. What would it be like to have Anteros buried inside him? He'd never taken a cock that big before and the thought of all that pressure squeezing his insides tight and rubbing against his prostate almost made him cry out. Imagine feeling all of that deep within and being able to pleasure Ella at the same time, pushing into her and filling her to capacity. He imagined her scream of release and the powerful contraction of her womb muscles around him even as the hot seed of Anteros flowed into him from behind.

"Ella." He cleared his throat. "Maybe we should work to put Anteros out of his misery. He hasn't had the pleasure of release with us, yet."

The words were simple but the meaning behind them was not, and he waited, breathless, to see how she would respond.

"You're right." She squeezed his hand gently. When he saw those gorgeous nipples rising to attention again his breath left his lungs in a rush. She wasn't repulsed by his suggestion. Instead, like a man with a hard-on, her body clearly demonstrated the depth of her need.

She really does like the idea of a ménage a trois with Anteros.

His limbs felt like jelly and as if she sensed his sudden relief her voice turned playful. "Poor Kade. You really think it's only Anteros who needs to be put out of his misery?" She turned to their companion. "Why don't you come here to us, Anteros? We all need some TLC right now, don't we? Including you."

The breath hissed out of Anteros and he moved so fast it was hard to fathom how he'd gotten there, directly in front of them. "I would like to be included," he said, and his substantial arms encircled each of them around the buttocks, drawing them close.

Kade leaned into the hardness of Anteros and felt that enormous slash of cock like a hot brand against his stomach, while the pliant curves of Ella draped his hip. Or was that his own member sandwiched between his stomach and that of Anteros?

He didn't know, and he didn't care. It felt like he'd died and found his own special brand of nirvana, with the smell of raw sex pungent around him, the softness of woman on the one side and muscled strength on the other. He was held in an embrace so tight he was powerless to move. His thighs shook as someone's leg insinuated itself between them and a harsh sound escaped his throat.

Ella's laughter vibrated his chest and the squeeze in his heart matched the physical ache in his loins. "I've never had a three-way kiss before," she said.

"Me either," he admitted, and Ella grinned up at him.

"Too vanilla for that, Kade?"

Anteros let out a snort of laughter. "Nothing vanilla about this."

A strong hand fisted in his hair and pushed him forward and his mouth met with Anteros and Ella in a wild exploration of lips and tongue and teeth. Hot sweet breath and pliable flesh ramped up a pleasure so intense he felt it right to the bone. Madness overtook him and he grabbed at hair both blonde and dark, pulling them closer, attacking and licking and sucking and being sucked and licked and tasted in return.

Groans mingled and he couldn't tell who was making what noise, nor even if some of those strange sounds were emanating from his own chest. All he could feel was damp heat and the delicious sensations in his mouth and across his lips that were mimicking what was happening below.

Someone's hand smoothed over his ass cheek and dug in, urging him nearer, if it were even possible, and his hips began to pump and thrust against whatever he could reach as the temperature of his cock threatened to boil over in a feverish release.

Ella too was bucking and grinding, one of her legs bent up and hooked now around his waist as she surged into his hipbone and moaned deep into his mouth. Anteros had somehow worked a hand in down there. He could feel it maneuvering along the mound she was rocking against him.

Then all of a sudden she yelped and froze. He broke away, breathing heavily, trying to regain some level of sanity, but when she let out a deep, primal growl and made a funny little movement with her butt his sanity flew right back out the window. "What the...?"

"More, Anteros," she said. "I want more."

His knees almost buckled when he realized Anteros must have entered her asshole with one of his digits. Without lube. And she was enjoying it.

"Do you want it, too, Kade?" Anteros regarded him with a raised brow, and Kade nodded so hard he almost put his neck out.

"Yeah. Do it. Please."

He sucked in his breath as he felt a thumb circle his anus and push gently, and then Anteros was in, plunging back and forth, even while he did the same to Ella with his other hand. Kade could feel her increasingly rapid gyrations against him and her panting breath rattled in his ear.

They were both being thumb-fucked by the same man, at the same time, and he'd never felt anything so delicious. Was it the same for her, this incredible sensation of fullness? The intrusion of someone else inside his body, stroking so fucking hard that he just wanted to scream and fall apart.

"Ella," he yelled and took her mouth in a kiss that tried to express all he was feeling. He wanted to be tender but her lips responded instantly and her gasps vanished straight down his throat and tenderness lost out to desperation. When they finally broke apart he clung to Anteros, inhaling the intoxicating scent of his sweat-slicked skin while Ella snuggled against the muscled chest then turned inwards to trace around the pink-brown pebble of his nipple with her tongue.

Beneath his cheek Anteros shuddered, and he realized this was not giving their god any relief. He knew that feeling intimately, the scorching ache that would cross over into unbearable pain if your hard-on ran on too long. The frantic race toward release before it became too much to bear.

Anteros was there already. He could sense it.

It was time to take control.

"Stop," he said, and felt the movement inside him and against his hip cease. "Remove your hands, Anteros. It's time for all three of us to make love. Together."

PART VI
ELLA

CHAPTER NINE

The ragged sigh that escaped from Anteros's lips at Kade's declaration gave her heart a lurch. He was finally at breaking point. How had she not seen that?

She was so focused on the new sensation of someone penetrating her behind and the joy of feeling Kade's lean body against hers that she had ignored the third party in this room.

This gorgeous man – or god if that's what he was – who had brought her to this moment with the one she loved, was in desperate need of his own. A wave of tenderness washed over her and she cupped his cheek in the palm of her hand.

"Kade's right. It's time. I want..." She felt the telltale flush of heat in her face spread right down to her chest, but she pushed on regardless. "I want both of you to make love to me. At the same time. Is that...can we...?"

Okay, some things really were too difficult to say out loud.

The men looked at each other and she felt their mirth surround her like a warm, safe cocoon.

Kade kissed her forehead. "We all want that, hon. But I need—"

"I know what you need, Kade," Anteros said. "You love her, and you need the lead role to prove it."

He really does love me?

Kade looked down at Anteros's cock and frowned. "But you'll...hurt her if you—"

"No." Anteros sighed. "What do I need to do to convince you both? This?" He flung his arms out and she found herself up near the ceiling, her arms and legs dangling down like an unmanned puppet while she stared across the room at Kade in a similarly undignified position. Sparks surrounded them both, though she felt no pain but instead just pleasant warmth.

Suspension of disbelief. She repeated it like a mantra, over and over, wondering if the gob-smacked, mouth-open look on Kade's face matched the one currently decorating her own.

"Sorry," Anteros said, bowing his head. "I know you don't have – well, what would you call it? Magic? – in your world. But I do. I don't get ill, I carry no disease, and I can adjust the size of my appendage to suit Ella, or you, Kade, and..." His hands flicked and she found herself lowered slowly back onto the bed beside Kade. She clutched at the silken bed covers, relishing the reality of the fabric in her grasp. "I just want so badly to be accepted for who I am and...I'm sorry."

The aching sadness in his voice called to her and she let out a long slow breath. "Well." Silence. She tried again. "Anteros. I trust you. I let you bind me and you didn't hurt me at all. That's a big deal in my life right now. I want to accept you for who you are, but...it's hard for us. This is all a bit strange. I'm sure...Kade...?"

She appealed to him for help. He was staring in wonder at Anteros. "Yes," he said. "I've never met anyone like you before, Anteros. You…appear to know the deepest part of me, that hidden bit I'm kind of ashamed of, and you make me feel as if you accept me anyway. I want to do the same for you. And I'm sure Ellie does, too."

When he glanced at her she nodded hard. "We accept you, Anteros, bizarre streaky power and all," she said. "Now please, please let's all make love." She sank down onto the luxurious bed sheets and looked up at the two men, one on each side of her. With their cocks thrust out in front and their balls hanging down beneath they looked like dueling swordsmen ready for a bout, but these swords were long and thick and tipped with shiny liquid. She seized one in each hand, learning their width and massaging along the shaft, spreading leaking pre-cum before it overflowed and began to drip down onto her stomach.

Slowly she drew them in towards each other until the ends of their members were touching and she could use both hands to run along their double length.

Back and forth. Hot stone encased in velvety satin. The scent of sex permeating the air around her. The sound of kissing, above her, as their mouths met and laved and frantic hands clutched at each other's rear. She moved her arms faster, left to right and back again as the men jerked and shuddered above her, their balls slowly drawing up tight in a telltale sign of impending orgasm. Her men were ready.

And so was she, her clit like a big fat cherry about to rupture between swollen labia lips.

"Fuck me, gentlemen," she said, and her voice came out like a rasp. "Before I slip away in my own juices."

Kade moaned and leaned down on top of her, kicking her legs wide and fitting himself neatly between her thighs. His eyes sparkled as he stared down at her. "I love you, Ella," he said, smoothing a tendril of hair from her face and caressing her temple.

"I know. And I love you, Kade. I always have. I think I always will. We'll work the rest out later. But please, enter me now before I burst."

He did, plunging into her with a smooth movement, and hot tears sprouted from her eyes at the sheer beauty of what she had been imagining for so many years.

Kade. Inside me. Filling me with his flesh. My beautiful, beloved friend, making love with me at last.

Slow movements at first, then faster, plowing deep until he pushed close to the very heart of her.

Oh, God. This is pure bliss. I love it. I love him.

She wrapped her legs around his hips and held on as tightly as she could, digging her heels into his butt and trying to force him deeper still, enjoying the weight of his body along the length of her own, reveling in the crush of her breasts and the rasp of his nipples like tiny little nuggets against her own longer ones. Mingled sweat between them made their movements easy. He was kissing her again now, kissing her so deeply it was like he was absorbing her very essence…taking everything she had to give…returning it a thousand-fold…

But Anteros. She craved him too. Where was her beautiful god? There had to be room for him, too, somewhere in this instant where lust and love connected.

I am here. And I will never forget that you sought to include me in this moment.

A hand touched the nape of her neck, caressing damp tendrils of her hair before moving to her shoulder, gently encouraging her and Kade to roll onto their sides. The warmth of another body heated her back as Anteros slipped into place, cradling her – and Kade too – in his substantial embrace. She felt his kisses feather-light working the pulse point beneath her ear and heard the thrum of desire in his whispered words. "Are you ready to feel what he feels when he makes love with another man, Ella?"

Her heart pounded and her clit pulsed against Kade's groin. Was she ready?

"Yes! I am." She was enveloped in heat from all sides, slick with perspiration, and she could hardly breathe for wanting.

I needed you to experience this first, Ella, before I give him what he desires. I wanted you to understand why he needs this.

Were the words being spoken aloud? They reverberated inside her head, and Kade didn't respond, so she guessed it was magic again.

I understand. She hoped he could read as well as project thoughts. But it doesn't matter. I know what he is, Anteros, and I love him anyway.

You are amazing, my Ella, and he is a lucky man to have you. I would prefer to be where he is, right now, sinking into you like a man usually does with a woman, but he is staking his claim on you, and it is his right. He loves you more than he has ever loved anyone.

She stiffened when she felt the head of Anteros's cock press against her rear, a flicker of fear mingling with the need. "Are you sure—?"

"I won't hurt you. I promise. I am a god and I will make this easy…see?"

Her breath hissed out as he penetrated her and she let out a little squeak. Kade had stopped thrusting when Anteros moved behind her, and his face only inches away showed both concern and desire. "It'll be fine, Ellie. I'm sure it'll be fine…oh, God, I feel him in there. I feel him!"

Slowly, steadily, Anteros had eased further in, and it was pressure without any of the pain she was expecting. "That feels kind of...odd...it feels...oh! That's good, Anteros. Kade. Please, keep going."

They were tag-teaming now, but gently. First one, then the other, it was exquisite torture to be so full of man and so close to coming, encircled by the one she had loved for so long, and the one who had brought her to this moment with such tenderness and understanding.

Is this what you feel, Kade, when Will is inside you? It aches and burns, like an itch that is too deep to be scratched. Like I need to move, and lunge. Like I need to gasp my last breath before exploding into a million starry pieces...

The grunt surged out of her like the sound of a strange beast and it seemed to galvanize the men into frenzy.

Kade was panting and moving faster now and he grasped at one of her legs as if to use the leverage to impale himself more deeply inside her. Anteros was growling in her ear, his balls slapping against her rear and his legs tangling with Kade's beneath her.

She was putty between them, boneless in her movements, thrusting and jerking and sobbing with lust until the turmoil built to an almost unbearable level. She lashed out blindly, trying to connect with some semblance of reality, her passion-slicked passages clenching on their organs and sucking them in until physical boundaries disappeared.

Three became one.

Rutting and panting and desperate for release.

The need grew until she could hold on no longer and with a mangled scream she fell over the edge into pure rapture, dragging the men with her into the abyss.

Reality returned slowly. Their bodies were entangled and heavy with repletion. She thought she'd never be able to move again, and they lay together in the confines of this deli-ciously comfortable bed until Anteros withdrew from her body. She shifted in protest. "No!" It was like losing a part of herself. She felt empty and bereft. "I need you both."

You have us both, my Ella. I am here with you, always. As I am sure that Kade will be, too. But now it is his turn.

Anteros was in her head, and Kade was still partly buried inside her body, and she knew their Adonis spoke the truth. She did have both of them, and it was Kade's turn to feel the physical intimacy of their god.

Anteros began to chuckle suddenly and she caught a wicked gleam in that aquamarine gaze as he leaned over them. "I will help you both recover more quickly than the norm, and then I think it's time to add a bit of fun to the mix. Don't you?"

PART VII
KADE

CHAPTER TEN

F un? It couldn't get much more fun than it already was, surely? The unbelievable joy of coming while he was deep inside Ella was a moment he would cherish forever. That look in her eyes when he entered her...

But Anteros had his hands on them both and was urging them apart. Did his own face reflect the confusion he could read in Ella's?

"Kade," Anteros said, "would you like to be fucked by Ella?"

"Well, yeah, but—"

"Good. Let's try something new, then."

Their companion moved behind Ella in one of those quick fire actions that seemed to defy reality, and then her delicious mouth parted as if in shock. "Oh!" she said.

What the hell?

Ella was growing a cock! Or at least, that's what it looked like as he stared at her mons and the head of Anteros's cock began to appear there, as impressively hard as ever. But as big as he was, when had Anteros ever been long enough to show three…four…no, about seven inches of hard-on beyond the front of Ella's mound?

His heart pounded so hard he could feel it right throughout his body. Anteros…and Ella, intertwined into the one physical entity. Her beautiful softness, her breasts with their delicious nipples calling for his mouth, the feminine curve of her hips and stomach…and a hard male cock primed and ready to fuck, right there at the juncture of her thighs.

They were all woman, and all man; everything he could ever want or need in life. Everything he had been searching for, and never quite found.

Until now.

They were both watching him carefully. He wondered what they'd make of the redness in his face and the clenching of his fists, or the sudden jutting of his own dick despite his orgasm only a few short minutes ago.

So this is what he meant about helping us recover?

Then Ella looked at the appendage between her legs and put her hand down to touch herself. No. Anteros. To touch Anteros. To stroke him. It looked like she was stroking herself.

His mouth opened but nothing came out. He coughed and tried again.

"So…" Still croaky, but working now. "There are definite advantages to making love with a god, then."

"Oh yes, Kade. Definite advantages." Anteros was grinning at him over Ella's shoulder.

"Turn over, my love." Ella's voice shook with emotion and the glitter in her eyes promised so much.

"No." He shook his head. "I want to see your face." He lay back and lifted his legs, assisting Ella and Anteros to position themselves correctly. He was somewhat acquainted with the slick heat of a man between his butt cheeks but the feel of Ella on top of him, so thin but unyielding as her body pressed into his, was new and electrifying. Her skin was so damn soft it felt like satin gliding against him and his cock laid out between their flesh pulsed in response. He presumed she was resting her weight on her elbows, but perhaps Anteros was supporting her for she seemed to have a freedom of movement that only added to the pleasure. Her hands began to caress him all over, stroking his hips then up the contours of his body to travel smoothly around the curve of his shoulders. The firmness of her touch was both achingly familiar and enticingly different. He'd felt that strength in the past, when she kneaded the muscles of his neck and shoulders after a hard day at work. Never like this before tonight, and never coupled with the feel of a rigid cock pushing into him. Slow, relentless and oh, so fucking hard.

But even without lube, it didn't hurt. Must be the god thing. Instead, it felt peculiar as hell, but so exhilarating to know it was Ella thrusting in unison with Anteros, her pussy mound spanking his loins in an ancient and increasingly fast rhythm. Her gasps mingled with those of Anteros until all he could hear was a roar of decadent sex noise and all he could see in front of him was Ella's face once again caught in the throes of passion.

Perfect.

Then his mouth opened and he too joined the cacophony of desire, a cry tearing out of him as he reached the pinnacle of pure sensation and fell over into the void. Cum squirted everywhere within the silken cocoon of their bodies as he finally released his load. "Yes," he screamed at the very moment of Ella's high-pitched squeal and the inarticulate roar from Anteros. She bucked crazily as a burst of heat inside him signaled his companions had travelled with him over the edge and into this eccentric yet orgasmic paradise.

His arms shook and sobs wracked him as the moment went on and on. Ella fell shuddering onto his chest and through her he could feel Anteros shivering as well. Beneath their skin he felt the thudding of their hearts, matched to his own still-rapid pulse. The weight of it all, both physical and emotional, was too much and a tear spilled out to wend its way down his cheek.

What would she think about him crying like a baby? He'd never done such a thing before. But when she smiled and leaned in to capture one of his tears with her tongue he began to relax. "Salty," she said, and he grinned back, wondering if she and Anteros felt as exhausted and as replete as he.

"I do," said Anteros. "It was wonderful."

Kade began to laugh. "Can you read everything in my head? Ella's too?"

Somehow he managed to maneuver around and fold Ella in his arms, and he tightened his embrace to include the other man, so the latter would know there was no resentment at the idea of their thoughts being transparent.

Anteros rolled onto his back and lifted an arm above his head as if pondering how to answer. "Read is not quite the right word," he said. "It is more...all of my senses are attuned, so I hear, see, feel, taste what you do. If I choose to tap in, that is. Is it...do either of you mind? I can stop if you prefer your privacy."

The tone was unusually diffident. No trace of arrogance whatsoever. Anteros lay very still, staring up at the fabric canopy above the bed, and Kade got the impression he was not used to asking permission.

"No. I don't think I mind at all, Anteros."

Ella turned in his arms and her gentle fingertips traced his jawline. Anteros was getting the same treatment. "After tonight, I think privacy is the last thing on my mind." Her tone was dry and he felt a swell of amusement at her words. "I like it," she added. "And I like...this." She gestured at the bed. "Is there any way...I mean, could we...?"

Her cheeks began to darken and Anteros rose up on one elbow to look at her. His sudden grin was infectious and Kade grinned too and began to play with some wayward strands of her hair. "Could we what, Ella?"

She slapped his arm, hard. "You know what I'm asking."

He took pity on her after several enjoyable seconds. "Yeah. I do." He looked at Anteros. "I think Ella is trying to ask if we could see you again. Would that be...could we...?" Now it was his turn to be tongue-tied and he felt the hot evidence of embarrassment in his own cheeks.

Anteros stared at them with those gorgeous eyes the exact color of the sea on a clear summer's day. "You..." He coughed. "You both want to see me again? Beyond tonight? Beyond the doors of Secrets? I sensed it in each of you several minutes ago but I was afraid. Afraid you might have been caught up in the moment of lust, and that once you left here you would not...need me anymore. I...I was afraid to...hope."

Ella sat up. "Gentlemen. This was going to be a one night thing for me. A night of indulging in whatever came my way, so I could put the past behind me and move on. From you, Kade. I was sick of waiting for you to notice me."

When he reached for her she batted his hand away. "I haven't finished." He heard Anteros snort. "But I found something special, tonight. I found happiness at last. Physical happiness in the arms of two wonderful men. And," she frowned, "it's more than physical. It's like, Kade is the one I love, but Anteros, you complete me." She grimaced. "Now I sound like that movie, don't I?"

"It was a good movie," Anteros said, and then the three of them were laughing.

"I know what you mean, Ellie," Kade said. "When I look at the two of you together, it feels like you're the two halves of what I'm looking for in my life. I've come to love you, and I only wish I'd been smart enough to realize it earlier, but I'm there now. I love you, Ell. But I also feel something for you, Anteros. It's as if my experience with the woman I love wouldn't be complete unless you were there, too. Is it possible that we could do this...more than once?"

"Oh, yes. It is more than possible. It is a certainty. I have never been wanted before, simply for me. Only for what I can provide to others. I..." He lowered his head for a moment, then raised it and his eyes blazed bright. "You are both stuck with me now, for as long as you need me. Forever, if that's what it takes. Would you like that?"

Ella's smile was wide. "Yes, please."

"Hell, yeah." Kade lunged forward and grabbed for them, these two amazing halves of his one love, and together, the three of them collapsed onto the bed in a tangle of arms, legs and laughter.

PART VIII
ANTEROS

CHAPTER ELEVEN

The door of Secrets closed behind his two favorite lovers and Anteros heaved a sigh of regret to watch them leave. But he would see them again this evening. Ella had extended an offer for him to visit her home.

His first invitation ever.

His shoulders straightened and his heart was unusually full. Was this what anticipation felt like? Not just physical anticipation, but that of the emotions?

Once again he had the urge to skip down the hallway but of course it would not be fitting, even though it was half past five in the morning and the club was now empty save staff. Perhaps, though, just a tiny one?

He tried it out and his heart hopped in unison with his feet.

"You're looking very pleased with yourself, my son."

Mother of the gods!

"Aphrodite!"

He felt the shock run through his system like a fork of lightning sent down from Zeus. Never had his mother descended from the heights of Olympus in her mortal form.

Never! At least, not since her tryst with Anchises.

Fear twisted in his gut. Something must be dreadfully wrong. Perhaps, in his focus on Ella and Kade, he had missed the signs.

"What is it, mother? Is everything all right? Are the others—?"

"Everything is well, my dearest Anteros. All is fine. I simply wish to visit my sons and see for myself what is keeping them here in this time, and this place."

She pouted and he laughed in relief and residual fear. "Nothing is simple with you, Aphrodite."

She raised a brow in a regal look that used to intimidate him when he was young. A very long time ago. When she saw it wasn't working now she shrugged. "The intensity of your emotions, Anteros, and that of your brothers. It has been calling me, that intensity. Some of you have found love, it seems. All of you have been significantly moved by your recent experiences. I wish to find out for myself what it is that you have discovered. Is that not enough of a reason to be here? And are you not pleased to see your dear old mother?"

He snorted. "Dear old mother! Have you looked in a mirror lately?" Aphrodite was the epitome of beauty. There was no one on this earth or in the heavens above who could hold a handle to her physical beauty. None. And she knew it, too.

But…he frowned. Compromise was needed when you fell in love with a human. If she wished to experience mortal love, she would need to understand such a thing. Was there anyone here who would be strong enough to take on the goddess of love and teach her how to compromise?

In all his time in this world he had never met such a one.

Perhaps one of his brothers…

"Yes." His mother spoke gently. "Call your brothers,

236

Anteros. I wish the erotes to gather and assist me in this game of love. I wish each of you to find me a mortal who can replace Anchises in my heart. It has been too long, Anteros. I am so…lonely."

"But mother—"

"No buts, my dearest. You and your brothers are to gather here with your choices," – she looked around the club and raised her brows – "well, no, here will not do. I will find somewhere suitable with a view of my ocean and I will let you know where once I've decided. Gather at midnight, two days hence. I wish to be thoroughly seduced by a mortal."

Ω Ψ Ω

Please read on for the next instalment in the GODS OF
LOVE series.

IMMORTAL SEDUCTION

BY JEN KATEMI

IMMORTAL SEDUCTION

APHRODITE, GODDESS OF DESIRE

Love. Power. For Aphrodite, the two are permanently entwined, and when the goddess of desire hungers for love, who among mortals could possibly resist her power?

Fire fighters Ashur, Kieran and Hugh are damaged men. A tragedy has left them scarred, both physically and emotionally. Love and power? Nothing to them but empty words.

Aphrodite's sons hope to reignite their mother's passion for life and love by bringing these three mortal men to Aphrodite's attention. But the darkness inside Ash, Kier and Hugh is growing. Will it take more than the seductive power of a goddess to save them...even when the goddess is .the undisputed Queen of desire?

A steamy Reverse Harem ménage romance featuring the goddess of love and three hot fire fighters!

PROLOGUE

Are we agreed on our three, brothers? At last?"

Anteros glanced across at Himeros and Pothos, both of whom were staring down toward the beach at a lone figure wobbling along the shoreline. From their vantage point up here atop the cliff, the view stretched for miles along this windswept terrain on the southern coast of Australia. Midwinter—close to freezing for those who were mortal—and yet still the man below limped determinedly through the night hours.

Even though it was well past midnight the moon was full, lighting the landscape with an eerie silver glow that he knew would appeal to their mother when she finally emerged from the sea.

Aphrodite. Mother of the ancient and powerful erotes, and goddess of all things love and desire.

He grinned. She might know desire, their beautiful mother, but she had not had recent experience in this mortal realm. A group of human lovers, such as the three he and his two favorite brothers had painstakingly chosen for her, may well offer a few surprises that even Aphrodite herself could not foresee.

It should be interesting, these next few days.

Himeros nodded slowly. "Agreed, brother."

"And Pothos?"

A muscle twitched in Pothos' cheek. "He is much damaged." Doubt clouded the words. "Are you sure…?"

"I am." He too, looked back down at their choice. Fighter of fires, hero to other mortals, and a stubborn man to walk so far every night when he was clearly in a great deal of pain. But that stubborn streak could be a useful weapon against a woman as powerful and as controlling as their mother. "More than ever with this one. The other two, Hugh and Kieran, will complete what is needed, but this one…Ashur…will be the pivotal influence, either way. He's the one most in need right now, and he's also the one with the greatest inner strength."

Himeros let out a small chuckle. "He's going to need it, Ant, to go up against our mother in the game of love. They all are."

"I know. But we felt it, right? Their need. Their collective strength. Their…possibility. Didn't we?" Despite his initial confidence, a spark of uncertainty wobbled in his chest as Pothos continued to scowl.

His mother had made this into a game, yes, but there was so much more at stake beneath the entertaining façade than simply winning or losing a game. Aphrodite needed this with a desperation they hadn't felt from her in eons. She needed to love again in this mortal realm, and be loved in return. Though, who among mortals would be strong enough to take on Aphrodite? If they had chosen incorrectly…

Indecision affected his control and his guard dropped. Her incessant loneliness washed over him with the force of a tsunami wave. Desperate. Dangerous. Drowning.

"Stop it, Ant!" Himeros grabbed his arm and shook. "When you do that it resonates through us all. Be strong. We need to stay positive, and know that we've made the correct choices here. You too, Pothos." Him stared hard at Pothos and finally their reluctant brother nodded.

"You are right, of course. You both are."

"This will work." Him sounded almost fierce when he spoke. "If a human can touch me...Gina touched my very essence..." His eyes lost their focus, looking inward, and Anteros felt an indulgent smile tug at his lips as the echo of their mother's loneliness receded and Him's joy took its place. Gina, the unique and beautiful mortal woman who had been born into a male body had been a remarkable influence on the god of sexual desire.

"I understand." Pothos ran a restless hand through his hair. "I have never felt such things as I have experienced with Jeannie and Jake. It confused me at first, but now..." The surge of emotion from Pothos rippled the air between them and Anteros shivered at its potent force. "I am still learning about love with my pair, but I am...happy for the first time in my existence. Really very happy."

A few days ago Anteros would have been as jealous as Phthonos himself at the knowledge that two of his beloved brothers had found love with their humans. But nothing of their fourth brother was here right now. Phthonos, the person-ification of envy and jealousy, had been banished from this realm for certain...indiscretions.

His thoughts boomeranged back to his own lovers, Kade and Ella, and he bent his head forward to hide the sudden grin that lit his face. Happiness? Yes, he was learning, too.

They were such generous mortals to let him in to their hearts and to make space for him in their lives. He ached for the embrace of their relationship, still only days old and therefore delicate and precious. He nodded. "I am beginning to understand this concept of happiness." Kade and Ella. I am only at the start of my journey with you both, and yet you have taught me so much already.

First he and his brothers must fulfill this pact to succor their mother's desperation. He prayed to Zeus that Aphrodite would be able and willing to open her heart to the same lessons of love that three of her erotes were learning. Please let her be strong enough to relinquish control and let a human in to her heart.

"There is no option for failure," he said, looking again at the determined figure down below.

Please let the mortal and his friends be truly strong enough to tame the passionate yet willful goddess of desire.

CHAPTER ONE

Midnight was fast becoming Ashur Dane's favorite time of day. Especially here on the beach, at the base of the cliff, where he could watch and listen in peace as moonlight caressed the waves that crashed relentlessly along the shore where he walked.

No one in their right mind would be outside in this remote spot in the middle of the night, and that's just the way he liked it. Empty of tourists, empty of families, empty of people altogether. Even the birds had gone to sleep. He was alone on the sand with only his thoughts for company, and he knew from having limped along this stretch of southern Australian coastline every night for almost a month that it would stay uninhabited until at least four or five in the morning.

His mouth twisted. Wouldn't it be handy if those soul-destroying thoughts put themselves to sleep as easily as the holiday crowds? But his mind wouldn't cooperate.

Maybe Kieran had the right idea. Stare down into a glass of whiskey every night instead of out toward the midnight sea. Tempting. So tempting. He'd been down that route before, directly after the incident, and it had only made things worse. Instead he was determined to conquer this his own way and...what...the...fuck?

There's a woman wading out of the sea. Right in front of me. Topless.

Instantly he was transported back to the time as a young teen when he watched his first James Bond movie on television. That image of Ursula Andress wading out of the water had populated his fantasies for several months afterward. Only difference now was that it was night, the sea was grey and rough, and this exotic beauty was dark-haired and light-skinned with no bikini in sight.

Had he finally flipped? He shook his head and blinked a few times, but the vision in front of him remained steadfastly real. She was actually standing there, hip deep in the restless water, with a shaft of moonlight turning her pale skin to silver.

"Hey, lady. Are you...all right?" He felt like an idiot, even asking the question. She certainly looked okay, but who the hell would venture out near these sharp rocks, on their own, and in the middle of the bloody night?

She tilted her head to one side as if studying him, before nodding calmly. "Never better," she said, amusement lacing her words. "Though the water here is a little colder than I'm used to." Her voice washed over him like a pulse of energy and the hair on his forearms stood up in response.

Whoa. Where had that come from? He hadn't had a notable physical reaction to a woman since Aiden died. Post-traumatic stress, the psychologist said, but Ash knew better. Guilt, more like.

The fact that his heart began to pound violently in his chest and his breath shortened when this woman continued her path directly toward him was nothing more than amazement at seeing anyone out here at this time of night.

Oh…kay. So maybe it had a little bit to do with the fact that she was more than topless. The woman was stark bloody naked. And built like…well…a goddess, for want of a better word.

He tried hard not to stare at the creased juncture between her thighs, where water was now streaming down in tantalizing rivulets over a hairless mound but…hell. He was only human.

Her face. Concentrate on her face. His eyes didn't want to cooperate. When he lifted his reluctant gaze upward it didn't quite reach the intended destination. Instead he stopped at her breasts. Big, and ripe, and jutting straight out at him, the globes were tipped with long rosy peaks that seemed to call for his suddenly hungry lips to close around them and suckle.

His dick began to swell as if with a mind of its own and he was grateful for the denim jeans and long winter overcoat that would hide any sign of his involuntary reaction to her nudity. He cleared his throat and shifted, willing his body to calm down. Why now, of all moments, had his body finally decided to wake up? Where in God's name had this crazy woman come from? There was no pile of clothing on the beach or any other telltale sign of her presence prior to her foolish dip in the sea.

Shit. Guess I'll be giving up the coat after all. He began to shrug out of the encasing warmth as he took a step toward her. "Here," he offered, holding out the jacket. "You must be freezing your…" He coughed. Freezing your tits off was too close to the bone. "Well, you must be freezing," he said again. Lame, but at least she was stepping into the jacket, slipping her arms into the sleeves, and those afore-mentioned breasts were now safely covered and out of his sight.

"Only a little," she said. "But thank you for your kindness." Her tone was laced with humor and something more.

Something inherently sexual and predatory. She rubbed her fingers back and forth over the material now wrapped around her as if enjoying its texture and warmth. Once again a lick of arousal tugged at his groin.

"You shouldn't swim here at night, especially alone. It's dangerous with the current and those rocks around the bluff. Not to mention sharks. This is Great White territory, you know. They go after the seals out there in the Southern Ocean."

Her sudden laughter trilled across his skin. Goosebumps followed in its wake. "Your concern is touching, little human. But the water holds no danger for me. I am Aphrodite."

She paused, tilting her head coquettishly as if awaiting a response, but he was stuck on "little human". Little? Me? I'm six foot four, lady.

When he said nothing her brow furrowed as if perplexed, then quickly cleared. "The ocean is part of who I am. I was born in its foam. So, what is your name, handsome one?"

Handsome? No one had called him that before, either. His lips curved up in a reluctant smile, his first in weeks. "I'm Ashur. And you're one interesting woman, Miss Aphrodite. Where did you come from? And where the heck are your clothes?"

"Here." She plucked at the sleeve of his jacket. "Though technically I suppose this warm wrap is yours, not mine, so… do you want it back? I am not cold, I promise. And what I want is better achieved without any clothing on at all."

A wicked shimmer lit her violet eyes as she fluttered her eyelashes at him. It took away the slight silliness of the action and highlighted both the enticing angle of her pale cheeks and a slightly regal arch of her brow. When the end of her tongue poked out to wet her lips, his mind filled with an image of her mouth slipping onto his now definitely hardening cock.

Would they be cold and fresh from the sea, those lips, or would the heat of her mouth draw even more of his blood to that hungry appendage between his legs? Would she suck and lick, or use her teeth to vary the sensory exploration of his organ?

Jesus! What was wrong with him? He blinked and shook his head to clear the lustful thoughts away, but she was there in front of him. Naked again, and laying his own overcoat down on the sand, bending forward as if offering up the valley of her sex for his own personal use.

"Um…" Where the fucking hell should he look? While his brain was still trying to be polite his eyes had other ideas and he couldn't help but drink in the view of those hairless folds of flesh rimming the enticing slash that separated her perfectly rounded butt cheeks.

A ribbon of faint male laughter tickled his senses and he looked up and down the beach in confusion. They were still alone, so where…?

Ah. The cliff top. Silhouetted above them for just a fraction of a second he saw three well-built men standing shoulder to shoulder. "You won't be able to help yourself, my friend," a voice whispered in his head, and then another, less amused, overlaid it.

"He will, Pothos. He's strong. Keep looking into your heart, Ashur. You'll know it's the right path if you just keep looking into your heart. I am Himeros, her son, and you are one of our choices. You must remain strong. For as long as you can."

Then the silhouettes were gone, the crazy voices in his head were gone, and he was left alone with this eccentric woman who was seated now on his jacket and patting the ground beside her.

"My sons are being very naughty and you should ignore

them. Come sit with me a while, Ashur. I want to…know you."

That word, and the ravenous way she lingered over it, weakened his knees and he dropped to the sand as if someone had bashed him across the back of the legs with a stick. He grunted at the sharp pain in his thigh but was grateful of the reminder of his injury. It cleared his thoughts.

"Look Aphrodite, I'm glad you're okay. You're obviously comfortable with being out here—" he looked around "—in the middle of the night in winter. But you can't just go around saying stuff like that to strangers. Especially when you're… you know. Naked." Thank God it was dark and she couldn't see the swift heat that burned his cheeks. "It could be danger-ous," he added.

She knelt up and pressed her body into his and a strange perfume assailed his nostrils. She smelt delicious, like a spicy exotic fruit, and he had to fight the urge to bend his head and test out her pale skin to see if it tasted as good as its promise. "I love a hint of danger. Don't you?"

"No! I mean…" He cleared his throat. Used to. Not anymore. "No," he managed more calmly, despite the fact that her breasts were mushed against his chest. Without his coat, only the fabric of his black T-shirt separated their bodies.

A very thin T-shirt. And very insistent nipples.

He shifted backward but she followed. "This is stupid," he managed. "We need to get you home. Where do you live?"

"Stupid? You dare to call me…that?" Muscle coiled against him in sudden tension and her lips thinned in obvious displeasure. But then she seemed to rally, taking a deep breath and huffing it out in a puff of warmth across his neck. He felt the rigidity leave her body. Everywhere that is, except for the nubs of her nipples which stayed hard. Very hard.

They poked into him as she breathed. What would she do if he leaned down and slipped one of those rosy tips into his mouth?

"I live a long way from here. I'm only visiting. And perhaps…" She narrowed her eyes and pouted. "It'll be a shorter stay than I expected."

"Why?"

"You are not giving me what I want, here. And I always get what I want."

The cold breeze off the ocean at his back was a stark contrast to the heat where her body touched his. She couldn't help but be aware of the hard meaty lump between his legs, no matter how he tried to play it cool.

"What do you want then?" His voice had morphed from normal into raspy somewhere in the last twenty seconds or so.

"I want…no, I need you to kiss me, Ashur. I ache with loneliness."

Her voice touched something deep inside him. It was as if, just for a moment, he knew her loneliness. He knew her. And suddenly, he didn't want to back away anymore. The memories had driven him for too long. It was exhausting to run from your own needs.

Lifting a hand, he traced the outline of her beautiful face. Those luminous eyes softened in anticipation. Those ruby lips waited for his kiss. That scent, powerful and heady, drew him in to closer proximity, whether he wanted it or not. "Who are you, Aphrodite?"

She turned her cheek toward his palm, snuggling against his cupped hand as if starved of affection. Her skin felt softer than any he'd ever known. "I am the goddess of love and desire," she said. "Listen to your heart. You already know me, and you will kiss me now."

It was a command, not a request, and yet the urge slipped

over him and gripped too tightly to fight off. Yeah. Hell yeah. He bent his head to capture her ready lips with his own. She was all softness, with a tensile hard strength beneath, both demanding and persuading all at the same time. Her tongue flicked his and the weird sensations washing over him ramped up ten-fold.

Who kissed like this? Dominant one second, then softening into submission the next. I should be the one in control here. He pressed harder, gripped the globes of her butt and squeezed, imagining red finger marks on her alabaster flesh as he thrust into her softness. Desire spiraled at the thought of marking her with his need. Having this woman at his mercy, writhing beneath him, screaming out for release and only achieving it when he gave permission...The crazy images filling his head gave lie to his control and he almost lost his load right then and there.

No. I am in charge this time. Not you. Not anyone else.

Bitterness filled him and he wound his fingers into the long dark hair snaking down her back and pulled, tipping her head to expose the delicate line of her throat. She opened her mouth and husky laughter spilled out. "Is that all you've got?"

His erection jerked and grew in his trousers and he knew a spurt of pre-cum had just leaked out to dampen the cotton of his briefs. "I haven't even started," he said, and tugged viciously at her tresses, forcing her backward into a deeper arc. The action pointed her breasts skyward and he paused above one long nipple, his breath rasping quickly in and out. What sort of woman had nipples this long? Like miniature phalluses, aiming straight up at his face to proclaim her arousal as obviously as any man.

"I love your eyes." Her voice was a mere whisper, constricted by his hold.

"My…eyes?"

"They've changed from hazel to green now that you're aroused. And they shine."

He grunted. "So do yours. Shine, I mean."

"They always do when someone ignites my interest."

His grip tightened. It must have been hurting her scalp, but she just lay there compliant beneath him. Eyes shining brighter than ever.

"Don't you want to taste me, Ash?"

His balls lifted and tightened as desire and self-loathing mingled. Why did the thought of hurting her harden his cock like this? She'd done nothing to deserve it, and he wasn't like this. Inflicting pain for sexual kicks did not turn him on, so what the hell was happening? He was no more in control of himself now than he had been the last time he'd had sex.

That night. The night he turned everyone's lives to shit. The urge to scream out his rage and despair against her throat warred with an equally strong need to sink his face between her beautiful breasts and weep.

A ragged breath escaped and he closed his eyes. Control yourself. Control her.

His breathing slowed, centered, and he opened his eyes. "Now I'm ready to start," he said, and extended his tongue to graze the very tip of her nipple. A moist flick, a mere second of connection, but she gasped and shuddered as if he'd thrust into her with his cock.

"More." Her voice had deepened to an almost guttural groan.

"Please?" Hmm, so had his voice, it seemed.

"Please, Ashur." She wasn't laughing now, she was panting. The action caused her breasts to shift upward to tease his lips and then down again. Over and over. Up and down. Like her nipples had become crazed little cocks and she was drilling him instead of the other way around. Resolve disappeared and he snatched her breast into his mouth, nipping and sucking at the pliant flesh with its hardened center until a cry tore out of her throat.

The need to assert authority forced his erection into her muff in a grinding action so fierce he expected her to give way. Instead she met him, thrust for thrust, squeeze for squeeze and he found himself capitulating. Submission was unfamiliar but surprisingly sweet and for a few seconds he let her take charge, allowing her to dominate. She dragged his head up from her breast and captured his mouth in another heated kiss.

When he tried to pull back, to analyze the experience and digest thoughts, feelings, vacillating emotions, she pursued him. A fighting dance of lips, tongues, and teeth ensued. One that drew his mouth back onto hers and called his very soul out of hiding.

He twisted away, struggling to breathe, still lurching his hips against her as she wriggled to better fit that hairless pussy around the long hot line of his cock, even sheathed as it was in his jeans.

"Wait, I—" But she was there again, purring against his lips, biting the bottom one hard enough to draw blood, and he sucked in one startled breath before bite turned back into delicate kiss. Give and take. Dominate. Submit. This time he could taste the metallic flavor of his own blood in her mouth. When she moaned, the deep sound summoned an answering groan out of his own throat and had him clutching at her hips to steady his shaking limbs.

Blood. Violence. Desire. This was utter madness.

Again he wrenched away, and this time managed a roll across freezing cold sand to put a couple of meters between their bodies. "This isn't right." He could hardly speak, he was panting so hard. "We have to…Jesus, put your legs together, woman."

"Why? I want you to love me." She lay back on his coat, leaning up on her elbows and with legs akimbo he could see the slick cream at her core. She was breathing hard too, though not, it seemed, with quite such a desperate rasp as him.

He wanted nothing more than to unzip his jeans and let his cock out into the night so it could do what it was meant to and fuck this woman senseless. His whole body shook with the effort of holding on. But one of them had to display a bit of sanity and it clearly wasn't going to be her.

"This isn't love, Aphrodite. We met like…what? Three seconds ago? This would be a quick fuck and nothing more."

"Quick?" She let out a faint chuckle and those tantalizing breasts jiggled. "It would not be quick, Ashur." If she pushed those mounds together he could drive between them and come all over that beautiful silvery skin, turning everything slick and wet.

No. Stop. He shook his head to try and clear it, but his voice wobbled a little when he spoke. "It would not be love, Aphrodite. I don't even have any condoms with me." His attempt at a laugh almost came out sounding normal. "Wasn't expecting to run into any willing women down here at…" He checked his watch. "Twelve forty-five in the morning. And as tempting as you are…" His gaze slid over her perfectly proportioned curves and his gut flip-flopped. "I can't do this right now. I'm too fucked up to…well…fuck."

"But…" She gaped at him, eyes wide and surprise turning her mouth into an 'o' shape. "Surely you don't really mean that. Do you?" Astonishment gave her a softer air and for a second he almost gave in. Until she added, "You wouldn't need a condom with me. I am a goddess. I carry no disease. In fact, I can cure it, if you wish."

She gestured toward his leg and he flinched as if she'd connected with his damaged thigh. "Leave it. Just…leave it. Please."

"Why?" Puzzlement shaded her features. "Can you not feel my power? I can use it to help you." She stretched out her fingers again and heat washed over him like a wave of comforting warmth. The sensation centered in his thigh and for an instant he relaxed into relief as the incessant ache began to recede.

Was this even possible? It really did feel as if she was digging out the damage to find and heal what was wrong. Muscle, nerve and tissue, her touch crept right down to his very bones. How was she doing this? Taking away his pain. His punishment.

"No! Stop! Aphrodite, please. I don't want your help. I don't need it."

"I am offering you everything, Ashur. I am offering you the chance to worship at the altar of a goddess." She really sounded like she meant it.

"Fuck this. I think you're psycho."

"But…I don't understand." Shocked hurt flared in her eyes and slackened her lips. Her confusion seemed genuine and a jolt of remorse went through him.

"Sorry lady, but…fuck."

How he managed to get to his feet and stumble away he would never know, but somehow he made it to the base of the cliff footpath. He looked back then, intending with the safety of physical distance to call for her to at least follow him back to the guest house, but she was gone.

What the…?

He shoved shaking hands through his hair and blinked

furiously, but she didn't re-materialize. So…what? Had he just had some kind of psychotic episode, or had he finally gotten to sleep and dreamt up his idea of a fuckable woman? He took a step toward where they'd just been sitting to check up and down the beach, but she was nowhere in sight. Surely she wouldn't have gone back into the water? No. The waves at that moment were unusually calm and in the bright moon-light he could see that the sea was empty of perfect phantom women.

Not quite perfect though. He scowled. Physically she'd been everything he could or would ever want in a woman. But emotionally, there'd been something missing. If she could appear out of nowhere and open her legs for the first person she saw and then think it was love…well, then clearly the poor thing hadn't had much experience of love.

Laughter tickling at the edges of his mind again. Deep, masculine, almost out-of-control mirth and, strangely, tinged with a hint of sadness. But it was gone as soon as he turned his head to try and locate the source.

Jeez. He really was going to have to figure out a way to get some sleep before he completely lost his mind.

CHAPTER TWO

At first Aphrodite was too stunned to be upset. He had spurned her advances! She had not been rejected since...ever. The man clearly hadn't had sex in a while; his lonely desperation – and the powerful echo from his friends – had called her from the water before she was quite ready to emerge. Even so, he had resisted her generous offer and actually left unfulfilled and full of misery.

How? Why? Her mind was full of speculation, but for the first time answers were not apparent.

"By the gods!" She lifted her chin and watched the figure ascend slowly up the cliff path. A tall, rugged, intensely physical man, with a powerful cut to his shoulders and the kind of short dark hair she favored. Neat at the back and sides, designed to stay mostly in place, but with enough kick at the top and around the fringe area to provide a perfect place in which to sink her questing fingers.

Clearly he had been wounded in a battle of some kind, with that limp giving him a slightly awkward gait up the rocky staircase, and a darkness in his soul that called like a friend to the loneliness in her own. A man who fought against fire and rescued other mortals. A hero among his kind. She could sense that much when she dipped beneath the surface of his skin. But something had gone awry and he was now very much in need of a rescue of his own. So awry, in fact, that he couldn't see her offering for what it was – a chance to lay with the goddess and worship her in the most delightful possible way.

Her brows lowered. He'd called her psycho. She knew that here it meant something completely different to what it meant in the realm of the gods. Psycho was the breath of life. Soul. It was everything Ashur needed if he wanted to begin healing. Here it just meant plain old crazy.

How could she prove him wrong? Earlier her sons had been there atop the cliff where Ashur was walking. She'd tuned in to their conversation and tried not to laugh at their smug expectation that she'd find it more difficult than she realized in this time and this place.

Bah! Males! She would prove them all wrong; immortal or otherwise.

Despite her annoyance, her heart swelled with pride at the difference the erotes had already made to so many lives here in this world. Yearning, desire, and the beautiful balance of both requited and unrequited love.

Pothos, Himeros, and Anteros. Her boys. Aspects of Eros. She'd never seen any of them so…what was the word? Content did not convey what she could feel beneath their skins. No. It was more like a completion. A sense that they had finally found whatever was missing in their souls, when they hadn't even known there was anything missing in the first place.

She knew, though. She could feel it in herself. A place of emptiness where emotion was supposed to fill her and yet instead, there was a cavernous void. Everything now had become physical, and the gods knew that she of all people could easily fulfill her own and others' lustful needs.

But she wanted more. She wanted love. Completion.

It had been so long since Anchises had lived, and loved her. And she had loved him back, more than she had ever expected. The goddess of love and desire, they called her, these humans, but little did they know that since her beloved had passed from this world into the next she had harbored a great black hole where her heart should have been.

Sending three of her sons out into the world of mortals to seek out those in need and help heal them had been a comfort, even if only a small one. Not wanting others to feel this aching emptiness inside had forced her loved ones to conduct an almost endless task. Find and cure the lonely. Teach the meaning of desire. Guide lovers into the path of their soul mate or mates. One after another, after another. An endless stream of lonely souls. It had almost destroyed even the powerful gods of love.

A lick of indecision crept through her veins and her breath suddenly caught in her throat. What if I am wrong and they are right? My beautiful erotes. Maybe I am incapable of truly understanding the fullness of love and desire. What if, here on this earth, I am simply a crazy woman that everyone pities? What if there is no one available to love me?

She wrapped her arms around her middle, feeling the bite of cold that she had blithely told Ashur did not affect her. Apollo Bay was just a little further up the coast and though she knew it would not be warm like her Mediterranean home, the name had appealed. Would this place named after a god who ranked healing among his many responsibilities, live up to its reputation?

No doubt somewhere back home in Olympus, Hephaestus

and Ares were laughing hard at her plight. Maybe I am the biggest irony of all.

She hadn't expected Ashur. He was clearly attracted to her beauty and her essence, but he was so damn stubborn that he wouldn't give in to his need. And that need was great; she could sense it. Something dark in his soul that called to the darkness in her own. So why in the name of Zeus did he not simply capitulate and sink that hot and ready cock into her willing body? If nothing else he would get a delicious physical release that would ease his body, if not his mind. As would she.

Her gaze followed as he made his awkward way across the top of the cliff face. An action man. Crippled like her husband Heph had been, but she would not make the same mistake twice and underestimate him. In Ash she sensed a determined strength in the way he held himself, despite the awkwardness of his injury.

Why will he not let me heal him? "Stupid, stubborn man."

She held out her hand and the flash surged forward. Seeking, finding his form, curling up and around him and learning the line of his body. She detected the heat of recent scar tissue on his thigh. Metal had passed through this flesh not so long ago, perhaps a sword, or…

No. Not a sword. She twirled a lock of hair behind her right ear and considered. In this time and place it would not be a sword, but rather…a bullet? No. The scar was too jagged, the area of injury too large. An edge of piping from a building. Yes. Ashur was carrying a wound in his thigh that stemmed from a building that had been collapsing around him at the time. Healing, perhaps a couple of months old by now, but still some way to go, and that damage went far deeper than his flesh. She closed her eyes and went further inside, seeking his essence, his core, and found—oh! Darkness.

Unflinching darkness. Set there in concrete by the pain of guilt and remorse.

Retreat. She must retreat before it consumed her, this darkness. She had enough darkness of her own to contend with. Reluctant tears pooled beneath her closed eyelids and her throat tightened, hurting her. The poor dear man.

Stupid, stubborn, and with a soul-deep suffering that would take more than a flash of her power to heal. Her safest option was to leave here now and seek out someone else who would benefit from her endless experience. Someone who would welcome her assistance. Someone who would be unable to resist her potent brand of desire. Someone who would ease this incessant physical ache in her womb as it squeezed tight, reminding her of its hunger.

There were...she concentrated. Yes. Several candidates within a mile of here who would welcome her with open arms. Several hundred, if she expanded her search. A billion lonely souls, calling out for her guidance and her love, if she wanted to abandon this moment and this man.

But did she? How could she leave him like this? So hurt, so...enraged. How could she justify walking away from that level of pain? Walking away would give truth to the nagging anxiety that her heart really had disappeared down a deep dark hole.

Perhaps I really have forgotten how to love. Heartless, or helpful? It is up to me to make that decision. I can choose, right now. One path. Or the other.

The night breeze crept across her skin like a sign from some of the gods, and in that moment she knew that Hephaestus was not laughing. Neither was Ares. The deformed god of blacksmiths and volcanoes, her one-time husband Heph who had been treated horribly at her hands, and her powerful lover Ares, god of war himself, both had hearts bigger than that of the goddess of love. She could feel their well-wishes in this quest to rediscover her essence.

Laughter began to bubble even as tears dribbled down her cheeks. When she flicked out her tongue to the side and caught one of them, the taste of the sea filled her mouth. Salt. A symbol of truth in some religions on this earth. There was no choice really, in the end. Immortality was a bitch if you had to live too long with self-loathing.

Another cool draught of air was a reminder that she should probably put on some clothing if these humans were to accept her amongst them. It had been fun to tease Ash with her nudity. His prudish shock warred with lust in a way that fascinated her, but it was time now to behave. More or less.

She sent out a flicker of power to see… yes. That woman would do. The one wearing a short white dress, hmm, very short, and was tottering on those spike-heeled shoes as she made her way back inside the guest lodging. Obviously she'd had a more than passing acquaintance with mead.

Aphrodite concentrated hard, getting all the small details correct in her mind, and then she was wearing a perfect replica of the dress and the shoes and was standing atop the cliff, looking at the big stone building where Ashur had disappeared only moments ago.

The flutter of excitement in her belly was both unexpected and strangely arousing.

I am going to help you through this, my friend, whether you want my assistance or not.

$$\Omega \, \Psi \, \Omega$$

Ash couldn't stop thinking about her. Those lush curves encased in that milky-white skin. The strange violet hue of her eyes rimmed with dark lashes and a hooded, almost sleepy look that spiked his blood with sensual heat every time she turned her gaze his way. And those lips. That beautiful mouth almost the exact color of the throw rug currently gracing the end of his bed. He'd thought it was hideously feminine when he'd arrived here at Stony Gables Inn almost four weeks ago. But now? He studied the rosy pink fabric, reached out to run curious fingers over its mohair softness. Now that color instantly brought to mind lips that were as luscious as any he had ever seen. Wide lips that would have wrapped themselves around his aching dick if he had only given the go-ahead.

Was he mad to have said no? Was he mad, having perhaps dreamt her up in the first place? Aphrodite. Like a goddess. No woman looked like that in real life. Hell, hardly anyone even looked like that in a magazine or on TV, even in this digital age where any image could be altered or improved.

Where had she disappeared to, the strange exotic beauty who was plaguing his thoughts and preventing him from sleeping? His lips tightened. Can't blame the insomnia on her. When had he last slept through the night like a baby? Not for a long while, now.

Restlessness filled him and he paced the room, pausing to snatch the throw rug off the bed and rub it against his face. Soft. Just like her hands, her lips, her cheeks. He nuzzled into it, imagining his head pillowed between her breasts…

Fuck!

He paced some more, wondering if Kieran or Hugh would still be awake, and toyed with the idea of dropping round to one of their rooms to while away the rest of this weird, restless night. But Hugh was probably asleep already, and

Kieran… That visit would involve alcohol. Probably lots of it, and at this point he couldn't risk getting back on the booze. Might not ever get off it again.

What would his best buddies make of Aphrodite? Would they be as turned on by her beauty, by her scent, *as I was? Still am*, he corrected, the need heavy between his legs. They'd shared women several times in the past, the three of them, often at the same time, and he was pretty tuned in to their needs. Usually, if one of them found a woman attractive, the others did too. Brothers on the job, and lovers who shared everything, even their women. One part of him wanted desperately to regain the old camaraderie, but in another, deeper place, anger flared at the thought of sharing Aphrodite with anyone.

She was different, like no woman he'd ever met before, and he really didn't want to share this one with anyone. Even Kieran or Hugh.

Or Aiden, if he'd still been alive.

Fuck sex! It had all become mixed up with the negative shit that was still toying with his head, and he couldn't bring himself to do anything about it, even when he was so desperate for a fuck. Even when the thought of sharing a woman he'd only just met, a woman who could well be a figment of his imagination – and if she wasn't, then she was most likely an escaped mental patient with delusions of grandeur – still filled him with yearning.

Kieran had gone the other way since the night of the accident. While Ash wouldn't have sex at all, Kieran couldn't seem to get enough of it. He'd had women in his room most nights over the past month, and a couple of men too, and at first he kept trying to get Ash to join them. Lately though, he'd gotten the message and finally given up asking.

Of the three of them, Hugh seemed the least affected, but

then, he hadn't been with them that night, and he'd always been the peacemaker in their group. The one who calmed the others and took the edge off their testosterone-fuelled orgies. Hugh had lost just as much, of course, but it hadn't been directly his fault.

The way it was mine.

He threw the rug back onto his bed but it missed and fell to the floor in a puddle of dusky rose. He wanted to throw himself down on top of it and rut like a crazed animal. Until the fountain of seed backed up in his loins gushed out and drowned that soft padded surface in a sea of cream.

Aphrodite.

You're one woman I would definitely want to keep for myself.

And in doing so, I could well destroy you with this black thing that's eating me up inside.

CHAPTER THREE

K ieran looked across at Hugh shifting restlessly in his sleep and the dark emptiness began to build again. Would it ever disappear, this yawning hole inside of him? Or would he be stuck like this forever?

Usually, when the shadows beckoned he either retreated into a drink or found a willing partner to take to his bed. Tonight at the bar there was no one who took his fancy. Except Hugh, of course, and so the two of them had ended up here, sucking each other's cocks in an attempt to forget.

A pity fuck. Or more technically, a pity suck.

He knew Hugh was bi and quite liked a bit of guy on guy, but he also knew tonight's little episode had been purely for Kieran. It had been Hugh's valiant attempt to bridge the dark chasm between post-dinner drink and sleep with a few minutes of physical distraction for his friend. While it wasn't the first time they'd made love without a woman involved, there was something missing in the encounter that left him feeling shallow and unfulfilled, despite spilling his seed into Hugh's mouth only a short time ago.

Hugh loved the taste of it, the hot heat. He'd told them

both once that it was one of his favorite things to do. Kieran enjoyed it too, on occasion, but Ash wouldn't have sex without a woman there. Never had, so there'd been no point asking him to join them tonight.

He twitched aside the sheer white curtain and looked out into the darkness of night. A canopy of stars greeted him, and even from up here with the window closed he could hear the crash of waves onto the beach down below. Strangely mesmerizing, that sound. He let it wash over him, sinking gratefully into the brief sense of calm that settled through his body.

A beautiful place, this, despite being miles from Melbourne, the nearest big city. And in the middle of the cold season, too. The Victorian coast in winter was stark and cold, with a breeze that swept in straight off the ocean and chilled you to the bone, if you stayed out too late or too long.

Not a place he'd ever thought to recuperate, but Ash had found the tiny hamlet listed on the internet, nestled on the coast near Apollo Bay, and they'd had a "pay for two, get one free" deal. With Hugh willing to come along for the ride it hadn't sounded too bad.

"It'll be good for us, Kier. Fresh air, surfing, some nice bush walking up that way. There's a resident physiotherapist too, who can help some more with…this." Ash had gestured angrily at his leg, and Kier had capitulated. As he always did with Ash.

Alpha male. That was his buddy all right. Older than Kieran, and Hugh for that matter, by a couple of years, Ash was definitely the leader of their little pack, both at the fire station and outside of it. If his buddy had been fully into BDSM Kieran would have been first in line as his sub. That's why it hurt so bad to see Ash weakened by what had happened. It wasn't how things should be.

"Fuck bush walking, man," he'd grinned. "But yeah. Getting away sounds pretty good."

So they'd booked the stay for six weeks, out here along the remote Victorian Otways region in the middle of winter, and four weeks into their stay Ash finally seemed less tortured. Where was he right now? Was he still pacing up and down that beach at the base of the cliff, or had he finally retired to his room down the hall to try and get what little sleep he could before dawn broke in a few hours' time?

Poor Ash. He looked at Hugh. Poor all of them. Would any of them ever be…whole again? At this point he couldn't imagine going back to his job as a firey. But he didn't know how to do…how to be…anything else.

A knock at the door was quiet enough not to wake Hugh, but demanding enough that he found himself across the room and answering its peremptory summons before he'd even had time to process who might be calling this late at night.

"Are you Kieran? Or Hugh?"

"Um…" He gaped at the beauty standing before him a moment too long before his wits reasserted themselves. "Kieran. Yeah. I'm Kieran." *And though I sound like a half-wit I'm not. Always.*

"I am Aphrodite. Ashur's need brought me here to—"

"Ash? Err, he's not here right now but I can go get him if you like." Trust Ash to scout out the most gorgeous woman in the region. He swallowed hard when he met huge violet-hued eyes framed by long dark lashes. *In the region? In the country, more like.* Her dark hair fell down over her shoulders in a silken cascade and he had to fight the urge to reach out and run his fingers through its length. Her body was somehow both lean and voluptuous, curving in all the right places in a dress so tight it looked like it had been painted on. *Was he goggling at her? Probably. But in an outfit like* that… "Would you like to…um…well, I guess you're already in."

She'd stepped past him into the room in a fluid movement that reminded him of a wildcat. Fast, smooth, and powerful with a transient body heat that he felt right to his bones. Especially when those breasts encased in the low cut white fabric scraped across his naked torso.

Despite his earlier tryst with Hugh his cock began to harden. Always ready, these days, it seemed, but rarely fulfilled, even after orgasm. Though he had the feeling that might change, if this woman had anything to do with it.

She leaned forward and the dark valley between those breasts called out to be fucked. He blinked and shifted, trying to maintain some level of politeness, but damned if the woman's mouth didn't turn up a little at one corner as if she knew exactly where his thoughts were right now.

"You won't need to fetch him. Ashur is on his way here already. And he's going to be mad as hell when he sees what's happening in here." She smiled again, a tiny Mona Lisa-style grin that hinted at secret satisfaction, and his heart began to race.

"So…what is going on in here right now?"

"Hey." A sleepy voice from the bed piped up and he glanced across to see Hugh sitting up and rubbing a hand through his blonde hair. Tufts of it stuck up randomly and Kieran couldn't help but grin. Hugh always had bed hair, whether he'd just woken up or not. It added to his boyish appeal, as did those deceptively innocent blue eyes that were now fastened on their guest with interest.

"My," she said. "You're all as good-looking as each other, aren't you?"

He promptly reached up to finger-comb his own light brown hair, wishing he looked half as attractive as Hugh. Or at least had a few less freckles. Even Ash, not traditionally handsome, had sex appeal oozing out of every pore.

"You going to introduce us, Kier?" Hugh was definitely wide awake, now.

"Yeah, sure. I…" But he didn't need to. She was making her way across the room, noiseless on the thick cream carpet, and holding out a graceful hand toward his companion. Long limbs. Smooth gait. He'd never seen anyone move like that before.

"You must be Hugh. I am Aphrodite, goddess of desire, and I am here to find love with the two of you. And with Ashur, if he will just let me in." Tight frustration laced those last few words and Kieran raised a brow.

"So, you've already met our friend?"

"I have."

His other brow joined the first. Ash must have really pissed her off. The tightness left her features. She slanted her gaze between the two of them and Kieran's breath caught in his throat at its seductive promise. Where the hell had she come from, this woman who appeared to be glowing from within with a strange golden light?

He rubbed his eyes but the effect remained. She was shining. He took a hesitant step toward the bed, wanting to get close enough to touch her.

"Ow!" Hugh had clasped Aphrodite's hand briefly then pulled back with a frown. "Zapped me."

"Oops." She laughed and the sunny sound washed over Kieran with the soothing cadence of a breaking wave. He shrugged his shoulders as the taut muscles in his neck began to relax. "Sorry," she said. "But I wish to make love with you, gentlemen, and I am so full of need I can barely walk."

Aphrodite touched her abdomen briefly, curling her fingers over the flat stomach, and the gesture sent a rush of heat to his cock. "I will try and…what is the term? Reel it in a bit before I harm you with my hunger. Here. Is that better?" She reached out again and this time connected with both of them. Energy from their linked fingers whipped through his blood like wildfire and the beginnings of his arousal became a fully-fledged hard-on that tented the sweat pants he'd pulled on earlier.

"Yeah," he managed. "That's good. Doesn't hurt a bit."

"Jesus!" Hugh knelt up quickly, the bed sheets falling away to reveal his nakedness and a boner even more impressive than his own. "Mine does. It aches." Hot and angry-looking, already tipped with pre-cum shine, and all from one caressing touch from this gorgeous woman.

Every man's fantasy come directly to life. He ran curious fingertips up the white skin of her arm, exploring her softness, and goose bumps formed in the wake of his touch.

"Nice," she whispered. "More please."

He grinned at Hugh, who did the same up and down her other arm. She shivered between them and a tiny gasp escaped her lips.

"You really like that?" Arousal tightened his vocal chords and it was hard to get the words out.

She shut her eyes and nodded once. Delicate shadow coated her cheeks beneath long black eyelashes and gave her a vulnerable air that fed his desire even more. Somewhere in the sensible part of his brain he knew he should care about who she was and where she'd come from, but it was like that part of him had been muted. Instead it seemed right that she had just turned up, walked in and demanded love.

"Then I guess we should do it some more," he said. "Don't you think, Hugh?"

"Why not?" His friend seemed bemused by the woman

between them, but his fingers were edging further, past her shoulder and down around the bodice line of her dress.

Kier extended his reach up the long line of her neck and across the angles and curves of her face. He traced near her eye, just around the edge of those lashes, and her eyes fluttered open again, their liquid depths mesmerizing at this range. The breath locked momentarily in his throat and he pressed his groin hard against her hip. Hugh did the same on her other side.

A man sandwich, one of their past lovers had joked when they got to this point, but Aphrodite said nothing so crass. She just let out another sigh, the ragged sound edged with anticipation. Her perfume filled his nostrils and a strange roar in his eardrums slowed his thinking until he couldn't concentrate, couldn't do anything except sip from her proffered well of moist sweet nectar when he leaned in to take the kiss. Her lips were both spicy and sweet at the same time. The taste was exotic and new, and it blended perfectly with the familiar whiskey-laced breath of his friend as Hugh joined them in a three-way kiss like none he had ever experienced before.

Time ceased to exist as he dipped into her mouth and supped. The ever-present vestiges of his anguish receded as hunger took its place. Desire. Craving. That was all he knew, especially when her moan vibrated across the back of his throat. First one, then the other of them plunged with a tongue here, nipped there with eager teeth. He sucked at the fullness of her bottom lip and felt in turn the delicate flicker of her tongue as she rasped it across his own.

Demanding, then asking. Dominating, then pleading. The dance went on and he couldn't tell who was in control. Or out of it. He didn't care. If she wanted to be in charge, that was okay by him. He would happily go wherever she led.

Her body was as soft as it had promised to be, and yet

somehow hard and unyielding. Earlier she'd been wearing a white dress, but now she was naked between them. How was that possible? He groaned and heard an answering sound erupt out of Hugh before his friend leaned down to take one of her long pink nipples into his mouth. Blindly he reached out and grappled the other breast, weighing its enticing heaviness in his palm.

Slow this down. Catch our breath. He inhaled deeply, willing his body to do as his mind insisted, and felt the heaving breaths that wracked Hugh's ribs when he paused, too. What the hell was happening to them both?

Aphrodite stared up into their faces with an expectant look softening those extraordinary eyes, and once again he was assailed by her scent. If he'd ever imagined the scent of sex, it would be this. Whatever perfume she was emitting, it drew him in like a moth to the proverbial flame.

"Will we be burnt, touching you?" He hadn't meant to voice the thought and instant heat flamed in his cheeks, but Hugh's strained chuckle didn't suggest ridicule. Far from it, in fact.

"We fight fires for a living, man. I'm sure we'll cope."

Aphrodite laughed and began to trace tiny circular patterns down his stomach. He shivered beneath the heat in her touch, but it was a sultry warmth, neither overpowering nor painful. "You would be burnt to powdered dust in the heat of my flame, if I willed it, Kieran. But I do not. I will keep you safe in my arms, you and Hugh. And I will help you both forget your troubles, if you wish."

"Um…no." His heart flip-flopped. "I don't want—" How to explain his need? He wasn't sure if Hugh felt the same, but they should never forget their friend and fellow firey Aiden, who had died without his buddies there to help protect him.

Aphrodite bowed her head as if listening to some internal

monologue, then raised her eyes. The intensity of her gaze made him uncomfortable. A glint of the predator that showed only for a moment and was gone just as fast. Looking into him, rather than at him. "Or I can help you learn to live with those memories, if you do not wish to forget."

Oh…kay. Who are you, Aphrodite?

She just smiled and watched him some more. Hugh let out a strange grunt, as if he'd felt the force of that stare too, and slipped around behind her on the bed. Maybe he's trying to escape it.

"Where did you come from?" Hugh spoke into the curve of her neck, snaking one arm forward around her waist. "And what magic wand are you waving over us?" His other hand was thrust out in front of her. "Look! Every single one of my muscles is shaking right now."

Kieran saw the truth in his friend's shuddering fingers. Hugh had clearly been as affected by her uncanny perception as he was. An equally unfamiliar tremble shook his own hand as he reached out to explore her mound.

A quick grab and she held him there immobile, tilting her hips into his now cupped grasp as if embracing the closeness. "The mound of Venus. Mons veneris. That's what they call it. And that makes it mine."

Had she suddenly grown? There was a ferocity to her stance that made her seem more substantial than before. He'd have sworn minutes ago that she was slightly shorter than his own six foot two by a couple of inches, which made her tall for a woman in any case. But now she seemed to soar over both of them. He blinked, confused.

"I am Venus," she said, and her voice resonated right through to the center of him. "I am Aphrodite. Goddess of love and desire. It is not magic but simply me. You cannot help yourselves, gentlemen. Though…" She shook her hair away from her face and it rippled over her shoulders and down her back. If he'd ever thought to visualize a goddess, this would be what came to mind. Except for that slight frown marring the perfection of her brow. "He resisted. Somehow."

He? Surely not…Ash? What the hell did you do, man?

She huffed out a little breath and the sound fractured the image of her as some kind of immortal being. She was back to being all woman. Normal size. As if he'd also been released from a spell Hugh shook his head and then reached down to touch her between the legs, threading his fingers in between Kier's in order to reach her slit.

No. For a second Kier's fingers tightened. Why should he share? But then shame washed over him at the unfamiliar urge and he forced himself to relax and let Hugh in. His friend was an expert when it came to touching a woman. There was a delicacy to his touch that usually delighted, a gentle swipe of the forefinger that he knew from experience would have her mouth parting and her eyes widening in startled pleasure.

He waited, watching Aphrodite's face, and…yep, there it was. The tiny gasp, the sudden widening of her eyes, the "ooh" that tripped out involuntarily from between her lips. She had enjoyed that, all right. Her thighs widened and now he too, slipped his fingers into her moist crevice, searching for and finding the already swollen nub of her clit. He coated himself in her slick juice as he circled and flicked the sensitive area in tandem with Hugh.

Her head dropped back and to one side, exposing her throat, and as he bent and kissed its vulnerable softness she let out a moan that vibrated against his lips. "You both have magic fingers," she gasped. "That feels so good."

Impossibly, her clit swelled even further, until he could see it peeking out from within the twin folds of her muff when he looked down. No, not her muff. What had she called it? Her mons veneris. There it was, poking out from her mons veneris like a cheeky tongue, and the urge to pull that extraordinary piece of flesh into his mouth and swallow the fluid giving it shine was too strong to resist.

He knelt on the carpet in front of her, grateful for the softness beneath his knees as he gripped her rounded butt cheeks and pulled her in closer to his mouth. In this position her delicious scent surrounded him and his whole body felt energized and full of hot, racing blood. Most of it was centered in his hard and ready erection.

Hugh had changed position slightly and was now working her from behind, thrusting up into her body with two of his fingers. As they slipped in and out Kier could see wetness coating his friend's digits. Impossibly, his cock thickened further as he imagined himself in their place.

Her remarkably large clit shifted and swelled right in front of his eyes, mimicking what was happening in his own body and a crazy growl burst forth out of his throat. Oh my God! I sound like an animal! He sank his tongue between the folds of her flesh, wanting to coax the same sounds out of her.

"Yes!" She thrust into his mouth, hips spasming without rhythm. He sucked her in fully and it was like taking a bite of some strange exotic fruit, full of salt, and cream, sweetness and spice, the most decadent thing that had ever tempted his taste buds.

Delicious.

Usually by now he would be touching himself, wanking a little to keep the momentum going. There was an inevitable ebb and flow that often occurred when there were more than two people involved in the sex, but if he laid a finger on himself right now he'd be shooting a jet of cum so high it'd probably hit the ceiling.

He halted, panting, trying to stop himself coming too soon, but from where he knelt in front of her, with her legs akimbo like that, he could see Hugh had now worked three fingers into her channel, pumping hard and fast. Was his fourth finger scraping across the puckered button of her asshole? Was that why she continued to moan and buck above him?

The urge to breach that asshole and fuck her, hard, almost overwhelmed Kier. Hugh had joined his deeper voice to hers and they were both making groaning noises now. He lay his head down on the edge of the bed, fighting for control as he felt his balls tighten in approaching release.

"Not yet." The gentle touch of feminine fingers in his hair and the whispered words above his head floated through him, just enough of a calming influence to prevent the creamy explosion.

"Hugh, please, you wait too." The bedcover shifted beneath his forehead and he looked up to see her twisting away from them both, reclining over on the far side of the bed. Hugh knelt panting in front of Kier, a sheen of sweat highlighting his abs and those sexy twin grooves that slanted down toward his groin. Hugh's cock appeared as ready to detonate as his own, sticky liquid dripping from the tip. Frustration was clearly paramount as hands fisted at his sides.

Kier's lips twisted when he realized pre-cum had also left a patch of wet on his own sweats. Just like a teenager, unable to control it. He ripped his pants down and shucked them off before throwing them to one side. It left his organ free, cool air warring with the heat within, and on impulse he slid a finger across the shiny head and brought it up to his mouth. A flare of excitement lit Hugh's face and he slowed the movement, sucking his finger all the way in and then out, enjoying the tease. Enjoying the taste.

The flavor of sex. The flavor of male desire. But it didn't taste half as good as Aphrodite had. Why did she want to stop?

He clambered awkwardly onto the bed beside Hugh and slipped an arm around his friend's waist. Both turned to study their companion and he wondered what they looked like to her, with their breath still coming fast, their thigh muscles shaking and their twin erections jutting out toward her, ball sacks drawn up tight. Hugh's member was longer, uncircumcised like their buddy Ash, whereas Kier, like Aiden, had been cut. Women had commented before on the thickness of his cock and he hoped Aphrodite liked what she saw in front of her. Together they would be able to pleasure her every way she wanted it.

If she still wanted it.

His brows lowered. Neither he nor Hugh could reach her now, but the wetness between her legs and the dark dusky color of those swollen labia lips was impossible to miss from any angle, with her legs spread-eagled like that. She looked almost inhuman lying there, so white and impossibly long-bodied and long-limbed. Like some kind of Amazon warrior but with the strength and power softened by those perfectly formed curves.

A predatory hunger sharpened her gaze as it swept over their prominent sexual organs and her fingers convulsed as if she wanted nothing more than to reach out and stroke them. But she didn't. The scent of desire rose around them and dizziness overtook him.

What did it feel like for a woman, to have all that blood rushing to her genital area and engorging those folds of flesh? Was she dizzy too? Did arousal feel the same for her as it did for a guy? Did it feel better? Her clit was swollen beyond any he'd ever seen, so big and shiny it reminded him of a plum. A juicy, ripe plum. Or an apple, like, Eve, tempting them with her flawless forbidden fruit.

A thread of delighted laughter flickered through his mind and he cocked his head, wondering where it came from. An apple? It was her voice, Aphrodite, but she wasn't speaking, only staring at him with a tiny smile lifting the corners of her mouth. It would be very hard for a woman to walk if her clit were the size of an apple, my friend.

True, I guess. His own lips lifted in a wry grin, even as he wondered how the hell he was conversing with someone without even opening his mouth. Again his eyes were drawn to her sexual parts and the urge to leap across the bed and sink his dick into her body became almost overwhelming. God, I want to fuck you so bad, Aphrodite. I don't know why we had to stop.

"Why?" Hugh asked the question hovering on Kier's lips.

"Because we need to wait for our fourth."

Ash.

A flicker of jealousy shot through him, unexpected, unwanted. But there nonetheless.

"Speaking of whom…" she said, turning to look at the door. The end of her tongue flicked out, wetting her lips and turning them to a glistening rose that matched the color of her pussy. "He's here."

A gesture of her hand and somehow the door was open and there was Ashur, looming large and glowering at them all with accusation in his gaze.

CHAPTER FOUR

Hugh's heart skipped a beat as it always did when Ash entered a room. He tightened his hold on Kier. If he only knew what effect he had on the people around him. The force of his personality was always so intense that every other guy in the room would fade into insignificance when he entered. Except maybe Kieran, whose tousled hair and light dusting of freckles gave him a charm that was hard to forget, even in Ashur's almost overwhelming presence.

That strength of character was what had elevated Ash to Station Officer well ahead of the others, and what made his angst and self-loathing over Aiden's death all the harder to witness. His once-strong friend was hurting badly, with no idea how to process his grief, and Hugh had no idea what to do to help him through it. He could do nothing for the angst tearing Ash apart except to shove his worry back into the hidden compartment in his mind where all his feelings now resided. That's how he pictured it, anyway. Like a little black suitcase of horror, somewhere deep inside, and if he could only keep it locked away it wouldn't escape and destroy him the way it was destroying his two friends.

He was their calm. The voice of reason, and they needed him to stay that way in order to somehow get past this tragedy in their lives.

Calm. Reason. He let out a spurt of laughter. Impossible, when this beautiful goddess who could seemingly perform magic had appeared out of nowhere to turn their boring man fest into a full-on orgy.

"How the hell did you get here ahead of me? There's only one path up from the beach." Ash was looking at Aphrodite as he spoke and understanding dawned in Hugh's still sex-hazed mind. They'd met already, down there on the sand, and clearly Ash hadn't been as cooperative as she'd have liked.

Well, well.

The tension in the room ratcheted up a notch as Aphrodite straightened from her reclining position and shook back her hair. Hugh's breath caught at the beauty of its dark mass cascading over one shoulder and curving around her breast. But there was a deliberate carelessness to the movement that rang false. She was watching Ash too closely, and there was something slightly self-conscious in her demeanor that hadn't been there before he arrived.

His stomach flip-flopped. This could get very interesting.

"I do not lie. I told you on the beach I am a goddess, but it is up to you whether you believe me or not."

There was a crazy buzz of energy in the air around them, like they were standing under high voltage power lines. Prickles swept over his body and the hair on his forearms stood up in response. Beneath his fingers, goose bumps rose on Kier's flesh and he automatically stroked his friend's hip, seeking to calm. He couldn't focus properly on Aphrodite. She was shimmering, he knew that much–a luminous silver-white effect that surrounded her and obscured his vision, but he could tell she still locked stares with Ash.

For an instant she didn't look human. Maybe she really is a goddess.

Of course I am. A lonely one. Will you help me, Hugh? Will you help me…help him?

His eyes widened at the pleading in his head. But she hadn't spoken aloud. He'd swear it. Neither Kier nor Ash had even blinked. What the…

If we push him hard, make him jealous, maybe he'll relent. Help me, Hugh. You and I between us, we can help him through this. We can help them both. And in doing that, maybe I can help you all.

She had moved closer on the bed and her fingers were entangled now in Kier's light brown hair, alternately clenching then stroking, while her fierce gaze was still locked on Ash. Help both of his friends through this mess? Nothing would please him more.

Okay. Can't believe I'm speaking back to a phantom in my head but…yeah. Okay. Let's do this. "Ash." He cleared his throat, praying for guidance. "You can stand there all night and watch if you like, or you could come in and join us, you know. Either way, the lady wants to be fucked. Kier and I are…in."

Jeez. Something was guiding his tongue, for sure. Something – or someone – who knew that the disrespectful words would goad Ash into action. But what kind of action?

Ashur's fingers clenched reflexively as he took a step into the room and the scowl on his face deepened. Yep. He's definitely pissed.

"I…can't."

Aphrodite stiffened. "You can, but you choose not to, and I don't understand why. How can you not love me? How can you…dislike me so?"

"You think I dislike you?" Ashur's voice was raspy, his

laugh short and painful on the ear. "I don't dislike you, Aphrodite. I don't even know you. None of us do. You can't just walk in and say fuck me, and then expect undying love. It doesn't work that way. Lust and love...they're different things."

"Not in my experience," she said. Curiosity and bafflement decorated her features. "I've never met anyone like you." Her tone was wistful. "I feel your need. Your sexual need. It's as strong...maybe stronger...than these two combined."

She gestured at Hugh and Kieran. The latter snorted and muttered quietly to Hugh. "Maybe that's 'cause, unlike us, he hasn't been laid in over two months."

But Aphrodite was still studying Ash, frowning. "Is it possible that mortals separate the physical from the emotional? Could that be how it works here? Could it be that even I could learn something from you all?"

Ash expelled an exasperated breath and Hugh saw the tension holding those wide shoulders tight loosen a touch. A good sign. "Look, man," he said. "Either step up and join us, or stand back and watch."

Kier shifted beside him. "Or leave."

He laid a hand on Kier's bicep, squeezed gently. A reminder to stay calm, to stay away from the impulsive responses that guided most of Kieran's actions. A reminder that if he wanted to goad their fragile friend it should be done in such a way as to elicit the right action without going beyond what he could take.

For an instant weariness overtook him and his shoulders slumped. How long would he have to perform this balancing act between two friends who both had darkness tugging at their soul? What if he wasn't strong enough to support them?

What if he never found a way to help them heal from this thing that was destroying them all? What if he faltered at some point, or wasn't there to deal with the situation if one or the other of them ever flared into full-blown rage?

Hugh. It is not your role to heal them. Not alone. I will help you. I will support you. I will be there for you as much as for them.

Aphrodite? Is it you in my head? Sudden tears pricked and he blinked several times trying to keep them from falling. Tough guys didn't cry. Tough guys sucked it up and somehow found the strength. He straightened his back. I do have the strength to do this. I know it. Whether it came from her support, or whether it was already inside of him, either way he would be there for his friends as long as they needed him.

"The lady wants this, and so do we." It was hard to get the words out. His throat ached with the effort of holding in the tears.

"What I want is all of us naked. And that includes you, Ashur." Aphrodite flicked a hand and he felt a whoosh of warm air skim through the room.

He let out a disbelieving laugh. "Um, what just happened?"

Kier's mouth had dropped open. "His clothes like... morphed off him."

They all observed Ash, who was standing there in the buff with a stunned look on his face and sporting an erection bigger than anyone else in the room. Longer, wider, and far more impatient-looking, his cock pointed skyward in a proclamation of extreme need. His dark-haired friend's body was visibly vibrating, clearly wound so tight it was a miracle he didn't spray all over the carpet, or perhaps the ceiling given his aim, but even as he lifted a hand to bring Ash into their circle of three, his friend took a deliberate step back and leaned casually against the wall. Fisted hands one each side of his hips gave lie to the casual stance.

"You want this?" Ash was watching Aphrodite carefully, a dark flush staining his cheeks.

"I want all of you," she said. "Please, Ashur."

A quick shake of the head. "No. But I'll stay and watch."

Her lips thinned. "Fine. Your friends have no problem accepting my offering. See?"

The urge to touch her grew until it overwhelmed all of his senses. Sight, smell, hearing, touch, all became attuned to Aphrodite. The air even tasted of her. On some level he knew this was not all of his own doing, but he couldn't seem to help himself. She exuded sex. Not sex appeal, but straight-out sex.

She was sex. How could anyone resist her curves, her statuesque body, or her beauty so pure and perfect? Yearning slackened Kier's features and Hugh knew his own face must mirror his friend's as sensation surged through his system and found a ready home in his groin.

Heat, and hardness, and devastating need. Ramped up one million times from anything he had ever felt before. His brain stopped working and all the blood in his body migrated instantly to his cock.

Blindly, he reached out and found her shoulder, gripping it hard and coercing her down onto the puffy coverlet. He dived on top of her, a position normally reserved for Ash or Kier, not caring about anyone or anything else except the need to force his desperate erection deep into her beautiful, perfect body. She was neither woman nor man to him in that moment, merely a willing partner whose need to connect enticed him in and held him enthralled. Her legs parted, showing the way even when he couldn't think for himself, couldn't concentrate on anything bar this woman, this goddess, who had suddenly become his universe. His everything.

"Aphrodite!" He thrust, impossibly hard, cramping his own butt cheeks in the process, and without even knowing how it happened he found himself home, inside her body. She cried out, a sound filled with joy, and want, and satisfaction as her pussy lips sucked him in and closed around his flesh. Tight. Hot. Wet. Like she would never let him go.

So she liked it hard. He thrust again, and then again, pumping harder and more violently than he'd ever dared in the past. Fear of splitting her in two should have tempered his movements but he couldn't help himself. She just laughed and wrapped eager legs around his hips.

"You can't hurt me, Hugh." Her voice was deep, elemental. "Not with anything physical."

The words centered him, brought some semblance of thought process back into his brain. Oh, God, Ash! And Kier! Where the hell…

A ripple of pressure along his dick showed him where Kier had disappeared to. He'd gone deep, driving into her body from behind. Her inner flesh clamped more tightly around him. They were lying on their sides, Aphrodite facing him, one leg hooked up around his waist. Hugh could feel the movement both within and without as her channel yielded to the thickness of Kier's erection. He had breached her asshole, at some point when Hugh was lost in his own sexual haze, and was now grunting and pounding and creating exquisite pressure against Hugh's cock as he did so.

How did it feel for her?

He moaned and tried to stop moving, to savor the moment, but it was so difficult when all he wanted to do was fuck hard and fast. "That feels so fucking fantastic."

"Yeah." Kier's voice was hoarse. His exposed leg cradled Aphrodite's and rested somewhere around Hugh's hip. He looked down at their limbs curving over his side, one white and slender and smooth, the other tanned and impressively muscled and with a light covering of wiry brown hair.

These two people were protecting him with their leggy embrace, and he slipped his hand beneath Kier's bent knee to pull their bodies closer. We are one. For these few seconds more, we are as close as it is possible to be, at least physically. The hair on Kier's thigh crackled beneath his fingertips and the hard nubs of Aphrodite's nipples poked into his chest. Her breath was sweet in his face. Somebody's hand whispered down his back, tracing along his spine and digging with their fingernails deep into his ass cheek, but he couldn't for the life of him identify whose it was. Breathing, harsh and uneven, filled the air around him.

"Argh." He couldn't speak for wanting, except to make these inarticulate gurgling noises. The thrusting began again though he couldn't tell who started it. Slowly at first and then faster, building in momentum and becoming almost rhythmical as he tag-teamed with Kier deep within Aphrodite's warm wet passage.

The feeling of energy, of light, of impending explosion, built until he could hold it in no longer. He let out a half-strangled shout as he came and Kier followed suit about three seconds later. He shuddered as his load released into this beautiful woman in a rush of seed that seemed to go on forever. His mouth opened, his neck muscles clenched tight and he arched his back as the feeling went on and on.

When the frenzy finally loosed its hold on his body, Kier's still gasping breaths permeated his haze, as did the pain in his bicep where his friend had gripped him when they came. Gripped hard, too. There'd be a bruise there in the morning, and… oh, shit! Aphrodite! He unclenched his hold on her hip and saw the imprinted red fingermarks. Had he hurt her in his thirst for fulfillment? It wasn't like him to do anything so rough. He was known for being gentle, for reigning in the more testosterone-filled passions of the others.

But there was no discomfort in her features. Instead his gaze met amused feminine eyes so dark with craving he couldn't tell what color they were. Not purple anymore. Closer to black. Then she turned her head away from him and looked across the room.

"See? These boys are mine, Ashur, and you should be, too."

Fuck! He'd forgotten Ash again. Just for a few minutes, he'd forgotten everything but his own need. His head whipped around and he realized Ash had made his way silently across from his place near the wall. He was standing over them, staring down with longing and envy sparring in his craggy face.

The beautiful strength of Ashur's body created an ache deep inside. Incredibly, his now sated penis stirred, still inside Aphrodite and wet with his own creamy cum. This close he could see that Ash was trembling, and he wanted nothing more than to slip his friend's dick into his mouth and suck. I want to taste you, Ash. I want to suck you dry, until there is nothing left inside of you. No seed, no need. And no guilt, or regret, or pain.

But he knew that wasn't going to happen. Ash was forbidden fruit when it came to him and Kier. And now, it seemed, he might even be off limits for the goddess of desire herself.

Her need surged through him, as did Kier's, or was it all still his own? He couldn't tell the difference. There was only one thing missing from the moment. One person who could make it all perfect.

"Join us," he said. "Please, Ash, it'll do you so much good. And no one's going to die, man. Not this time. It'll be okay, I promise."

Aphrodite's here to help us.

CHAPTER FIVE

Ash couldn't take his eyes off them. Off her. She was beautiful, flawless, and her presence drew him in like nothing he'd ever felt before. Usually he liked to dominate during sex, and down on the beach he'd sensed that she liked to do the same. Even here, though she had not taken the lead with his friends. There was a muted strength and power that was paramount in every gesture, every movement, and every slanting look of those unusual eyes, yet he could tell that she was holding her power on a very tight leash.

Waiting for me.

He knew it. The coil of its presence licked at his bones. It should have had him running, but instead it excited him in a way he hadn't felt in...shit. *I've never felt like this.*

Why? What was it about her that kept his gaze fixed on their rutting bodies? He couldn't look away. Why was she taunting him with his two best friends who would never be strong enough to say no to someone like her? Was that why she'd chosen them? Because she knew they would be powerless to resist even when they must know how hard it was for him to be here, watching. How wrong it felt.

Like a betrayal of Aiden's memory.

It didn't look wrong, though. It looked like perfection, the three of them lying there, connected physically as if they were one. Strangely, the two men appeared both sated and wired, while the woman sandwiched between them moved with a hint of restlessness. Her physical needs were still unfulfilled and it gave her beauty an edge of voracious hunger. If he had joined in as she wished, would she still be unsatisfied? Or would he have been able to fulfill her craving in a way that the others had not?

If he'd thrust into her with this darkness driving him, instead of the more tender Hugh, she might have bucked madly beneath his hips and screamed her orgasmic release to the world. He ached to fuck her, just like he'd done to other women in the past without even thinking about it. But every time sex came into the equation, all he could think of was Aiden, and how he'd died because Ash had been busy with a one night stander he'd met at a club, instead of being on duty and ready to assist his men.

Station Officer. Jesus. Fat lot of good he'd done them all. If he'd checked his phone and read the message earlier, he might have gotten there in time instead of at the tail end when the building was already beginning to collapse. Aiden had always been reckless. And it had been Ashur's job to keep him reigned in.

His leg throbbed as he leaned against the wall, curling his fingertips back and forth over textured wallpaper. The pain was a grim reminder of everything there was to hate about this situation. But still he didn't move away. Instead he remembered the softness of her skin when he held her in his arms on the beach, and took a step toward them. Then again, closer still, compelled by God knows what to inch slowly in toward the threesome.

There was a strange beauty encapsulated in the sight of their bodies moving in unison that he had never realized before. Always, until now, he'd been in the center of the action, caught up in the throes of passion and with no idea what they might actually look like as they all made love together.

Now he knew. The revelation sent a wave of eagerness rippling through his body and his already hard member jerked up until it was angled almost vertical. The veins on his cock were engorged, the skin so constricted he wondered if he might split right out of it. His balls were pulled tight with the force of his erection.

Even his asshole throbbed. Like someone was thrumming a practiced thumb over the entrance, pressing at the flesh around it, teasing his prostate to join in the pleasure of the moment.

Control. I want it back. But his body refused to cooperate and an agonized groan escaped. Every muscle twitched and shook with need, readying for climax whether he willed it or not.

Kier and Hugh looked up at him with an unfocused mix of both sheepish regret and rekindled desire. They'd just come, for Christ's sake. And they were ready to go again.

He wanted to answer Hugh, and to tell them both it was okay, to just forget him and go for it, but the words caught in his throat. It wasn't okay. This commanding woman had dually seized his interest and raised his ire, tempting him to break his sexual fast with her long powerful body and generous curves. She should have been laying beneath him, pliant and submissive, her wrists captured in his impenetrable grip and her heels drumming madly on his glutes while he plowed her so deep she would feel it all the way up into her throat.

His lips parted and pre-cum squeezed out and dribbled down his erection. God, it would feel so fucking good.

Instead she lay there between his friends, her head thrust back on the pillow and locks of shiny hair decorating Kier's chest and shoulders as if proclaiming ownership over his body. In that position, the pulse point in her neck was exposed to his view and he could see how rapidly her heart was beating. Impulse had him bending to press his lips to that spot but Kier got there first, ducking in from behind and nipping at the join of flesh where neck curved into shoulder.

He snapped back into place, hoping no one had noticed his futile lunge toward her and took a tiny step back, afraid of the intensity of his emotions. Afraid of what he might do if he climbed onto the bed and touched any one of them. Afraid of why.

"I don't know what's happening." He clenched his fists, short nails digging shallow crescents in his palms. Something in him enjoyed the sudden pain. A reminder, like the incessant ache in his thigh, that he didn't deserve any better. In the aftermath of their orgasm all was quiet bar their breathing. "Hugh, Kier…I…"

"Shh." Hugh as usual reached out first, stroked his arm, and clasped his hand. "It'll be okay."

"Yeah, man." Kier was more awkward than Hugh, but the sincerity shone from his eyes as he added, "It'll be all right. Join us. Aphrodite wants you. We all do."

He didn't think his cock could get any harder. It'd be gushing like a broken water pipe in a minute. But there was no space for him to join in this cozy ménage a trois, even if he'd wanted it.

There is always a place for you here beside us. Beside me. In me. We can learn from each other, Ashur. We can learn to heal.

That voice in his head again, and he knew it was hers. What magic was she weaving in this room tonight, that he would even consider…

"Here. Take my place, Ash." Hugh slipped out of her and rolled off the bed, coming up to stand beside him. His member glistened at half-mast in the golden light cast by the reading lamp. Kier must have left it on when he went to bed earlier. He knew that Kier didn't like the dark, since that night.

Then Kieran was there too, and Aphrodite. He was surrounded by people who reached out to caress him. He closed his eyes. It wouldn't hurt for a moment, surely, to just give in and enjoy the sensations. Questing fingertips skated across his arms, his chest, down to his groin. A hand gripped his cock, too large and indelicate to be hers, but he could fight this urge no longer. His head fell back and he gave in to the feel of moist lips and tongue sucking him in, not caring whose mouth it was, and yet also caring too much. Who had control of his manhood, of his sex? Who had such exquisite expertise as they licked and sucked and pulled the ready juice out of him and down into their throat?

A male body was behind him, the slick wet head of a cock prodding between his ass cheeks with a persistence that made him want to bend over and be fucked for the first time in his life. And then…oh, God! There were lips on his thigh. On his scar. Someone was raining tiny kisses all over the disgusting puckered flesh before dragging their moist tongue back and forth across his skin.

How could they face doing that?

His eyes flashed open. It was Hugh who had sucked him in deep, so deep that the top of his cock hit the back of his friend's hot throat when his hips shuddered in an instinctive thrusting response. It felt so fucking good. He couldn't believe he'd made such a big deal about not doing this in the past.

Hugh. He wanted to laugh, and cry at the same time. Who knew?

Breath laced with a familiar whiskey smell was hot and hard against his neck, identifying Kier behind him. His buddy was busy back there, stroking his body and caressing the crease where his butt cheek met his leg, teasing his ass in the most delightful way possible.

But his senses honed in on Aphrodite. She was kneeling in front of him, side by side with Hugh, and she was touching his scar. Celebrating the mutilated flesh on his leg with her lips, and tongue, and even her fingertips.

"Aphrodite," he whispered. And that's when the shaking began. Real shaking, as if he had a fever of some kind and his body was no longer his own. "I don't want...I want..." He couldn't get his tongue around the quaking words. Couldn't get his brain around the thoughts. "I don't know what I want."

Tears squeezed out of the corners of his eyes and an ache formed deep in his ears and throat as he held in a sob. Jesus. I'm better than this. I'm stronger. But he just stood there, unresisting, tears falling silently as he let them all love him. One hand became lost deep in the softness of Aphrodite's hair, the other gripped a fistful of Hugh's shorter locks to assist the movement back and forth. He was desperate for release and terrified he would find it.

Damn. The man's pretty good at this.

Even with Hugh's compelling action Aphrodite kept calling his attention back to her, just by her presence in the room. Her breath on his leg was like a zap of energy that went well beyond the surface. It burrowed deep into the darkness inside of him. "I want to heal it, this scar," she said between kisses. "But I won't. I understand now. It's a symbol, isn't it? A symbol of your heroism and sense of responsibility. Your ability to be the one to go in and rescue others. Even when it's not your place to do so."

"No." His denial sounded weak, even to his own ears, yet who the hell could blame him? Hugh kept sucking hard and Kier was now sliding his member all the way along Ashur's butt crack until the rounded head touched the back of his balls and smeared them with wetness. Jee-sus. And overlaying it all, her breath, her touch, consuming him.

He lurched inside Hugh's mouth. "It's…" The attempt at laughter came out wrong. "It's a symbol of my failure. My inability to save him. To save Aiden."

His voice cracked and the damn sob escaped despite his best efforts. Then he was crying for real, weeping like a woman, and he wished the floor would open and just suck him away. He couldn't do this. Not in front of the guys. They didn't need to see him like this. Still the sobs wracked his body, and he just…couldn't…stop…

In his peripheral vision he detected Kieran pushing Hugh off him before both guys stepped back and away. It was just Aphrodite in front of him then, standing up in a quick fluid movement and reaching out to push his fringe back from his face with a tenderness he hadn't experienced since childhood.

He was struck once again by her unusual height. Not many women could stand almost eye to eye with him. With his stupid, wet, crying eyes. His mouth twisted and heat washed from his chest all the way up to the roots of his hair.

"I'm such a fucking weakling." He couldn't even look at Kier or Hugh.

No. There's not a weak cell in your body, gorgeous man. I know it. And so do the others. "It was not your fault, Ashur." She followed him when he shook his head and tried to step back. She was good at doing that, he was beginning to realize. She slipped her arms around his waist as if to hold him in place, and cradled her head in the hollow of his shoulder.

Damn annoying woman. But his arms came up to hold her in return. "You weren't there," he said. "You don't know."

She sighed and her breasts pressed into his chest like living cushions. Her fresh perfume wound through the room, reminding him of the herb garden at the rear of this property. He'd stumbled into it one night early on, before he'd taken to walking the beach, and been assailed by oregano, and rosemary, and mint. Other exotic spices were there too, but he had no idea what they were. He could smell them all and more in Aphrodite's breath and in her hair, and it was an intoxicating aroma.

"I see it in here." She cradled his face in her hands and tapped a light finger at his temple. "I relive it every time you do. As do your friends over there. And you owe it to them to start putting this behind you at last. It's not about trying to forget. Nor about moving on without heart or soul. It is time to begin the healing process."

"I owe it to them?" He glanced toward Kieran, who'd been with him in a threesome that night and who'd driven with him to the incident when they both got the text message. And Hugh, who'd been alone at home, oblivious to the unfolding tragedy until he'd turned up for his shift the next day.

Was his behavior contributing to their grief? Was his black despair destroying these two men as well as himself? The answer was evident in their stricken expressions as they sat thigh to thigh on the edge of the bed and stared back at him.

"So, I have that to answer for, too?"

"Ash." She clicked her fingers to bring his attention back

to her and his brows came together at the action. Bossy even in this moment. "You do not need to answer for any of it. Aiden was on duty that night. You were not. He chose to take the extra shift. His decision. Not yours. The Acting Station Officer told them not to go into the building at that point because it wasn't safe to do so. Aiden ignored that directive. Again, his choice, not yours. His intentions were good, of course they were. Your wonderful friend Aiden was brave as well as reckless. He wanted to find the person who was still trapped in the building, and he did not know that the man had already been dragged out one of the windows at the back. It is not fair that he passed from this world too soon, trying to do good and save a life. But this tragedy is not down to you. No matter what you were doing at the time. No matter who you were…" She bowed her head, caressed his face with soothing fingers. "…fucking at the time."

His own thoughts were being flung straight back at him. "How can you do that? How do you know?"

Fingers burrowed into his hair and clutched tightly, no longer soothing but pulling instead at his scalp. "Come with me, Ash. Come with me into my world, into my space. Learn me, and then you will not need to ask such questions."

"I don't know what you mean." But even as he said the words he was falling. Falling into space, and light, and infinity, all the while held tight by the woman whose embrace was never-ending, and whose grip was the only thing separating him from the abyss of despair.

CHAPTER SIX

Aphrodite bit the inside of her lip, even as she concentrated on holding Ash aloft. Had she stepped over the line, exposing herself to his awareness like this? What if he took the knowledge and used it against her? Against every god or goddess in existence?

Even as her mind formed the thoughts she knew she was on the wrong track. Stupid, he'd called her when they first met, and yes, he had been correct. She was stupid to think that Ashur was a man who would take knowledge and use it for betrayal or harm.

He was a hero, this man she held suspended within her energy and her power. The man she had invited in to her core. He deserved everything she could show him and more, even if he and his friends had nothing to give her in return.

A thread of shrewd laughter tickled the edges of her mind and she tried to shut them out, needing to concentrate on Ash. Later, my beautiful erotes. I will speak with you later. But somewhere deep inside, the floodgates had opened and their approval and love began pouring in to fill her.

Channel it, she thought. Use it to fill him. Don't keep it for yourself.

She built the light, golden and warm, and sent it barreling through Ash; an endless supply of love from every aspect of Eros. There was yearning from Pothos, and her beautiful desire in Himeros, and finally there was her love both requited and unrequited. Thank you, Anteros. Thank you my sons.

All of it channeled through her essence and into Ash. Her soul, he might call it, if he cared to give it a name. It would feel like a blast of electricity, she knew, zipping through his blood and energizing every cell. His eyes were full of shock and awe as he stared back at her from the center of her being, and joy filled her as she met his gaze.

"I'm not used to showing myself," she admitted, her voice huskier than the norm. "But it feels right." This was based on emotion, not lust, and she wasn't used to dealing with emotion. But regardless of what happened, she would not change her decision to let him in.

He nodded. "Feels right to me, too."

Hesitantly she opened her mind to her sons. "You are doing it, Mother." Their voices would not be silenced and she allowed the soothing words to wash over her. "You have gone beyond the physical, Aphrodite, and now you can begin to heal."

Ω Ψ Ω

They were falling backward into his memories. There was Aiden, laughing and carefree as they played a game of cards during down time at the station. There were his parents, grinning widely when he completed his training and qualified as a firey. There was his first day in the program, the newbies all lined up in the yard looking like scared little rabbits, and they found themselves standing between Kier and Hugh. "We can be the four musketeers," Aiden had joked, and Kier had snorted.

"Weren't there three?"

Hugh had smiled quietly and leaned forward. "No, he's right. There were four, actually." And that was that. The four musketeers, who had stuck together from that moment on through the good, the bad, and at times the downright ugly.

There too was the high school teacher who had changed the course of his life. "You boys have to stop mucking around and start thinking seriously about what you want to do with your lives. Ash, we talked in careers counselling about the Metropolitan Fire Brigade, and you might be interested to know I've organized a rep to come out to the school next month. But Aiden, you can't just do whatever Ash chooses. At some point you need to find your own path in life."

"Why can't I do what he does?" Aiden had grinned his irrepressible grin and followed Ash into fire training after all. Just like everyone had known he would.

"Ah." Aphrodite shifted against him. "That's why," she murmured. They fell further then, deeper, and earlier. He was a small boy once again, playing airplanes in the garden, running with his arms outstretched through his mother's flower beds even though she'd told him not to. But the flight path went that way. Surely Mamma would understand. Happiness flooded him, the joy of youth and innocence.

Heat from the sun on his cheeks. The sound of the dog barking as it scampered along the flight path behind him. The feeling of freedom, of a weightless time before responsibility for others took its toll. He breathed deeply and it felt like his first real breath in forever. He could smell the perfume of flowers in his nostrils and it all seemed so real.

"It is real," she said.

"I forgot what it felt like. To be happy."

"I know, gorgeous man. Soak it up, soak it in. And remember that feeling, when we return to the present once again."

Do we have to return?

On impulse he leaned down toward the nearest bush and was only partly surprised when his fingers actually connected physically with one of the flowers growing there.

Magic? Yeah. He could believe in anything, at this moment.

He plucked it, the tiny perfect frangipani blossom with its white outer petals and bright yellow center, and tucked it into her hair just above one ear. "Thank you," he said, and was rewarded not with her usual bright laugh but with an astonished look that swept across her face.

She reached up and touched the flower, gentle fingers exploring, wonder in her eyes. "No mortal has ever given me a gift before."

His brows lifted. "I find that hard to believe."

"No. I mean it." Her lips were parted and she was staring up at him with luminous eyes. Liquid violet, with shock still bright in their depths. "Other than physical gratification, of course, but for me that is as natural as breathing is for you." She touched the flower again. "This…makes me want to cry."

"Why? It's just a flower."

"It is so much more than that, Ash."

Now it was his turn to cup her face. "No crying. Not here in this happy place." His tone turned wry and he gripped her chin a little more firmly. "Wherever here is."

She chuckled. "We are in your mind, Ash. Your memories. And my tears…are ones of joy, not sadness. It is a happy place here, isn't it? It can be again, you know. You've proven it yourself. The darkness…it will always be there, but if you can just remember this part of yourself, when we return to the others, there can maybe be a balance, between the two."

His heart thumped painfully. I want to. I hope I can.

She grimaced a little, as if she'd heard him. Most likely she had. Of course you can.

He bent and touched his lips to hers, a gentle caress. "Only if you promise to remember this." He tapped the flower gently, traced the outline of one of its petals, and then tried to secure it more firmly in her hair. She brought up her hand to cover his.

"Of course. This is a moment in time, past, present and for all time to come, that I will never ever forget. I promise you that, Ashur Dane."

The light grew around them, impossibly bright, and a warm blast ruffled his hair and skin. "So it's time to go back, then?"

A quick nod signaled her answer. "Your friends are waiting, and they take their cue from you. I know what a huge responsibility it is, to have two men – once three, when Aiden was still in this world – looking to you for guidance. You are like their parent in a way, but one whose children have chosen a dangerous path as fighters of fire. What do you call them? Fireys."

She tapped his temple, then moved down and pressed her hand over the left side of his chest. "If you can remember the nature of happiness, and hold onto that memory here in your heart, you will learn to be whole again. Your strength will return and it will help Kieran and Hugh to recover, too. Especially Kieran. He doesn't share the inner peace that keeps

Hugh sane, so he looks to you for emotional stability, as Aiden once did."

"What if I fail Kier too?"

"You didn't fail Aiden. You were always his friend, his guiding light, his happiness. You made your decisions, and you know what? So did Aiden. He chose to become a fire-fighter because that's what he wanted to do, not because you forced him into it. He chose, just as you did, and just as you will choose the right path, when we return to your friends at the inn. You will not fail Kieran."

"And if I pick the wrong path?"

"Oh, Ash." She touched the flower and her essence surrounded him. Warmth and safety. Love. Astonishment. Joy. "You gave me this, when I needed it most. My sons trusted in you and they are being proven right by your actions. You will follow in their example, and you will not choose wrong."

Dizziness blasted his head and he closed his eyes to block it out. Then Aphrodite was shaking him by the arm and he could hear Kieran murmuring to Hugh. "He looks better, don't you think? Kind of shiny, like her. But definitely better."

His eyes popped open and they were back in the bedroom at the inn. Everything looked the same as it had only minutes earlier – had it really been only minutes? – and yet everything was changed irrevocably.

"So I look shiny, Kier?" He managed a grin at the two of them, sitting on the bed gaping at him like Tweedle Dum and Tweedle Dee, and he wondered how long it had been since they'd actually seen his smile.

"A bit," Kier said, hesitation in his voice.

"But in a good way," Hugh added quickly.

"Ash." She spoke quietly, with an uncertainty that he

imagined did not come naturally, and he extended his smile to include her, too.

You don't need to say my name, Aphrodite. Can't you tell I'm hyper-aware of you?

She was standing only a few feet away, and his body still zinged with whatever she'd blasted through him in that weird nowhere land. It was as if he was bound to her essence, soul to soul. Her predatory need was still there, he could feel the pull of it even now when she was trying to tamp it down. But her generosity of spirit—her love—shone just as bright.

Ashur, I want so much to be a better person.

Don't you know that for us, for humans, the very act of trying makes it so?

Her eyes widened slightly. *Wise man.* "Will you fuck me now?" she asked. "Will you…fuck with all of us?"

He snorted. "No," he said. "I won't fuck with you." *Is this the right path? I think so.* "But there's nothing I'd like more than to make love with you, Aphrodite. With all of you. If you'll have me."

CHAPTER SEVEN

I f we'll have him? Kieran's heart constricted painfully at the blast of adrenalin from Ashur's capitulation. At last. "Whoa, that was…unexpected."

Hugh hissed in a breath beside him. "Finally," he said, the boyish grin spreading wide.

When Aphrodite and Ash had disappeared in a haze of light and vibration, leaving him sitting on the bed holding hands with Hugh and wondering what the hell was going on, he found himself praying that whatever this was, it would somehow turn out right. For all of them. Now they were back, and Ash had a look on his face that Kier hadn't seen in months. It was a look of hope. There was new life in his eyes too, so that instead of a flat hazel they seemed to flare with hints of vibrant green. A tight squeeze around his palm as Hugh mushed his hand bones together signaled that he wasn't the only one to have noticed the positive change.

Then his mouth dropped open when Ash lunged for Aphrodite and lifted her up into the air and around in a circle. Holy shit. That was something Kier might have done, or even Hugh, but…Ash?

Her delighted laughter rang out through the room and resonated right through to his core. Excitement began to build, but it was different this time. Before it was purely physical, but now, with the knowledge that something had shifted within Ash, it felt more real. Bigger somehow. Like he had permission to relax and properly enjoy it.

So this is why they call it butterflies in the stomach.

Whiskey had been his best friend for the past couple of months, but maybe that friendship was coming to an end. He wouldn't want to blur this moment out of his memory for anything. Even with a twenty year old single malt.

Aphrodite's beautiful scent grew around them and his cock, which had grown flaccid in the time that Ash disappeared, suddenly came charging back to life. Hugh shifted on the bed beside him and he realized they were in a race for the biggest erection. A cock race.

He chuckled. "Which one of us is gonna get to the finish line first?"

Hugh reached out to capture and stroke him and his breath caught. Now that felt pretty damn good. I'll be racing over the finish line well ahead of the others if he keeps that up.

But Hugh gestured with his other hand toward Ash. "I'm thinking maybe him, this time." When Kier glanced up at their friend, who was holding Aphrodite suspended above his cock, he was inclined to agree.

Her legs were wrapped around his waist and in that position her pussy was spread nice and wide. Ash was magnificent in his nakedness, his cock hard and pointing straight up toward her exposed channel entrance. His eyes were wild, his dark hair disheveled, and Kieran loved the way it fell in that careless sweep over his forehead. The normally harsh lines of his face were softened a bit, like a darker version of Hugh and his bed hair.

His dick shifted again as Hugh increased the tempo of his stroking, reminding him of its profound greed. What else could he do but reciprocate? He reached out and gripped the satin-skinned hardness of Hugh.

"Then we'd better catch up to him, man," he said and felt the vibrations of Hugh's laughter through his fingers as he began to pull his friend.

$$\Omega \, \Psi \, \Omega$$

Ash couldn't believe he was about to make love with a Greek goddess. It seemed surreal, this whole experience, and yet there was nothing about the moment he would change. She sat ready in his embrace on a makeshift chair of muscled arms, her hands gripping his shoulders tightly to help maintain balance. In that position her sex was wide open, lined up almost directly over the top of his erection. His leg hurt like hell and it was beginning to twitch, but damned if he was going to lower her yet. Let her squirm for a few more seconds. Let her need it as much as he did right now.

I am already desperate for it, stubborn man. There was gentle laughter in his mind. She ran a thumb slowly across one of his nipples and it hardened instantly. Smaller and flatter than hers, but clearly no less sensitized. He bit his lip to hold in the groan.

"Please," she said. "We've waited so long. Don't make us wait any longer."

He sucked in a ragged breath, imagining her scent as a

tonic for his soul, cleansing and renewing, seeking out the black bits and destroying them with its fragrant beauty.

"Yes," she whispered. "That's it. Let it go. Let it all go."

His straining muscles started shaking in earnest. "I'm afraid." He said it quietly into her cascading tresses as its satiny softness snaked across his lips. For a moment he wasn't sure if she'd heard him. Wasn't sure if he wanted to be heard.

Her embrace tightened. "I know, darling. But I will protect you. I will protect all of you. Lower me."

It was a direct command and a plea all rolled up into one. How could he refuse her? Conviction filled him. This was right, at last. He clutched at her hips and in one swift movement forced her body downward onto his cock. All the way down that long length she slid, until she hit the end of his rod and her pussy slapped against his flesh.

She let out a low moan. "You're so big. You've filled me right up."

"Good." He thrust once, holding her immobile. Warm wet heat embraced his manhood. "Is this what you wanted?" He took a step toward the bed.

She moaned again. "Yes. I feel you, at my core."

"And this?" He plunged again and this time she jerked at the force of the impact, her heels digging into his lower back.

"Yes. More." She was sobbing now, tiny whimpers that ignited passion in his blood, and when he reached the bed Hugh and Kier automatically shifted aside to make room, as if they could sense how close he was already.

He turned and fell backward onto the covers, awkward as hell but somehow managing to keep his body impaled inside her. She wriggled into place until she was sitting astride him with her back slightly arched and the rounded breasts heavy and full above him.

The mattress shifted as Kier knelt beside him and leaned over to suckle at one fleshy globe, Hugh doing the same on her other side. His eyes narrowed as he watched their devotion to her breasts, the breath hissing out between his teeth as he willed them to suck harder. Make her scream.

Kier was dancing around her nipple and flicking its extraordinary length with his tongue, while Hugh had a different response, teasing the edge of her flesh, licking at the seam between breast and rib and then darting upward to take her nipple deep into his mouth. They were driving him crazy with their movements and he could only imagine what it felt like for Aphrodite. He began to buck in a more frenzied pattern as her vagina clamped tight around him.

Hugh let out a groan, then Kier, and then Aphrodite fell forward over Ashur's chest until her breasts—still wet from their lips—squashed against him. "Kieran," she gasped, "I want you inside me, too. Hurry, please…"

She leaned so far forward her luscious butt must have been right there in front of Kier. He could imagine the rim of that tight little pucker at her rear, clenching in readiness and an aching shudder went through him.

Kier maneuvered quickly into place and then stopped. "Without lube? What if this—"

"You won't hurt me. You didn't last time, remember?" Her voice was breathless. "Go deep, Kier, and please go fast."

Ash felt the shift in pressure when Kier's cock head breached her and he let out a grunt of pleasure. "Yeah, man, that feels fucking good."

But Kier stopped. Aphrodite squirmed back and forth, the movement both encouraging Kier and bringing Ash to within a hairs breadth of coming. "Do it," she demanded.

The sudden plunge into her body constricted the moist grip holding Ash prisoner and he let out a strangled yell. It was heaven, and he could no longer control the bucking movements as the need to come overtook him. He began to tag team in a crazy back and forth rhythm with Kier, the thin membrane of her flesh the only separation between them.

Just like in the past, only a million times more meaningful. Especially when it was Aphrodite riding him, gazing down with those amazing eyes, her lips parted and her tongue poking out just a tiny bit to one side as she concentrated on moving her pussy. Her inner muscles gripped him like a pair of grasping hands.

He was being milked. Hard. "Keep doing that," he gasped. "Just like that. It's…argh…"

More weight pressed on his chest then, and he realized Hugh was readying above him to enter Kier from behind. Three of them above him? Yes, he could take the weight. He was strong enough now, especially sunk deep inside this amazing woman and leaching power from her seemingly endless reserves.

You can do this. She was speaking to him from the very center of her heart. He'd been there. He recognized it. And he could never thank her enough.

I know. The anxious need in the faces of his friends began to fade as he reached out to try and fit them all within his embrace. I can support you all.

You don't need to, gorgeous man. I am here to do it with you.

Aphrodite. "Thank you," he whispered. It was so inadequate, that phrase, and yet she accepted it from him with love shining in her eyes. A secret moment, when she was looking just at him. His heart swelled as it began to revisit long-forgotten joy, and then the boys and their needs were back and the moment grew to encompass them all.

"Ready, man?" Hugh's voice was hoarse, desperate, and

Kier nodded frantically behind Aphrodite, bracing for entry. Ash knew the second Hugh pushed inside of his friend. Kier's mouth opened wide and an animal-like groan rolled out of him. Hugh's features were set in a rictus of concentration as he pressed relentlessly forward, and that in turn forced Kier deeper into Aphrodite. She gasped and dug her fingernails into his shoulders and he bucked so hard he lifted all three of them off the bed with his thrusting hips.

"Yes!" She cried out and clenched her channel around him. "I'm coming, Ash. I'm coming right now!" The twin pressure on his cock from her movements, and from Kier, and even vicariously through their bodies from Hugh finally sent him tumbling over the edge into heaven.

"Oh my God!" He let out a strangled cry and shuddered violently.

Then Aphrodite was screaming too as they all tipped together into an amazing, simultaneous orgasm that went on, forever it seemed, in a wild frenzied ride. Thoughts and fears were gone. Black despair was gone. Everything was gone but the image of a white flower with its golden heart imprinting itself on his now closed eyelids, and an incredible sensation of completion that only ended when they collapsed in a boneless tangled heap of limbs and light and breathless laughter.

Ω Ψ Ω

Aphrodite lay replete amongst the jumble of male bodies, the scent of spent semen like a calming tonic to her soul. It was a scenario she had experienced countless times over too many years to admit to, but this time it was different. So different that she couldn't find the words to describe it.

He had given her a flower. A piece of his memory. Maybe he hadn't fully realized the importance of what he'd done in that moment of impulse, but it didn't change the fact of it happening. Ash had moved her to tears in that moment. The recall had her tearing up yet again.

"Hey," he said. "Crying again, Aphrodite?" Gentle lips touched her forehead and she looked up into his craggy face. Ashur. It meant "the beginning", that name, and perhaps it was, for all of them.

Kieran. Hugh. And Ashur. Her mortal lovers. Her heroes. Her new beginning.

She smiled through the tears. "I'm happy," she admitted, and for the first time in eons those words carried truth. "These are tears of joy."

We are happy too, Mother. The echo of her sons washed through the room, their approval and joy an almost tangible presence. She reached out with her essence to embrace them.

Thank you, beautiful boys. But...I guess I proved you wrong in the end, didn't I?

Exasperated laughter swept over her, just as a large thumb smeared the wetness of her tears across her cheek. Ash. "You and I both know a night of passion won't fix everything, Aphrodite. Not really."

"No." She ran her hands over Ashur's chest, enjoying the feel of hard muscle encased beneath soft skin, wanting to ease the pain that was still so ingrained. "It won't. You still have a difficult road ahead of you." She shifted to look at the others and include them in her words.

"So do you, Kieran. And Hugh." She reached up in turn to caress their strong jawlines. Three heroic men who had lost their way for a time. "But today was the beginning of the process of healing. For all of you. You took that first step. The one that is always the hardest."

Arms tightened around her. "One foot in front of the other." That was Kier, beautiful Kier. She snuck a quick kiss on the point of his chin.

"Exactly."

Hugh cleared his throat. "But what about you, Aphrodite? Have you found what you were looking for, tonight? With us?"

She considered his question carefully before answering. "I am at the beginning of my journey, too. Before I arrived here I believed I had lost something vital. I convinced myself I had lost the ability to love."

She let out a self-deprecating laugh. "And that is not good if you are the goddess of love. But in meeting the three of you I have discovered that I still have a working heart after all."

She bit her lip before adding, "And I would really like to stay here awhile and continue this journey with you. If you'll have me, of course?"

It was Ash who answered for all of them, bold and sure. "We wouldn't have it any other way."

Ω Ψ Ω

Please read on for the next instalment in the GODS OF LOVE series.

DEMON OF ENVY

BY JEN KATEMI

DEMON OF ENVY

THON, GOD OF ENVY & JEALOUSY

What's a girl to do when the man of her dreams appears on the doorstep... and it turns out he's a fallen immortal trying to claw his way back toward a state of grace?

Thon holds the petty jealousies and passions of all mortals in his heart. In the beautiful yet damaged Olivia he may finally have found his savior, but his lover's very presence incites the demon inside to escape.

How can the Greek god of envy possibly protect a mortal woman from the grim darkness of his own reality?

"Oh, Liv. If I love you, I might kill you."

CHAPTER ONE

"You want me to walk through the fires of Hell to save you? Phthonos, you ask too much."

"Not to save me, Olivia. To save yourself." The dark tone of his correction shivered down her spine in a sensation that was equal parts fear and desire.

She knew this was a dream; had relived the sleep-induced fiction every night this week. She needed to wake up before the bit where he started to burn, where she reached toward him and...oh God, the flames were consuming him already. It was too fast, and too powerful. His beautiful face twisted in pain and the clear green eyes flashed desperation as he stretched out a clutching hand. She leaned in, connected with his fingers, and the greedy flames engulfed her too...

For the sixth time that week Liv sat bolt upright in bed, the scream still lodged in her throat and the bedcovers in a twisted mess around her legs. Sweat coated her body. Not the heady exotic scent of post-coital perspiration, either. No. This was the sharp acrid scent of sheer terror, of illness. Of something wrong at her core.

She reached for the brown hair tie on her wrist and

snapped it. Once. Twice. A third time. Count to three, then snap again, over and over, the rhythm so familiar by now she didn't need to think. Gradually her heart stopped its uncomfortable thumping and her breathing began to even out. The anxiety attack was receding.

One last snap of the wrist band, the one for luck that she always had to finish with, and she was back in control once again. A swift kick with her left foot removed the sheet and she climbed wearily out of bed before turning back to straighten the tangled covers. Phthonos. Whoever the heck you are, whichever little piece of my imagination that you sprang from, you need to let me get some sleep, hon.

The thought of her sexy dream companion sent an ache directly to her belly, and for a moment she wondered what it would be like if he were real. Would he gaze at her the way he did in the dream, before the flames took him? With those green eyes softening into hungry desire as if she were the only person on earth who really mattered. Or would he look her up and down, note her sweat-soaked flannel pajamas that highlighted rather than hid the extra pounds she'd gained recently, and turn away from her in disgust?

A tiny laugh escaped as she caught sight of herself in the mirrored wardrobe door. Suspicious hazel eyes stared back, the faint vestiges of fear still visible if you knew what to look for. Yep. Her lips twisted. Prime fantasy material to capture the imagination of a sexy god right there. Especially with her new haircut—the supposedly always sleek pixie-do—now sticking out unevenly in every direction and looking nothing like it had when she left the hairdresser a few days ago.

She reached up a hand and tried to smooth out some of the dark brown kinks, but gave up after a moment with a defeated shrug. There was no point. She'd never be a beauty, and her gorgeous Phthonos, who'd begun visiting her almost a month ago now, was merely a recurring dream that for some reason this week kept turning into a nightmare right before she awoke.

You need to save yourself.

Liv frowned and shook her head to dispel the last of the panic. It was after five in the morning, and she knew from previous days that sleep would elude her if she went back to bed now. Instead she headed for the shower to wash away the sweat and the panic. For some reason though, the taint of wrongness remained this time instead of disappearing down the plug hole.

The water cascading over her body was warm and comforting. She closed her eyes, trying to forget the dream. The memory of his eyes stayed with her no matter how hard she scrubbed at her scalp with the vanilla-scented shampoo. That sex-filled gaze set free the crazy butterflies dancing inside her stomach and woke the ache of desire between her legs. It had been so long since a man had touched her there. Oh yes, just there, circling and teasing at her clit. Right there where the gush of water from the hand-held shower head was now concentrating its tickling stream.

A ragged sigh escaped, and she braced her other hand against the tiles to steady herself, directing the jet even closer between the swelling folds of her flesh. Her clit ached for a man's touch, for a man's lips to close around it and suck.

No. Not just any man. It had to be Phthonos. She yearned for her sexy dream companion to be real, and to be here right now, kneeling in front of her and kissing her sex in the most intimate way possible. Or even more enticing, to go exploring with his fingers. To part her vulvar lips, then tilt her hips upward and thrust into her with his long, darting tongue. The shower was a double one, so there would be plenty of room for them both to do whatever took their fancy.

What would it feel like to have Phthonos prepare her with his breath, his mouth, his fingers, and then rise from his knees and lift her up and then down onto the water-slicked head of his hot, hard organ? He'd do it without any effort at all, despite her weight, and he'd tell her he loved the way her curves were full and lush. He'd say how much he adored everything about her, from her unruly brown hair right down to her slightly crooked pinky toes.

She moaned, imagining her channel full of him, and rocked back and forth beneath the gushing water before dropping the shower head and taking over with her fingers. The release was too quick. She shuddered, her pelvis jerking in spasms and leg muscles quivering as the last vestiges of anxiety fell away and welcome sensation rolled through her body.

Hell yes. Oh, Phthonos.

When her heart rate began to slow to a more normal level, she bent to pick up the discarded shower head. A rush of sadness brought tears to her eyes. Her body might be replete, but the ache of loneliness was stronger than ever. It was always this way after she'd brought herself to orgasm. Especially this past month, when she imagined it was Phthonos right there beside her. Inside her.

Unfortunately it was just a dream, and this empty apartment in the cold light of dawn was her reluctant reality. She took a deep breath and let it out slowly. Reality sucked, but this year it was going to be different. This was the year she was determined to become the mistress of her own destiny at last. Enough with sitting on the sidelines watching everyone else and envying what they had. Now that her anxiety was pretty much under control, even to the point where she might be able to consider dating again, it was time to stop watching and start living the life of which she dreamed.

A wry grin twisted her lips. Minus Phthonos, I suppose, but imagine if he were real. My God, I'd love to have him right here in my life. And my bed.

She'd put fresh grounds into the coffee machine and was toweling dry her hair when the doorbell chimed. Whoever was on her doorstep was feeling impatient, that was for sure. They had a finger on the bell and clearly weren't letting go till she answered.

"All right already! I'm coming." She slanted a look at the clock. Seventeen minutes past six. No one she knew would be up at this ungodly hour, unless there was an emergency of some kind. Her heart thumped painfully and she took a deep breath. No. It was fine. Everything would be fine. No need to panic. Regardless of her self-assurances, there was a wariness to her movements when she opened the door and peered around it, the safety chain still in place.

Her breath caught in her throat. "What the—"

"Liv, you need to let me in. Quickly." Green eyes set in a darkly handsome face stared down at her. The severe slash of his cheekbones was apparent as he turned to glance toward the elevator and then back to face her. The cords of muscle in his neck stood out at the movement and his wide mouth, one that she had imagined in a sultry grin only hours earlier, was tight with tension.

She was still dreaming. She had to be. Phthonos wasn't real.

"Of course I'm real." Impatience laced his tone. "Let me in."

"I beg your pardon?"

His gaze softened and one corner of his mouth lifted slightly. "Sorry, Liv. Let's try this again. Yes, I am Phthonos. Yes, I am real. I would be grateful if you would please let me in. And…um…better close your mouth. It's gaping."

Her teeth snapped together as she did as instructed, and even while her mind was screaming at her to turn and run, her fingers unfastened the chain and swung the door wider to let in…who? My imaginary lover? A sexy dream god? A demon of Hell? Or maybe he's a serial killer who's just found his next idiot victim.

Her heart catapulted into overdrive as she followed him into the kitchen, just in time to catch the faint snort of laughter as he turned and leaned his butt against the edge of the sink. The room was her favorite in the apartment, centrally situated and with a large skylight that let in lots of cheerful sunshine during the day. Its pale green walls, white units, and granite bench tops usually gave an impression of openness, but with Phthonos standing there in jeans and a black T-shirt, arms folded across an impressively wide chest as he studied her, the space seemed far too small for two. She pressed backward against the island bench and reached behind to grip its polished edge. The stone finish was smooth and cool beneath her fingers. Solid. Comforting. She gripped tighter.

"A serial killer, Liv? You can do better than that after the month we've just shared. Even if it was during your dreaming state. And I'm certainly not imaginary. I'm as real as they come. Can't you tell?"

Between one blink and the next he was there in front of her, his body molded so hard against the cushion of her breasts and all the way down to her thighs that even a strand of hair couldn't have made its way between them. He now held the bench as tightly as she did, one hand each side of her hips, effectively imprisoning her in a circle of finely muscled arms and shoulders. Arms that looked as if they belonged in a world-class body building contest.

She hadn't bothered with a bra beneath the loose white

blouse she'd pulled on after her shower, and the abrasion of rock-hard pectorals as he shifted triggered instant hardening of her nipples. Only his T-shirt and the thin material of her top separated them.

Heat flooded her cheeks at the realization that he would know his proximity had aroused her. The embarrassing response wasn't only confined to her breasts, either. The feel of a man's cock against her abdomen might be rare but it wasn't completely new, and yet she'd never felt anything quite that size before, even contained as it was within tight denims.

Holy crap, he's big. And he wasn't even hard. Well... She shifted experimentally and it was like a lightning strike directly between her thighs. Yep, maybe he was hard, at least a little. The smug grin that lit his face said he knew exactly what effect his partial erection was having on her nether regions. Her vagina clenched involuntarily and a rush of moisture dampened her panties. Luckily, she was wearing loose harem pants or the sudden wetness slicking her pussy would be blatantly obvious.

Breathe, she told herself. Even that simple act was difficult, though, when his scent rose around them both and invaded her nostrils with every labored inhale. Lemon, and mint, and something more exotic that she couldn't quite identify. Clean and fresh, and yet infinitely carnal at the same time. How could that be?

Okay. Doesn't matter that he smells like sex. Just breathe. Nice and even. Not so deep that my nipples will scrape against him again and show him exactly what I'm feeling... "Stop moving! Please." Her urgent request emerged low and husky and she felt an answering jerk against her belly. Hmm, maybe three-quarters hard, now. And when had her voice ever sounded like that before?

"I don't want to stop." His tone was slightly contrary, with a deep sultry cadence underlying it that wouldn't let her take offence. "It feels good, Liv. Better than a dream, don't you think?" He sounded sexy as hell, and when he shifted again her nipples instantly responded. Was it even possible for her nubs to poke out any further?

He stared down at her, those cat-shaped eyes so eerily familiar and yet with a strange, glittering hunger that she'd never seen before. Better than a dream? Damn right. Her lips parted as she struggled to inhale any breath at all.

Was he real? It certainly felt like it, and yet it didn't matter where he'd sprung from. Whether real or a figment of her overworked imagination, she was letting him stand here and practically assault her in her own kitchen without doing anything other than holding her breath and staring up at him like a love-starved teenager. It was the catalyst that finally got her moving.

"Step back, um, Phthonos. This is way too close on first acquaintance, don't you think?" She punched gently at his upper arm, and then with more force when he didn't move immediately. "Now, please." It felt so weird to call him that name from her dreams, and even more so when he responded.

"Liv." Her name flowed across his tongue, slow and seductive, and he stayed molded against her a moment longer, as if emphasizing an unspoken claim. When he did finally move away, it was as if all her unwanted loneliness came crashing in and, perversely, she craved him back again. "It's hardly first acquaintance, my beautiful one. Don't you remember our nights together this past month? You saved me from myself. You will continue to save me. I hope. And I will do my utmost to save you in return."

He was back across the room and she could finally think. But it all made as little sense now as it had seconds earlier when he was still pressed against her and the urge to wrap her legs around his narrow, masculine hips was almost over-whelming.

"I really don't understand what's happening right now." She brought a hand up to her neck and began to rub the knotted muscles down one side. She'd been to the osteopath only two days ago and been told to steer clear of computers and stress. Yeah, right. As an administrator she couldn't steer clear of her computer. And as for stress... A grin curved her lips. "You visited my dreams, Phthonos. You...well, we made love. Lots of times. In ways that I never imagined would even be possible." She let out a faint giggle, disbelief rather than humor lacing the sound. "And now suddenly you're here in my life—in my kitchen for heaven's sake—talking about saving each other. From what, exactly? And why am I even considering this in a rational way?"

His head tilted as he studied her. "You're considering this because deep down you know it to be genuine. You're trusting your instincts, even though you don't realize that, yet. As to what's happening...your desires brought me back. I felt you and your need. Even from where I've been—" Despair lit his face and was gone almost as quickly as it had appeared. She blinked, wondering if she'd imagined it, but then he was speaking again and the momentary flash of emotion was hidden. "It's been a long time since the path to this realm was open to one such as me." A tiny chuckle accompanied his words, as if he'd made a small joke. If so, she didn't get it.

"So you've been in another realm, and yet somehow you know my innermost desires and needs."

"Oh, Liv." This time when he moved toward her it was slow and steady, with one inexorable step at a time. He brought up a hand to stroke her cheek, the touch so gentle and affectionate it took everything in her not to respond and lean in to the caress like a love-starved woman.

Who was he, and why did it feel so right to have him here in her home? "I don't understand," she repeated, as the urge to touch him, to stroke him back the way he was now touching her, had her fingers twitching and her whole body lit up with energy. It was zinging along her veins, and she'd never felt more alive, nor more confused. What's wrong with me? Am I so desperate that I've conjured up the perfect imaginary lover? A man like this would never understand that level of desperation. There was no way on earth he would get what it felt like to want for another's touch, to envy everyone because their lives were more complete than your own.

He shook his head, just the once, and one corner of his mouth spasmed. "Perhaps there is no way on earth," he said. A thrill rippled as her thoughts were repeated back in a gentle tone. "There are other places, other experiences, which you will never know or understand, that can lead the way to Envy." A shudder shook his frame and her heart lurched at the contained violence of the movement. "You brought me back from my own private torment, Liv. You brought me back from a place where nothing is everything, and everything is nothing. Want? Oh, yes. I am intimately familiar with that concept. And envy?"

A grey-green haze misted across her vision and his voice hardened until it felt like a reverberation across her skin. Sudden fear clutched at her innards and she turned to run, but she could no longer see her surroundings. Couldn't tell forward from back, or even pinpoint where Phthonos stood, anymore. She flung out an arm and yet he wasn't there. Only the mist curled around her body, obscuring everything, and holding his voice at the center of it all, deep and loud, seething with dark emotion. "I am Envy. I live and breathe it. Once it consumed me, and I was lost for longer than even I can know. Now…"

A sob escaped as she balanced on the edge of panic. No! She reached for the elastic band on her wrist. Snap. Do it again. Keep going, snapping, over and over, until…it's not safe here. It's not safe…

The mist receded and she was enveloped in a strong embrace. He was rocking her back and forth just like one might do with a small child. Stroking her hair, shushing her, whispering in her ear that she was all right, that he was sorry, so sorry…

The horror left her as suddenly as it had arrived and she realized that not only were tears dripping down her cheeks, but her nose was running. "Oh my God, Phthonos, I'm so sorry, I'm so embarrassed. I—"

The last time she'd lost control and had a full-on panic attack had been in the middle of a busy intersection while at the wheel of her Ford Fiesta. She'd sold the car shortly after and now caught the train to work when she wasn't working from home. To show that level of vulnerability in front of anyone else…in front of Phthonos… "I'm sorry," she repeated, and he scowled and shook his head.

"Shush, darling woman. It wasn't you who lost control, it was me. It is I who owe you an apology. It took me by surprise and I wasn't ready. I'm sorry, Liv. So sorry. It's been too long." His voice choked as he spoke into her hair, testament to his angst, and yet still he caressed her gently with one hand while the other held her tightly around the waist.

"What happened?" That sounded relatively normal. Well, close enough that she could feel some pride in how quickly she was regaining control.

He lifted his head and she felt him gather a lock of her hair, no doubt one of those short sticking out bits, and tug at it gently. She stared up into eyes that looked deeper and darker than anything she had ever known. Despair. Desperate hunger. Remorse.

"Envy," he answered after a long pause. "It lives within me, and I've not been here in the mortal world in so long that it is desperate to get out. It hurts. Pushing hard from within, forever, all the time, while out here—" He gestured widely. "The need wrenches from every direction. So many sad, lost souls. So many people coveting what others have, without even realizing that what they truly need is almost always right there under their own noses."

"People always think the grass is greener." She tried for a light tone, but his mouth tightened.

"Then people should learn that it isn't, always." Her pulse rate accelerated at the realization he was fighting back tears. "What if I'm not strong enough to hold it in?"

Her panic had receded enough that she felt confident to reach out and trace a pattern along his jawline. Light stubble abraded her fingertips in a pleasant roughness. "It's okay, Phthonos." What was okay was still a mystery right now, but the words and the comforting action felt right. She cupped his cheek, then hesitantly dipped her fingertips into the dark mop of his hair. It was as soft as satin. "I'll help you find the strength."

Deep down within the pit of darkness that shadowed his eyes a faint light flared and the zing of an unspoken connection spread like a comforting warmth through her body. The effect in her dreams had been nothing to the reality of Phthonos standing in her kitchen and holding her in his arms. A real live sex god. Needing her support.

A tiny smile shifted his features from stark despair to dancing sunlight. "A sex god. I like that idea. It makes me sound more like one of my brothers." His embrace tightened briefly. "Now I finally have a second chance, Liv, and it is because of you. We are going to make love, you and me. Not in your dreams, again. This time it will be in your physical world, where it matters. Right here in your apartment, and most definitely today. And through our coupling, somehow we will help each other fight off the darkness of Envy and move toward the light."

CHAPTER TWO

We're going to make love? Today? She shrank back against the kitchen bench as her heart threatened to jump out of her chest. "I...um..." What could she possibly say? No thank you, I don't want to make love with anyone right now? Or maybe...get the fuck out of my house or I'll call the cops, you crazy bastard.

"I have work." Okay, so maybe that wasn't the sanest thing she could say in the circumstances.

He stepped back and crossed his arms in front of his chest. "Call in sick."

The space he'd just given her wasn't helping to make things any clearer. It simply filled her with an almost over-whelming urge to run at him, push him down to the ground, straddle his magnificent body, and start riding.

The most sensible thing to do was to ask him to leave. Or, failing that, maybe run from the room herself and scream for one of her neighbors. Either response would be a lie. Even as nervous tremors began shivering through her body and her mind was screaming at her to do the right thing, a flutter in her belly heralded an unfamiliar and growing excitement.

"I could do that. Or, I guess I could go in late." Her whole body was shaking now. She had never in her life played hooky from work. In the past two years she'd only taken three days sick leave from her job at the Foundation, and that was when she'd been unconscious in the hospital.

He chuckled. "Late? It will have to be very, very late, if I do my job properly."

"Phthonos, I don't want you to leave, but it's not my work that's the issue. Not really. That's just an excuse. It…oh, it's so hard to explain." How to tell a man like Phthonos that I live my whole life these days around managing anxiety. She wanted to be as honest as possible, right from the start of whatever this might turn out to be.

"I understand exactly how hard this is for you, Liv. It's partly why I'm here. Even though I inspire enormous unease, you still want me. You can't help it."

She let out a little snort at the arrogant-sounding words. Damn it if he wasn't right. She did want him, more than anyone she had ever met in her life.

He shrugged. "I am a god. Not quite a sex god unfortunately, but the blood of Aphrodite herself runs through my veins and it draws you in whether you want it to or not."

"So, am I being manipulated against my will? That doesn't sound like a good start to anything involving sex."

"No. You're strong, Olivia, even though you don't recognize that trait in yourself. Even I would not be able to make you do anything against your will. Woman, look at what you're doing to me." He cupped the huge bulge at his groin and her mouth parted slightly. As an emphasis for his words, the action definitely worked. What would his penis look like, free of the denim restraint? Her fingers itched to find out. "I'm aching for you, Liv. You've been dreaming of me for a month, yes? Well, I've been dreaming of you too. And in the reality I had until now, your presence and your delicate, loving touch, quite literally kept me going. Kept me sane. I couldn't believe that I would ever get the chance to see you in person, and yet here we are. I want you. Desperately. Let me love you."

He was wearing the face, the body, even the scent, of her fantasy hero, and he was standing right in front of her with a raging hard-on and those seemingly heaven-sent words coming out of his mouth.

Phthonos. Who are you? And do I really care? With a deep, slow breath she unclenched her hands and reached up to undo the buttons of her shirt. One at a time, slowly, while she stared across the room at him and trembled. "What's a woman to say, then, after that little speech?" Even her voice was quivering, but he seemed to hear her okay anyway, judging by the intensifying look of hunger on his face. "I do want you, Phthonos, with every fiber of my being." It felt awkward, being the initiator, and yet she wanted this so much. "I don't even know why, but that's how it is. Please, come here and help me remove my clothing."

$$\Omega \, \Psi \, \Omega$$

The need to engulf her with everything raging inside flooded over him with such force he went deathly-still. Get it under control. The darkness was too all-consuming, and she couldn't withstand him if he lost it. She was so delicate and easy to break, despite that elusive core of inner strength, and he had to remember at all times to hold himself back.

She was human. She was fragile. And she was about to

become his if he could only control his demon long enough to keep her safe.

He shucked off his T-shirt and threw it to one side before moving forward to take over for her fumbling fingers. "With pleasure." Remember. Do it slowly.

He managed to release two more of the tiny buttons before a waft of her perfume teased his nostrils. It was a musky scent that reminded him of hot nights and seductive need, so long-forgotten that its sudden effect on his senses blasted his self-control to pieces. With a groan that rattled his throat on the way out he grabbed the two sides of her blouse and yanked them apart, the remaining three buttons flying off in all directions with a ripping pop, pop, pop.

"Oh!" Her gorgeous mouth formed into a round of surprise. He clutched at her wrists before she could cover her breasts, then released them slowly when he felt her peak of embarrassment begin to subside.

"No! Don't ever cover yourself when you are with me. I must look at you." She was solidly proportioned, with more flesh than was the current fashion, judging by what he'd seen in his brief time back here. Good. He liked it better when there was something substantial to hold onto.

His fingers trembled as he traced around first one large globe then the other. Her skin was so white he could see the blue network of veins peeking through from beneath. Her life force, so close to the surface. So tantalizing. His touch raised instant goose bumps on her skin and pleasure filled him as she inhaled sharply and caught her bottom lip with her teeth.

"You're beautiful," he whispered. "You feel warmer than I expected. And more soft. A little like my memory of a satin sheet."

"A satin sheet? I have some of those on my bed, if you'd,

well…" She sounded out of breath. "If you'd like to check them out? And, I guess you feel kind of satiny too. Only hard underneath the soft." She was exploring him while she spoke, cushioned fingertips tracing in a hesitant fashion across his pectoral muscles and down over his abdomen. It tickled a little and he grinned, until her hands stopped their wandering right at the top of his jeans. "What about here, I wonder?" She unclicked his top button and left the zipper alone, instead touching his bulge with a slow, teasing rhythm. "Are you soft here? Or are you hard?"

She brushed him again and now it was he sucking in a breath. An inhalation that became stuck somewhere between his throat and his chest. "That doesn't tickle, Liv." It feels like I made it home to the gods.

"Good. I don't want it to tickle."

There was laughter in her voice and his eyes closed briefly as a further rush of blood pulsed into his cock. At this rate he'd last only about as long as one of the younger gods. Dionysus, perhaps. He would have to release himself from the rest of this mortal clothing, soon. It was unnatural to keep his sexual organ confined when the rigid ache of need sat so heavily upon him. "Keep doing that and I won't be able to stand upright in a minute."

"Hmm, I think you're doing a pretty good job of standing upright already." He opened his eyes and caught the mischief lighting up her features. "How about we check to see if I'm correct?"

She seemed more relaxed in this moment than he had ever seen her, even in their dream state, and something deep within him released its tight hold just a touch. "If you insist." Zeus, he sounded like a boy at his first deflowering. Felt like it too. Especially when she tugged at his zipper and released the teeth in one quick downward movement.

His growl of relief at the freedom combined with her gasp of shock as his cock shot free. "Holy moly," she said.

Well. That did not sound like she was impressed. And her tension was back. Ten-fold. "Do you wish me to increase the size? I can if you—"

"No! Definitely not. I, um, I don't even know what to say." She was frowning, and when he tried to read her mind this time it only gave him the beginnings of a headache. There was too much stimuli to be able to focus on one coherent thought.

"Then what—"

"You're so freakin' big, Phthonos."

She stumbled over his name every time she said it. He wanted to make it easier for her. "Thon."

"Okay. But Thon, you're too big for me. How am I ever going to…?"

Ah. He reached out and lifted her chin. "It's all right." He stared into her eyes, willing her to relax. When she was in a non-anxious state it gave him enormous pleasure. "I told you, I am a god. When we make love it will not hurt you. Unless you wish a little pain. See?"

He adjusted his size slightly and saw the instant relief take hold. He gripped her upper arms and shook her a little. "I will never knowingly hurt you, Liv. You could be my savior. You are my present and I wish you to be my future."

"Okay. I believe you." *And even adjusted, you're still bloody impressive!* Her thought shot into his mind and it was as if she had created it knowing he would hear. His heart beat faster than usual, and he focused back in on her body, wanting to show her that he meant what he said.

Pleasure. His brothers, the erotes, knew instinctively how to give and receive pleasure. His mother, well, pleasure was her middle name. Not that Aphrodite had any need of another.

As the recipient of all the genes in the family relating to the darker side of love, seduction did not come naturally to him. During his time away from this realm, in the place where nothing was his everything, he had almost forgotten how to pleasure a woman such as Olivia.

He had forgotten how to pleasure anyone at all. Even himself.

He studied her body. Her nipples were the only part of her still standing sentinel to tension, it seemed, only their tension was obviously sexual rather than nervous in nature. They jutted out in a rosy counterpoint to the softness of the flesh surrounding them and he couldn't resist their entice-ment. He flicked one with his thumb and she let out a tiny moan. The sound caused a spurt of pre-cum to adorn the tip of his cock.

Another flick, across both nipples this time, and he let out a satisfied chuckle when she responded with an even louder moan and tipped back her head to expose a tempting expanse of neck. Her pulse beat there, fast and furious, and he leaned in to press his lips over the life force beating through her veins.

Delicious. She tasted even better than her scent and he drank her in, running his tongue up the line of her neck to hover above her mouth. Her lips were parted and he caught a glimpse of white teeth within. What would it be like to have her bite at his flesh? To scrape her teeth along his skin before following up with the moist lick of a warm tongue. What would it be like to have her lave his organ, sucking him deep and working at his erection with every part of her mouth? He groaned.

Her breath was hot and sweet. She must have brushed her teeth already this morning with some kind of mint flavored paste. He was savoring the anticipation of the kiss, ready to swoop in and claim her, when he felt the clutch of decisive fingers tangling into his hair. She pulled him in toward her.

"You took too long," she whispered, the words vibrating right into his mouth. Then she was kissing him and he was lost.

Sensation like none he had ever felt before. Sweet, moist, hot. Forget claiming her. It was too late. She had claimed him the moment they met.

Ω Ψ Ω

This was one thousand times better than their dream kisses. The feel of his lips on hers, the dance of their tongues as she tentatively swiped hers across his teeth and felt the surge of response as he thrust into her with his own. His hands were on her buttocks, squeezing the glutes and lifting her up and over his jutting cock until it rested almost horizontally along her vulvar lips. Hot, and hard, and a perfect fit.

The denim jeans bunched down around his hips added delicious friction to their connected bodies and she began to thrust with her pelvis. Sensation spread outward at every press of her clit against his groin. She deepened their kiss, taking a firmer hold on his dark hair, and reveled at the tiny rumble of noise in his throat. She absorbed the sound, and made one of her own. A little mewl that she didn't even recognize as hers. Again, it was swallowed up somewhere deep within their connected mouths.

She had never taken the initiative before—with any man —and it was unbelievable to be the one to elicit that level of response from Thon. His kiss was just like his body, a mix of hard urgency and sweet moist softness.

When they broke apart she felt naked, but not in a physical sense. "Don't leave me, Thon," she begged. His laughing eyes told her not to worry.

"I only want to rid us of the rest of our clothing. I'll try not to rip it this time." He flicked a hand and a wave of warm air washed over her. Just like that and they were both stripped bare.

Embarrassment once again rippled through her and her hands jerked instinctively, only this time she managed to resist covering herself. Instead she lifted her chin. "That was a little more pleasurable than having them torn off."

"Did you not like that, Liv? I will buy you a new top, if you wish."

"No, it's okay." Strangely she had enjoyed that hint of violence. Being on the brink of control. It was a place that often had her in panic mode, but right now panic was the last thing on her mind.

He was gorgeous. There was no other word to describe the perfection of his undulating muscles and smooth tanned skin. Though his chest was hairless, there was a faint scattering of dark on his thighs and a neat circlet of hair around the base of his genitals. The last man she'd been with, a couple of years ago, had shaved his pubic area on a regular basis and had an unattractive rash as a result. She secretly thought Sean had done it to make his penis look bigger, though Thon clearly had no need for such illusion. His erection was in full force, long as well as thick. His balls pulled tight and neat beneath the blood-engorged cock that poked out and upward with impressive rigidity. That erection was all because of her.

Her clit swelled in immediate response and she wondered

if he could see its round head glistening between her pussy lips. Her slit was creamy with fluid and her whole body was heavy with need. He was stunning to look at, perfect in every physical sense and her body was responding wholeheartedly.

Oh, God, I want to taste you, Thon.

Without further thought she dropped to her knees and took him deep into her mouth and throat. Velvety smooth skin, ridged with veins. Hot. Hard. The very essence of everything male. She sucked him in, working back and forth, stealing the sticky fluid from the tip of his cock with her greedy tongue. The taste was divine, like...like... There was nothing to which she could compare. It was the headiest aphrodisiac she'd ever placed in her mouth.

"Like the nectar of the gods, Liv? It is exactly that." Thon's voice was hoarse above her, and she smiled around his organ and let her lips, tongue, and teeth continue to explore. "By the gods, that feels good."

Fingers tangled in her hair, encouraging the sliding move-ment up and down his cock. She cupped his balls with one hand, squeezing lightly, and with the other slipped her fingers behind them to press into the springy flesh between his testi-cles and anus. She'd read on the internet that men liked such a move. A sharp hiss sounded above her head and he jerked in her mouth, then sudden pain assailed her shoulders and a greenish grey mist surrounded them. What the...

She lifted her head and let him slide out of her with a moist sucking noise. She knelt there, inhaling his musky scent and panting, blinking to try and clear her vision. Why was it suddenly so shadowy?

He was bent forward a little over her, fingers clutching so tight around her upper arms and shoulders it felt like claws digging in to her shoulder blades. So that was the cause of the pain. A wave of lust swept through her at the sting and a yelp filled her throat, but she refused to let it escape. No. Don't let him see it.

Pleasure and pain. The double-edged sword that was her deepest secret and one she had only revealed once before in her life. To disastrous effect.

It was too late. He knew. "Oh, my God, Thon." The words burst out of her when he squeezed again and a betraying gush of vaginal moisture coated the top of her thighs.

"You like that?"

She whimpered and closed her eyes, and then snapped them open when he slid his hands under her elbows and lifted her seemingly without effort to her feet.

"Liv? You like a bit of pain?"

She spoke through clenched teeth. "I don't want to."

"But you do."

"Yeah. A little. Not a lot. Just…just a little bit." A tremble started up in her limbs. It's all right, she told herself. Breathe. Just breathe. Thon's probably not even real anyway. He's just a figment of your imagination. It's not going to turn bad. He's not going to do what Sean did…

"Who's Sean, and what did he do?" Thon was standing very still, and he had captured both of her now-shaking hands in one of his and was holding them secure. "Hey." He shook her a little when she didn't immediately respond. "Lots of people enjoy a touch of pain along with their pleasure. I do. It makes things infinitely more intense, walking the knife edge between agony and desire. It's not something to be ashamed of, Liv. Who's Sean?"

Her heart did one of those sickening bumps in her chest— the lurch that always occurred right before she went into a state of anxiety. "I don't want to talk about it." Despite her resolve she couldn't control her memories, and knew from his sudden flinch the moment he gleaned the thoughts from her mind.

"Yes," she confirmed, jerking free of his hold and reaching for the elastic band on her wrist. Snap. "Sean was my lover, for a short time." Snap. "He's also the man who put me in hospital and gave me two years' worth of panic attacks."

CHAPTER THREE

"Deep down I already knew what he was like." She was proud of the way her voice stayed so calm. Maybe she was finally getting past it. "He threw me into a wall once, after we'd only been together a week or so. I should have left him right then and there, but he was so contrite. I decided to give him one last chance, and when I finally opened up and told him what I like..." Okay, maybe she'd been too optimistic about the getting over it part. She snapped the safety band again and again, her wrist stinging, until Thon reached out to stop her. She cleared her throat and tried again. It will be okay. He's not like Sean. You know him, already, even if only from your dreams.

"What I like in the bedroom, I mean," she continued. "He...um...he took it completely the wrong way. He went nuts. He said people like me deserve to be punished. And he did. Punish me. A lot."

There was so much more she could say about what had happened, but it wasn't the right time. Thon began to pace, controlled violence in the movement, and his fists kept clenching and unclenching. Murky darkness coiled again at

357

the edges of her vision and yet when she turned her head there was nothing to see. "Calm down, Thon, please. It happened a long time ago, and I heard that the next woman he went after had a brother in some kind of gang. Sean lost one of his hands. The one he used for punching."

He didn't answer at first but he did stop pacing. His rage, though palpable, didn't scare her for some reason. It felt different to Sean's anger, like it was on her behalf rather than directed at her. Perversely, his discomfort soothed her and the last of her tremors eased away to nothing. Panic averted.

She took a deep breath and let it out slowly. "I mean it, Thon. I don't want to talk about it anymore. At least right now." What could she do to distract him? She reached out and ran her hands over his abdomen, then further down to take his cock in a firm grip. It had lost its rigidity during their discussion, so she ran her hands up and down, teasing him back to hard.

"Liv, stop! I—"

"No, Phthonos. If you want to please me, then give me this." She jerked her hand and felt his surge of response. "I want you. I want to create new memories in the bedroom. Real ones, not dreams. And I want to do it now, today, with you."

His eyes were sparking so bright it was like looking right into the center of twin emeralds. Green fire. She caught her breath at the beauty. I know you. I look into your heart and I don't see the darkness that I saw in Sean.

He let out a ragged sigh and reached to cup her cheeks. "I am real, Liv, and I am not like this Sean. I do not take pleasure in pushing any woman past the point of pain at which she is comfortable. And that is what he did, isn't it? More than once." When she nodded mutely, his wide mouth thinned and the muscles in his neck tightened again. "So terrifying for you." He kissed her on the lips, the connection butterfly soft. "I wish to bring you pleasure, Liv. And if we cut ourselves just a little on the knife's edge of pain, it means our pleasure will be all the sweeter. I would never wish to break you. But..."

"But what, Thon?"

His concern intensified. "I have the demon Envy in me, Liv. My heart is not pure, despite what you think. It is black. Evil. I am trying to hold it in, but what if..." He half-turned away, lifted a hand, and ran it roughly through his hair. "What if I can't control myself? What if it escapes? How will I protect you?" He was muttering now, as if to himself. Then he cocked his head to the side, obviously listening, yet she couldn't hear whatever it was. "What to do? Mother, she is so fragile."

Now Liv could hear it too, the faintest hint of female laughter and a short snatch of words that made no sense "... would not place you with such a delicate flower..."

It was just a second or two of exquisitely beautiful sound, and then it was gone as if it had never existed. She was still processing what Thon had said. "Fragile?" She stepped forward and smacked him in the shoulder, enjoying the sudden shock that lit his face. "I might have an issue with anxiety, but that doesn't make me weak. I'm not fragile, Thon. I've been to Hell and back in the past couple of years and you know what? I survived it. You said earlier that I'm tougher than I realize, but you didn't really believe it yourself, did you? Well, I am strong. Not fragile." She hit him again, this time in the chest, hard enough to make her point without really hurting him.

He caught her hand in his fist, a twisted grin that she didn't understand turning his features from handsome into a grimace. "Then we've each been to the same place, Liv, and as we are both standing here, I guess we are both survivors. We will discuss this further, I promise you. You do not make an announcement such as yours and then leave it alone. However not now, if that is your wish."

"It is."

"So be it." He nodded and released her hand. "Then right now I have a burning need to make love to you before I spill my seed all over your kitchen floor instead of inside your body where it belongs."

When he swept her off her feet and up into his arms she let out a surprised yelp. "I'm too heavy—"

"Which way to the bedroom? My bones are ancient and prefer the comfort of a supporting mattress when I plough into you."

"Oh, well, I guess…that way." She gestured wildly. "The door at the end of the hallway. Don't you know where it is? We've already used the bed more than once." And the floor, and up against the wardrobe door, for that matter.

He cocked a brow. "I've never actually had the need to walk into your bedroom before."

"Oh." True. He'd always just materialized, during the time she'd been sleeping. Though, as she bounced up and down in his arms, she decided that he wasn't really walking this time, either. Instead, he strode with determined purpose, carrying her weight with seeming ease, and then threw her down onto the mattress with such vigor that she rebounded a couple of times. When he knelt astride her, thigh muscles rippling, she saw that he now had hold of some kind of implement. It had a short handle and multiple strands of supple leather-like material draping down toward her. Her belly flip-flopped with a combination of excitement and tension. He let the implement fall lower, the ends touching her skin, and drew it slowly across her breasts. Goose bumps raised themselves in its wake and her nipples hardened into peaks.

"Do you know what this is, Liv?" He did it again, only this time the leather ends went lower, much lower, caressing her stomach and then down to kiss her pussy slit.

She clutched at the sheets, the silken material sliding through her fingers and making it hard to keep a firm grip. "It…it looks like a whip."

He nodded. "This is my flogger. She and I are old friends, and I want to introduce her to you."

It was suddenly hard to breathe. A tightness in her chest constricted her lungs as apprehension threatened. What if it happens again? What if he can't control himself? She started to sit up, but it was too difficult with him looming over her. "No, I…I really don't think—"

"Liv. It is all right to be true to yourself. You can give in to your desires without fear, if you have the right partner by your side. You do not have to be afraid, anymore."

Her anxiety had no time to take further hold. A flick of his wrist and the ends of the flogger snapped, catching her across the mons and just above the nub of her clit. The sting was sudden and sharp and sent throbbing signals directly to her core. She gasped and arched her back, panic forgotten in the shocking rush of intensity.

When he bent and placed his mouth over the slight red mark that raised itself on her skin, her craving increased tenfold. His breath was hot, his lips gentle, and his tongue slid out to circle her nub in a movement that created instant sweat all over her body. "Yes, Thon, that feels…oh my God…" His kiss had deepened, and when he sucked on the center of her being with such force she began to buck against his face.

"There," he said when he finally lifted his head. His lips

were swollen and slick and his tone was gruff. "That's my brand of pleasure and pain. Better, don't you think?"

She nodded hard. He was still crouched between her legs, hovering above her wet mound like a predator over its prey. Need grew within until she perched right on the edge of release. A betraying spurt of fluid escaped from her channel. She felt its expulsion and let out a little moan. "I'm sorry." She was panting and it seemed ridiculous to be so embarrassed by her body's reactions, but his mouth was only inches away from her snatch and she was so sensitized that even his breath threatened to bring her to a screaming orgasm.

His gaze softened and he ran his thumb over her juices before darting in briefly with his tongue to lap up the remaining moisture. She shuddered at the sensation and when he spoke in a muffled voice the vibration only increased the delight. "Delicious. You taste like musk and sunshine. My beacon of light in the darkness. Don't ever apologize for your need, Liv. I find everything about you incredibly erotic. And remarkably innocent. I love it."

At the top of her pussy lips she could see what looked like the tip of a tiny pink tongue sticking out. Her clit, so swollen she didn't even need to part her flesh to show off the extent of her desire. She had never seen it look like that before. She had never felt like this before, either, so full and tight and ready to explode.

"I need you inside me, Thon. I want to come around your gorgeous organ."

"Soon, my love. First though…" He knelt up again, his member jutting hard and clearly ready above her. "Is this what you had in mind?" The leather thong tickled her inner thighs yet again, and she tensed, waiting for the lash. "It's not too rough?"

"Yes!" Her pelvis was starting to thrust a little, almost as if it had a life of its own. "I mean no. I mean..." Coherent thought was becoming more difficult by the second. "Yes it is exactly what I had in mind, and no. It isn't too rough. But no rougher than that. Please." Again a tiny trickle of anxiety threatened, though for some reason it wasn't taking hold. Thon was so different to Sean there couldn't really be any comparison.

"Trust me, Liv. It will be just this much, and no more." Another flick of his wrist and exquisite pain stung her thigh. She clutched at the bed sheets.

"I do trust you," she managed to gasp. "I don't even know why, but I do. And trust me, Thon. If you do that again and then kiss the spot, I'm going to come, right in your mouth."

"Excellent," he said, and flogged her again, right across her clit, before plunging downward and consuming her pussy with hot lips, teeth and tongue. She shrieked at the influx of pleasure which was too much to contain, and broke apart beneath his suctioning ministrations. Waves of electrically charged energy rolled through her body and time lost meaning as a violent orgasm rocked her, releasing her tension as effortlessly as the ejaculate from her vagina. Eventually, when she came back down to earth, gentle hands were stroking her and she was being held safe within strong male arms. She relaxed into him, savoring the moment, every part of her trembling. "Beautiful, Liv," he said. "The look on your face when you climax...we will have to do that again shortly. For my pleasure as much as yours."

Right now she felt as frail as the time she'd decided to take up swimming as exercise, and got out of the pool after several laps to find that her legs would barely hold her up. "Thon, that was amazing." She reached up and traced his cheek, running her fingers into the dark hair. He seemed to enjoy the caress, arching into her touch as if he were a cat. "It was just the right balance."

"Between agony and ecstasy? Yes. You want the whole experience of love, and in order to do that you need to open yourself up to the vulnerability that comes with loving someone. Both an emotional vulnerability, and a physical one."

Tears pricked at her eyes and she blinked hard. He got it. Finally she had met someone who got it. It wasn't about being a victim, or being punished. It was about opening yourself up in every respect to the other person. It was about trust. Giving it, receiving it. Protecting it.

"Thank you," she said, trying to wriggle around in his arms so she could fully return his embrace. In doing so her hip grazed against hard flesh and she sucked in a breath. "Oh, Phthonos, you've been so patient with me, and you...you're..."

"I'm ready to burst," he admitted in a gruff tone. "And I want to do it inside of you. Are you ready?" When she nodded enthusiastically he shifted over her until he was supporting himself on his elbows and the tip of his cock rested at her entrance. It had been so long since she'd lain with a man anywhere except in her dreams, and this was her fantasy lover in the flesh. A renewed rush of excitement ignited butterflies in her stomach. Her slit was still slick with cream from her earlier orgasm, and he was already dripping with pre-cum. Entry would surely be relatively easy. An exploratory tilting of his hips and the wet tip of him slid into her, proving the truth of her thoughts.

"Am I ready?" Her laughter turned to a gasp when he followed the gentle breach with a hard thrust. Once, twice, then a third time, and he was in. So big, and yet so right. In the beginning she'd been scared she couldn't contain his enormous size, but now that her vagina cradled his flesh it felt like a perfect fit. Pressure deep within triggered an immediate resurgence of desire, only this was different to the stimulation on her clit. This need was profoundly stronger, more elemental. More raw. "Hell yes, Thon, I'm ready. Please make love to me. Now."

Ω Ψ Ω

The moment her vagina parted and then closed around his eager flesh was one that would be seared into his memory forever. Perfection. He was afraid to move at first, in case he came too fast. He wanted to savor this feeling of having finally found his mate.

Two halves, together at last.

He grunted as her desire rose around him in a musky scent. Control. Keep control. Don't lose it. Even more important now that he knew her past. She'd been through so much horror already. If he lost it to the darkness...No. I won't let the darkness win. Think of her, smell her need, taste her love, be whatever she wants me to be. Oh, Liv.

He plunged into her, hard, and a deep groan ripped out of her throat. She wrapped her legs across his buttocks and met the bucking of his hips thrust for thrust. Her hands were everywhere, frantic. On his upper arms, then his shoulders, before grabbing at his back. Nails dug crescents into his flesh in a welcome return of his own sweet yet painful medicine.

He could feel the trembling and thought it was her, but then realized it was he who was shaking, he who was now groaning, as he continued to thrust into her. "That's so... damn...good!" Her voice was low and husky when she spoke, her eyes had closed and her back arched up and into him. He bent and took her lips, fucking her mouth with his tongue as hard and as desperately as his cock rammed itself home into her pussy.

Liv, my Liv, you taste so fucking good...

She was kissing him back with the same urgency that drove his need, biting, and sucking, and licking so hard and so fast that his walls of control began to tumble. The rhythm of their love-making intensified, like a drum beat in the jungle getting faster, stronger, and louder. He seized her by the buttocks, adjusting the angle, pounding into her, losing himself...

Blackness compelled from within, like a pressure cooker about to explode. It was desperate to escape, desperate to devour whatever was light and good...Fight. Fight it and win. Don't let it out. Protect her. Hold it in...

He broke off their kiss and cupped her face, wanting to connect and yet not like that, not with the pain. It has to be purely pleasure now, it has to be joy and brightness. The dark can't survive, if I concentrate on the light.

She opened her eyes and gazed up at him, the implicit trust in her expression filling him with confusion. Why did she trust him so? He had done nothing to earn it.

"I see you," she whispered, and his heart flip-flopped painfully in his chest. "I see you fighting it. Whatever it is. It's kind of murky, though it seems to be thinning out and going away. You can do this, Thon. Make love to me, darling man."

Unexpected moisture began to leak from his eyes. Tears? Zeus! So this is what it feels like to love someone. A surge of joy expanded within his chest and the pressure eased. Tuck the dark back into its fortress. Throw away the key. Do not let it out.

When he bent to kiss her this time it was as gentle and sweet as he could make it. She deserved that. But... "I can't wait much longer, Liv. It's been so long." A thousand of your lifetimes, my love. And more.

"Then don't wait." I'm about to come again, and I want it to be with you. Her thought sprang into his mind and her grin told him it was a deliberate communication.

The growl started deep down inside him and grew until it burst out in a shuddering roar that echoed her higher-pitched scream as she fell over the abyss once again. With one last thrusting pump he followed her blindly into sensory overload, emptying an eternity's worth of seed into the woman he loved. Even their orgasms were paired to perfection as their uncontrollable jerks and shudders fed each other. Her vaginal spasms clutched at him, prolonging the ecstasy and milking every drop of fluid from his cock.

He could feel, as if it were his own body, the ripples of pleasure still working their way through her. With a sigh he relaxed into it, learning what it was like to have an orgasm as a woman. The sensation was more heightened than a man's. Next time he would use that knowledge to bring her even more pleasure. Right now, sated and happy, it was almost impossible to move. He rolled to the side so as not to crush her beneath his weight, then slipped a hand under her neck and pulled her close. She snuggled in and drifted off to sleep.

Just before she did, a tiny kiss landed like a butterfly on his chest and a drowsy voice whispered, "Love you, Thon," then she was truly asleep and he was left holding her, his heart swollen with something he could not remember having felt before. He thought maybe it was hope.

CHAPTER FOUR

"How old are you, Thon?" They were under the bed covers in a cocoon of warmth, and she was tracing an aimless pattern on his chest. His skin was a duskier tone than hers and she enjoyed the juxtaposition of dark and light as she moved her arm across his torso. His face from this close vantage point was so smooth, not a single wrinkle, and no grey strands marred the perfection of his dark tumble of hair. "I'm thirty-two," she offered. "Are you younger...or...?"

His chuckle was quiet but full of genuine mirth. "I am ageless, in mortal terms," he said. "I am whatever age you would like me to be." Then he sobered and his brows shunted together. "In truth I have lived an eternity, and yet for so long it felt as if I did not exist at all."

"What do you mean?" She rose on one elbow to better study him.

He rolled back onto the pillow and raised an arm above his head, staring up at the electric fan light fixed in the center of her ceiling. The autumn weather was mild and sunny and she hadn't needed the fan for a couple of months, and he seemed to be studying its intricacies so intently that it could have been the most important item in the room. The hesitation was so slight it was almost non-existent, but the visible tick pumping fast at the base of his throat gave away his ratcheting tension. Curious, she ran her thumb along the line of his collar bone before resting it over the pulsing hollow. "It was a simple question, I thought."

He huffed out a breath. "Nothing is simple. You should know that by now. I told you, Liv, I am not pure of heart. I was sent away from here—from this realm—so long ago I can hardly remember it. And where I've been since—" He shuddered, the movement sudden and violent, and despite his muscular physique a sense of his inner vulnerability washed over her. There was something deep and dark lurking just below the surface, threatening to consume him if he let down his guard. She'd had that same impression right before he climaxed earlier, as if there was an unwholesome shadow on his soul and he needed to fight to free himself from its cloying grip.

She pressed her thumb down into the hollow of his throat and the beat vibrated beneath her thumb tip. Fast and strong. As if his life force were quite literally at her fingertips. He needed protection. From what, she wasn't sure, but the urge to wrap her arms around and hold on tight was so overwhelming she gave in. He sank into the embrace, gripping her forcefully in return.

"I cannot go back, Liv. I would rather be mortal and facing death, than have to return to—" His face was in her hair, inhaling. "You smell so delicious. Like vanilla."

"To where, Phthonos?" She didn't want to push him, however the need to know more about him and his circumstances drove her to ask. His blatant distress fed her own, and yet not in the way she expected. There was none of the overwhelming anxiety that normally laced through everything she did, and that caused her to assess and categorize every situation for potential disaster so she could plan in advance to avert it. Her counsellor called it catastrophizing, and the effort of it usually exhausted her.

Right now, though, she had no need to break the cycle of rising panic by snapping her stupid wristband, or counting to a hundred, or remembering to bring her focus to the present experience as part of her mindfulness training. Not that she wasn't focused on the present, and yet the disquiet in this moment was completely different. Like she was on the cusp of an important decision, one that could be life-changing. The right choice and she would save him, and maybe herself. The wrong choice, and what would happen? Why was she even thinking like this, and how could she make any choice at all when she didn't know what the choices were about?

"To where?" There was an unattractive edge to her voice, but she couldn't help it. She had to know more. "Answer me."

His hair rustled against her pillow as he shook his head. Then his jaw firmed. "To Hell, Olivia." The simple words were wrought with agony. "I said it earlier, and I'm sure you thought I meant it figuratively. I didn't. It was like…nothing. It was just grey. Gloomy. Full of anguish and desolation." He shuddered again. "It was so empty of life." His skin had paled as he spoke, the cast turning his olive complexion almost yellow. He looked as if he had some kind of fevered illness.

Now it was her heart creating a fast pulsing tattoo in her throat. She swallowed hard, forcing herself to touch him, even though the taint of wrongness was growing. "Shush. It's okay. It will be okay." She tried to speak gently, while tracing the chiseled planes of his face then down his neck to his shoulders and chest, feeling the heat of his body beneath her caress. How can I fix this for you? How can I distract you from whatever inner demons you're wrestling with?

A faint sheen of sweat lay upon him and with her fingers moist with his fluid, sudden inspiration hit. She raised her forefinger to her mouth and licked off his flavor. Salty. Musky. Still deliciously sexy, despite whatever he was fighting inside.

His gaze had followed her movements, and as she sucked on her finger his eyes flared bright. The impression of unwholesomeness began to recede and his color returned to a healthy glow. Good. She sucked some more, going deeper, grinning at him around her digit and enjoying the disturbance against her thigh that heralded his mounting interest. She slid her finger out of her mouth and leaned in to trace her own moistness around his lips, which he curved up in a wry smile.

"See, Liv? You're good for me." He captured her hand in his, surprising her with his speed, then turned her palm and pressed his lips into the fleshy mound at the base of her thumb. It was as if wild fire ignited in that spot. Scalding. The heat traveled through her veins as fast as a lightning strike, all of it centering between her thighs. "It is within your grasp to decide the fate of Envy. Do I stay? Or do you send me back?" She jerked as his teeth bit into her.

"Ouch!" The sting followed the blistering heat equally as fast, finding its home in the flaming bud of her clit. The pain slid away, leaving only pleasure. She shuddered and bit her lip, fighting against the response. Desire and pain. The double-edged sword, as he had called it, and one that had remained her deepest secret. Until she found the courage to share herself with Thon.

His hot tongue laved her palm and then he bit her again. Yes! A moan escaped. This was utter madness. She didn't understand where he'd come from, and whether this was just an extension of her dream world or something completely out of left field. Had she truly gone mad? Her body was insisting more loudly than her mind, craving what he had to offer, and when she finally spoke it was in a voice gone husky with so many emotions she couldn't begin to process them all.

"I don't want you to go anywhere, Phthonos. I couldn't bear it. I want you to stay and...oh!" She didn't get to finish. Instead she was enveloped in an embrace so constricting it was as if they were already joined as one.

"I knew it!" His eyes blazed emerald. "I knew you were the one. I heard your call. I heard your desperation. I heard your loneliness. And I knew you would understand mine. The need to respond was just so overwhelming. She finally let me back in."

"She?"

"My mother. Aphrodite, the goddess of desire. The goddess of this." Strong fingers found her breasts and tweaked the nipples until they stood out hard and pink.

"Not fair." She was breathless again, but found the energy to push at his chest until he lay flat. "It's your turn." When her nail flicked one of his nipples experimentally he inhaled sharply and the flat pink-brown nub hardened instantly. "Hmm." She did it with the other one and he growled.

"Liv, don't do that unless you want more of what we've just been doing all morning."

She smiled and flicked him again. "Okay. If you insist."

He grabbed her wrist. "Devil woman."

"Demon."

"I am." When he grabbed her by the back of her neck and pulled downward she allowed him to claim her lips in a kiss both punishing and sweet. There was no hesitation in letting him in. The frantic connection of their mouths fuelled an urgency in her body as the faint flavor of her sex, and his, still lingered on their breath from previous love-making. The taste was an elusive reminder of all they had done, and a heady aphrodisiac guiding all they were about to do.

When she eventually broke off the contact, they were both panting and he was fully ready to fuck. She swung a leg over his hips and slid down onto his cock, the walls of her vagina welcoming him in with greedy hunger. She sat still astride him, cupping a hand over her abdomen and smiling down at him lying there between her legs. "You're mine, Thon, and you're not going anywhere." Her fingers curled. He had embedded himself so deep inside her it was like he'd breached her womb, and yet it couldn't be more right.

"Ride me, Liv," he urged, his hands resting on her hips, and she finally began to move, slowly at first and then more urgently. Heaven. The ache in her clit was only part of it as the reaction deep within her grew to almost unbearable levels.

"Oh God, yes, that feels so...fucking...good, Thon." He met her grinding gyrations with hips driving so hard that she lost control of the rhythm. She bounced up into the air and back down at his every grunting drive, his balls stinging as they slapped into her ass and his cock head doing God knew what damage inside her. She was sobbing at every thrust, but she couldn't get enough, wanting it deeper, harder, and faster.

His mouth was pulled tight now in a rictus of effort and grasping hands were on her breasts, grappling with the bouncing globes. Does my face look like his does right now, so sexy and animal-like? She fell forward, intending to give him better access to her breasts, and he took advantage and twisted her nipples hard. It was the catalyst that sent her over the edge. A keening noise that she didn't even recognize seared her throat as she climaxed, her whole body rigid with the intense sensory wave that was pounding her. His guttural groans grew louder, signaling the end of his journey was near, and then he joined her with a primeval yell and a shudder that reignited the tail end of her orgasm into full-blown ecstasy once more.

She was nowhere, and everywhere, all at the same time, and somehow through it all they stayed joined in a coupling that didn't want to end. When focus finally began to return, she was wrapped in Thon's embrace. Their bodies fit so perfectly together. She knew—whether demon, god or man—that she had found the one who had stolen her heart.

Ω Ψ Ω

"Morning, Olivia. Or should I say afternoon? It's not like you to be late."

Janice, her supervisor, was chewing on the end of a pen and frowning at Liv over a document as she slid into her seat at the workstation opposite. The new, open-plan layout was supposed to be advantageous for social interaction with work colleagues, but right this minute it would have been much less embarrassing to have the old arrangement where Janice was enclosed in her own office with a solid wall between them.

Could anyone tell she'd had sex? It had been so long since she'd been with a man that she couldn't remember if there'd be signs. And with a man like Phthonos, who'd left her feeling so replete she could barely walk, who knew what might be revealed if anyone looked too closely. Finger marks and bruises, probably. Flogging and bite marks, definitely. Thank God they were all in private places currently hidden beneath her clothing.

She scanned the room. There were six staff other than

Janice and herself currently working away at their computers, and no one seemed particularly interested in their quiet little administrator who didn't have a life outside work, and therefore could not possibly have an interesting reason to be late. She bit her lip to curb the urge for evil laughter.

"Sorry, Jan. I did leave a message earlier at the front desk. I...um..." Had a stomach bug? Slept in? Had one of my panic attacks? She couldn't bring herself to straight out lie, but what on earth could she say? "I was indisposed." There. That sounded okay, surely. The surge of heat in her cheeks gave lie to the words and she instinctively ducked her head, only to remember too late about her recent haircut. She could no longer use her hair as a screen behind which to hide.

Her boss was already turning dismissively back to her work, but then her eyes narrowed and she did a double-take. "Indisposed?" She let out a small chuckle. "If I didn't know you better, Liv, I'd say you've been playing hooky with some guy."

God damn it. More heat? Get yourself under control. You'll be breaking out in a full-blown sweat in a minute.

Jan's eyes widened suddenly and her mouth dropped open a little. "No. Way. A guy? You? No!"

Liv scowled, unaccountably hurt. "Why is it so hard to believe that I might be able to attract a man? Everyone else seems to be doing it. Why not me?" Then, as Janice continued to stare at her wide-eyed, she sighed and her shoulders slumped a little "Okay, maybe it is out of character. I guess. But—" How to explain Phthonos? What if he wasn't even real, and she'd just had the best morning of her life with a figment of her own imagination? Would that count as fucking yourself? If you were convinced your imaginary lover was real, was it still called masturbation? Or madness? Wouldn't that put the icing on the cake of Janice's shock?

Especially if she saw into the depravity of Liv's mind and realized what she really wanted from a lover.

I want a bit of fifty shades without the contract. I want a lover who dominates with ease, and who knows instinctively when he's about to go too far. I want a lover who lets me take over sometimes. I want a lover who understands that pleasure and pain are two sides of the same coin. I want dominant and submissive in the one partner.

She let out a tiny sigh. Pity someone like that didn't exist in real life.

Her boss was smiling now, before throwing her chewed up pen onto the desk. "Well, I'll be a monkey's uncle. You really know how to keep a secret, my girl. How long have you been hiding your man from us all?"

"Oh, no. He's not my—"

"I know." Janice jumped to her feet and papers slid everywhere. "It's the Foundation's charity ball this Saturday night, which you know about, of course, since you're helping us organize it. You could bring him along as your date! I'm sick of seeing you always turn up at our functions alone. And you always leave on your own, too. Can't wait to meet him! What's his name?"

Her stomach lurched. "It's…um…his name's Phthonos. And, no. I'm sure he wouldn't be interested in coming along to the ball. He's…he's very busy." How on earth had the conversation reached this point? All because of an out-of-control blush that made her look like an inexperienced school girl. Oh, Thon, what am I going to do?

"Phthonos? That sounds exotic." At least Janice was sitting down again, but she was leaning forward in her chair, studying Liv, still interested in the topic. "It sounds a bit…I don't know…"

"Greek?" The male voice cut in to their conversation

smoothly and this time Liv felt the blood drain away from her face altogether. "It is. An ancient name, Phthonos. Your modern tongues find Thon easier to handle, I believe." Phthonos was here? At her work? And he was speaking to her boss? "I am Liv's lover," he said to Janice, flashing Liv a quick glance and a mischievous grin, as if he knew the turmoil roiling around inside her. "And I do wish to attend this ball you mentioned. She was very naughty not to tell me about it, wasn't she? But she can be a little devil at times. We will have to see about punishing her for that, later."

Oh my God. Just let the floor open up and swallow me now.

"You're Olivia's lover? But…you…you're…are you by chance a model?"

"No. I am a god."

"Well, yes, that's one word I would quite possibly use to describe you."

Her boss was talking to him? Did that mean… Liv's mortification eased into hope. "Wait. You can actually see him, Janice?"

She glanced around the room and realized that not one, but seven sets of wide eyes were on her and Thon. Janice's gaze slanted into confusion. "Well, yeah. What sort of question is that? Maybe you should put your specs on, hon. It's damn sure worth having clear vision right this minute." She turned back to Phthonos and held out her hand. "Pleased to meet you, Thon. We'd love to have you at the event. I'll make sure there's an extra ticket at the door. And if Liv decides not to bring you along after all, give me a call. Please. My, it's suddenly hot in here." She flicked her hair away from her neck grinning like the Cheshire cat, and irritation flared through Liv at the easy way her boss's long blonde locks flowed down her back. Why, oh why did I ever have that stupid hair cut? I can't preen in front of an attractive man anymore, even if I wanted to.

Phthonos appeared to consider Janice's words, then slowly shook his head. "No, thank you. I will attend with Liv, or not at all." He stepped across toward Liv and handed her the phone that she knew had been safely tucked in her handbag only minutes earlier. "You forgot your mobile, gorgeous woman. I want to be able to text you when I'm not with you in person. I want to be able to remind you of the things we have done, and all the things we are going to do—"

"Yep." She cut him off with a quick hand gesture. Since when did he need a mobile phone to communicate? They both knew that all he had to do was creep inside her head.

He let out a little snort and instantly her mind was filled with an image of Phthonos kneeling over her on the bed. She was on her stomach, facing the mirrored wardrobe door, and in the reflection she could see they were both naked. His cock was extended, proclaiming his arousal in no uncertain terms, and he held his leather flogger in one hand. "I don't creep, you naughty girl," he said, and with a quick flick of the wrist he smacked it across her bare buttocks.

"Oh!" She jerked in her chair, the sudden sting of the blow as real as if they were back in her room and not sitting in an office with several others watching on with speculative looks. The whole team was now staring across as if she'd suddenly grown an extra head.

Her clit throbbed in tandem with the pain. She had to fight to keep from jumping to her feet and rubbing her ass cheeks to ease the tingle. He did it again in her mind's image, those green eyes sparking with laughter in the mirror and equally full of fun as he stood here in the office in front of her with a faux innocent expression on his face.

I know exactly how to arouse you, Liv. The thought

flowed into her mind like a slow caress. And today is only the beginning.

Well. Two can play at that game. She raised a brow, sent a tiny smile his way, then bent her head and started moving papers around on her desk. I want to taste you, Thon. I want to wrap my hungry lips around your vein-ribbed cock and suck in your flavor. Mmm. Sticky and salty. Delicious. She deliberately parted her lips and ran the tip of her tongue around the edge. Her reward was a hissing sound as he sucked in a strangled breath.

She looked up, ready to smile innocently at him, and her heart skipped a beat. He was leaning over the desk, right up close, his eyes promising punishment later. The knuckles of one hand rested on a white folder marked "Finance" and the muscles in his shoulders and upper arms flexed in high defin- ition, making the black T-shirt he was wearing look positively too tight.

"Don't be late home, darling. I can't wait for our next liai- son." Hmm. Maybe this had backfired. Concentrating on work for the rest of the day was going to be a bitch. His tone turned low when he continued, the words clearly for her ears only this time. "And I love your hair the exact length it is right now, Liv. It's cute. I don't like preening. I like cute." He brushed a lock off her cheek and the zing of connection trav- elled right through to her bones. If he didn't leave soon she'd have an orgasm right in front of her work mates.

She gave him a pleading look. "Please. I'll see you later. This is my work." Despite her words she wanted to jump into the air and fist-pump. He was real? Janice had actually seen him, and spoken to him. He wasn't just a figment of her imag- ination. He was damn well, fucking real. And now, for however long this would last, he was actually hers.

CHAPTER FIVE

Bringing Thon into your work life is a bad idea. The words kept drumming through her head as she got ready for the function Saturday evening. Never mix business with pleasure. Work had been her savior over the past two years, as she struggled to recover from the disaster of her private life. She had worked hard to keep everything compartmentalized in an attempt to retain control.

And now Thon had come crashing into her life and was knocking down barrier after barrier. Trust me, he'd said, and she was trying. Though it was difficult. She fingered her elastic band and realized with a shock that she hadn't needed it at all since that first morning with Thon. His presence, while challenging her to face some difficult memories, was perhaps more positive than she had been willing to admit.

At least tonight he would finally see her looking her best. She put the finishing touches to her make-up with a swipe of red lipstick and stood back to look at the effect. Not bad, except for the hint of worry that was still deepening the furrow between her brows.

Give it a rest. He's been nothing but good for me. Trust him, and enjoy yourself tonight.

Her ivory dress was designed to flatter a woman of generous proportions, the floor-length flowing skirt decorated with curving black lace cutouts down the side that gave the impression of a narrower waist and hips. The high neckline was both modest and alluring, with another lace cutout down the center of her décolletage, perfectly placed to highlight her cleavage without flaunting it in everyone's faces.

She fluffed a little at her hair. Overall it had come up nicely, thanks to the efforts of a new hairdresser who had styled it in a short, flicky look that was modern and yet still feminine. A smoky-grey shade of eye shadow and liner had given her hazel eyes a green tint. Not as intense or attractive as Thon's, though the effect was pleasing. She hoped Thon felt the same.

"No, I do not feel the same."

She started and turned. "What?" He was leaning in the doorway, watching her with a predatory look.

"The effect is not pleasing. The effect is stunning. You look beautiful, Olivia Stratton. I am proud to be your partner for this evening."

"Oh! Well, thank you." The butterflies were back in force in her belly and when she turned to study him in more detail her legs developed an instant wobble. Wow! "You look amazing, Thon."

The word was inadequate to describe the perfection of the man who stood before her. He was wearing a black tuxedo over a white dress shirt, the suit's exquisite cut showing off the width of his shoulders and emphasizing his long body and narrow hips. His hair was neatly slicked back for once and his jaw was clean-shaven. A waft of scent, not aftershave but a fragrance she was beginning to recognize as his and his alone, drifted into the room. It was divine, and her pussy threatened to spill its creamy fluid in a spurt of yearning. For the first time she was grateful for the thick shape wear that lay beneath her dress. It would protect her dignity should her lust threaten to get out of control during the evening.

In an instant he was across the room, gripping her by the hips and tugging her into the cradle of his legs. He was hard. "I can smell your desire." The gruff words puffed against her hair. "It is going to drive me near insane tonight, your need. I can almost taste it in the very air that surrounds us."

"I'm going to be the same, Thon."

"I know. And I'm not going to make it easy for you, either." His eyes narrowed. "Your lust will be out of control this evening. I'll make sure of it. I'm going to give you a gift, and you will wear it, and every time you smell its fragrance, you will think of our need and how much we want to be alone and pleasuring each other instead of standing among the unknowing crowds making meaningless, boring conversation."

"A gift? Thon, I don't need a gift to know how much you—oh! It's…beautiful." Tears pricked at her eyes as he slipped a delicate-looking corsage onto her wrist. The central flower was an ivory lily, surrounded by smaller flowers, and a hint of greenery to frame it. The arrangement sat on an elasticized black velvet wristband, and it matched her dress to perfection. No one had ever given her a corsage, before. "Wait," she said, and reached underneath to hook her old brown worry band with one finger. "I don't think I'll need this, tonight." Removing it after all this time should have felt abnormal, but with the corsage in its place instead, and Phthonos smiling down at her with approval in his expression, it seemed right to drop the band into the trash.

"Well done, Liv. You are strong, after all. Amazing woman."

A waft of scent rose around her and her vagina clenched. Was this what she'd be exposed to all evening? Her pussy lips were already engorged and if this was a preview, it was clearly going to be a form of torture.

"I'm not going to be able to walk, you know, by the end of it."

He snorted. "And you think it will be easier for me? I have to work doubly hard to hide the effect of arousal. It will be fun. Every time I look at you tonight, my gift will release its scent, reminding you of my cock primed and waiting to find its home in your body." He ran his thumb briefly over her lips and then let her go. "And I intend to watch you a lot, Liv. All night long, in fact."

Ω Ψ Ω

Phthonos looked for her among the crowd. Where had she gone? There were several hundred people gracing the main ball room right now, and with a group of musicians up on the podium during this break between courses of their meal, at least half of the occupants had decided to get up and dance. Where was his Liv amongst the throng of all these ordinary, tiresome mortals?

As one of the event organizers she had been in demand the moment they walked through the front entrance, sorting out a spate of minor hiccups that owed their existence more to the nerves of others than to anything that had been organized incorrectly. She was an oasis of calm amongst a sea of anxiety, and he had been fascinated to see her in that role. Where was the woman who needed to snap a wrist band to stop panic spiraling out of control? Where was the woman who had let anxiety rule her life for so long she had almost forgotten how to live?

She was gone, and in her place was his beautiful Olivia, doing just as her name suggested and finally learning to live. Flitting here and there, soothing ruffled feathers and ensuring that everything ran smoothly for her employer's fundraising event.

The Foundation. How appropriate that she would work so hard for an organization that strived to protect the heart health of her fellow Australians. He was so proud to be her partner. Liv had the biggest heart he knew.

It had been fun to see her squirm whenever he laid eyes on her, knowing that his pheromone scent was drifting in the air around her, tuned in to her and her alone. To know that her clit was swelling beneath that gorgeous dress despite her best efforts to ignore the longing. To know that she was finding it more and more difficult to walk, just as she had predicted, when her pussy lips grew heavy and swollen and the tortured flesh began to rub together whenever she moved.

Are your breasts sensitive and full, Olivia? Have your nipples grown hard, rubbing themselves into rosy rigidity against that strange contraption you call a stick-on bra? Is the heat of that sticky substance against your flesh creating patches of sweat that I can taste when I finally strip you bare?

He wanted nothing more than to drop to his knees, lift that long skirt, rip away those unfortunate-looking undergarments, and expose her slick, creamy fanny for his tasting. Liquid coated the tip of his organ as he pictured the ease with which he would penetrate her.

It was taking everything in his power, and then some, to

keep his own arousal hidden. A glamor concealed his erection from the prying eyes of all these strangers, but if anyone looked too closely they would see how desperately his need sat upon him. Every time his pheromones released at Liv's wrist, her sexual scent intensified. It had reached the point where he didn't know if the lust within could be controlled at all. It struggled, just like the darkness, clawing to be out in the open.

He could sense her growing unease as she tried to concentrate on her job, and in the end he conceded, letting her off the hook so she could do what she was here to do. We will have our time later, Olivia. And you will pay for making me wait, my sweet. He sent the telepathic message and smiled a little when he felt the answering lurch deep within her womb.

If you let me be for now, I will make it worth your while later.

Cheeky woman. She was getting quite practiced at communicating without words. Tonight, he would make her beg, before he would relent and fill her with his seed. His heart thumped at the knowledge that she would be his again, so very soon.

It was so hard to hold in his own craving while pretending to be interested in this inane conversation with her boss, Janice. The woman kept touching his arm and stroking it, leaning in close to flash her cleavage in a low-cut yellow dress and making it more than clear that she was interested and available, should he wish it. Interested and available was good, but only if the woman in question was his Liv. Where is she? I need her.

He removed Janice's hand from his arm for the eleventh time and interrupted her mid-sentence. "Sorry. I need to find Liv. She promised me her first dance."

"Oh." The woman pouted. "Sure. If that's what you really want?"

"Yes, it is. Otherwise I wouldn't have said it."

He stepped away, scanning the crowd, and his heart jumped when he found her. Yes! But...

"Seems like you might have missed the boat on the first dance, Thon." It was Janice, back by his side again, and she was looking directly at Liv on the dance floor.

A grey mist hazed his vision and his fists clenched. I'm already strung too tight. Holding everything in. Hiding my need, surrounded by the smell of desire. The petty jealousies and passions of a whole race, calling to everything inside. Keep holding it. Don't let it...don't... She promised me first dance...she promised me...

At that moment Liv twirled in the other man's arms and looked straight at him with an unreadable expression, then her gaze slid to the side and she was staring at Janice, who was once again holding onto him, her breast brushing his arm in a fairly obvious display of availability. Liv's eyes narrowed, and when she glanced back at Thon her lips tightened.

He took a step toward her and she moved closer in to the man's embrace, wrapping her arms around his waist and twirling away from his reach. The last view he had of her was her white face, eyes blazing hazel green, and the man tightening his hold and swooping in toward her mouth.

Mine. Mine. Mine. No. Brothers, help me. Zeus, don't let it free...don't let it...

He started to shake, but it was too late. Far too late for containment.

Envy broke loose in the world.

Ω Ψ Ω

Liv stood there on the dance floor, horror creeping over her as an oily darkness roiled around her lover. What was it? Why was it leaching out of him like that in spurts and patches of ugly greenish grey? He didn't even look human anymore. She wanted to run to him but her feet were rooted to the floor, eyes wide and her hands covering her mouth.

He stared directly at her with desperation in those clear green eyes, clutching at his middle, then reaching out toward her with fingers clawed in a rictus of tension. *Oh God, it's just like my nightmare, only there are no flames in which to burn.*

The dark burst forth from Thon in a streaming gush of grey and black. His mouth was stretched wide, like he was screaming in pain, though no sound emerged bar the rushing noise as the shadow whipped past, around, and between each of the people swaying on the dance floor. She stood without moving at the center of the rushing gloom, filled with terror as tendrils of it scrabbled hard trying to grab at her, then it was past, smashing headlong into the wall with a loud crack.

No flames? There they were, all around them, whipping up the wall in a lightning fast flash of orange and yellow as the decorative drapery took hold. The screaming began then, and the rushing stampede for the door. Through it all she continued to watch Phthonos who suddenly hunched over, shaking his head, moaning, beginning to weep. *I'm so sorry, Liv. I tried. I tried so fucking hard...*

And then she was caught up in the rush, too, someone grabbing her arm and shoving her toward the door. "Thon!" She began to scream, joining the others in growing panic as she tried to look back, but her panic was not for herself this time. It was for him. She struggled to remove grasping hands from her arms as she was carried out on a tide of humanity toward a safer place away from the flames. She attempted to go back against the sea of bodies, desperate to find her lover. Was he still alive? Or was he burning in the flames of his demon, with no one there to save him? "No! Let...me... go..." It was impossible to return, and though she strained to stay connected with Thon the energy was gone and his mind was no longer there for her to sense.

Ω Ψ Ω

Was it eons later, or perhaps only a couple of hours? Liv had lost all track of time. She stared in through the window frame at the charred ruins of what was once the Foundation's charity ball. The glass along some of the ground floor windows of the hotel housing the massive ball room had disappeared sometime during the blaze, and fire fighters still moved back and forth among the smoking debris, doing whatever they usually did during the aftermath of an incident.

People milled around, shocked and dazed, calling loved ones on their mobile phones, hugging each other, crying. Janice stood several meters away, mascara running down her face and soot decorating her dress that was no longer jaunty yellow. A media crew had arrived and were setting up for some kind of interview. She saw it all as if through a bubble, strangely numb. Shock would take hold later, probably, but for now she just watched and took it all in as if completely disconnected from the horror of what had happened.

My fault. If she'd not allowed Phthonos into her life, if

she'd not flirted with her colleague when she saw him standing there with Janice and the flame of jealousy flickered within… She knew it would annoy Thon, and she shouldn't have done it. If she'd stayed sensible, then none of this would have happened. God of envy, or demon of Hell? Her knees suddenly gave way and she sank down onto an upturned planter tub, clutching at the ceramic edge to avoid slipping all the way to the ground.

God in heaven, how will he and I possibly move beyond this moment?

At least no one had died, thanks in large part to the quick-thinking hotel staff who had coordinated the evacuation, and the emergency services who had responded so quickly, containing the blaze to the ground floor of the building only.

Phthonos. What have we done?

Strangely, the panic she would have expected at this point had not kicked in. She looked down for her elastic band and remembered it was in the trash at home. The wrist corsage that had taken its place was still there but now it was merely a piece of black velvet, the flowers torn off somewhere in the stampeding rush toward the exit. No doubt the once-beautiful lily was a handful of ash by now. Nausea roiled in her stomach as she fingered the velvet. With a sudden, violent twist she ripped it from her wrist and threw it as far as she could.

"Olivia." She jumped up as Phthonos appeared before her, looking human once again, his voice in that one word managing to convey the depth of his sorrow and regret. When he reached out hesitantly her heart lurched. For an instant she considered pulling away, and then it was too late. His fingers were entangled in her hair and she couldn't help but relax into their gentle and loving caress. It was instinctive, her response to his touch, despite the devastation surrounding them. How could one being contain so much good intention, so much capacity to give and receive love, and yet also be the cause of this level of pain and destruction?

"I couldn't stop it, in the end, though I tried to direct it away from you. Away from them all." He gestured briefly around them, then his shoulders drooped. "I didn't see the candelabra standing in that corner near the drapery. It should have just blasted out one of the walls."

Her eyes widened. "It should have?" A laugh slipped out of her, but it held bitterness rather than mirth. "It'll be all right." A lie, and yet what else could she say? "We'll work this out." Or not.

"No, we won't." His grip tightened and he forced her head to tilt upward. There was agony and self-loathing stamped across his face. His eyes seethed with unspoken emotion. "Dear Liv, you and I both know it will never be all right. Not while I am here with you. I need to go back. Back where I came from, in order for you to be safe. I thought I could contain it, my demon. I was wrong."

She sighed, the sound as ragged as her dress. "I'm sorry. It was my fault. I saw you there with Janice and I felt jealous. All of a sudden I wanted to make you feel the same way." Nausea threatened and she would have vomited if there had been anything left in her stomach. But she'd thrown up earlier, while watching the fire fighters work to douse the flames.

His lips twisted. "I am jealousy." His voice was flat. "And what you felt was me. The destructive part of love. It was never your fault, Liv. I drove your actions, as I drive every-one's jealous actions in this realm. I try to hold it in, but sometimes... No. Not your fault. This one is all down to me."

He let go of her so suddenly she almost lost her balance, tripping on the edge of her dress. Where her shoes had disappeared to was anybody's guess and without them the skirt was too long. She rubbed her hands down the sides, uncaring of the fabric now that it was covered in soot and dirt, trying to contain the urge to weep. *If you go, I'll be all alone once again. Only this time, I will know what I'm missing, and I don't know how I'll survive it.*

Her throat ached with the effort of holding on. *Tell him. Tell him how much he means to you. How much you need him to stay.* She opened her mouth, took a deep breath, and then hesitated. "I..."

A flurry of movement within the burnt premises caught her eye and then a voice was calling out, "Back. Everybody back now. This section's about to go." A small piece of ceiling collapsed into the room in a frighteningly loud rumble of noise.

She folded her arms across her stomach, and the rest of her sentence refused to come out. She just stood there, staring at Thon, silent. Her heart felt like it was about to break in half. *I'm sorry. I don't know how to get past this. What if it happens again? What if next time someone gets hurt, or even worse? Sean hurt only me, but you...*

He nodded, glancing around and then back at her. "Yes." His eyes were pools of misery. "I could hurt them all, Liv. I don't want to, and yet...I could."

Oh, God. "I don't think I'm strong enough." *I don't think I'm the one meant to save you.*

He let out a groan that was half growl, half sob, and right before her eyes began to fade. "I wish it could have been different." His voice surged over her, full of sorrow, and the flow of energy that had heated her blood since the moment they met finally began to dissipate. In that last moment before he vanished a desperate hand reached out toward her. "There is only you, Liv. I love you," he mouthed, and then it was just his eyes, like a green blazing beacon proclaiming his agony, until even they winked out to leave her alone in unbearable darkness.

The ache in her chest finally let loose and she began to cry, silently at first and then louder, deep wrenching sobs that threatened to split her in two. She wrapped her arms more tightly around her middle and hunched over, weeping for the loss of this building, for the danger in which everyone had been placed, and for the terror they had all endured. She wept for her charity, who did such amazing work and didn't deserve the flames that had destroyed everything.

Most of all, she wept for Phthonos. Whatever he was, whether man, god, or demon, he had desperately wanted to be good. He had wanted to rejoin this world and be a part of her life in a meaningful way, and he had placed his trust in her to help him achieve that dream.

But she had not been able to save him from the darkness in his soul. In the end, unlike her dream, she had not walked through fire to drag him from the flames. Instead she had let him go, all alone, and in so doing had ultimately failed them both.

CHAPTER SIX

L iv slept roughly all week and if she dreamt at all, it was not memorable enough to stay with her till the morning. Since the "terrible accident," as the media were calling the fire, she had stepped back into the routine of her life as if Phthonos had never existed, getting up every morning and making her way to work, coming home each evening and falling into bed.

It was as if her days were the dreaming state, when she went onto auto-pilot and did everything by rote. Her colleagues didn't seem to blame her for what had happened, nor did they blame Thon. The police had dozens of witnesses who had all told the same story. An unexplained gust of wind that blew open one of the side doors and blasted through the room had tipped one of the tall candelabra into a satin backdrop draping the wall, and the blaze had spread from there.

Liv didn't know how to counteract that explanation with the truth. *I woke the demon of Envy and he let loose when he discovered me flirting.* If she told anyone it would probably score her a stint in a psychiatric facility, and she'd come very close to that already in her life when she'd first been crippled by panic attacks.

So instead, she kept quiet and did everything people expected of her during the day, working doubly hard for the Foundation by personally contacting all five hundred people on the guest list. Most were wonderful, willing to stand by their previous donation pledge despite what had happened. There would be enough to achieve their aim of funding the first year of a new early screening program for relatives of people with cardio-vascular disease. The program could potentially save hundreds, perhaps thousands of lives, and it was an enormous relief that at least something positive would come from that night.

Without Thon by her side, though, nothing had the same meaning as before. It was only when she got home each evening and bed time grew near that she began to feel alive once again. She craved sleep, when she might escape into her dream world and possibly catch a glimpse of her lover. Was he missing her, the same way she was missing him? Was he all right? Or was he burning in some kind of eternal self-torturous Hell for what he'd put them all through?

If he can't be with me in the real world, at least let him visit my dreams, she begged whoever might be listening. Aphrodite, he'd said, was the one who had let him back in to this world. "Please, Aphrodite," she said aloud, as she climbed into bed one night. "We never had the opportunity to work out a solution together. Let him come to me. He never had his second chance, not really, because in the end I didn't even try to help him."

When she'd been standing amongst the wreckage of her event, thinking about how much worse it could easily have been, and surrounded by a sea of faces all registering differing degrees of shock, it had seemed an impossible, heart-wrenching choice. Love a man who embodied this level of violence, a man who personified everything she'd been trying to escape from for the past two years, or let him go and spend the rest of her life alone and lonely.

I didn't think I could risk it.

Now, several days on from the angst of that moment and with time to reflect on all that had happened, she could see that Thon was nothing like Sean. The latter was an abuser, pure and simple. He had reveled in acts of violence without regard for his victims, taking pleasure from hurting others and only showing contrition after, not during, the episode.

Thon, on the other hand, worked his ass off trying to control the darkness in his soul. He took no pleasure from letting out that part of himself, and in fact had tried to direct the violent outburst away from her and everyone else in the room. Despite what had ultimately transpired, Thon had actually tried to protect them all. A demon of sorts had been unleashed that night, and yet thanks to Thon, no one had died or even been injured.

It was done; it was over. And instead of walking through the fires of Hell to save her lover, she had left him to burn. Alone. Forgive me, Phthonos. I was wrong to leave you.

She was desperate for sleep, for the chance to reconnect, but night after night she slept alone, and dreamless. He was truly gone, and even though he'd only been here for a short time, the impact on her life—on her heart—was immeasurable.

I love you, Thon. For the first time in my life I let someone in past my barriers, and I fell for you. Head over heels. I should have spoken up when you wanted me to. I should have insisted you stay and we could have worked it out. I don't know how, but together, I'm sure we could have made it work.

A month after he had first appeared in the flesh, she slid under the satin sheets on her bed and switched off the bedside light. Would he visit tonight? She was naked, just in case. It wasn't to be. Once again she was disappointed; there were no dreams that she could recall.

This time, though, it was different when she woke. It was near dawn, still dark, and her heart was pounding as if she'd just run a sprint. She sat bolt upright, her hand at her throat, an awareness that she was not alone energizing her system but unable to see who it was. "Phthonos?" It was a feminine scent that assailed her nostrils, though, a perfume that reminded her of some spicy, exotic fruit, and even as her muscles tensed ready to flee her mind was telling her to stay calm. A woman whose fragrance envelops you like a warm caress is unlikely to be a crazed drug addict after cash for a quick fix. She stayed frozen in place, ready to bolt, eyes wide and strafing the dark until the voice vibrated through her mind.

Beautiful Olivia, is your resolve still firm?

My resolve? Liv let out the breath she'd been holding and fell back into the pillows. "Aphrodite? Is he all right?"

He is suffering, and he will continue to suffer, unless...

"Unless what?" She clenched her fists and pounded the mattress. What sort of mother refused to protect her son from Hell itself? "If there is something I can do to help him, then tell me."

She felt rather than heard the sigh reverberate through the room. *I'm trying to protect him.* Even though it was an unspoken thought rather than anything said aloud, Liv sensed the acerbic edge, but quite honestly, at this point she couldn't care less. Aphrodite was not her focus. Phthonos was.

Child. This time the thought was gentler. Do you know how hard it is to make room for love when you hold Envy in your heart?

Liv sighed too, releasing some tension. "I think I'm beginning to understand. But..." She paused for a moment, gathering courage, then plunged ahead. "I love him. Every part of him, even the demon within. I accept who and what he is, and I want to help him navigate this tricky world of ours, if I can. Please, Aphrodite..."

There was the faintest touch on her hair, like a gentle caress, and then the presence was gone. She growled in frustration and then with a hiccup she was crying, her mouth wide open and sobs wrenching painfully at her body as she gripped the bed sheets. "He needs me," she managed to choke out. "He does."

"I do need you. So desperately, Liv." The deep masculine voice reverberated right through to her bones.

"Phthonos!" She shrieked and jumped out of bed, launching herself in the direction of her lover's voice. When they connected she clung tight, afraid he would dematerialize. I won't let you leave this time. The room lightened as dawn began to break and at last she could see him. His grin had a lopsided slant, and she saw shiny tears marking snail trails through streaks of dirt adorning his face. "Where have you been?" She began to giggle through her own tears, the combination of laughter and sorrow causing hiccups. "You look so dirty."

"Do you think I need a shower?"

"Yes. Definitely."

"Hmm." She felt his kiss like a flash of heat on the top of her head. "Well, your nose is running, so maybe you should join me and wash it clean."

"Oh gosh." She grabbed for a tissue from the bedside table and swiped at her nose. "Not very dignified. Sorry."

He tilted his head. "I like that your tears are for me, and that you have cried enough to make your nose run and your eyes swell up like that."

"Oh." She ducked her head but he chucked her under the chin, forcing her face up.

"Don't hide. I'm telling you that it pleases me." He shifted a little in an awkward shuffle. "You don't..." He swallowed hard and her brows lifted. His cheeks were flushed. He was blushing? "You don't hate me, then?"

"Hate you?"

"For, you know, what I did."

He was so still and unsure that she got the impression he was ready to disappear once again. She attached herself more securely and spoke as gently as she could. "I don't hate you, Thon. I love you. What happened didn't change that."

There. It was said. And it was easier than she'd thought, so she said it again. "I love you, Phthonos; god, or demon, or whoever you are. I love everything about you, the good, the bad, and the ugly. And yes," she held up a hand to still his protest, "I saw it. I know what is in you."

He must have been stretched so taut. As soon as she finished speaking he slumped in her arms, his relief so patently strong it rolled over her own skin like a wave.

She smiled. "Somehow, we'll work out a way to deal with your green-eyed monster. I'll be honest, Thon, I don't actually know how, yet. We'll figure it out, together. Perhaps with a little bit of guidance from Aphrodite."

"I don't know what to say."

"How about, I love you too. That would be nice to hear at this point."

"Cheeky woman." He smacked her on the butt cheek. "Of course I love you, Olivia. More than you will ever know."

He leaned in and planted a nibbling kiss against her neck, the delicate movement of his lips creating a shiver down her spine. "Now I need my shower." Impatience laced his tone. He grabbed her hips and pulled her in and she felt the surge of hard heat against her belly. "See?"

A frisson of current sparked around them and then he was as naked as she was. Her clit throbbed and dampness lined her slit. Instant hard-on of the female variety. It was suddenly difficult to draw in a breath. "Hmm, so there are some advantages to having an immortal being as your lover. No need to waste time on buttons or zips."

"Some? I will show you many advantages, woman, starting tonight."

"Good. And you know what? I've changed my mind. I like you dirty, Thon. Let's have our shower later. Right now, I want you to fuck me." She turned in his arms and bent over the bed until her ass was in the air. She met his hungry gaze in the mirror across the room and knew the same appetite was probably there on her face. There was an urgency in her that she couldn't explain. She just knew that she had to have Thon inside her. Now.

He smacked her again, first on one cheek and then quickly on the other. She sucked in a breath at the sting. "Naughty," he said. "I won't fuck you. I will make love with you, Liv." His correction was punctuated with yet another quick slap, and when he dipped a thumb into her slit and ran it along the seam her pent-up breath released in a low whimper. He stopped at the sphincter of her ass and pushed in. "Do you like that?"

"I do." Her voice was muffled as she pressed her face into the mattress, trying to contain her desire, trying to stop her ass from quivering. Trying to delay the moment when she would explode into a million pieces around him.

"Ah. I can see that you do. Your pussy is glistening with sex fluids. You are all ready for me, and we've only just this instant begun to play." Pressure from his thumb as he played with her asshole created an answering ache in her core. Her labia lips felt so engorged that it was a miracle he could see anything at all down there. She moaned, her hips twitching as the tip of his thumb finally breached her.

"Thon, I know we've just started, but...I can't hold off for much longer." Desperation laced her words and he laughed above her, clearly delighting in her torment.

"Do you think I want you to hold off? Oh no, Liv, I want you writhing in ecstasy as I enter you. And I am going to enter you very soon. My cock is so wet with need that I could fuck your ass without lube, if that's what you wanted. But right now, I think...I would rather...do this." He punctuated his words with a thrust and his hot cock slid straight into her waiting pussy.

"Yes," she sobbed. "Oh, yes. That feels so good."

"I love you, Liv." He drove again and the pressure inside built to breaking point.

"I love you too, Thon." She could hardly speak for gasping.

He bent over her, capturing a handful of her hair and tilting back her head. His lips were right beside her ear. "Now it is time for you to climax." He drove a third time, the loud slap of his groin against her fanny testament to the strength behind his movement.

It was too much, all at once, and she began to keen as her body shifted over the edge and into the most exquisite orgasm of her life. It started deep within her womb, like an aching clench that expanded until her whole body was on fire and nothing existed except the relentless pounding of his flesh inside her own.

"Phthonos, I can't...it's too much..." Her scream was muffled in the bedclothes as she came, shuddering in an explosive response that went on and on until his roar above her and his crazed bucking as a rush of seed squirted heat into her womb sent her straight into the black pit of unconsciousness.

When she finally came to it was disorienting, until she realized they were spread-eagled across the bed, lower limbs still entangled, and a gentle hand was stroking up and down her spine in a touch designed to relax.

She sighed, and rolled over to find him leaning up on one elbow and studying her. "I've never blacked out before," she admitted.

His smile had a touch of pride, and she couldn't help but reach up to trace around his gorgeous lips. "There will be many more orgasms as intense as that." He spoke against her fingertips. "If you want them?"

Even now was that hesitation, as if he were unsure of his place in her life. "Thon, I hope we can do that every day, maybe for the rest of my life." She frowned a little then. "I'm not sure how we'll work it out, you being immortal and the carrier of envy. But—"

"We will work it out together, as you said. That's the most important thing. I can't wait to start building a future with you, Liv."

Joy filled her. "And I can't wait to have that shower, demon lover." She rolled to present her rear for a reprimand, and was delighted when he obliged and then followed up with a kiss.

Pleasure and pain. Light and dark. Demon and god. Phthonos might be all of these things, but above all he was her mate. Somehow, together, they would build a future. I'm the luckiest woman in the world to have discovered love with you, wonderful man.

He cupped her cheek. And I you, beautiful woman. "Now. Let's have that shower."

Ω Ψ Ω

I hope you enjoyed these steamy novellas in the GODS OF LOVE series. If so, please consider leaving a review at your place of purchase. Reviews are lifeblood for authors. Thank you!

ABOUT THE AUTHOR

Jen Katemi is an award-winning and international bestselling author of steamy contemporary romance. She is published with Evernight Publishing, Naughty Nights Press and as Jennifer Lynne with Red Sage. Jen also has forged a successful indie career starting with her popular GODS OF LOVE and FORBIDDEN series of steamy romance novellas.

When she's not writing, Jen works in admin, looks after the family, pampers various cats, and tries to find a smidgen of time for her husband. She lives in Melbourne, Australia.

Read more from Jen Katemi
www.JenKatemi.com

Also:

Touch Me Not (Naughty Fairy Tale), *Evernight Publishing*

Crossing the Line (A Ménage Romance), *Evernight Publishing*

Tempt (A Billionaire Romance)

Heart's Destiny

Educating Ethan

Titles by Jennifer Lynne:

Pandora's Gift, Red Sage Publishing

Secrets Vol. 28 Sensual Cravings Anthology, *Red Sage Publishing*